THE DELICATE BALANCE

THE DELICATE BALANCE

A novel by

VICKI TURPEN &
SHANNON HORST

Golden Word Books
Santa Fe, NM

Library of Congress Control Number 2019902745

Printed in the United States of America

Published by Golden Word Books, Santa Fe, New Mexico.

ISBN 978-1-948749-42-8

It takes a month to starve to death, weeks to thirst to death, but only moments to suffocate.

—*Buckminster Fuller*

~1~

MATTHEW WAS DEAD. THE GENTLE DAD WHO HAD TAUGHT HIM TO love the land and all its creatures, was gone. Jesse didn't know when or how. The official memo from the Essentials in Iowa said only that he was dead.

Sick with fear and self-doubt, he felt there was only one person he could talk to—Hannah.

But she was at the hospital volunteering—rocking terminally ill babies or something like that, she'd mentioned to him once. He'd have to go find her.

It seemed a strange activity for the Hannah he'd come to know. The hospital reception area felt cold and empty. A nurse came scurrying past.

"Can you tell me where I might find Hannah Koenig?"

"She'll be in Ward Three, upstairs."

Ward Three was packed with babies and toddlers. Surely, he thought, not all of these were diagnosed terminal. The toddlers in beds with rails and play pens followed him longingly with their eyes. Even the babies in cribs turned in his direction. They held out their little hands and babbled or wailed as he passed. Then it hit him. They were hungry. There wasn't any food being shipped in. And where were their parents?

Hannah was in the last room, sitting on the edge of a bed, her back to the door. She was holding a child in her arms, rocking back and forth, humming.

It wasn't the right time to interrupt her, so he sat in a chair by the door. His discomfort grew. How could he help these children? He'd never really thought about physically caring for any children but his own. He'd convinced himself it was enough for him to focus on saving the environment so they might have a chance at a future.

He remembered going home that night after the U.N. vote on temperate forests and going into the boys' room. The night light flickered warmly on their little bodies. Though each had his own bed, they seldom stayed in them. The bed clothes reflected late night wrestling. In the shadows the plump roundness of Troy shone in stark contrast to Ethan's sinewy length. Their bodies were intertwined into mounds of softly breathing, other-worldly flesh.

He tried to rearrange the covers to protect them from the cool morning. Troy opened one eye and said, "Hi, Dad," closed it and rolled over, flinging his arm across his brother. How protective he felt that night, ready to defend his family from the world. Looking back, he wondered whether he really had given the time needed to truly know his boys. Or had he simply allowed his crusade to save the environment rob him of what mattered? All that counted now was what was happening to his family. But where were they?

Hannah put the little bundle down on the bed, drew a sheet up over its face and stood up. The sight of Jesse and the thought that he'd been watching her unnerved her.

"What are you doing here?"

"Hannah, I need to talk to you about some of the new data . . . ."

"No."

"No?"

"No, I don't want to talk right now. Jesse, these children are dying. Take a look at them; all of them. We're letting them die. This is our fault."

"Hannah, it had to be done. We were all going to die unless someone did something."

"We don't know that. It's only a theory. This is real—real death. Oh, what's the use, you don't care about these children. You only care about your damned data." She moved at him with her fists raised.

Then she sidestepped and rushed to the hall door. He caught her and shook her, forcing her to lift her head so he could see her face.

"The ones who survive will live in a better world. You were just as convinced as I was. Something had to be done. Don't lay all this on me. We did it because we had to. No amount of recrimination now will stop what we have put in motion. We have to go forward and trust what we are doing is right."

They left the hospital, the silence between them as cold and penetrating as the wind and rain whipping New York City.

Jesse was unsure how to deal with this new, vulnerable side of Hannah. She tried to leave him at the entrance to the massive concrete barricade that had been erected in front of the apartment block where she now lived with other international U.N. Essentials. But he flashed his own "Essential" badge and pushed past the lone guard standing at the only narrow opening to the main door. He followed her to her rooms. "I don't want you to be alone right now," he said, settling onto her sofa.

"I just need some time to mourn little Nicholas. He was such a fighter, and I'd grown to love him so."

Hannah put on a woolly robe and drew a shawl around her shoulders. She heated water on a Bunsen burner.

Jesse looked at the contents of her room. Like her office, not one bit of clutter. Unlike his wife, Karen, whose stacks of books eclipsed their whole apartment, Hannah carefully shelved hers: international law, human rights, law and international borders, German and French philosophy, a few classics, and two that surprised him, on parenting and motherhood.

His mind filtered back to how he and Karen always argued over things like the law, philosophy and parenting. The fiery intellectual wrestling would burst into cherished moments of sharing and sexuality. He watched as Hannah sat down, curling her legs up under her as she sipped the coffee. He moved closer and put his arm around her shoulders.

"We must keep trusting that by the end of this decade, it will be a better world for all children."

"All the children who are left alive."

"There is a place in the Bible where it states the sins of the fathers will no longer be visited upon the children. I don't believe our children must continue to suffer for our mistakes . . . .Are you listening, Hannah?"

"I just can't deal with that right now, Jesse. Where are Nicholas's parents? Why weren't they there tonight? How could they leave the city with him in hospital? I guess I don't understand. What would you have done if Nicholas were one of your boys? Would you have abandoned him when Wave I went into effect?"

Jesse got up and walked slowly to the window. The rain had turned to snow. He wasn't sure how to answer. Finally, he turned around.

"I would never abandon one of my boys to save myself. But if I had to abandon a very ill child to save a healthy one, or to save its mother . . . . I would probably do it in the end. Wasn't Nicholas going to die anyway?"

"That's not the point," she choked as tears streamed down her cheeks.

"Hannah, haven't I, in a way abandoned my wife and sons by staying here? Every day I am hit with a wave of fear that something has happened and they are not safe anymore. Perhaps, I'm no better, really, than Nicholas's parents."

For the first time she was looking directly at him. When he met her gaze, she lowered her eyes. He watched as she heated more water, only as an afterthought asking him if he too wanted some coffee.

Everything about her had become so familiar. Her walk, her voice, even the way she poured coffee. He remembered the pine smell and warmth of her body as he put his arm around her. He was hit by more confusion—a longing for Karen and the boys mixed up with a growing familiarity with Hannah.

~2~
NEW YORK CITY

JUST TWO YEARS EARLIER, JESSE, A SENIOR ATMOSPHERIC SCIENTIST with the U.N. whose job it was to track the effect of climate change on the atmosphere, had received data indicating the delicate balance of gases that make up oxygen had begun to shift. His first step after cross referencing the data from each of the stations around the world, was to take the information to his superior, the head of the United Nations Environmental Program (UNEP), Miriamu Mirza.

Jesse walked in on her in the arms of a handsome, muscled man. Embarrassed, he tried to back out of the office.

"Jesse Forester, this is John Cunningham, a friend of mine. John, Jesse is a colleague who heads up the group at the U.N. that pays attention to global climate change. John and I were just finishing our business."

Cunningham flashed Jesse a wink, kissed Miriamu on the cheek, patted her on the rear, and sauntered out. Jesse sensed something more than just sexuality, almost a threat in the encounter. Miriamu pulled herself up to her full six-foot-two and shut the office door. She composed herself, rearranging the colorful African drape that hung from her shoulder. Then she moved behind her desk.

"Dr. Mirza, I'm here to discuss my concerns about data my unit has recently received from our stations throughout the world. It's not good. There's now a hole in the ozone twice as big as it was when everyone started tracking it in the '80s. We are getting more and more data out of South America on the amount of carbon dioxide build-up and the shifting ratio of carbon, nitrogen, and argon to oxygen. And the reports coming from New Zealand and Australia substantiate our conclusions. The ice is melting, throwing tons of carbon dioxide into the atmosphere."

"Is it just the Southern Hemisphere?"

Jesse hesitated, losing his train of thought completely, as the nightmare that jarred him in his sleep flashed before him. His two little boys were stacked with dead bodies like cords of wood on a mountain side. Their little chests were rising and falling and their faces were pink and rosy in contrast to the ashen faces of the others. In the nightmare, he had tried desperately to reach them but his legs wouldn't move.

"Mr. Forester, is it just the Southern Hemisphere?"

Her voice pierced the images and he shook himself back to reality. "Funny you should ask. Yesterday we learned there's been another tragedy with climbers, a report from Nepal. Twelve experienced climbers were found dead. Even the sherpas were dead. The authorities say there was no weather-related event or avalanche. They were just lying on the side of the track. Their oxygen tanks had emptied before they got to 22,000 feet. The initial investigation indicates maybe there just wasn't enough air to breathe."

She shuffled several papers on her desk. "Do we have more data from the North Pole?"

"Yes, Theodore Sands and his supervisor, a fellow named Many Horses, report that oxygen levels they're registering at the poles are making it necessary for the fly-boys to use oxygen even at lower altitudes. The lab at Boulder reports that increases in carbon dioxide are showing up all over the place."

"Good. Our information to the Security Council will be accurate; the data confirms our decisions and the need for the recommended actions you will propose tomorrow."

"Secretary Mirza, I would rather you speak directly to the General Assembly. I don't feel qualified, and I am not a public speaker. In fact as you may notice, I have a slight speech . . . .

"Nonsense, of course you are qualified. You can make it all more easily understood to a lay person. I will see you tomorrow at the General Assembly." She dismissed him with a wave of her hand.

Jesse always felt uneasy when dealing with Miriamu. He was sure she should make the presentation. Why did she refuse? Even with hard data and a flawless presentation, could anyone make the assembly understand the urgency of this problem? Wouldn't it need to be someone of her rank among her colleagues?

~3~
NEW YORK CITY

"THE MASS OF MEN LEAD LIVES OF QUIET DESPERATION." JESSE WENT to sleep with Thoreau's quote running through his head and woke up with it still there. His life would never be the same. Would he be able to keep the promise he made to Troy? He was trying to drift back to sleep when the alarm screamed at him. More panic stirred in his heart. He rolled over to Karen's side of the bed and fumbled to shut it off.

Some of the butterflies in his stomach were caused by the anticipation of once again encountering the secretary-general's senior legal counsel, Hannah Koenig. Jesse knew what needed to be done to restore the balance and he needed the very best international lawyer—one who had written the bulk of the last decade's treaties and agreements on environmental regulations the U.N. nations would agree to—on his team. Instead of moaning about his family, he should be thinking about how to explain the gravity of the situation to her. He sure had to do a better job than he had with Karen.

He cut himself shaving. *Damn, I can't go to my appointment with her, looking like I've been in a brawl.* He reached for his favorite sport coat and selected a tie Karen had given him last Christmas.

Jesse's prejudice against lawyers in general was an obstacle he had to control. Whenever he saw that blindfolded female symbol of justice, he knew the environment he cherished and defended would suffer. His first encounter with Hannah Koenig, two years earlier, had been typical.

She had stormed unannounced into his office. "Jesse Forester?"

A whiff of strong soap and a bit of pine hit his nostrils. "Yes, Ms. Koenig?" *Damn it,* he thought, *what does she want?* Her reputation had preceded her. In the corridors of the huge labyrinth of the U.N., she was whisperingly called "the Gestapo."

"Mr. Forester, your proposal to sustain the world's temperate forests is not in line with the economic development needs and policies of any of the Western nations or the emerging nations for that matter."

Jesse had seethed during her five-minute lecture on the fine points of his temperate forest code and its effect on Third World economies. She outlined a barrage of reasons she intended to counsel the secretary-general not to endorse it.

His first impulse had been to strangle her and throw her out his eleventh floor window. As she ranted, all the past jibes he had endured on endangered species and environmental wackoism flashed through his mind. He remembered "nuke a gay whale for Jesus," "marinate a spotted owl," and "sauté a silvery minnow." He moved around his desk and looked down at her with all the disdain he could muster.

"Ms. Koenig, I can certainly understand the economic ramifications of these steps in the short run. However, all of our data shows these steps will result in the stability and health we need in forests, and therefore in the surrounding communities for hundreds, perhaps thousands, of years. I don't know about you, but I'd like my kids and my future grandkids to have just a small crack at a decent life."

She headed for the door. "Your plan is unsustainable, Mr. Forester. If the United States and its allies will not comply, how do we ask the rest of the world to comply?"

He followed her, blocking the doorway. "Well, Ms. Koenig, a large part of the world refuses to comply with a variety of its own laws. As far as the U.N. is concerned, I suggest you begin working on initiatives that will force member nations to create laws with teeth to sustain the temperate forests. A law that is unenforceable and regularly defied isn't really a law is it? You may as well be whistling Dixie." He realized the reference would be totally lost on a German even if she had a sense of humor.

"And Ms. Koenig, isn't that really the problem here? Our countries are engaged in a grand delusion, developing and adopting laws and regulations we have no intention of adhering to and cannot even enforce."

He saw the slight smirk disappear from her small mouth as his complete dismissal of her life's work sank into her head and then her heart. She raised her chin, hesitated a moment, edged around him and walked out. Jesse had basked in what he saw as a verbal triumph over the banality of the world's environmental legal treaties and regulations. Two weeks later, he sat in the General Assembly as a year of his hard work went down the drain with her hand stamped all over the Drano.

So why was he so sure she was the person to help him now? Would working with her make an insurmountable task even harder? He already had to deal with Miriamu. Two strong women might be a disaster. But he had witnessed Hannah's mastery of international law. Then he remembered his own words, "adopting laws you can't enforce." Would those words come back to haunt him now, when so much more was at stake than just temperate forests?

~4~
NEW YORK CITY

THE FEBRUARY WIND OFF THE EAST RIVER BELTED THEM, MAKING conversation impossible. The gray smog left grimy residue on all the surfaces around them, threatening to deposit a film on Jesse and Hannah if they stood in one place too long. The temperature had dropped below zero. Jesse had chosen an obscure cafe blocks from the United Nations Building. He steered her to a booth away from the cold blasts of the entrance.

He had to hide a mild feeling of self-righteousness, knowing that the battle he had lost to her over new regulations to revive and sustain temperate forests had, along with others, led to the dilemma he was about to share with her. Now, he desperately needed her to be on his side and it was crucial he avoid another confrontation.

"Non-fat latte for me, and make it really hot," she instructed the waiter, then rubbed her chilled hands together.

"Just coffee for me. Ms. Koenig I appreciate your willingness to meet with me. I'll get right to why I called you. As you already know, my U.N. department monitors many of the scientific factors related to climate change using a vast array of technologies and equipment placed in strategic locations around the globe. We are now convinced that the balance between oxygen, nitrogen, argon, and carbon dioxide is shifting. The oxygen crucial to human survival could rapidly decrease if it continues the shift it is now making and we do not do something."

"What?"

"Oxygen is disappearing. Data in reports from all around the planet forecast that we are slipping toward a future without enough oxygen."

"Reports? From where?"

"Atmospheric stations at the north and south poles and in numerous places around the world run by the U.N. or other government authorities in conjunction with my division."

"And why are you sharing this with only me at what feels a bit like a clandestine meeting?"

"Well, I've been meeting with the secretary general and a small group of other senior U.N. people to discuss what needs to happen and what role the U.N. might play to reverse the human activities throughout the world that are leading to this slide toward a shift in our oxygen. At this time, the group and I feel that the U.N. will need to oversee a worldwide effort to avert this balance from shifting further and it will need to do so immediately. Our actions will inevitably require a wide variety of coordinated mandates, backed by international treaties and agreements.

If the data is accurate, and we have no reason to believe it is not, there is no time to further debate or discuss plans. We have to act now, or the atmospheric trend will be irreversible. And you are the senior most legal counsel to the U.N. You will need to play a crucial role in helping formulate the actual legal basis for our actions and the international agreements and treaties we will need to put in place."

"And just what kinds of global actions do you propose we will have to undertake to reverse this trend, Mr. Forester?"

"We need to stop all burning of fossil fuels, waste, and agricultural fields, etc. and any other activities that contribute to the buildup of carbon dioxide in the atmosphere. We'll have to do it fast and it will have to be a global effort. We will also need to immediately ramp up all efforts to create truly benign forms of energy and to get city dwellers—really anyone who does not grow their own food and have access to a working well, natural spring or clean river—access to food and water."

The waiter came to ask if they needed food, but Jesse brushed him away. Hannah took a large tissue from her purse and blew her nose.

"That, Mr. Forester is the most outlandish story I have ever heard. You want me to provide the international legal basis for plans your group will create to force every nation to halt the use of fossil fuels. On whose authority will you implement these actions? The U.N.'s? You'll create chaos. What nation is going to buy into the data and adopt the steps needed without a fight?"

Jesse felt foolish even attempting this encounter. What if she refused to believe or trust him?

He took a deep breath and tried to be more forceful but not in anger. "Ms. Koenig, I have a briefcase full of the figures that substantiate what I am predicting. I know it is hard to believe we have been pushed into such a corner. Several years ago, we knew the tipping point of carbon dioxide overload—four hundred parts per million—would land us in trouble; we just didn't know what it would be. But we are there now."

"Who else have you told?"

"The secretary general and those closest to him on his staff. Ms. Mirza will be glad to go over the figures and substantiate our findings. You must realize this is much more urgent than the latest economic treaty between nations or another peacekeeping force."

"Mr. Forester, I'm not stupid." Someone opened the cafe door and the chill wind caused her to pull her coat closer around her body and put both hands around her coffee cup. "All right, Mr. Forester, let's say I believe there is a problem, where does one start when dealing with an atmospheric crisis?"

"Well, I've been pondering for a few weeks how to go about it. I've decided we need to implement changes in three "waves" of action. First, we will calmly initiate the announcement to all people of the data and help them understand what it will soon lead to. We must give them about six months to figure out how to water, feed, and shelter themselves without burning anything. Then in the second wave we must shut down all fossil burning human activity—manufacturing, industrial agriculture, communications, etc. anything not driven by nuclear, solar, wind or hydropower and distributed by that same power. Simultaneously, we must develop or retrofit all our sources of energy, food, transportation and communication, but in ways that require no burning of fossil fuels. The third wave includes gathering and distributing information about solutions—rebuilding our civilizations without any dependency on fossil fuels."

"Wouldn't it be better to just mandate the changes like renewable energy before we take away what people rely on now?"

"We don't have time for that. Twenty years ago, five years ago, yes—but now we are about to run out of oxygen, and we are out of time. In reality, it may be too late already."

"And Mr. Forester, given that I would not even support your efforts to sustain and renovate the temperate rain forests by putting in place international agreements to cut harvesting percentages, why did you choose me?"

Jesse took a deep breath. "Well, I've watched you at many sessions. There is no one else with such a command of international law."

"There are others."

"No one else has your persistence in the force of formidable opposition. You are a person of moral courage and we will need a lot of that. Ours is a daunting task."

"And if we don't initiate your three waves?"

"Then we will cease to live on this planet."

~5~
NEW YORK CITY

KAREN FORESTER STOOD ON THE SIDEWALK AND WATCHED AS HER husband struggled to fasten the bikes to the top of the suburban. "Jesse, I still feel this is unnecessary."

"I don't know how you can say that. You've seen the data. Tell the families of those folks who lost their lives in Nepal last year when they ran out of oxygen way before they should have that this isn't necessary. Tell those in the Southern Hemisphere who barely survived the typhoons and the rising oceans."

"We don't live on a mountain in Nepal or in the southern hemisphere! We live in a beautiful apartment in New York City. This is my home, where I want to stay."

"Karen, New York—all cities—will be dangerous places as soon as the people know about the shift in oxygen. We have to stop all burning. People will panic and all hell will break loose."

"Why can't America just cut back and . . . ."

"I told you. This is a world problem; we share the Earth's atmosphere with all of mankind. Nothing America does now on its own, no matter how big, will be sufficient."

Jesse walked into the street to tighten the bungee cords on the driver's side. A motorist honked for him to get out of the way and then threw him a finger. Karen just stood there, with hands on her hips in her latest familiar pose of consternation.

"We went through all this last night. We are dealing with tons of atmospheric carbon dioxide and decades of shortsightedness." Jesse came around to where she stood on the sidewalk and tried to take her hand. She pulled away. "Karen, be reasonable."

"No, you be reasonable. Nothing about this move makes sense to me. If all that sweet talk and lovemaking last night was to convince me, well, it didn't work. All these New Yorkers get to stay, but I get shipped off to Iowa. I don't want to live on a farm. I want to stay here with you . . . . Oh, Jesse you're being unfair."

He came up behind her to put his arms around her. "Karen, I'm so scared. I'm afraid for you, for our sons. I'm afraid for all these New Yorkers. I need some kind of assurance that at least you are safe. You can also help my parents cope with the changes that are inevitable. Can't you understand that?"

"What about you? It won't be safe for you, and I want to be with you."

"What about the boys, are you willing to endanger them?"

He turned her around and held her at arm's length. They stared silently into each other's eyes. Finally, weary of the old argument, she shook her head and kissed him softly until a cacophony of stomping and loud voices interrupted them.

Two boys erupted from the apartment house yelling at each other. The bigger one, Ethan, was followed by Troy, who sported a long face. Ethan was obviously getting the upper hand in their argument. "Troy, you know I'm older and will get to ride the horse. You're too little to ride by yourself."

"I'll get to ride too."

"No. They probably don't have enough horses for both of us to ride regularly!"

Troy skirted around Ethan and grabbed Jesse at the waste. "Dad, Ethan says I'm too little to ride the horses at Grandpa's, and there won't be enough of them. He's wrong isn't he, Dad?"

Jesse caught them both, swinging Troy around, and shaking his head at Ethan. "No, you're not too young. I was just your age when I got to have my own horse, and I was riding the farm horses long before that. Ethan, there will be plenty of horses for both you and Troy. You'll have to learn to ride, but I'm sure gramps will teach you. I promise it will work out.

"See, Ethan, I told you so."

Ethan stuck out his tongue, shrugging his shoulders.

"Boys, kiss your dad goodbye and get in the car."

Ethan gave Jesse a peck on his cheek and climbed into the suburban. "There's no place to put my feet, Mom. Where do I put my feet?"

"Just rest them on the boxes."

"Gee, I'm hungry. Can we stop at McDonald's for a Big Mac and fries?"

"No, you just had breakfast. Maybe we'll stop for lunch."

Jesse leaned down as Troy gave him a hug and a smacking good kiss. "Is my erector set in the car?"

"It's in the U-Haul with the extra supplies for Grandpa."

"Where's my bike?"

"See it right there on top of the Suburban?"

"Oh, yeah, I guess I can go then. Bye, Dad." He started for the car.

"Bye, son."

Troy hesitated and turned back to Jesse. "Dad, will you come to the farm too?"

"Yes."

"When?"

"As soon as I finish my work here, I'll come."

"Promise, Dad?'

"Promise."

~6~
NEW YORK CITY

JESSE PUSHED ASIDE PAPERS AND PUT THE SACK OF SANDWICHES AND drinks down on the table. It was 9 p.m. and they had been at it since noon. Hannah was down the hall at the wash room. The winter months they'd spent preparing the U.N. mandates had been draining. The issues were written on a white marker board. The actions for Wave I were identified and mapped out.

On April 1

• The public—in cities and rural areas—in every nation will be advised of the shifting ratios of carbon dioxide to oxygen and informed that they have 180 days to find a source of food, water, and shelter that does not depend on fossil fuels.

• Each nation will designate a small group of officials, including at least one U.N. representative, to be the Essentials for that nation. Essentials will have centralized, limited access to transportation and communications. They will be housed in centralized apartments and provided with clean water and sufficient food. They will have all authority needed to enforce the implementation of Operation World Salvation in their nation. They will have police and military protection and service to enforce the mandates if need be.

On April 15

• Churches, schools, and government offices will begin distributing detailed instructions and offering whatever assistance they are able to in helping people find and secure the basic essentials quickly.

On October 1

• The sale of all petroleum products will be halted.

• The burning of all and any types of waste will cease.

On October 10

• All burning of fuel for cars, buses, trucks, and planes will be off limits except to those designated by the U.N. as "Essentials"; all burning of any material for waste, heat, or any other reason will also be prohibited.

On October 25

• The military and police of all nations will begin to enforce the ban on the use of carbon-based fuels and any and all burning to the full extent of international law, which in this case can mean violators will be put to death.

The Mandates for Wave I were further fleshed out:

• People must find means to grow food themselves or work in communities to grow and share food; any and all empty lands within city spaces will be made immediately available, by international law, for food production; private ownership of such spaces is suspended till further notice.

• People must find means to provide housing that does not depend on any source of carbon or burning for a heat source for the coming winter.

There were ten pages of further instructions to go to government authorities who would get them out to the public. Within a very short time the Emergency Declaration and Instructions for Wave I would be translated into every known language of the world and stand ready for the first announcement on April 1.

Wave II was similarly outlined, but some details were still sketchy such as what nations should do if citizens refused to stop using gasoline—shoot them? On what authority? Wave III really bothered him. They had just a hodgepodge of information gathered about ways to shift the whole of human society to civilizations not dependent on fossil fuels. They needed ideas that had been successful, but where in this day and age would they find communities flourishing without fossil fuel? And if they found such examples, would it be possible to recreate those examples quickly all around the world? The task felt more daunting each day.

Hannah returned, looking a little fresher, and dug into her sandwich.

Jesse smiled at her eagerness. "You were hungry."

"Starved, I exercised in the gym this morning and skipped lunch."

"That's not healthy."

"No, but I'm inclined to eat and sit too much, especially now that it's difficult to find time to exercise."

He shook his head. "I need you healthy."

"Not to worry, I'm like a cat, I have nine lives."

"Why do you say that?"

"I'll tell you someday."

"Tell me now. We both can use a break."

Hannah carefully wiped a dab of mustard from her lip and took a swallow of tea. "I was not expected to live as a child because of an early bout with TB and pneumonia. My parents were very frightened and sent me to Spain for a year to live with another family. I came back fully restored. When I was sixteen, I was in a horrible accident on the autobahn. My little Volkswagen ran under a big lorry, and I should have been decapitated. The physicians couldn't believe that I came out almost unscratched."

"How?"

"I ducked. Then, when I was twenty-seven, I was supposed to be on that TWA flight that went down off Newark, but I missed the plane and had to take a later flight. So you see, I lead a charmed life. Like my cat, I have many lives."

"Impressive. Is it a thing of faith?"

"No, actually I'm agnostic. I have always felt I'm in control and can reason my way through any situation. How about you? Do you believe in God?"

Jesse didn't answer right away. They'd never talked about anything but the Operation, and he was afraid a flippant answer might blow what so far had been a smooth relationship. He wanted to avoid any confrontation.

"I believe there is a divine source. Most scientists do believe in a supreme power. It is hard to see all of the beauty and majesty around and not believe in something beyond our mortal efforts. I know I didn't create the stars or the planets or the oceans, nor did any other mortal. I guess I tend toward the intelligent design theory a little. Still I'm just not sure how we can know for sure. Even less sure how we can trust we are receiving help from that source. I'd like to think when I make decisions like we are making now that they are the right ones. Do you know what I mean?"

She moved back to the marker board to correct a figure. "Making decisions logically, intellectually is not good enough for you?"

"No, I guess not. You must admit that humans have been making decisions in what seemed to be logical ways for centuries, and look where it's gotten us. I would like to think there's a better way. If there's a divine intelligence, maybe we need to learn how to tap into it better and use that source."

She turned to face him. "That frightens me."

"Why?"

"I'd like to know you're sure of what we're doing without help from some mystical power we can't depend upon."

"Fair enough. If it's any consolation, I am making decisions according to what makes sense and seems scientifically and ethically right. Does that help?"

"Some. Let's get back to outlining Wave II."

They returned to hammering out the plans for food supplies, fuel supplements, and alternate transportation modes. By midnight, the Wave II mandates were satisfactorily sketched out on the marker board, ready for Hannah and her secretary to type out and put into a packet to share with the secretary-general.

Jesse stretched and walked around the table while she gathered up papers.

Hannah handed him a booklet. "Have you read this?"

It was entitled "Our Responsibility to the Land" by an Irishman named Paddy Freeman.

"No, have you?"

"Most of it."

"And?"

"Our office received it months ago. I stuffed it away and came across it yesterday. You might want to contact him. His ideas could help with Wave III. There is also a female agricultural minister in Argentina: Camilla Olivas, I heard her speak at a conference last year. She may also be able to help us form Wave III. Or her ideas are really from some old guy named Hendrik Johnson—not sure if he's still around—who came up with an intriguing way for agriculture producers to restore their farms, ranches and even communal lands while making good money and building social capital in their community. Let's see if we can track down both of them too."

"Yeah, I recognize that name. Some years ago, Karen gave me an article about his work. Thanks."

She stopped sorting papers and looked him in the eye. "You see, I believe our help comes from each other, not that mystical source you were talking about. The answers are there."

"Yeah, but what's to say that mystical source isn't telling us where to look or bringing us all together at the right time?"

~7~
BELFAST, NORTHERN IRELAND

"MR. FREEMAN WOULD YOU LIKE A CUP OF COFFEE, OR SOME TEA?"

Paddy Freeman looked up from the papers he had been handed. "Thanks, no. I had a sip o' tea at station. I don't like Belfast, wire and concrete barriers down now that the troubles are over, but it be a dirty city. Now where in heavens name be me glasses?" Fishing them from his sweater pocket, he cleaned them. Paddy skimmed four sheets of statistics and an addendum covering some of the ideas he had developed over a lifetime career in agriculture on self-sufficiency, renewable energy and family farms—pamphlets and papers he had written in the '90s.

Paddy looked over his glasses at the man speaking. Aye, he's the kina pompous statesman like them that's in Parliament. The other three be a strange lot, the U.S. senator fellow, the Spanish-looking man, and the African-looking woman in the beautiful batik suit with a matching multi-colored turban. They make me nervous. An ol' fool, that's what I am. An ol' fool that has not a speck a trust left.

"Mr. Freeman, have you had a chance to consider the request we made in our letter of two weeks ago?"

"Aye. But why on God's green earth did you want me to travel all this way? Me writings, they be speaking for me. They're available to you and anyone else at wants to read 'em."

"Well, we were hoping your presence would encourage our Dutch friend, the CEO of BDM, here to retrofit his facility so that wind energy machines could be moved in his shipping containers which right now he uses only for grain and other foodstuffs. You are revered by those very writings and the work you've done at all levels of E.U.

agriculture and conservation and we felt your endorsement would be useful." For the first time, Paddy considered the bulging Dutchman at the far end of the table with distaste. The other American—Manuel something—was passing out more papers.

Paddy recognized some of the statistics on the documents as his own predictions for the collapse of soils and crop failures as well as the ensuing soil carbon build up in the atmosphere. He'd predicted the drying up of the Ogallala Aquifer in the U.S. and the increased spread of the Sahara Desert. He knew that soon the rest of the world would reap what the oldest cultivated societies had already experienced—collapse. And even before that happened, thousands of years of food production without regard for soil fertility had released carbon into the atmosphere for centuries, producing 30 to 40 percent of the carbon legacy load. Caught up for a moment in his own past, Paddy remembered how angry his writings made the other farmers in the early days and how often he'd been hissed from a stage despite sound data to back his predictions.

"Mr. Freeman, can we count on you? Our friend from the Netherlands values your work, as we do. We would like to use your numbers and name to document the necessity for people to move toward sustainable practices, not only for Europe but also for others around the world.

"What makes you think they'll listen? I've talked till I'm blue in me face and been thrown outa the hallowed halls of Parliament and Congress on me tail."

"Well, we don't know that they will listen. But we have to try; the fate of the world is at stake, and your support of this effort will make all the difference."

He peered over his glasses at those around the table. "I be as sure that things can't go as they have been as ye. But men be afraid o' change. Most o' me Irish farmers and fishermen know what they be doing is wrong, but first they need to be taught what is right. Then they might change. It's reeducation that's needed or ye may have people freezing to death and starving."

"That's exactly where you come into our plan, Mr. Freeman. Even though you may not be respected so much in Ireland, your writings have been read all over the world. Your name on these business documents will help our company convince key international financiers and politicians to support this effort."

As the black woman continued to address him directly, Paddy wished for the second time he could remember her name. He knew the uppity American was Senator Cleveland like the American president, but the woman's name was too strange for his old ears.

"We are anxious for those who are knowledgeable like you to help us to, as you say, re-educate the public and decision makers to make a wholesale shift toward renewables. Of course, we hope no one will starve, or freeze to death in the interim."

Cleveland pushed another document toward Paddy. "Mr. Freeman, we are ready to put other sources of energy in place and of course we are going to promote quick re-education for agriculture production which should prevent most of the foreseeable crisis."

"Aye. You can use me name and me ideas. Canna hurt to try again, but experience and failure has been me teachers, and nowhere in this here plan can I see a surefire way o' saving this old earth from lots o' pain. Sorry if that offends ye, but being eighty makes me a pessimist. Now, I have a train to catch."

"Before you leave, Mr. Freeman, could we get you to sign some releases on several of these documents?"

As Paddy signed the papers, the rest of the group got oddly quiet. He noted the bold letters at the top of each page referred to a company called SOLYNDRIX. He didn't remember much these days, but he'd try to remember that name if he could. Then he struggled briefly putting on his worn Macintosh and left the room with a wave of his hand.

~8~
NEW YORK CITY

Hannah Koenig slammed the phone down on the table. Her frustration over the conversation was obvious. Her brother-in-law would not believe her warnings. She was grateful Jesse didn't understand German. Legally, she had no right to pre-warn her family, but she knew Jesse had done the same by getting Karen and his boys off to the farm. She pushed wisps of hair back into the combs that held her bun in place.

"Trouble at home?"

"My brother-in-law Ali can be so difficult. He's a Turk, and sometimes it is just communication and sometimes it is his bull-headedness." The ease with which she avoided the whole truth made her uncomfortable, and she began sifting through papers. She needed all her wits about her for their meeting with Miriamu.

Jesse walked to the window and gazed out at the horseman statue in the little United Nations Park. Lunch time, and the spring heat was coming much too early. Trees in the small grassy area were already budding, and the sun felt too hot for March. U.N. employees sat on the concrete benches eating lunch or just soaking up the sunshine.

"Hannah, as Dr. Hageman, my old philosophy professor, would say, we need to exercise a democratic imperative here."

"What?"

He turned and walked back to the desk. "We have the choice to act as individuals for the safety of our loved ones. How we deal with this is something we must both agree on. There must be some advantage for all the sleepless hours we have spent—for our families to suffer more would be doubly cruel. How we deal with our families in private need not go beyond this room. Karen has already left with the boys, headed to my family's farm in Iowa."

She threw him a warm smile of relief. It was the first time he could remember her whole face smiling. Usually, the mouth turned up but the eyes remained cool. Jesse noticed she was actually quite lovely.

As the two of them went through the reports on the carbon dioxide buildup, she questioned Jesse on everything, trying to find any possible fault or discrepancy in his data and calculations. The marker board was replete with question marks.

"Trust me, Ms. Koenig, it always comes back to the simplest fact. We have hit an imbalance. We are a suicidal society. Either through ignorance or conscious choice, we have placed ourselves on the precipice of our own demise."

"Well, Mr. Forester, human populations with time on their hands do one of two things. We explore and create great art or we sink into decadence.

Hannah paused from writing on the marker board and turned to face Jesse. "Did you know before the wall fell in Berlin, philosophers who looked at the western side with the brothels and pubs and flashing lights decided that the calm on the east side, the quiet poverty, created in large part by lack of technology, might be better? Now, both sides are virtually the same, and we have come to this. I have my doubts that technology is real progress."

"Well, I don't think we should throw the baby out with the bath water. The only reason we now know there is a problem we must address and the only way we can communicate to everyone what needs to be done is through very advanced forms of technology, right?"

* * *

"Secretary Mirza to see you."

"Thank you, Peta. Send her in"

Miriamu entered the room with her usual air of grace laden with superiority. No one could possibly ignore the tall, shapely Kenyan.

She wore a bright red and orange kanga that Jesse had seen often, and her abundant braided hair was fastened by a large golden clip. Jesse held her chair out for her and then sat down across the table.

"Miriamu, I am concerned that the United States will not get the full impact of our information soon enough. I know that our U.S. scientists are aware of most of the data, but for some reason, they are ignoring it. I hear rumblings from our scientific center but nothing solid. We feel our findings should have been shared with the U.S. government yesterday if not sooner. I propose . . ."

"And I suppose Ms. Koenig feels the same about Germany?"

"I can't speak for Hannah, but I think so. If we are to be successful, there must be countries who lead the way. Others will then follow. We all know that if one powerful country decides not to accept the data and join with others to lead the way, it could be fatal. The mistrust among governments at the U.N. has grown every year, especially since 2001. The U.S. has refused to sign almost every single climate change treaty over the last twenty years, the international tribunal court has fallen apart, and votes of the Security Council are regularly unable to achieve what is needed for the body to act as a whole.

"Won't your own U.N. ambassador be reporting to the president as soon as the Security Council approves our plan?"

"Yes, but he was a weak appointee from the start and is not trusted by many in Congress. By now, the information should have been shared with the entire U.N., and therefore at a minimum the strongest nations. There are many scientists who will deny all this—they will create havoc and delay. Industrialists will refuse to comply.

"If we, as you say, have countries who are leaders and those that are followers, which do you see as the followers?"

"Ms. Mirza, the more industrialized the nation, the harder it will be for that nation to comply with the Operation, especially with the mandate to mobilize the military to force compliance. Those nations will also experience the greatest turmoil because they are the most heavily dependent on fossil fuel infrastructures. The less industrialized will be less impacted, but they will, in many cases, be suspicious that this is a ploy by the Western world to force them to cut emissions while the West continues with its own coal-consumptive party."

"Mr. Forester, all of this has been discussed. We need to be sure information is not leaked to the press. If the facts are leaked before we are ready to implement the plans, it would be suicidal. I will be out of town for several days. When I get back, I will discuss it again with the secretary-general, and I will let you know." She stood up to leave.

Hannah came around the desk to stop her. "Director Mirza, I think Jesse is right. We must begin to let people in power know before it is too late. Up until now, the U.N. has not been known for its accomplishments. If we sit on these facts, we are doomed. This is an emergency. How can you ask us to wait? Why are you not willing to admit the urgency of this? You must . . ."

"Ms. Koenig, I am completely aware of the seriousness of these findings but we must wait for the secretary-general to decide how to handle the timing of information, the designation of the Essentials for each nation who are also U.N. officials or staff, and whether the U.N. will follow your suggested solutions. Now I have . . ."

Jesse stood up, grabbing papers from Hannah's desk. "Damn it, I don't think you've been reading the reports. It's all there. We can't wait any longer! Any plan will fail if we let more time go by. The U.S. authorities must . . ."

"Don't push me, Mr. Forester. I will let you know!" Miriamu swept from the room, slamming the door behind her.

"Now, maybe I know why my niece Gretchen who has asthma has to fight harder, it seems, every year to just breathe. And why Donald, a friend in the legal department, carries oxygen around with him. His love is the Colorado mountains, but they told him he had to live at sea level. Now even here, his breathing is difficult. He wasn't even a smoker."

"So people like you knew this was coming. Most of us ignore what doesn't affect us directly, don't we? We just go on living our lives, paying our bills, raising our kids without any real thought to what each action does to the life-support system around us."

~9~
NEW YORK CITY

CHINATOWN WAS WEARYING. CHINESE NEW YEAR EXPENDED MOST of the natives' energy. Street hustlers smoked, leaning against the buildings. Tourist groups were their main targets. Miriamu, modestly dressed and alone, was not approached. In her casual suit and comfortable shoes, she was any working woman or housewife shopping in Chinatown.

She hesitated at the Noodle House, glancing back over her shoulder. She opened the door to the aroma of fried fish and pungent Chinese cabbages.

A small, furtive man just inside the door took her arm and guided Miriamu to a table in a far corner away from the handful of other diners. A pot of tea was already steaming on the table as they sat down.

"Ms. Mirza, I am so honored that you came. How are your family, your mother and father and brothers and sisters?" Haile Gebremichael, assistant to the ambassador from Ethiopia, was nothing if not the essence of African hospitality, propriety and respect.

"My family is in Kisumu, and they are fine. This is not about my family. What is it, Haile? What do you want; what do you need to tell me?"

"Miriamu, you have become too Western. Are you not going to at least first ask about my family?"

"You didn't come to talk about our families. You know it is dangerous for me to be here. You have made yourself known as 'difficult,' and I am risking my reputation by meeting with you. What do you want?"

"Miriamu, I know you are a more important person in the U.N. than I, and my country needs you to be on our side."

"What makes you think there are sides, Haile? Why can't we all be in this together?"

"Miriamu, look around you. This is not Kenya. This is not Ethiopia. This is a rich country where a machine gives you dollars, where doors open for you without you moving them, where the stores are bigger than a mosque, and people sit around with their feet up pushing buttons on talking boxes. This is a country where there is food; no mass famines have ever occurred here." The waiter appeared and quickly took their order.

"Haile, these people also work. They have families; they don't get all this free."

"But they get it, and our people do not. Is it not reasonable to do something to put our people on the same ground?"

"A completely even playing ground is not possible; there are vast differences in natural resources, the development of technologies, the availability of education, governmental systems and many other things. There are differences in cultures."

"Miriamu, I am speaking only of food. I am talking about people, my people, your people, and a way to feed them now and in the future." He leaned forward, lowering his voice. "We both know you are working on a plan that will create havoc in the Western world, havoc that will result in opportunities for our people."

"What are you talking about? Why would I become part of a plan to create havoc? And how do you think such havoc would relieve the suffering of your people? I know your country is struggling as mine is but . . ."

"My country has had famine, half of the middle age adults have died of AIDS, and the International Monetary Fund says we are once again in default. What is default to an Ethiopian sitting in front of his hut? You are here with all this power. You are the Rhodes scholar, a big person in the white world. Are you not doing something about Kibera town, where thousands live in poverty? You are in a position to level the playing field and loose the bands of those who hold us in slavery."

"I have a job to do, but it doesn't include solving all of Africa's problems."

"Then why are you here? Of what use are you to the African nations? We will help you with your plan—to change the tide of prosperity and opportunity."

"I am unaware of any such plan, and if one exists, it certainly is not being masterminded by me."

Haile stood up, and leaned over the table to grab her arm, "I know about the monies collected, the many fishes; I know about the other players, those you are in contact with, those who will help this leveling. I know there is a plan. There is a plan to rob the West of its advantage." His voice was soft but forceful as his grasp on her arm intensified. "I will help you. We, my country, will be a player in the game. We must not be left out. Miriamu, listen to me. My people are hungry, they are sick, they . . .'

"Let go of me! You're making a scene! You have obviously been given false information. Someone is trying to set me up perhaps."

His black eyes blazed, venom spit through the words spewing from his mouth. "Ethiopia will not be left out. We must reverse the ancient and modern oppressions of the white man. You will hear from us." He turned, abruptly knocking the tray from the hands of an astonished waiter. Egg rolls, sweet and sour soup, and noodles cascaded down the waiter's front and ended up all over the floor. Haile paused at the door and pointed an accusing finger at her, then disappeared down the street.

~10~
WASHINGTON, D.C.

B.J. Cunningham was on leave from Quantico when he met the senator. Actually, he didn't know the man was a senator. All he knew was the man must be very rich because he was paying for drinks and invited B.J. to join the party. B.J. was used to people making friends with him just because of how good he looked, especially in uniform. The next morning when he scanned the card the man had given him, there was the Senate insignia and a note on the back: "call me if you want a job."

At the interview, the senator asked him "What are you trained to do?" B.J. responded, "Play basketball, protect America, and kill her enemies." The senator laughed as though it was a joke. Then he looked directly into B.J.'s eyes and nodded. From then on, B.J. knew they had something in common—a burning desire to get what they wanted and to conquer anyone who got in the way. The first time he had felt that burning inside, he was six sitting on their broken down porch in Harlan County watching the leaves fall and hearing his daddy yell obscenities at his momma. The burning increased every time his momma sent him to the store with food stamps to pay for groceries and whenever he watched his parents sit around and wait for the welfare check to come in the mail. The mountains around Harlan County, Kentucky, represented the grinding poverty his family endured, and once he left, he never looked—or went—back.

B.J. Cunningham's real name was Brother John. He hated that name. He knew it was stupid to be called Brother John by strangers or even people he knew. His big sister, Naomi, had given him the name.

"Why'd you want to name me Brother for?"

"Because that's what you are, you're my brother."

"I'm not everyone's brother. I'm just brother to you and James."

"So don't you want to be everyone's real brother? Reverend Matthews say we're all brothers.'

"I ain't his brother. He's too old and fat!"

In the Kentucky hills where they lived, the term brother was a sign of affection and belonging. To him, the term and the place were things he just wanted to be free of.

Brother John was a beautiful child—even if everyone did think he was a girl when he was little. His momma had been so beautiful she was crowned Laurel Festival Queen when she was seventeen. He got her wavy auburn hair and his daddy's deep blue eyes. When he was twelve, he looked in the old mirror in the bathroom and knew he was pretty—no, handsome, really handsome for a boy. At thirteen, he was over six feet tall and decided that basketball was his way to climb out of the mountains.

But he wasn't just handsome and tall; he was smart too.

"B.J.," Naomi would say, "help me with this algebra stuff. "I just can't make sense out of it."

"I have practice, you know that. Hit me again tonight when I'm back, Naomi."

But usually he didn't have time to help her or his younger brother. He was busy being himself. When the captain of the cheerleading squad came to him a few months after they began having sex, he didn't have time for her either.

"B.J., I'm pregnant."

"So?"

"Well, you devil, it's your child."

"So?"

"You got to marry me."

"I don't got to do anything. You too stupid to protect yourself? Why you think they gave us those sex education classes last year anyway? Get yourself over to that family planning place in Baxter."

That attitude didn't work with the next girlfriend. Her Catholic daddy sent her off to an aunt in Elisabeth Town to have the baby. B.J. never admitted the child was his, and the girl's parents didn't press it for fear of the gossip it would create.

B.J. averaged twenty-seven points a game as a high school senior and the Kentucky Wildcats recruiter was at the state finals. He signed a four-year promise to play for them. But in Lexington on the third day of practice, he got into an argument with Coach John Calipari. When the coach told him to spend an hour doing suicides, he refused. A week later, they dropped him from the team, and he lost his ticket out of the mountains.

Dejected, he told himself being a big fish in a little pond was Harlan. But being a little fish in a big pond was different, and he would have to adjust. Walking around Lexington, he saw a Marine recruiting poster. It had a big, handsome man with an M16 in his clutches. The poster told him there was more than one way to skin a cat. He passed both the physical and written tests with ease, and two months later was in basic at Quantico. During firing practice and maneuvers, his enemy wasn't the other soldiers—his enemy was always somewhere and someone else. He might never play basketball again, but he sure was good at killing.

~11~
WASHINGTON, D.C.

B.J. KNEW HE WAS BEING FOLLOWED. HE NOTICED THE SMALL, dark man as he left the Hart Senate Building. He saw him again as he swept down the escalator. B.J. pretended to read his paper while waiting for the train. The man stood about twenty-five feet away, so blatant, obviously not a professional, certainly not a threat.

B.J. waited until everyone else had gotten on the car before he stepped into the train, noting that the man did the same. He sat perusing the evening news, pleased to see the increased focus on news about pollution, the ozone, and growing rates of asthma.

He exited at Dupont Circle. Taking the steps two at a time, he almost ran down a mother and her baby. "Watch out, move to the right, why don't ya?" he growled. "Damn to hell these tourists who don't understand D.C. protocol and how to handle the escalators." At street level, he walked up Q Street to 17th and began window shopping past boutiques, cafes, and bakeries. He could see the man off and on reflected in the windows.

Then he remembered—he's one of those U.N. fellows, working on the same floor as Miriamu. B.J. sauntered half a block and ducked into an alley, kicking papers, garbage cans, and a solitary dead rat. Ten paces in, he slipped into the shadow of the wall, holding his breath to ward off the putrid garbage smell. He caught Haile as the slight man stepped gingerly through the alley looking right and left, pinning his arms to his sides.

"Why are you following me, little man? Who are you and what do you want?"

"Careful, son, I'm staff at the U.N. and I work for the ambassador from Ethiopia. And I'm just interested in why you keep showing up at Ms. Mirza's office and what business you have with her."

"Well, buddy, she and I are having raucous sex a few times a month, and that's none of your business and nothing else is either."

"Are you involved in the plan she has cooked up to change those who are on top and level the field for the black man?"

"I have no idea what you're talking about. Do I look like a guy who cares about black men?"

"You work for that senator—what's his name Martin or what? I know—I have seen you meeting with him and others at offices at the U.N. too."

"So what if I do. It's my job to be close to him. I pretty much go where he goes." B.J. dropped his arms, and looked past the man's face to be sure their loud voices hadn't attracted any pedestrians.

"I don't want to fight with you; I just want to help with your plan. And if you won't cooperate with me, I'll reveal what I know of your plan to the press, Congress, and the U.N.

"That's an interesting threat since there is no plan. You damn cocky Africans think just because you have access to the U.S. and diplomatic immunity, you can do whatever you want. Well listen and listen carefully. Stop following me. Do you hear? Make no mistake, I don't like being followed by anyone and especially not dirty, shiftless foreigners. I don't like being threatened either. And just to make sure you got the message—here's my plan for you."

He raised both his arms and let them fall with force on Haile's shoulders. As the Ethiopian slumped over, he buried his knee in the man's stomach. Haile hit the ground with a thud.

B.J. Cunningham returned to the sidewalk and headed back to the subway station, pausing now and then to window shop.

~12~
CINCINNATI, OHIO

KAREN COULDN'T HELP THE RESENTMENT SHE FELT. THEIR MARRIAGE had had its ups and downs, but this was the worst. The farther west she drove, the angrier she became. Her whole life had been put on hold. The move to New York from California just a few years ago had been so exciting. She loved her editing job at Harper's, and the apartment and the museums; she even loved the subway. All her life, Karen had been a people watcher, and the subway was a fascinating place for this. There were all those people reading and sleeping or staring, pretending to be alone in their own space.

One day, she'd watched a Jewish boy with his eyes squinted and his face screwed up memorizing the Talmud. He looked up and mouthed the words, and looked down to confirm the passage. Another night, she and Jesse had been coming home from a play when a young man entertained them, singing traditional religious songs. He sang "The Old Rugged Cross," "In the Garden," and finished with a chorus of "Amazing Grace." Then he smiled, bowed low while they clapped, and got off the train.

They all enjoyed Radio City Music Hall and the skating at Rockefeller Center. They attended the parades, especially loving the Macy's Thanksgiving Day parade, They would sure miss the Broadway musicals and the Yankees games.

"Mom, when will we get there?" Ethan asked, interrupting her thoughts.

"Tomorrow night. I told you this morning. You know it takes over two days by car. Please be patient."

"There's still no place to put my feet."

"Be grateful you're not walking beside a covered wagon, okay?"

"Like you had to, Mom?"

"Don't get smart with me young man. I'll cut off your french fries."

"Ah, Mom. Boy, I'm hungry."

"Eat another apple."

The Suburban and U-Haul were packed with things Jesse thought might eventually be hard to come by in Iowa. He'd collected canned meats, candles, extra bedding, batteries, strong gardening tools, and an old but sturdy small hand plow he'd picked up in the New Jersey farm country.

How was a wife supposed to react to a plan that could keep them apart for months, maybe years? How was she supposed to feel stuck away in a farmhouse in nowhere, America? How was she supposed to respond when she knew he would be spending lots of time with another woman—an attractive, intelligent woman?

Jesse told her he disliked Hannah Koenig. She was way too severe, not at all feminine. But she couldn't help wondering why, among all the U.N. personnel, he was so sure she was the legal person to help him. Karen had never felt jealousy before, but now her doubt grew with each passing mile.

Outside Indianapolis, the fuel light went on. She stopped, made both boys use the restroom, and bought coffee. An hour later, when Troy and Ethan were finally asleep, she switched from the rock station that was giving her a headache. NPR was reporting a precipitous increase in alternate energy stocks. Sales in wind- and solar-power equipment had gone up drastically. And the market value of a few companies that manufactured alternative energy systems was skyrocketing.

The report was puzzling. Neither the market nor the general public had any knowledge of the U.N. operation. Why this sudden demand for renewable energy? She made a note to mention this when she called Jesse that night. Switching to a country-western station, she sang along with old tunes. The melancholy love songs made her ache, especially when she thought of how long her separation from Jesse might be. She turned to a classical station and tried to concentrate on the white lines in the center of the road.

~13~
NEW YORK–WASHINGTON, D.C.

"THIS IS YOUR CAPTAIN. WE WILL BE FLYING AT THIRTY-ONE THOUSAND feet. Our flying time to Reagan International will be forty minutes. Visibility at Reagan is less than one mile. Expect the usual turbulence; do not leave your seats as long as the seat belt light is on." Jesse tuned out the pilot and reached for his briefcase under the seat. The turbulence made it virtually impossible to read, and he knew the information by heart anyway.

The earliest report was dated October 1948, when residents of Donora, Pennsylvania, woke up in a stagnant cloud of pollution. Four days later, twenty people were dead and half the seven thousand residents were sick. The next set of files summarized the 1960s fight against hydrofluorocarbons from spray products. They were all there: 1970, 1980, 1982, 1983, through to 2012.

He pulled an item from the 1990 file. The *New York Times* front page read, "Mysterious crib death related to breathing difficulty" He knew the article by heart. Forty-five children had died inexplicably in their cribs that summer. His 1998 folder was full. An article from *The Scotsman*: "The London Health authorities stated that 24,000 British children were dying each year from asthma related to fossil fuel exhaust." It was the first year of massive fires, out of control, in Sardinia, Greece, Italy, Florida, the American Southwest, Mexico, and Australia. Almost always, they were followed by rains, flooding, mudslides, and socioeconomic mayhem.

Looking out the window, Jesse remembered a sermon from a revival when he was a boy in Iowa. What was the minister's threat? First there was the flood—and then there would be fire. Maybe the old boy was right.

It would be 7 a.m. at the farm in Iowa, and his boys would be getting up. He wondered if they had learned how to milk the cow yet. Would they skinny-dip in the same spot of the creek he had? He closed his eyes, imagining the feeling of freedom as their lithe bodies slid through the cool water of the pond. No need for goggles or even swimming suits in a mud pond. How different their lives would be at least for a while now. For how long?

He wanted to wad up all the papers in the brief case scatter them to the four winds from thirty-one thousand feet, forget all about oxygen levels and ozone layers, and just go be with Karen and the boys. Part of him regretted sending them away. But he knew he had no choice, and the world had no choice. It had to change. Could he and Hannah make even one little dent in solving the problem humans faced? Would the measures for Wave I that he was about to present be accepted in Washington? Would it halt the growing imbalance of oxygen fast enough?

He rifled through the files reading at random. It was a history he knew well, and he'd tried to make it simple but compelling for his presentation to Congress:

• As early as 1896, Svante Arrhenius had begun calculating the effect of a doubling of atmospheric carbon dioxide to increase in surface temperatures by 5–6 degrees Celsius;

• In 1938, a British engineer presented evidence that both temperature and the CO_2 level had been rising over the past half-century;

• By 1972, a fellow named Sawyer published his findings that a CO_2 increase of 25 percent would correspond to a six-degree rise in world temperature; And in 1975, a three-dimensional model of global change confirmed the numbers already developed.

• As public and scientific concern rose, the UNEP supported the creation of the Intergovernmental Panel on Climate Change, which became the most powerful body looking at the effects of climate change on the Earth and all its species;

• A few of the salient points in the IPCC's 2007 report simply had to be shared:

• Eleven of twelve years in the 1995–2006 period ranked among the top twelve warmest years on record;

• Average arctic temperatures increased at almost twice the global average rate in the past hundred years;

• The ocean has been absorbing more than 80 percent of the heat added to the overall global atmospheric system; polar ice was melting at rates never recorded before, destroying billions of acres of polar habitat and producing a rise in sea levels.

Most of that was pretty dry stuff unless you were a climatologist, but by 1990, other agencies of the U.N. and scientific organizations had begun to better track the human impact of climate change other than buildup of heat and temperature. The data they gathered included:

• Billions of tons of soil each year are losing their carbon matter and other minerals that make them fertile and most of that carbon is going to the atmosphere as a contributor to the carbon buildup;

• Cataclysmic weather events—hurricanes, drought, fires and flooding—were increasing like a sigmoid curve, causing untold human suffering, especially on poor communities with limited resources and funds to clean up the mess that followed;

• The American Lung Association indicated in 2013 that there'd been a 12 percent rise in asthma rates over the last decade, and European and Asian statistics were following suit;

• By 2016, scientists could track that there had been a slow decline in atmospheric oxygen over the last eight hundred years as a result of fossil fuel burning, deforestation and desertification.

Jesse sighed. All the signs had been there for more than a century, but the world had simply ignored them or fought over the source of the changes people were experiencing. For decades politicians, scientists and the public had simply played the blame game. The IPCC set the threshold for carbon buildup at 400 ppm. And that threshold was surpassed in May of 2013.

For three decades climate change scientists and minister of state who were assigned to the IPCC had been telling the public it needed to adapt to climate change and had poured billions of dollars into research and technologies that might give humans a few more years or decades. It was a stupid suggestion from the beginning. If climate change was caused by human activity and you didn't stop the activity causing the change, adapting to the change was no more than rearranging the deck chairs on the Titanic. Eventually, something like the shift in oxygen—something humans just can't adapt to at all—was bound to happen.

The next-to-last folder in the stack held the original data of all the oxygen statistics that had thrown his department and his U.N. working group into panic.

Satisfied with his review of the "why we must do something" part of his presentation, he pulled out the small folder in the last compartment, "Operation World Salvation." He and Hannah had fought over the title as they had fought over many aspects of the Operation. He had first come up with the name, and she had balked.

"Salvation is such a big word. It means God and heaven and all that, not of this world. It just doesn't fit in our world, Jesse."

"So Miss Smarty Lawyer, what title is better?"

"World Conversion, Operation World Transformation, Operation World Change."

"Those words aren't strong enough, Hannah. They don't grab. We must sell this to the politicians and the people. Some don't even know there's a problem. They don't know they need saving. But they do. We're looking for order and meaning to life, trying to save humans from extinction. Salvation means an affirmation of life. Doesn't it?

"Doesn't this world deserve salvation here and now? So why are we afraid to say so in the name of our operation? For our use, salvation is a perfectly good word and doesn't need the belief in a heaven to make it profound."

She gave in. Operation World Salvation it would be.

Jesse read the opening paragraph. Even to him it sounded like something from a sci-fi thriller, something Asimov or Clarke or maybe Bradbury would have written.

Jesse felt tired—every muscle and bone screamed from months of sixteen-hour days and conflicts with Miriamu and Hannah, as well as his own doubts. He closed his eyes and pressed the button, leaning back in the seat. Who will believe it? They didn't revere poor old Galileo until 1985. They laughed at Rowland and Molina in the '70s. Before 2000, Clinton couldn't get support for Kyoto, and Bush and the Energy Department mocked the science behind climate change. How long would it take for the world to wake up? His boat wasn't much different, and then there were all those being paid by the oil companies to make hash of his proof.

Could they reduce the levels of carbon dioxide and increase the amount of oxygen? By 2020 there would be 5 million hectares of re-forested areas. But the rest of the world was burning up that same amount of biomass every four months in crop residue, grasslands, and thinning of forests. South Africa waged war on pine trees as "an invasive species" with no thought for the impact on collateral species or the soil. Japan and the U.S. fiddled while the world burned.

"We're beginning our descent into Reagan National. Please be sure your seat belts are fastened and see that your seat is in the upright position."

"Excuse me sir . . . sir, could you please put your seat in the upright position"

"Sorry, I must have dozed off."

"That's all right, sir; you must have been dreaming, something about Rome burning?" The stewardess smiled over her shoulder as she moved down the aisle.

~14~
SYDNEY, AUSTRALIA

"MARK, LISTEN TO ME; WE'VE GOT ANOTHER PROBLEM. THE U.S. can only send half the shipment. We can't meet our contracts of food supplies from Australian stations, and the U.S. grain we've been getting is falling. The Dutch BDM guys are going to be really pissed.

"Jerry, I'm sorry, mate, what were you saying?"

"Grain supplies from the U.S. are dwindling."

"Well, they could've found another buyer who'll pay them more. Or maybe they just don't have enough to send us because they need it there. Or maybe they're moving a different product that has better value? Maybe the days of milk and honey for grain and foodstuffs being shipped all over the world are really over."

"What in hell are you talking about? The shipment was corn and wheat. We don't deal in milk and honey?"

"You know, from the Bible—Hendrik used to use that quote and always had to remind me it was a promise to the Children of Israel that they would be led into the 'land of milk and honey'."

"Sorry, mate, you've lost me."

"Jerry, did you know that thirty thousand animals died in three weeks in Kazakhstan when the Soviet Union fell and no grain was being shipped in?"

"No, and who the hell is Hendrik?"

"My dad."

Jerry pulled a chair to the other side of the desk. "Come on, mate. I didn't even know you had a dad, and what does he have to do with the work we are doing?"

"Everyone has a dad, don't they? Hendrik and I, we just see things very differently, so I don't talk about him much. He lives in Zimbabwe in a little village with the natives. He's actually a world-renowned, environment and sustainable agriculture expert."

"One of those doomsday guys?"

"No, he at least has some solutions. He's written stuff ever since the 1950s on the problems that occur when the Earth loses plant and animal species and the impact of soil collapse on build up of carbon in the air and what this all means for humans. He says it happens because of the way we make decisions and live our lives. It's sort of like saying we have faulty software in our head and we just act out of that faulty software. He developed a different way to make decisions and trained people all over the world to use his management approach. This is his recent letter warning me some sort of collapse is coming."

Mark shoved the letter across the desk to Jerry and leaned back in his chair. He rubbed his ear and watched Jerry's face as he read.

"Wow, do you believe this stuff?"

"I don't know; that letter, on top of our supplier being able to only ship half the order, makes me nervous. Also, a buddy of mine here who launched a solar and wind-energy manufacturing company a few years back was recently approached by some U.S. fellow from a company called SOLYNDRIX, I think, to build more machines than he could ever imagine. The investor has already sent him his first check. Why would that be? Is there something going on with energy we aren't aware of? There will be some major crisis if we reach a stage where there is no more fuel to ship things across the oceans or even from one town to another. Maybe individuals, or governments, have begun to stockpile for a rainy day."

Jerry threw the letter back on the desk. "That sounds pretty far-fetched to me. We still have plenty of petroleum coming in. On the other hand, we're pretty isolated from the rest of the world. Well, since the drought and fires, Australians and their animals depend on shipping to eat.

Mark, we can't solve the whole world's problems; you and I just have to decide what to do about filling our orders. So?"

"Make some calls and see if anyone else—Argentina or Brazil—has any reserves."

"Should I call Jacobs?"

"No way, mate, not until we make an effort to fix the current shortfall. If Hendrik is right, by the time we have to face Jacobs, our jobs won't be worth a damn anyway."

Jerry headed for the door and turned. "Mark, if you hear anything more from your dad, will you let me know? I have my family to consider, okay? Oh, and I won't be able to go to the soccer match tomorrow. Connie informs me we have a birthday for one of the boys. Catch ya later."

Jerry's friendship meant a lot to him. Still, even with all his money and his luxury apartment at Finger Wharf, Mark Johnson was a lonely man. Nothing could replace Lisa. He had taken secretaries, file girls, even a few older company VPs to all the posh places, and some home to his bed. But when he woke up and faced himself in the mirror, all his other senses gave in to the faint smell of Lisa's powder in the bathroom. He missed her round face and wide eyes, her fresh smile, but mostly her intelligent way of cutting through the bullshit of life. Closing his eyes, he saw Lisa jogging along the wharf, her long red hair blowing in the wind. Her scent came over him like a stiff drink.

He began trying to cut an order for the dock workers. Not too long ago, everything began to go wrong. Every year, his job buying grain became more complicated because of the erratic weather that increasingly led to crop failures, market fluctuations, and government subsidies that supported the shipping industry.

The stress of the last few years had boiled into conflict in his marriage. At one moment of crisis, he had bargained with her old man for a thousand head of cattle to ship to Indonesia. The deal went south quickly.

"You promised my father 90 cents on the hoof, and you're going to pay him 65?"

"Lisa, the price of beef went down, I don't control the market."

"BDM could pay him $1.10 and you know it."

"I'm not the company."

"Yes, you are. In Sydney, you are BDM, whether you admit it or not."

"I can't do anything about the world market or company policy."

"The damned bloody world market, that's what's wrong with this whole picture. What's he supposed to do if he can't sell them at such a loss? Bury them in pits like they did with thousands of sheep in the '80s?"

That really was the straw that broke the camel's back. But deep down, he knew it wasn't really the company or the cattle or the messed up deal with her dad but Sydney that she hated. She loved life at the station. He loved life in the city. The outback was just so totally boring for him. And Sydney was dull for her.

He had thought he could change her with the excitement of fancy restaurants, clubs, theater and the world-famous opera house in Sydney. Her voice reverberated through his mind. "I can't live in this dirty city. The only soil here is in pots on the balcony. I have to be where I can smell the acacia trees and hear the padding of the 'roos. I need to see the baby calves and lambs and the green shoots coming up in the spring."

About six months ago now, he'd come home one day and she was gone. She left a note on the kitchen counter. "You hate the outback and I hate Sydney. I'm not sure our love can bridge that gap." No matter how much money he made, how exciting the city was, he couldn't buy what she really loved. In the end, even her love for him wasn't enough to fill her own empty spots.

~15~
WASHINGTON, D.C.

Senator Elena Villanueva frowned at the proposal in front of her. "Mr. Forester, you are convinced the extreme measures suggested by the data you're getting and your research really are necessary?"

"The data and conclusions in my report are real. If you want me to suggest another route for solving this crisis, I know of none."

"Have we been asleep, that this would come upon us so suddenly? Why now?"

"Scientists for years have been aware of a lot of carbon dioxide they couldn't account for. Well, it is there, and we have to decide what to do about it. The Earth's atmospheric balance is shifting. The chaos evident in other places has been somewhat avoided here because of our paper wealth. You and I know that disaster relief has skyrocketed around the world. And we know the U.N. has been twiddling its thumbs at every climate change conference since Kyoto."

"Why is this coming from the U.N. and not our own government scientists?"

Senator Clifford Martin interjected: "Madam Chair, Elena, all know that's because the oil industry controls climate scientists in the U.S., paying other well-qualified experts to rebut anything a scientist says that warns us of the danger. They will make mincemeat of this report. Mr. Forester, are you convinced the extreme measures suggested in Wave I are necessary?"

"Yes, sir. If you are asking me whether humanity will be safe after these have been put in place, or whether we will have functioning societies, that is any body's guess. United Nations countries devised a plan in 2005 to halt the destruction of the rainforests and that's gone fairly well, but nothing can stop the growth of cities and the massive spread of fossil fuel use throughout the world as long as petroleum is widely available and reasonably priced."

Martin slammed his fist down on the report. "Mr. Forester, how is the U.N. responding to this information? If the U.S. is to go to extreme measures, will the other countries follow? Or will half the nations stand aside with their: 'We're too poor to implement these changes' whine and leave us standing alone?"

"Senator Martin, in the next few weeks the European Confederation, the Asian Assemblage, and the new Soviet Democratic States and all of NATO will have the report. At this moment, the head of the U.N. Environmental Program and the Security Council are sitting on it."

The junior senator from Texas, a handsome Latino with flashing eyes, jumped in. "If this is so damned urgent, why haven't we heard about this before now? Why would the U.N.'s leadership be sitting on it for any time at all?"

"As Senator Martin pointed out," Jesse replied, "it's politics as usual, Senator Romero. I've urged the head of UNEP to move forward. I don't know why she will not. Now, I've taken a risk of losing my job with the U.N. to bring it to your attention at this time. I'm here because I believe it is crucial for the U.S. to take a lead. You can't do that if you don't know what's going on.

"There is a great advantage in U.S. leadership at this time. More importantly, we are the society most at risk of collapse when these changes become mandates. It's crucial that you keep this quiet and confidential as far as the press and the public is concerned until the U.N. announces the plan. There are some measures in my report to help our country be more prepared when the word does get out to the public. Madam Chairman, gentlemen, it is my hope that the U.S. will take a lead when the United Nations meets to discuss this crisis and the recommended course of action."

Martin nodded, "I quite agree with Mr. Forester. Like the last two military encounters putting our men in harm's way on foreign soil under United Nation officers, if we wait too long we'll end up taking orders from some other regime. If Mr. Forester's figures are correct, and I have no reason to doubt him, we must proceed immediately to design how we'll implement the mandates of Wave I and II.

Senator Villanueva shook her head. "Mr. Forester, you ask a great deal with no guarantees. Fear will run rampant and we'll have chaos and bloodshed."

"Yes, there will be chaos and bloodshed and famine. But the better prepared we are, the quicker we move forward, the better we can avert some of it. The second part of the report is an outline of suggestions for a third phase; it focuses on how to rebuild our lives without fossil fuels while we begin massive revegetation of the planet."

"Mr. Forester, you're talking about shutting down airports, train stations, bus terminals, gas stations; about putting all electricity companies which do not run on solar, wind, hydro, geothermals, or nuclear out of business. There will be no way to move food. You are talking about a complete collapse of our current economy, of our lifestyles, our communities!"

"Yes, madam senator."

"But Mr. Forester, people will have to start walking."

"Yes, senator. In exchange, they will get to keep breathing.

Later, as he waited for Senator Villanueva to get back to him, he walked around his nation's capital. The meeting he'd just left had gotten him to thinking about his days at U.C. Davis and the first time he had to convince one strong individual and a committee to act quickly and trust that he was right about the importance of the biological and atmospheric environment that sustains human existence.

The fight, oddly enough, was what introduced him to the man who would become his best friend, good old Kim Soto. He could see Kim's face as though it were yesterday, his fiery black eyes, that unruly lock of black hair swinging back and forth on his forehead as he made point after point.

Early one morning, Jesse had encountered this small Japanese student with a tripod, transit levels and tape, trudging right through critical estuary habitat. Jesse confronted him with a fury he always felt for those who seemed oblivious to the biodiversity that was home to other living things.

"Hey, get out of here—this is university property. Whad'ya think you're doing?"

"I'm going to build a building here."

"Over my dead body."

"If you insist, but it is my sincere hope that will not be necessary."

"Listen, you little pipsqueak this is important estuary habitat, and no one in his right mind would allow you to put a building here. So move on—get lost, buddy. You hear?"

Kim gave a slight bow, folded up his transit, and walked off.

The next afternoon Jesse was called into the dean's office, and there was the same pugnacious young man. Jesse again lost his temper completely, and they argued for half an hour. Jesse knew the proposed site of the building would put many of the species he was studying in jeopardy. Kim believed it was a perfect site for the university's new agriculture building. Jesse had to admit the guy was not just persistent but also smart as a whip. He just wasn't about to lose any sleep over threatened fish and birds.

Jesse won, and the building was postponed while the study was completed. Eventually, the building was located some distance from the river so as not to disturb the estuary.

Jesse was glad to say good riddance to Kim. Then, one evening several weeks later, he was out gathering data on the site and there was Kim. He approached cautiously. "I'm interested in what you are doing. I am curious about your concern for the land. I know we got off on a wrong foot—but I wish to apologize and start fresh. You know a great deal, and I want to learn."

They ended up at Clancy's Pub and talked until 3 in the morning. Kim's family had orchards in Japan. And one of his goals, while getting a graduate degree in architecture, was to bring back any information on American agricultural technologies he could gather that would make their work easier and more profitable.

After that first night, the two spent many holidays and weekends exploring the mountains of California and the Northwest, trudging up and down the valley orchards of Washington and Oregon.

The hiking was fun, the information gathering discouraging—massive agricultural production systems and their aftermath, soil erosion, the collapse of underground and fresh water systems, and endless cycles of pests, chemicals, and more pests.

Even when Karen began to take up a lot of Jesse's time, he and Kim continued to explore and have rousing debates over development versus preservation, economic growth and global warming. In the end, they both concluded that Japan would be better off not to adopt any more U.S. agricultural methods. The American way might produce more for a period, but in the end, it would be disastrous for Kim's small island home. They also argued a lot over the fine points of American versus Japanese beer. Kim was at the altar next to him when Jesse married Karen.

The telephone was ringing in his hotel room when he turned the key in the door.

"Well, how did it go?"

"I don't know, Hannah. I think it scared the shit out of most of them."

"So are they going to sweep it under the table, ignore the inevitable, or do something?"

"No way of telling this early in the game."

"Jesse, it's not early. It is late, really late, and this is no game."

"Hannah. It's a figure of speech. Relax. Don't hassle me, I'm very tired and I just want to lie down and forget the whole mess for an hour or so."

"I had a call from Miriamu. She's back in town and wanted to speak with you."

"What did you tell her?"

"That you were out of town. I told her you were visiting family but would be back tomorrow"

"Are they ready to put Wave I in motion?"

"She wouldn't say. I didn't tell her you were in D.C. What if she finds out? I know she'll be furious, but that could get the ball rolling, as they say."

Jesse lay back on the hotel bed. "I need time to think. I'll call you at home later, or we'll discuss it when I get back."

"I think we need to demand a response from the U.N. The plan should have been implemented yesterday. You know that Jesse. I'll see you when you get back."

Jesse hung up the phone and stretched back on the bed. He knew it was Hannah's honest persistence that had led him to her. But he was so tired. He closed his eyes and tried not to think about Miriamu. She was his boss, and way above him on the VIP scale. She would be pissed if she discovered why he went to D.C.; that was for certain. But why did she seem to be dragging her feet on the Operation? It just didn't make sense.

Jesse ordered a ham and cheese sandwich and a Samuel Adams from room service and took a long shower. When the meal arrived he was sitting in his underwear watching the 6 o'clock news. The headline story was about a speech the president had given in California about how successful vouchers had been for education. How strong and secure America was. Jesse flipped through the channels and turned off the TV in frustration.

After some tossing, he fell into a troubled sleep

The phone bolted him upright.

"Mr. Forester, this is Senator Villanueva."

"Yes, senator."

"Our committee has set up a meeting with the president and the Cabinet at 9 o'clock in the morning. Could you bring your report and recommendations to my office at 7 so we can make copies? And bring all your files. I think they need all the facts so we can make a fair assessment of the situation, and I need you to stay for the meeting to help them understand the charts and statistics. Grant Malone, the senior private adviser to the committee, will, well—simply put—eat you for lunch. Be prepared."

"I'll be there, senator, and thank you."

"For taking you seriously, Mr. Forester?"

~16~
DIMBANGOMBE, ZIMBABWE

KATHRYN WAS TEACHING THE CHILDREN A NEW SONG IN THE RONdoval. Hendrik watched as she wrote the words to the song in Ndebele and then in English. The children laughed at the meaning. It was an argument between the wind and the sun. The wind challenged the sun to a duel. Which one could make man take off his coat? Half of the children wanted to be the wind, while the other half the sun. The children especially loved it because they got to puff up their cheeks and blow at intervals between the words. They blew and blew and eventually exploded into squeals of laughter.

One very tall boy was the man and as the wind blew he wrapped a blanket more tightly around his body. When the sun, represented by twenty-two waving black arms, began beaming down on him he pretended to be sweating, eventually removing the blanket. They all hooted and clapped and cheered. They begged to do it again, and those that had been the sun wanted to be the wind.

Hendrik wove his way through the puffing, shining children and turned to speak to them. They immediately became quiet in a show of deep respect for the old grizzled man their parents admired so much. He bowed, asking their permission to talk to their teacher. Older children murmured their approval, and quietly began reading to the younger ones.

They walked a short distance to a bench under a mopane tree. There was an awkward silence; she knew he would only interrupt her work for something important. Something she would not be happy about. "Where are you going this time, my love?"

"I have been asked to give a talk in Johannesburg and then another in Cape Town."

"And you are the only one who can possibly talk at these important meetings?"

"Can you not answer that question yourself?"

"I can, but when you're away, I'm lonely."

"How can you be alone when sixty children and their parents clamor for your attention?"

"There is a difference between being alone and being lonely. Without you, I'm lonely—but, of course, never alone here in the village."

"Kathryn, I've been getting communications from some of my former colleagues around the world that the world is beginning to be more open to my ideas—articles about the successes some producers are having restoring their land and increasing their profits are appearing everywhere. People feel that having me talk also about what we are doing here in this remote village in Zimbabwe will be welcomed and important to turning the tide. I feel I must go help where I can and while I am still able."

"Any chance others who have trained with you, such as people from Argentina will also be on the platform with you?"

"No, just me and my own dog-and-pony show. Camilla's last letter from Argentina indicated she was doing very well, but things are hard and she is having to monitor her situation closely. She has developed her husband's land just as we planned and been instrumental in influencing others. There is great success there, and we can be proud of her work. She has become the first female minister of agriculture ever in a Latin American nation and is now getting our practices and policies implemented throughout her country."

Kathryn got up from the bench moving around the tree so her response was hidden from him. He caught her by the arm and turned her around. "Kathryn, I love only you—you must know that. My friend—*our* friend in Argentina—is happily married."

"Then why do I feel a deep emptiness whenever her name is mentioned? I don't feel that when you mention Mark's mother. I'm not a jealous person, Hendrik. Oh dear, I'm being too sensitive. Are you planning to visit Mark and Lisa anytime this year?"

"No. He has made it very clear that my ideas are anathema to him. Sadly, the awakening world does not include my own son. You can go with me to South Africa if you want. You know I would love to have you with me."

"No, we're in the middle of a term. And if I were to go, who would answer the villagers every day when they want to know when you will return? No, I have no desire to see the outside world anymore."

"I'll be leaving for Harare in a week. Friends in Johannesburg are booking all my travel round-trip out of there." He kissed her on the forehead and she watched as he made his way through the huts toward his beloved Dimbangombe River.

~17~
BUENOS AIRES

Camilla Olivas had begun her work on the Committee for Agriculture and Climate Change more than a decade ago. She ducked when her male counterparts blew cigar smoke in her face or spit tobacco within a few feet of her head. Their anger grew with every presentation and discussion on the impact of agriculture on carbon buildup in the atmosphere or how imports had swamped local markets. They often unleashed their fury when she stepped to the podium.

"By God I will use force if BDM ships in one more load of beef. My guns are ready. Tell Minister of Agriculture Melindez he will have a revolution on his hands."

There was always a hush and then a shifting of bodies when Camilla was handed the microphone. It was not because of what she might say, even when her production numbers were astonishing. The hush was largely simply because she was a woman in a man's domain. In the past there had been no breaking through their stubborn resistance to change. She hoped this time they would really listen. This time had to be different. The future of her country depended upon it.

"Gentlemen, fellow farmers, remember what I told you last year and the year before. There is no wealth in cattle or crops without rich land." This time, Camilla used her computer and PowerPoint graphs as well as pictures she had prepared as back up.

"This is what my land looked like ten years ago. Year after year, no matter how severe the droughts, it has improved. You can see how both the grassland and the cattle are fat and happy. Here is a graph on our profits from animals raised and sold.

"Señora Olivas, how did you do this? Why isn't everyone using your ideas? Are people in the United States, China, Brazil using these methods?"

Camilla answered a barrage of brutal questions, but she held her ground. Hendrik would have been proud of her quiet resolve.

"Señores, a lot of Argentina is empty land. Together we will make that empty land productive. Argentina could be a model for food production for the entire world."

When the session broke up she hurried to the restroom to douse her face in cold water and breathe. As she left, one of the president's senior aides approached her. "Senora, I have just received a call from our president, who was listening to your presentation via the web. He would like to meet with you. Would tomorrow be convenient?"

Camilla had never trusted President Mateo Jesus Almeida de Rio. But then she had only ever trusted two men—Hendrik and her husband. She shook the hand the aide offered, but his crooked smile seemed a warning.

As she dressed for the appointment the next morning, she knew it was crucial to be properly Argentinian and feminine as well as strong and businesslike. Not an easy thing to do in the choice of one outfit for one meeting. As she sat in the waiting room of the president's office, she rehearsed the key points she needed to make during the meeting, no matter what the president wanted to know or discuss.

"Please, sit down, Señora Olivas. I have just listened again to the taped transcript of your presentation with the stunning pictures."

"And?"

"I am impressed and skeptical, as are all of my ministers. We face a crisis of unparalleled proportion. Our nation must boost its food production to feed our people. And we cannot exist economically without selling food to other nations that can no longer feed themselves. We need to expand our domestic economy. The food production systems we have used clearly are not enough to keep the 'lobo away from the door' as they say. We have rationing in the cities. We have tried to change eating habits to adjust to the lack of production on the ranches and farms. Last year was a bad year for agriculture."

"President Almeida, we were in trouble long before last year. Our soils have been steadily declining for years. You came into power and pushed the same ideas that were already destroying agriculture around the world. Vast monocultures sustained by chemicals. I tried to assist your agriculture minister, Señor Melendez, but he ignored my offers and continued with his own agenda."

"Señora, I do not wish to offend or argue. I am in hopes that we can blend your methods with our existing government policies and programs."

"President. If we are to survive, we will need to convert as quickly as we can to more sustainable practices on both our farms and estancias. That will take, initially, some blending of the existing and the new. But I must be honest with you. I could never work with the present minister. He is truly a bobo.

"Señor President, may I be candid with you?" She leaned forward just enough to allow her blouse to gape. The result was as she expected; he leaned forward and caught his breath. "My ideas and practices are anathema to those in your Cabinet. They will ignore me as a farmer but more so because I am a woman. I could never, as an adviser or counselor to your existing minister, help make the difference you desire. You understand?" She placed her hand over his just a second before straightening the silver clip that held her long black hair.

"Señora, I have no intention of making you work with the old bobo, as you have called him. I have asked for his resignation. Tomorrow you will be appointed as minister of agriculture for Argentina."

He took hold of the hand she had so gently laid on his and slid his hand up, grasping her wrist. "However, Señora, I must ask that you guarantee you will deliver for the whole of Argentina what you have accomplished on your own estancia. Do we understand each other, Señora?" The painful pressure he placed on her wrist portended what her future would hold if she failed to deliver.

~18~
TAUSHIMA, JAPAN

KIM SOTO CLIMBED DOWN THE LADDER AND STEPPED BACK TO LOOK at his pruning job. Pruning trees was torture. Each piece of fruit might be vital in feeding a hungry nation. That was the commitment he had made when he left his architectural practice in the U.S. to take over his family farm in Japan. The trees must be pruned, but inside his head there was always that deep sadness at having to cut away part of any tree. Fukuoka was right. Trees should never be pruned but left to find their own shape and produce as much fruit as possible for the nature of that one tree.

He climbed back up to get branches he had missed. Last season, they'd all bloomed and the fruit was plentiful. It was unusual for every variety to do so well. Kim had supplied both local and national markets. Abundance last season could mean the opposite this year. Who could predict, given the vagaries of the last decade's erratic weather patterns?

Kim had recurring visions of his work in North Korea as an agriculture adviser to Japan's foreign aid services. In North Korea, he saw first-hand how the politics of the county's supreme leader was allowed to snuff out children's lives. And the rest of the world—Japan included—had for decades sat idly by allowing it to happen. He was able to help North Korean farmers increase the production in their orchards for a time, but it had not come close to addressing the "guns versus butter" issue. He was a farmer, not a politician.

Jesse always said, "The only real wealth is in the land and growing things. The sun, soil, and water are our real sources of life. But you need to remember that economists, business leaders and politicians don't actually understand that. They think we can create vibrant economies on manufacturing and service industries while we deplete the soil resources and still have an actual economy. But we can't. In the end, if the soil is gone, we are toast."

"Kim, one of those top-secret, encrypted emails from Jesse just came through." Lee smiled up at him from under the dead limb he was about to cut. "Good news, we hope?"

They moved from under the trees to sit on a patch of grass where the soft February sun had already dried the early morning dew.

Kim, old buddy. It's happening. The first of April the UN will advise everyone to find a source of food and shelter that does not require fuel. Six months later, it will put a halt to the use of all fossil fuels, cooking fuels, biomass burning, etc. You know the rest. You're in pretty good shape. But there will be mass exodus from Tokyo, Kyoto, Hiroshima, and all cities. I sent Karen and the boys to the farm in anticipation of a mass exodus here. Make plans to deal with a lot of scared, hungry Japanese. Be sure to go into our contingency plan. The world needs you buddy. Kiss Lee and the kids for me. Sayonara, Jesse

"I do not understand, Kim." She touched his face with her hand. "Why is this happening? What is Jesse saying, the food we can buy now and what we can produce is all we will have in the future?"

"Yes, and we must grow all of our own from here on out, dry it, somehow preserve for the winter to get us through the year. When Jesse and I were hiking the trails of California we both hoped the public would wake up before it came to this. We worried about what kind of world we were leaving for the children."

"What about the children, our children, Kim? What will we tell them?"

"Maybe Niko is old enough to understand if we tell her the truth. For the little ones, we must try to make it all a game as long as possible, so as not to scare them. How stupid we have all been."

"Kim, maybe, just maybe there was nothing we could do. We needed this to make us stronger to learn to use what we can grow." Lee wound her arm around his waist and held tightly.

"So, what is your plan, general? Your second in command awaits her orders." She gave him a little salute, her black eyes flashing with another warm smile.

"Food is important. If the masses can't get it shipped in they will roam the country for it. Get out your old preserving books. We will can and dry everything we can this summer. We need to figure out what we can't make and either substitute or buy enough now to supplement until we can do without. We need to figure out where we can hide and store anything we produce. We must be sure we have warm blankets and clothing for the coming winter."

"Won't people get suspicious if we stock up on lots of food? They surely will if we do not sell all our fruit, as is our custom. I suppose we could tell the neighbors that we just had a visit from two of those young men in black slacks, white shirts and a tie and we've converted to Mormonism and are now beginning our practice of 'self-sufficiency'."

Kim threw his head back and laughed, kissing the top of her head. "I love you Lee; that is a great idea, it would give the whole village something to gossip about. Meanwhile, we know our little orchard and gardens will be in demand; let us pray for a great harvest this year."

He looked up through the limbs, trying hard to imagine the profusion of pink clouds of seasons past. "If no ships are bringing food to the port, people will have to rely on fishing and farming."

"Oh Kim, people in Tokyo, Kyoto—the cities—those people don't farm. They have money but no land. Most of them don't even have relatives who still live in the country. Many of them have no idea how to fish anymore."

"They will have to either find some land or find someone who will let them share their land if they want to eat."

"They'll want ours. It all reminds me of my great-grandmother and the potatoes."

"What potatoes?"

"Great-Grandmother Mai Ling was in Tokyo when Doolittle's planes flew over and bombed. The people had been told that it was the Imperial Japanese Air Force. When the bombs began to fall, they realized they'd been lied to; they panicked and ran for cover. My family was very wealthy, so great-grandmother filled one sack with money and another sack with potatoes. But in the stampede, she got to the cave in the mountains with only one sack."

"The money or the potatoes?"

"The potatoes, of course. Otherwise, she would never have been my great-grandmother."

Kim slipped his arms around her and kissed her mouth. "And I am so, so glad she was your great-grandmother."

~19~
WASHINGTON, D.C.

Senator Cliff Martin took his time getting to his destination, bought a ticket on the tour bus in front of Union Station, got off at the Vietnam Memorial, and then caught another bus for the Roosevelt. He'd been in Washington for fourteen years but never been a tourist. He had a vague sense that perhaps he had missed something. He saw the big monuments—Washington, Jefferson, Lincoln—from his car each day, but had never read the inscriptions.

When he got to his final destination and checked his watch, there was still twenty minutes to kill. Wandering among the waterfalls and fountains, he found the etchings were a history lesson in stone. The WPA, the labor movement, and Second World War inscriptions told of a big country puffed up about its existence and wanting the world to pay attention.

A large group of elementary school children in blue and white uniforms were splashing each other and running up and around the statues while a couple teachers tried to keep them dry and control the mayhem. One little boy stood motionless in front of the statue of Roosevelt in his wheel chair. The senator lit a cigar and stood next to the child watching him out of the corner of his eyes.

"Hey, mister, do you think he could have been a better president if he hadn't been crippled?"

"I don't know, son. I suppose he could have moved a little faster when there was a crisis, but I don't think it would have made him any smarter or helped him to make better decisions to have two good legs. And maybe his being crippled made him feel more compassionate for people who weren't so perfect."

"That's what I think. I don't guess he ever saw all these big rocks that tell about him, did he?"

"No, son, he was dead long before they put this thing up. But it's almost always that way—we wait till people are dead to tell them thanks for all they did."

"That's sad." The boy stood there with his head cocked to one side. Finally, a teacher came around from the next exhibit yelling.

"Samuel, Samuel I've been looking all over for you. You must keep up with the class." She grabbed his arm and pulled him away.

"But why was he crippled, Mrs. Morgan."

"He had polio."

"What's that?"

"Just a disease never mind—Samuel don't ask so many questions—come along; stay up with the class."

Martin skirted a group of tourists and read what the stones had to say about Eleanor. He listened and chuckled as a group of Spanish speakers argued about the meaning of the inscription. He selected a bench near the water in the shadow of the memorial, stretched out his legs, and relit his cigar.

After a few puffs, he caught sight of the person he'd been waiting for moving slowly along the shore. The little man had on a khaki slicker and a St. Louis Cardinals cap backward on his head. He walked with a slight limp, casting and recasting his line into the tidal basin. Martin strolled toward him just as if he were continuing a friendly walk along the promenade and stopped as any stranger might to have a casual chat.

"How's the fishing?"

"Just caught a big one. How's it going with you?"

"Caught a big one too."

The man opened his fishing creel wide so Martin could see inside—there was a large dead carp at the bottom of the bag and a small envelope wrapped in a plastic baggie. The stench was so pungent that Martin had to hold his nose as he reached in, remarking "Wow, that is a big one." He dropped a larger packet he'd pulled from inside his jacket pocket and quickly grabbed the small envelope.

"Impressive, keep up the good work."

"Sure thing." Lenny wandered on down the shore, casting his line here and there.

Martin had his doubts about these meetings. Why couldn't they just do it all through the internet? But now that it was in motion, he had to comply. He watched as the little man disappeared around the bend of the tidal basin. After carrying the cigar butt to the nearest refuse can, he sat down on a nearby bench and opened the packet. Inside were all the figures on the SOLYNDRIX purchases and sales of solar and wind equipment, the shipping through BDM, and the growing amounts of profit. Both companies were running smoothly.

He put the papers back in the envelope and caught the next bus back to Capitol Hill. Unfortunately, it was full of white and blue uniforms and screaming school children. Martin crowded into a seat with a lady whose girth was as large as his. At the next stop when she got off, he found himself next to that same little boy he'd chatted with at the Roosevelt Monument. The lad was writing in a note pad.

Mr. Rosevelt was very smart man and even though he had polio and was crippled he helped people find food and work.

~20~
SYDNEY, AUSTRALIA

"JERRY, THOSE SHIPS WERE SUPPOSED TO TAKE FOOD TO ETHIOPIA, people are starving there. Now, they are carrying machinery to America. How can we justify that?"

"I don't have to justify anything. I just collect my paycheck and feed my *own* kids."

"Jerry, I know you better than that."

"Maybe the grain they need is being supplied from another source. It's probably being shipped out of the U.S. right now."

"Do you really believe that?"

"No, but I can't fix what is out of my control. The company doesn't give us the leeway to object, now does it? How about that father of yours, what do you hear from him?"

"I haven't heard from Hendrik since that letter I shared with you. He was so sure that the crisis would be food, but now the company isn't shipping food. Why?"

"How do I know? Maybe BDM just got tired of the food business."

"Or maybe the alternate energy business is a better deal now. Maybe now there is money to be made in these machines. But why?"

"Your guess is as good as mine."

Back in the office, Mark reread his father's letters from the past few years. They always followed the same pattern.

Their disagreements had accelerated the last time he visited his dad in Zimbabwe. He got off the plane in Harare the cocky graduate with a master's in international finance from the Fletcher School of Law and Diplomacy, and announced he had just taken a job with BDM in Sydney. He was so proud. He hoped his dad would be too.

Hendrik wasn't.

The argument began the minute they were walking to the vehicle, and continued throughout the drive. "Mark, don't you know what BDM does? They ship food into poor countries and undercut the farmers there until they can no longer afford to grow, even for their own families. Then they have farmers and the country by the throat and they strangle them with higher prices. Meanwhile the lands lie fallow, people forget how to farm, and everyone becomes dependent on the big corporation. Think Mark, do you really want to be a part of that?"

"Dad, BDM isn't like that; they are trying to feed the starving world. They just ship food into regions where there is drought or famine and people can't grow food themselves anyway. And once the famine's over, they send technicians in to help the people learn and adopt farming methods that will give them bigger harvests, and they are . . ."

"And those new methods are destroying the soil and the environment with chemicals. I used to test those chemicals. Soils that depend upon chemicals eventually collapse; we will have to grow food in space." Hendrik gestured into the air and then turned the key and punched the gas pedal several times before it responded.

"BDM is doing that too, actually growing food in the air." Mark threw his duffle bag into the back seat.

"Yes, and at the same time, they are peddling inputs and chemicals that farmers become dependent on and buying up the native seed banks, creating hybrids that don't reproduce, so the poor farmer has to keep buying both inputs and seed from them and can't buy from anyone else or save his own seed from year to year. It is all one big money game Mark, think!" Hendrik jerked the wheel, avoiding a run-in with a cart pulled by a donkey.

"No, they're just trying to create new seeds that will produce more, resist pests, and help feed those that are starving. Don't drive so fast; you're scaring me."

"Africa fed itself until we started meddling!"

"Africa, Africa, what about India, China, Indonesia, South America, the Middle East? Anywhere there is starvation, I will be helping to bring food!"

"Damn it, Mark, you're a young blind fool, and there's nothing worse than a young blind fool who can't see the truth." They were stalled while a herd of goats slowly crossed.

"Yes, there is. It's an old blind fool—you just can't stand the fact that someone else might have a better idea than yours. You're so self-centered and arrogant, believing that no one has an answer but you. That's why no one can live with you; that's why Mom . . . ."

Mark remembered with pain the look on his father's face when he threw that at him, and wished he could have taken it back. That visit ended in a sad standoff. There were no long walks, no confidential talks about the improvements in the land and the volume of water in the river, just a polite, somber silence.

In the ten years since that last visit, Mark had made more money and been successful at BDM beyond his wildest dreams, but with Lisa's departure, his life had fallen apart. And throughout his own slow demise, those periodic emails arrived from Africa, reminding him that it did matter what kinds of decisions and actions—and the impact on others—we each took in our own lives. He once again read his father's final sentences.

> *BDM has dumped grain in Zimbabwe, destroying the local market. Meanwhile, there is famine in Ethiopia once more. I told you BDM's approach would not create lasting sustainability and would lead to more starvation sooner or later. Think about what you are doing. Mark, evil can only be stopped one individual at a time. You can make a difference. I regret our past differences, but must warn you once more. Your company will become obsolete, and you will have to figure out again who you are. The world will be warring over food and clean water, not petroleum or money, in the very near future. Love, Dad*

~21~
WASHINGTON, D.C.

GRANT MALONE, SENIOR SCIENTIFIC ADVISER TO THE JOINT CONgressional Committee on Climate Change, was seated at the table with Senator Villanueva, the president, and members of his Cabinet when Jesse entered the conference room. Malone had been advising Congress on issues of fossil fuels and climate change for over fifteen years. His salary for his congressional advice was $100,000 a year. No one really knew how much he earned in under-the-table "gifts" from three major oil companies and several of the larger energy conglomerates.

Malone spent the first forty-five minutes tearing into each statistic in Jesse's report. He had conflicting data for each item. He had graphs showing the weather as no more violent than it had ever been and certainly not a result of human activity. His conclusions were cutting, and delivered in a belittling tone.

"So you can see, Mr. Forester, we have no way of really justifying your Operation World Salvation. What is happening may have nothing to do with fossil fuel or burning. It's more likely this old world is changing by itself. You and your staff should go back and start again. I'm sure you will come to a different conclusion." Malone couldn't help smiling broadly at everyone, exuding the self-satisfaction of one who never doubted that he was right and the rest of the world helplessly ignorant.

Jesse, livid by now, forced himself to breathe deeply. He poured himself water from the pitcher in front of him and took a long drink. He tried not to appear condescending as he began to rebut the man's obvious stupidity and faulty reasoning.

"I am sorry that Mr. Malone has taken it upon himself to so cleverly disavow all of the information I have brought to you. The environment was out of balance long before this data came across the screen, but we turned a blind eye to the obvious signs and did not have the technology to see the others. We no longer have that luxury.

"Mr. Malone knows that the human-induced isotopic fingerprint of carbon is rising much faster than it should. The figures speak for themselves, but it is time for us to look around and think beyond the data. We need to look at the whole of our Earth's processes, not just individual statistics concerning greenhouse gases. We must look at the extremely disruptive and record-setting weather events, the advance of the deserts, catastrophic fires, increased and prolonged starvation and disease, massive increases in crop and cattle insurance schemes, the economic burden of cleaning up after repeated droughts, floods, and hurricanes.

"These things are not isolated environmental events but a long series of symptoms of the deterioration of every single biological system on the planet. As this deterioration advances, it will cause more economic and social chaos. Now, the data we must concern ourselves with is the fact that the mix of oxygen and other gases—crucial to human survival on this planet—is shifting. Our only guess is that this is the result of the buildup of carbon in the Earth's atmosphere."

Jesse extracted from his files the news articles and reports tying each one to his data from the points around the world. His figures had been put together in a packet for the president and each member of the Cabinet so they could follow the facts with their own eyes. After sharing with them the more obvious data and examples, Jesse moved into the more technical data.

"Pre-industrial levels indicate that CO_2 was at 170 ppm. In March 1958, when high-precision monitoring began at the Mauna Loa Observatory in Hawaii, atmospheric CO_2 was at 315.71 ppm. This means," he reminded them, "for every one million molecules in the atmosphere, 315.71 of them on average were CO_2 molecules. Today, atmospheric CO_2 has recently passed 400 ppm, the threshold beyond which all scientists indicated we would be in dire trouble."

Many of these statistics had already been revealed to the public by the U.N. and other international bodies. Jesse's ace in the hole was the data they hadn't seen: the more recent levels of oxygen versus carbon that had come in from the atmospheric tracking stations around the world. That data showed conclusively that the balance of oxygen and carbon was moving toward conditions in which humans would not survive.

"In summary, can we really write this off as 'the old world changing by itself' as Mr. Malone would ask us to? Ladies and gentlemen, the U.N. does not intend to do that anymore. It will announce Operation World Salvation in the very near future. I am here at risk of my job and reputation, and I am begging the U.S. to get on board before the announcement and play a leading role. From this point forward, we are either going to move into what can only be described as a 'war-footing' mode to avert the collapse of life as we know it. Or we are not. With power comes the responsibility to lead change. Today we have no choice. Mr. President, members of the Cabinet, senators, can we take a chance on whether we will or will not have fresh oxygen to breath tomorrow, next week, next year? You, alone, need to answer that question today." He looked each one in the eyes as he came to his conclusion and then sat down.

The room went deadly quiet. Finally, Senator Villanueva broke the silence. "Mr. Forester, the private and corporate scientists I asked to review the data last night have concluded that the data does indicate the shift in oxygen. Although there is some disagreement as to how we got in this dire predicament, there is no question that we are there. As chair of this committee, I am prepared to support the U.S. taking a lead on the implementation of Operation World Salvation."

Malone rose to his feet. "Madame Chair—I beg to differ with you. There is not enough evidence to proceed with this outlandish proposal. My own team of scientists will also quickly review the data presented by Mr. Forester and the U.N. team. We need to be double sure if we are going to cause this country to go to such extreme lengths as to ban all use of fossil fuels immediately. I suggest that the proposal be tabled until we can further study the data."

Jesse saw from their faces that Malone's associates were not so sure the conclusions were off-base. They were leaning his way.

"Mr. Malone, why would we need to further study this data. We have many of the top scientists from around the world, including many with whom you have worked your entire career, on the U.N. "hole watcher" team of which Mr. Forester is the lead scientist," Senator Villanueva responded. "I just can't fathom why we would delay and certainly I can't justify paying more money to investigate what has already been documented."

Malone shifted uncomfortably at the mention of paying him more money. "As the senior scientific adviser to this committee, however, my counsel must be taken into consideration on this matter."

"You are nothing more than a paid mouthpiece of the fossil fuel industry," Jesse countered. "You lack any moral courage! Your delay tactic today is the same one you have used for a decade now so that your clients can continue to pump the black stuff out of the Earth no matter what the cost to our air supply. Your measurements and guidelines for deciding on anything and then taking action are based on profit, enriching yourselves, nothing else." Jesse returned to his seat and reached for the pitcher of water on the table, knocking it over instead.

There was dead silence in the room. The water soaked the tablecloth, and soon everyone could hear it dripping to the floor. The drip, drip, drip was a sobering sound like the ticking of a clock steadily counting away life as each one searched for an answer to the dilemma in front of them.

The meeting ended when Elena called for Jesse's proposal to be voted on. The proposal passed, and a plan for the committee and president to begin laying the foundation for U.S. leadership on Operation World Salvation was hammered out. Jesse spent the rest of the day trying to calm down enough to have supper, by invitation of the president, at the White House. As he arrived at 1600 Pennsylvania Avenue, he couldn't help but think: "What strange circumstances have brought me to this point and place in my life."

~22~
NEW HAVEN, CONNECTICUT

SHE UNPACKED HER OVERNIGHT CASE, PLACING TOILETRIES ON THE dresser and carefully hanging up the extra coat. She hated coming any farther north than New York. Even though it was already warm for March, she felt chilled, and she had grown nervous once again. She found the heavy white bathrobe provided by the hotel and ran a tub full of very hot water. Closing her eyes she asked herself for the hundredth time what she was doing in this cold climate. Why had she not stayed where the balmy breezes were warm even in the winter and one had to ascend high on the mountaintop to feel any kind of chill?

She was dozing when she heard him unlock the door and come into the room.

"Miriamu?"

"I'm in the tub, trying to get warm."

"Ah, I'll build a fire out here to help when you get out."

"Thank you, that will be nice."

The fire was crackling and the room had a warm glow when she finally came out of the bathroom, wrapping the robe tightly around her. She smelled his aftershave and felt his eyes on her as she stood in the doorway.

"You're most beautiful, as always."

"You don't need to flatter me. I'm here. Were you followed?"

"No."

"Are you sure?"

"Woman, I flew in from D.C. with an Army pal to some obscure field in upstate New York. Then I spent today hiking around before I wandered up here. No one knows I am here; believe me, no one."

His backpack was on the floor—socks, shoes, and shirts spilling out of it. He had taken off his jeans and shoes and put on some loose sweatpants. He grabbed and kissed her as she headed to the fireplace. She was stiff at first as he rubbed her back and shoulders.

"You must relax, my darling. No one knows we are here. No one knows we are lovers. Even if they did know, no one would care."

Miriamu pulled away from him and moved to the fireplace to warm her hands and feet.

"You're wrong. My every move is watched. I'm not sure anymore who is friend and who is not. I am frightened. Everything is going so well, but still, I have this premonition, this feeling of being watched, that everything will come crashing . . ."

"That's your superstitious African witch doctor hocus pocus nature. This is the twenty-first century. There are no spirits watching us. The U.N. and those who you know are running around preparing for Wave I and are too busy saving their own skin to care about us. No one in Washington cares if I come or go. Besides you're black—you forget that blackness is a cover. Just like old Ellison said, blackness makes you 'invisible.' "

She spun around and threw her hands up. "Who is Ellison? How foolish you talk! I'm not invisible to those at the U.N. whose lives are going to change forever through Operation World Salvation! I am being pushed to the forefront! I am responsible for change; no, some say even for chaos!" She shakes her head at him. "I am being watched. I must be very careful."

"Ah, my love, of course you are being watched—I am watching too, to keep you safe. Now come here and let me show you how you are cared for."

He grabbed one of her uplifted hands and led her to the sofa, pulling her down into his lap. He kissed her face and neck, loosening the tight belt of the robe and admiring her limbs in the glow of the fire. He ran his hands down her slim side and then back up to her breasts. Finally she gave a sigh and pulled his face down to meet her lips. As always, their lovemaking was a combination of tenderness and violence—always an occasion when she felt so out of touch with the control she normally demanded of herself. It was the only place and time anymore when she was able to completely forget, though briefly, the tremendous weight she felt pulling her down.

They ordered food from room service, and she turned on the TV while he was in the shower. Two senators were to be on Mitch Larimore's talk show later in the evening to discuss the details of the latest Israel-Palestinian peace accord. She was about to flip it off when a voice announced:

> *A United Nations staff member of the Ethiopian delegation was brutally murdered yesterday. The police are calling Haile Gebremichael's death the result of robbery. He had returned home to his apartment in lower Manhattan from a reception at the British Consulate and surprised the assailant in his apartment. His body received multiple stab wounds. A cleaning lady found the body this morning . . . . The president of Ethiopia is offering a ten-thousand-dollar reward to anyone who has . . .*

Miriamu gasped and quickly flipped the TV off. She looked through the items B.J. had left on the dresser, and there it was—a New York City subway stub from yesterday. Clearly, he was lying to her. When he came back into the room, she was gathering up her clothes.

"I have to get back to New York."

"No. You promised me the weekend. I flew all the way here and walked around in cold muck. You are not going to desert me after one quick tumble!" He reached for his jeans on the floor, realizing she was still throwing things in her suitcase.

"What happened? Miriamu, look at me. What makes you think you must go back?" He came up from behind and grabbed her shoulders. "I won't let you ruin our weekend. He turned her around so he could see her face. "What has frightened you? What is it?" He tightened his grasp on her "You're not going anywhere! You're staying right here with me!"

She looked into his face for reassurance, but what she saw was anger and violence. Her fear increased. She wanted to trust him but accepted really for the first time that she couldn't. She felt like a lion falling into a pit—one of her own making.

He held her gaze without flinching. "Miriamu—what is your problem, woman?"

"Nothing . . . nothing happened. You're right. It's just my superstitious nature. I'm being so silly."

WAVE I

When people are ready to, they change. They never do it before then, and sometimes they die before they get around to it.

—*Andy Warhol*

~23~
PHOENIX, ARIZONA

Jason Ford looked at his paycheck in wonder. It was three times what he made in March the year before. In fact, all his pay checks had more than doubled since the New Year. He was soon going to be a rich man. He thought about all of the things he had always wanted to buy for Anita, the kids and himself. They could have it all now. He had always laughed resentfully at that old saying "He who has the most toys, wins." Now he could have all the toys he wanted.

He had asked the CEO point blank who had ordered all the solar energy units they couldn't sell even one year ago. The answer had been vague, something about being on the inside with the powers that be. The look on his face told Jason not to pursue the answer any further. And he didn't.

Jason put the paycheck in his pocket and locked his office door as he stepped out for lunch. It was ninety-five outside, consistently ten degrees hotter than late March last year. He made a dash for his Toyota hybrid and turned on the air conditioning. He decided to stop by Nautical Super Sports and pick out a boat. They'd always wanted a boat to take over to Lake Powell. If he got one, they would need a really powerful truck to pull it. So be it; they could afford that too.

He chose a beautiful blue and white Supreme waterskiing boat. It had a hundred-horsepower engine and would hold six comfortably. He put the boat on his credit card, scheming how he would bring Anita and the kids by casually and then surprise them with his purchase. During lunchtime tomorrow, he'd go out and find that new truck to pull the boat and then bring it to the boat shop and have them hook it up in anticipation of his family's visit the next day.

At the end of the day, Jason stopped at the Red Box at the grocery and rented several of last year's Academy Award winners, ones he and Anita had wanted to watch. He swung by Whole Foods and filled the cart with delicacies—imported Greek olives, French wine, a four-pound lobster that the man behind the counter assured him had been flown in from Boston just that day, and as an afterthought, he added Anita's favorite Belgian chocolate. Jason paid for the groceries with his credit card and hurried to the car. He turned on the radio just in time to hear the newscaster say there would be an unexpected announcement from the White House at 7 p.m. He thought to himself that by then, they would be watching a movie and wouldn't want to be bothered with any political spiel.

"What has gotten into you, Jason Ford? Lobster? Olives? French wine? Oooh, my favorite chocolate. What is the occasion?"

Jason showed her the paycheck. "You can quit work whenever you want to. We don't have to have two salaries to keep the kids in the academy. I can afford the tuition on my own—that is, if you want to quit."

"I don't know—the kids are both in school for a good part of the day. I'll have to think about whether I really want to be a stay-at-home mom or continue my career. But it's nice to have a choice, isn't it?"

Dinner was a huge success. The lobster turned out to be as fresh as the butcher had assured him it would be.

When the kids were in bed, they turned on the big screen in the den and plopped in one of the new movies. It was after eleven and the video was over when Jason flipped over to CNN.

> *Tonight's announcement from the White House has the country in an uproar. Scientists around the globe have informed us that the very oxygen we breathe is lessening to the extent that there will soon be too little oxygen for humans to survive. As such, there will be a worldwide ban, implemented and oversee by the U.N., on the burning of fossil fuels in the very near future. Citizens of the United States and the rest of the world have six months to find access to water, food, and any other needs they have that can be*

accessed regularly without the use of fossil fuels or any form of burning. Transportation, communication, and all human activities will be limited to non-fuel-burning efforts.

Jason slumped back into the cushions of the leather sofa and stared at the screen in disbelief. All those solar panels and wind turbines made sense—but that new boat he had just put on his credit card would never hit the water.

~24~
WASHINGTON, D.C.

THE PHONES WERE RINGING OFF THE WALLS AT SENATOR MARTIN'S office. The aides took turns answering the constituents' calls from New Mexico. Following the U.S. announcement, the U.N. had moved quickly to launch Wave I, and the details on that phase had been released the day before. Irate citizens were calling in alarming numbers. The young staff could only repeat what they were hearing on the radio and TV. They didn't know any more than that.

Other than the sound of the phones and the pat answers being given, the whole Hart Senate Office Building was like a tomb. The officers at the entrances had strict instructions to allow no visitors. The staffs, usually congenial among themselves, were somber. No jovial plans to go to lunch; no notes being passed concerning future beach outings or volleyball games on the mall; no teasing the youngest staff member. A tidal wave of anxiety and unease engulfed them.

"Mr. Gonzales, I can only tell you what the radio reports are saying. We have to stop using fossil fuel. The scientists are telling us that our oxygen is in short supply . . . . I'm sure statistics on this crisis will be forthcoming . . . . I can't tell you when the ban will be lifted. I don't have that information . . . . Yes, sir, I realize that your business depends on fossil fuels. Almost all businesses do. Remember, I worked with you in getting your last memo to the senator concerning that defense contract . . . . I just don't know what companies will be able to continue operations because they are strategically necessary . . . . Yes, sir, I promise to call you as soon as we have that information."

Miguel Sandoval, one of Senator Martin's staff members, hung up the phone and threw his hands up in desperation as it rang again.

"Senator Martin's office, this is Miguel Sandoval . . . . Yes, Mrs. Kent, I have heard the radio reports . . . . No, I don't know how you will get to the grocery store . . . . Do you have a bicycle? . . . No, ma'am, I'm not being impertinent; the government directives ask all citizens to revert to non-motorized vehicles for transportation . . . . I know it's been a long time since you rode a bike. Do you have access to one? . . . No, I can't guarantee that the grocery will have supplies after August. Do you have a garden? Even if you live in Albuquerque, you can still have a garden . . . . Mrs. Kent? . . . Are you still there?

At 5 p.m., the senator recorded a personal message on the answering machine. It was supposed to be comforting yet firm. It told New Mexico residents of the opportunities available to them for complying with the mandates of Wave I. It assured them their government was doing everything possible to promote their safety and well-being. The senator told the staff to go home, and he left.

Miguel decided to take the time to clean up his desk. It was piled high with budget memos and unanswered calls from lobbyists. He tried to call and order a sandwich, then remembered the guards wouldn't let the guy from the carry-out place in. On the way down to the Senate snack bar, it felt like he was in a morgue. The feeling sent chills down his back. He imagined it must be like the 2001 anthrax scare. His favorite ham and cheese on wheat was out, so he had to settle for tuna on white. He decided to make a night of it and ordered a Coke and some black coffee.

When he returned to the offices, the outer door had been locked. He remembered distinctly that he had left it unlocked but was glad he'd remembered to bring his key. He opened the door and let himself in. As he entered, he heard loud voices coming from the senator's private office. Crossing the reception room with its Indian pots, rugs, and comfortable furniture, he pressed his ear against the office door and tried to hear what was being said. There was a violent argument taking place in there. Miguel heard an unfamiliar voice cursing in Spanish about energy and large amounts of money. How much money? Who was being paid? What and when?

He figured there must be at least three people with the senator. He could hear Senator Martin arguing violently with someone who sounded like a southerner. As the voices became angrier, he was tempted to knock to see if the senator needed help—or protection. Suddenly, the voices went quiet and it was impossible to hear what was being said.

Returning to the piles on his desk, he tried to forget the incident. But he kept ruminating over the enormous sums of money they were yelling about. Nothing the senator was working on, not contracts for constituents or appropriations for specific part of the U.S. budget, as far as Miguel knew, was bringing in or costing that kind of money. He began shuffling through the most important pile on his desk, making notes to himself about whom he should contact the next day, and tossing the less important ones in the wastebasket. A half-hour later he returned cautiously to the reception area, noting that the lights had been turned off. The door to the senator's private office was locked.

Miguel went back to his own desk and punched up the senator's emails on the office computer. He ran through them, finding nothing about any renewable energy contracts or enormous amounts of money. He realized if there was going to be any information on this in the senator's emails or electronic files, it would be under another name. He hit another location but it demanded a password. He tried various code words he thought the senator might use, the senator's daughters' names, his wife's name, the name of his boat, and his street name in Alexandria. No success.

Remembering the senator's love for cigars, Miguel went through all the brands he could remember: White Owl, Tampa Nuggets, some Cuban black market ones. The last one he tried was the one he had heard the senator regularly put down as the worst, cheapest on the market, Swisher Sweets. That was it. As he read through the emails under that password-protected file, emails about SOLYNDRIX and BDM, the director of UNEP, and some Irish guy, he became more and more uncomfortable. Miguel shut off the computer, picked up his sandwich, and headed for home. He was just too confused and discouraged to pull an all-nighter.

~25~
DEERING, IOWA

"I'm sorry, Elsie, didn't expect it to rain today."

"Summer rainy season, does this most afternoons, can expect it. Don't let the heat from the sun go to your head girl. If we're to feed ourselves we better keep alert."

Jesse's parents' root cellar was already stocked with tomatoes, potatoes, onions, carrots, applesauce, peaches, and plums. Before the electricity went out for good they canned the food left in the old square freezer. The cherries, peas, beans, and corn were reprocessed. Sweat poured from their bodies for days before the no-burn law went into effect. Karen decided canning was definitely the pits.

Elsie insisted they must dry every piece of this year's fruit. It was Karen's job to put the food on the big screens, cover them with another big screen, and turn the pieces as they dried. Obnoxious flies buzzed all around the sweet fruit, trying to get at it each time she took the screens off.

She was too caught up in her own moods to really appreciate her mother-in-law. She hadn't heard from Jesse in two weeks. She felt deserted. When the rain shower came up, she had been down cooling her feet in the creek.

The boys helped Matthew put the slaughtered pig and steer on the hooks in the smoke house and salt them down.

"The way I figure, boys, we can easily get through this first winter what with this meat and a few chickens now and then."

"Grandpa, how long will meat keep salted down like that and still be good?"

"A couple a years, Ethan. 'Course, we could make jerky; that would keep a real long time, but we can't do it till the rains quit; too humid. You boys be praying for good rain so the corn and beans come in like they should."

Karen had only one pair of useful, work jeans, so she bought another at a local Walmart, and some worn overalls in a second-hand store in Deering—clothes she would not have been caught dead in before. She couldn't bring herself to wear the gingham dresses and printed aprons Elsie usually wore. She felt so Dorothy-and-Toto in them.

A few days later, Matthew and the boys walked to town and came home with a second horse and a wagon. "Brewers are moving to California; they figure the climate is better out there for year-round farming," Matthew offered.

Karen considered the reasoning poor. "Not a good idea. Anyone who moves there will be fighting millions of Californians for the land."

"Just what I told Justin, said he was foolish to pack his family and head into the unknown. Lucky for us he had a horse and an old harness and wagon he hasn't used in years and couldn't take."

Several weeks later, Karen came downstairs to find Elsie busy repairing frayed covers and quilts.

"What we need is a treadle machine. Where do you suppose we could find one?" Karen asked.

"I've seen them in the past at Grisham's Antique Emporium. But he wants a fortune for them."

"Well, it may be worth a fortune if we have to make all our own clothes next year. Where are the boys?"

"They went over to Boone to get us some bees."

"Why wasn't I told? I don't like it when the boys are off the place. What on earth do we need bees for?"

"For honey, that's what for. When the sugar runs out, you'll be grateful for the bees."

Karen panicked when they didn't get back till midnight, even though Elsie kept assuring her that bees can't be moved till dark. In the wagon sat two large hives with a couple of "supers" at the top of each. It had been a good year already, and the bees were busy putting honey in the supers. They watched as the boys and Matthew carefully untied the boxes and placed them halfway between the barn and the orchard.

"Fellow said we had good strong queens and around forty to fifty thousand bees in each of these hives; should be enough to make lots of honey before winter. Said we can take one super of honey this year from each and more next year. Just got to make sure they don't get mites or get to swarmin'. Don't want to lose these little girls."

"Honey lasts forever," Karen volunteered. "Did you know that they found some in pyramids that was put there thousands of years ago, and it was still good?"

"Is that so?" said Matthew, who continued his work in silence.

Karen wanted desperately to have someone to talk with further about the wonder of this long ago cache and the people who deposited it. She and Jesse had so enjoyed discussing ancient civilizations and world discoveries. "Seeds too. Did you know they discovered corn that could still be planted? They proved that noodles came from China, not Italy, when they found a two-thousand-year-old bowl of them."

But Matthew couldn't be caught up in an intellectual conversation at midnight on a Saturday or any night for that matter. He just yawned and headed off to bed. Loneliness engulfed her.

After attending the community Christian church with her in-laws the next morning, Karen made the boys sit quietly and read on the big wraparound front porch of the farmhouse. They squirmed and fidgeted until she had to let them go to see about the bees. She breathed a sigh of relief as she watched them run across the lawn. Then her eye caught Matthew coming down the road from the fields talking to a large stranger in a plaid shirt. They hadn't had any visitors since the announcement of Wave I, but they had listened to the news of people beginning to flee out of Sioux City and other larger towns and cities. Alton was south and had a bit warmer climate and lay near a river. It would become a prime target for those seeking food and shelter. Red flags went up in Karen's mind even as the stranger came through the gate with Matthew and then headed to the orchards.

When Matthew came in for Sunday dinner, he explained. "Fellow out there just wandered in from the city. Asked could he help around the place for a meal or two? We're going to repair the fences over beside the orchard."

Karen disapproved. "It's dangerous to take in strangers. We know people will be desperate for food and they will . . . ."

"Out here we got a code, Karen. There's got to be a helping hand to those less fortunate or we can't expect the next one to help us." He filled a plate of food for the man. All afternoon, they worked side by side on the fences. When the afternoon showers came, Karen was moving the screens where peaches and cherries were drying. She noticed that the man was watching her from the shadow of the barn. At sundown, Matthew took out another plate of food.

"Told him he could wash down at the trough with the spigot and sleep in the barn, and we'd finish the fencing in the morning."

When Matthew gathered up the fencing tools the next morning, the man was gone. When she went to throw grain for the chickens, Karen noticed the door to the smoke house was ajar. The pork and beef that had been hanging was gone too.

~26~
BUENOS AIRES

TWO YEARS AFTER HER APPOINTMENT AS MINISTER OF AGRICULTURE, Camilla once again begged Hendrik to come look over her work and give her advice. He flew in a month later. On the way to the airport, she mused over the past few years and the changes in her life. It had been no use trying to convince the government or her husband to let her meet his flight on her own. She was a married woman with children in a Latin country still clinging to its Catholic heritage.

Her rise to power in the government had been swift. Mateo Jesus Almeida de Rio had kept his promise, making her the first female minister of agriculture in a nation where all food production was still a bastion of machismo.

She'd had early success with policies to move the country toward self-sufficiency. The president was pleased and the people were, on the whole, better fed. The country was no longer even remotely dependent on the U.S., Europe, or its volatile neighbors for food or other essentials. Her determination that all agriculturalists begin producing "regenerative" yields was taking hold.

But each time she remembered the pressure of Almeida's strong hand on her wrist, it always made her heart jump a little. She needed Hendrik to help her with the next steps. The dismantling of dependency on chemicals and pesticides was daunting. She needed help not with the technical proof that the land was suffering from past decisions but with the politics of power. How could they help powerful industries dismantle their empires, and build new ones, yet keep labor employed throughout the transition? What did she need to think about in terms of future policies to sustain and continue what she had started—even if something happened to her?

Yes, she'd become a powerful minister and a confidant to the president, but she lacked the political savvy to take the next steps. She was a bit surprised and very grateful that Hendrik agreed to come. Camilla knew that though her intimate relationship with Hendrik had been over for years, Kathryn wasn't big on his spending time anywhere near her.

Protocol demanded that there be an entourage to meet the important scientist from Africa. That entourage included no fewer than ten people standing with her at the international visitors' arrival gate when he came through the automatic glass doors.

The last time she'd seen him was ten years ago, and before that there was a gap of five years. At that visit, she'd just been called on to be a policy adviser to her predecessor. There'd been a trade mission to America, and the two of them had carved out a few hours at the Dallas airport. They sat before a huge window sipping wine and talking rapidly to savor each moment together. He was in his mid-sixties, ever wiry, a twinkle in his eye as he looked her up and down, taking in the woman she had become in the last decade. He was still desperately trying to get policy makers and leaders all over the world to listen to his ideas. She remembered the brief look of exasperation, almost resignation, as he talked about the ever escalating stubbornness of the scientific world in its opposition. On top of that, there was the constant effort to keep the non-profit that had been formed to promote and further develop his work funded and stable.

"Here in the West, there are small pockets of people using my ideas to restore their land, also in Australia and Mexico and southern Africa. But it is a pittance in light of what must be done if we are to avert a worldwide crisis in food supplies that will follow the rapidly increasing loss of biodiversity everywhere."

"Where do you go from here?"

"Back to Africa, I am trying to alleviate the tragedy in my own country left over from the politicians that allowed the farms to be taken over, the crops to fail and animals to die en masse. But here I am talking about me. What about you?"

"My lands are improving. I'm making some inroads with other farmers. I'm gaining some influence over some in . . . ."

He took her hand at that point, and she was at a loss for any more words. They did not talk about family, his wife, or her husband. They just sat there holding hands until she had to leave.

Now, as she caught her first glimpse of him, Camilla found herself glad for the entourage. It would force a certain formality, saving her from slipping anywhere near the once too familiar. As customary, Hendrik was first to bound through the door. She smiled, remembering all the tricks he had shared with her about how to be the first on and off a plane, even when flying coach. His eyes swept the room quickly, finding her easily amid the pack of all-male military and diplomatic greeters.

He came forward with his arms outstretched and the grin that had always disarmed her. The agents moved to surround her, but she called them off, giving him a stiff, brief hug followed by the kiss on both cheeks customary in her country. As she brushed his cheeks she whispered, "Remember, we will be watched at all times for any improprieties."

"Let me look at you, Camilla," he said, pulling away while still holding both her hands. "Ah, motherhood has been good to you. One might not even know but for a certain wisdom that fills your eyes and a softness that turns your mouth."

"You're not trying to find a nice way to say 'You've aged well' are you, old man?"

"On the contrary," he rebutted, looking mortally wounded. "In my eyes, you will never be older than that twenty-something girl who picked me up one night after a terribly dry lecture about grass!" He winked, and she felt a blush rise to her face, remembering the first time she heard him speak and the many years now that they had cherished each other, first as lovers and now as dear friends.

"The civil service agents will ferry you to your hotel to allow you the remainder of the day for rest. You are dining this evening at my casa with the president, his wife, and of course my husband, Enrique, and the children. I am looking forward to seeing what happens when my two favorite men in the world meet. Remember, absolutely no musing over my past! I was twenty; you were my idol. And neither my husband nor the president would understand the workings of that twenty-year-old female heart."

"Ah, but they would understand the lust of an old fool."

"Hush! I'll see you around 8 p.m. And Hendrik, try to stay out of trouble until then." She laughed as the agents escorted both of them along the corridor toward baggage claim.

~27~
DEERING, IOWA

JESSE CALLED KAREN ON AUGUST 20, THEIR FIFTEENTH WEDDING ANniversary. After talking briefly to his mom, he heard Karen's voice on the phone. Just as they were about to launch into catching up in depth on what had been going on in New York and Iowa and around the world following the announcement of Wave I, Karen remembered that strange radio report about the precipitous increase in renewable energy stocks that she'd heard on her way to Iowa. It had seemed such an insignificant thing in comparison with her trying to resettle herself and the boys in Iowa. But now, it seemed important for her to tell him what she remembered.

"Of course they went up when the announcement was made, Karen."

"No Jesse, this was when we were driving out. It just seemed too soon! . . . Jesse, did you hear what I said?"

"Yes, I heard. It doesn't compute. I'll have to do some digging around. How are you and the folks getting on?"

"Okay"

"Just okay?"

"Well your dad wants to bring in every stray animal and human on the planet and feed and clothe them. Your mom is a bit more reasonable. I don't think either of them has a clue as to how dangerous that is. Right now they think I'm just being pessimistic about the whole thing—I guess I deserve that after all the doubting I did."

"Be patient with them, it's easier to change drastically when you are young. It's bound to be harder when you are so set in your ways."

"If you think going from a Manhattan publisher to an Iowa farm girl is easy—think again."

"Karen, I'm sorry. I know it hasn't been easy. I think about you and the boys all the time. I know we made the right decision. Things here are rough. The National Guard keeps watch over us Essentials and our makeshift apartment building. We get escorted from there to the U.N. and back. We have hot water twice a week. We buy what the P.X. calls food these days—mostly canned stuff—and eat it cold. Sometimes the only thing that looks palatable is oatmeal. We don't dare ask what kind of meat they are serving. The streets are almost deserted and fewer and fewer people are bringing in food. There are a few open air markets near neighborhood gardens; the grocery stores are all abandoned.

"We get reports of riots and killing. It's the same in Berlin, Paris, London, and other cities around the world. We won't even come close to preventing mass chaos. Lots of people didn't take us seriously and aren't finding or creating alternative sources of food. In the next few weeks, as we move toward Wave II, it's going to get worse. The streets aren't safe for man or beast. Believe me, Iowa has to be better."

"Iowa is without you."

"I dream about you at night. I reach for you and then imagine how it was, how it will be when I can hold you again. Never forget that I love and need you, Karen."

"Don't. It's too hard to even think about us. I try not to let my mind go there, or I will go crazy. Jesse, how long . . . when will it be over?"

"Well, right now we are just trying to maintain order. Get all those alternative forms of energy in place. We have to begin to rethink our use of resources and consumptive lifestyles. I plan to visit that guy Hendrik Johnson. Remember? I did research on him after you shared that National Geographic article about his work a long time ago.

"But that Johnson guy is in Africa. Are you really going there?"

"His ideas may help us formulate Wave III—a practical way to sink some more carbon in the soil while we rebuild food resources and create a more sustainable world. Hannah also put me in touch with Paddy Freeman in Ireland—good ideas on how to proceed. There is a woman in Argentina that may help."

"Africa, Ireland, Argentina, what about Iowa?"

"Karen, you know Iowa is not on the list that would make sense for using fuel."

"How long do you think all this will take?"

"Hannah and I are looking at a year, maybe two before we can get mass re-education systems put in place and policies to sustain them around the world that make sense."

Silence . . . . "So it is safe for Hannah but not for me?"

"Karen, I can't bring you back here the way it is now. It would be foolish. People are panicking in the streets. Give me time to stabilize things. Then I may not be needed here. I may have to be a farmer too.

"Jesse, you could come here now and let someone else be in charge. I hate this! Jesse I need you more than . . . more than Hannah!"

"Hannah? She has nothing to do with this. It's my responsibility to be here and see this thing through. I can't leave now … for the first time in my life I am doing something that makes a difference. All those frustrating years of fighting in the past are coming to fruition. I simply can't abandon this effort. I put forth the overall plan to the U.N. I won't now let someone else become responsible for it. I can't give up. You know it's not in my nature."

He talked to each boy, briefly. They seemed to be almost completely adjusted to the farm and their grandparents. They talked about riding the horses and milking the cows and fishing in the creek. They complained about weeding the garden and church on Sundays. He commiserated. They discussed whether school was even an option for that year. When Karen came back on the phone she seemed less hostile.

"Well, Mr. Essential, let me know when you have some free time. I'd love a date with someone so important. We'll picnic on fried chicken and corn and okra and tomatoes down by the creek and skinny dip and then lie out in the grass and I'll show you my esteem for you."

"Oh, darling—you are making my mouth water, and not for food. I miss you so. It's a date. I love you, Karen.

"Oh, Jesse—you don't know how much. What is it they say—we don't appreciate what we have until we lose it. I'm not going to lose you . . . you understand, Jesse? I'm not going to lose you."

~28~
NEW YORK CITY

When Jesse hung up the phone, he felt like he had been put through a ringer. He was sweating and breathing hard. For the hundredth time he reassured himself that he really was doing the best thing for everyone—Karen and the boys as well as millions of other innocent people. Yes, he was right to send them away. So far, the farm was a safe place for his family.

He felt a little jealous. Here he was in the middle of daily chaos while they were surrounded by the comforts of the farm. Didn't Karen realize that? Did she understand at all why he was still in New York? Jesse closed his eyes and mentally wandered through the garden and down the hill to the creek. He could see exactly where they had put the bees and imagine them buzzing around his mother's roses.

That day, he called Kim, anxious to listen to a friendly voice and somehow glean encouragement, even from someone thousands of miles away. It took several hours for him to make the connection. He'd forgotten the time difference, but once Kim realized it was Jesse, he was wide awake.

"Jesse—how's it going, my good friend?"

"Slowly, Kim, slowly. I guess we were trying to change the world overnight, and people don't move that fast. I hear Japan is still receiving shipments from BDM and others operating in the Orient?"

"Yes. The implementation of your Wave I mandate has been slower on the Pacific Rim. People are moving out of the cities, and there was one incident recently of refugees overwhelming a small village and attacking the residents, trying to take over their farms. Only nuclear trains are still running, and I see handcarts and bicycles being used. How soon do you think shipping will stop completely?"

"I don't know—your guess is as good as mine. In June, we closed down the wells in the Mideast and Alaska, and those in South America and off the North Slope were scheduled to close by July 1. Whatever fuel and food they are using was in storage, and it's bound to run out soon. When that happens, your people will have no choice but to seek alternate means. Are alternate power sources being revved up?

"You know, that's funny. Even before I got your first email warning me that this was coming, I read in the Kyoto paper how some individual members of the Pacific Rim Federation, especially Australia, were upping their production of wind and solar equipment. I thought to myself, "It's about time." But now that I think of it, seems the timing was off. Was increased renewable energy production part of the plan?"

"Yes, sort of. Do you remember what the date was?"

"Oh, let's see, I think it was about eighteen months ago. Why?"

"No reason, just curious. How are Lee and the kids?

"Just fine. They send their love. Hey, Jesse, when this is all over, let's get together in Hawaii and have some fun. Let's all have a vacation, Karen, you boys, and Lee and the kids—how about it? We can debate Coors versus Sapporo like old times.

"That sounds great to me. Kim. Are you following my instructions? Is your famil. . . ?"

"We're all set. Not to worry. Lee and I have at least a year of provisions stored and know how to dry and store whatever comes in this fall. Believe me, we are very safe here. The farm is off the beaten path. I don't expect any trouble at all. I am sharing any extra we have this year through the local growers market. I will continue to do that so as not to raise suspicion. How are Karen and the boys?"

"I shipped them off to Iowa this spring. I just talked to them. Karen is most unhappy, but that can't be helped. I think deep down inside she still doubts that this is even necessary. I know she is feeling deserted and alone. I have to know she and the boys are safe. You understand."

"Yes, and she will come to understand."

"I hope you are right. I probably won't call again until we get into Wave II. Kim, if you get into any trouble . . . well, I hope there will be a line open to the Essentials. Call me."

"Will do friend. Sayonara"

"Goodbye, Kim.

~29~
KILKENNY, IRELAND

Paddy searched his desk for his glasses, moving a pile of agriculture notes and a stack of pamphlets from agriculture firms. He found the glasses in the pocket of his old wool sweater. They were streaked with mud. He breathed on them and wiped them clean with his handkerchief. He reread the email from New York. Something about a message being on paper made it more real than on the computer screen.

It just said, "Paddy, just want you to know that I really appreciate your ideas about the important project we are working on. Thanks again, Jesse." It was from that nice young man who had stopped in about a month ago to talk about how to get the entire mass of humanity to shift to using entirely renewable resources and regenerative agriculture practices. So nice of him to reconnect amid the turmoil of Wave I. It occurred to Paddy that he'd never even heard back from that group of high muckety-mucks he'd met with a year ago and signed off to endorse their plan. Wasn't the beautiful African lady from the U.N. too? Did she know Jesse? Ah, he thought, too many people to keep track of for an old man.

The initial cut backs in fossil fuel as Wave I came to a close and Wave II was about to kick in had thrown Ireland into chaos. There were no signs of alternate fuels being developed, food was disappearing in cities like Dublin and Belfast. People were streaming out of the cities inundating the countryside. They were already beginning to fear winter, and Wave II was not even yet in effect. Any so-called "help from the government" hadn't materialized. Oh, well, he was just an old man on a farm. What right had he to threaten them? What could he do anyway? He probably should just concentrate on getting himself ready for the winter and whatever lay ahead, given the shutdown of all the fossil fuel systems that was imminent.

He stuffed the glasses back in his pocket, put on his old hooded jersey, and shuffled out into the twilight. The sun was a warm filtered spot in the otherwise gray sky. The mist was still lukewarm, unusual for autumn. He looked with pride over the fields he had nourished for half a century. He had eliminated erosion, never plowed in rows or used chemicals. His land was pristine. No other farmer in Ireland could say as much for his or her land. He knew a third of the Irish farms had gone under, and the knuckleheads continued to ignore his ideas. Why couldn't he just be happy with his land and let the rest of bloody humanity be hanged?

Paddy opened the near pasture gate to let Maggie in. She was bawling, anxious to be milked. The chickens had already begun to roost. He stuck three more eggs in his sweater pocket. Sticking the milk can under Maggie, he methodically stroked her teats, enjoying the sound of the milk as it splattered on the tin and then the mellow music of it swishing in the pail. He patted her on the rump and shoveled several pitchforks of hay into her stall. She flipped her tail and watched him leave from the corner of her liquid brown eyes.

As he left the barn, the chill from the wind caused him to pull the sweater tighter around his body with his free hand. Rounding the barn, he saw a strange vehicle parked in front of the cottage. Any vehicle would have seemed strange. No cars passed, much less stopped. The occupant of the auto wore an unfamiliar uniform. It was all very puzzling. Vehicle use was becoming daily more scarce since only select officials were supposed to have the use of petrol for the last few weeks leading up to Wave II. Why would someone in uniform be coming to County Kilkenny and his farm this late of an evening?

He stood there in the gloaming wondering. He'd done nothing that anyone in the military would be interested in. Years past, he'd been verbally abusive toward the stupid Green Party and Parliament, and was thrown out of committee meetings on a regular basis. But that was long since over, and the new Irish government didn't even know he existed. His inclination was to just ignore the visitor. But as he was about to pass the driver's door, the uniformed fellow got out and stood in his way.

"Paddy Freeman?"

"Aye."

The uniform seemed to be a combination of police and military, not Irish, perhaps a branch of British military, but he couldn't be sure. And the man had a soft accent that Paddy couldn't place. He didn't seem at all threatening.

"Could I have a few words with you?"

"And what is it you be wanting to talk about?"

"It's about your farm." The man waved vaguely at the hills behind the cottage. "The National Forestry Institute will be expanding its reforesting as part of Operation World Salvation. We will be using your neighbor's land there on the east and we think maybe your upland pasture will provide space for us. We'd like to show you some plans and ask your help."

"It's balmy they are, these hills will be needed to feed the people, they be for sheep and cattle and the low lands for vegetables." Paddy hesitated, peering more closely at the uniform, trying desperately to make sense of its meaning and the man's request. It remained enigmatic. However, the visitor seemed sincere, and it was colder now that the sun was almost down.

He turned toward the cottage with a shrug of his shoulders. "Come inside. I'll look at your plans—but I'll not be promising anything." Paddy took two steps toward the cottage door before the prick of the blow dart hit his neck and the poison began penetrating his body. He started to spin around but slumped to the ground. His left hip crushed two of the eggs, and the third rolled out onto the grass. The milk from the pail spilled onto the ground, pouring over the rosemary and thyme he had planted along the path. His last sensations were their sweet scent and the feel of his beloved Irish soil against his cheek.

The killer slipped on gloves and entered the cottage. The old coot had left the computer on; an email from New York was still on the screen. He wiped it out and removed all evidence that Paddy Freeman had been in touch with anyone in the United States. He left the computer on. Outside, he carefully removed the dart from Paddy's neck. There was no sign of breath when he placed a mirror over Paddy's mouth and nose. He methodically brushed away any imprint of his own shoes on the path.

Then, he moved his car onto the pavement and grabbed a random branch and brushed over the tire tracks and his footprints till he reached the pavement. Up to this point, all he'd had to do was pass papers back and forth with some senator, and he was earning some pretty good money. Pretending to be Irish M.P. and killing someone was a whole other step for him. He hoped it would be the last time he had to do something like this. Then he drove off, just another important official on his way to Dublin.

* * *

"Paddy died of natural causes, probably some kind of attack, Mona. I was just making my normal Monday morning rounds, checking on folks on the farms to be sure everyone was getting ready for Wave II, when I found him just in front of the kitchen door. Looked as if he just dropped dead right there."

"Natural causes hell—that's a bleedin' lie. My father's not been sick a day in his life. You must be mistaken. There is no record of a heart condition, advanced diabetes, or any of the things that someone might suddenly drop dead of. Yesterday morning, he was the picture of health. There is bloody well something wrong with this picture."

"Now don't get uppity, Mona, just doing my job. His body is right there, and my initial exam which I did while you were coming down from Carlow earlier today says he died last night. I'm no coroner, but I have a few skills in telling things about a dead man after twenty-five years on the police force, ya know."

Mick was right. Paddy lay on the kitchen table. He was definitely dead. There were no marks to indicate any foul play. Mona stood over her father, caressing the stubble on his cheek with the back of her hand.

Her anger at Mick kept her from crying. Fact was, she just didn't want to admit that Paddy could be gone. An old fool. But the only one who helped her make sense of life. Wave I had thrown her for a loop, and now this. She'd been planning to vacate her apartment in Carlow and move in with him in just a week or so. It was the best option to keep them both as safe as possible as Wave II hit.

He had been so alive just two days ago. He'd sown grain in the south field all day Friday, repaired fences on Saturday. She had helped him clean out the chicken house Sunday before heading back to Carlow. He had not complained about feeling bad—but then her da had never complained about his health.

After the coroner's wagon arrived and stripped and took away the body and Mick finally left, Mona began going though Paddy's clothing. In the pocket of an old sweater were his other reading glasses, filthy with a white filmy substance. She put them to her nose; they smelled like the earth and spoiled milk. Poor Maggie. It was then that she knew she was going to cry, whether she wanted to or not.

Mona found the overturned milk pail on the path and heard Maggie bawling. The cow had bashed the side of the stall. "Calm down, Maggie, old girl. I'm going to feed and milk you just relax." Mona stroked her until she calmed down. Fluttering on a nail stuck to the wall was a piece of paper, an email printout. She had set up the computer and printer for Paddy but didn't think he ever used them. The email was from someone with a ".UN" address, probably one of those young U.N. trainees her dad had worked with a few years ago. She read it several times but couldn't make any sense of the message. Was the old man involved in something he'd never shared with her?

She took the milk to the old icebox on the porch, grateful the battery-operated generator was still cranking. Soon she'd have to just get used to warm milk, blah. Then she sat down at the computer. Based on the date, he must have received the email just before he died. She punched in the password they had decided on when she showed him how to use his email service. There was nothing in the inbox. And a quick analysis of the "history" indicated there had never been any email from someone with this address. She checked the date and time on the paper again. He'd received the email Sunday at 3 p.m.

Running some further diagnostics, she could see that the machine had been wiped clean of any mail coming from or going to Paddy Freeman at about 8 that evening. Who had wiped the computer clean? Who was this Jesse? Who and what was behind this address? Why was her father in contact with someone in New York?

~30~
GEORGETOWN, D.C.

THREE MEN WERE SEATED AROUND A LARGE TABLE, SHUFFLING PAPERS, while a fourth man leaned casually against the wall. A large marker board showed lists of alternative fuel equipment in countries around the world being shipped from place to place. Three cigar butts were smashed into the last piece of cheese pizza. A bottle of tequila and several bottles of stale beer stood on a side table.

"Coffee—I could use a cup of coffee." Martin stood up stretched his legs and walked over to the window. The early morning light was just beginning to filter beneath the drawn shade. "Lenny, why don't you go to that little bodega on the corner, you know the one where the Pakis have decided to stick it out and see if they can survive and get us some coffee."

"I don't think that's a good idea," Cleveland warned.

Lenny picked up his baseball cap, looking uncertainly from Martin to Cleveland and back again.

"You're probably right. Sit back down, Lenny. Let's not take a chance on someone seeing you. We're almost finished, aren't we? Can't we call it a night? I need to get back to the Senate building, and I'll have to shower first." Martin's distaste for these meetings had grown, and he had become more and more impatient as the hours lengthened. "Are we in agreement? Manny? Cleveland?"

Cleveland shook his head no. "We need to decide on the transport for the last of those Australian goods. Melbourne is the holdup. It might make more sense to just leave the last order of goods there in Australia. Australia will need it just as badly as the U.S., and if we transport it this late, it will cause suspicion. Speaking of suspicion, all hell broke loose in Saudi Arabia when Peter and others started shutting down the oil wells for the U.S. and British petroleum firms. I've tried to contact him, but he has disappeared from the face of the Earth."

Manuel jumped in. "Geez, that's not good, dude. Sorry about your brother. But back to the topic at hand. We promised to bring that last load here. SOLYNDRIX told the Appropriations Committee we had enough machines for the U.S., but now the civil situation in Australia is beyond our control. *Jesucristo,* that Forester fellow has things moving too fast."

Senator Martin lit another cigar "It's not the Appropriations Committee we should fear. If the government doesn't get enough alternative energy sources into place, the public will revolt and put the oil and gas companies back in charge. The companies and Malone will put Forester's head in a vice and his U.N. buddies on trial."

"What do we care? Let the world go back to the way it was. We've profited. Let's take the money and run."

"Cleveland, further investigation could backfire on us. We can't close down. It would look suspicious as hell."

"Not true, Martin. Think. If SOLYNDRIX can't meet its commitments, they can just say transportation became impossible."

Manuel jumped in again. "Let's not be greedy. We've done much of what we set out to do. We've destroyed the hold the Arab oil machine had on the U.S. and made environmental NGOs very happy. Along the way, we lined our own pockets. *Es bueno. Es suficiente. ¿No?* Martin? Cleveland?

A cell phone that had been tossed onto the side table began to quiver and then ring. The senator picked it up. "Yes. No. I'll return her call. I'll take care of it." Martin turned to the others. Well, gentlemen, I have an important call to return. I'll go along with your decision. Maybe you're right, Manny, we've done enough." He gathered papers that had been scattered around the table, shoved them into a large leather briefcase, and walked out.

The room was quiet for a few minutes.

Cleveland broke the silence. "Martin is getting a little too jumpy. It's time to cut him out of the loop. It's time to dissolve the U.S. portion. Manny, tell the government acquisition people to buy directly from our Belgian contact at SOLYNDRIX, and we'll blame any transportation problem on the U.N. It's time for us to get out of the middle."

The two men settled down to wait as Lenny carefully wiped the marker board with chemical cleaner and emptied the ashtrays. He dumped the remaining beer down the sink, wiped the bottles and all other surfaces clean of fingerprints, and carried out the trash.

~31~
NORRIS DAM, TENNESSEE

ON NOVEMBER 5, SALLY WYNN'S PROPANE TANK RAN OUT OF GAS. She softly scolded herself. "Now why in tarnation did it have to be the morning of the first snow?" Outside the kitchen window she saw the clumps of white lying on top of the black walnut trees like glue. She hauled out her black galoshes looking for the *Knoxville Herald* in the yard. It wasn't there, another bad sign. Joe Morgan's son had been delivering for the past twenty years, just like his dad before him.

Finally she found the number of Tennessee Gas and Oil and grimaced at the slogan with the listing: "Propane is our Specialty—Serving all of Tennessee." She lifted the receiver to call. The line was dead.

Outside the kitchen window, a bright red sticker covered the intake valve on the tank.

> *This will be your last tank of gas. Our Company can no longer legally supply you with propane. We thank you for many years of patronage.*

"Now, why in the name of creation didn't I notice that before?" Hoping there was a little bit left, she tried to light the stove and make herself a cup of instant coffee. There was only hissing in the line. Sally munched on a stale biscuit from breakfast the day before, smeared with the apricot jam that won second prize at the Powell County Fair. Looking out the window, she saw some blue through the clouds and murmured to herself, "The sun will be out soon and it will get warmer. I'll just hunker down and read."

She went to the thermostat and once again lifted the lever and pushed the dial up above seventy-five. Nothing. The thermometer hanging with the bird feeder outside the kitchen door read thirty degrees. The house was still warm, though, and there was no way for her to call for help. Sally had never been one to cry wolf, and the troops from the National Guard hanging around the 'Get and Go' Market surely had more important things to do than help an old lady.

Sally opened the door to the spare bedroom, and the cold hit her in the face. Inside the old trunk was the afghan her Grandmother Ida had crocheted, the one her mother Sarah crocheted, and an old quilt frayed around the edges whose origin she couldn't remember.

Folded on the bed was the quilt the Methodist ladies helped her stitch some years back. She hauled her old rocker to the south window in the front room where the sun would shine first, if it decided to make an appearance. She stacked her reading material next to the rocker. On top was the National Geographic on pyramids from October, not even opened yet. She put one quilt under her for the draft already creeping in through the floorboards. The other she stuffed around her body along with the two afghans, then began reading about Egypt.

The sun shining on the sides of the pyramid was the last thing she saw before dozing off. Her dreams began with the feeling of warmth and light all around. She was back on the farm in Pennington Gap, and Papa was killing two chickens for Sunday dinner. The blood was warm and oozing from their necks as they hung on the clothesline. She smiled as she saw her brothers and sisters all around the table and smelled the yeast from the hot rolls Momma got up at 6 a.m. to let rise and bake for dinner.

Sally woke up, startled by bone-chilling cold, and wrapped the covers more tightly around her thin body. It had begun to snow again, and the little bit of blue sky had disappeared. She dozed off but couldn't quite recapture the warm Sunday afternoon. In her reverie, she relived the night in September when she went swimming in the old reservoir with the Duke boy. They had gotten so cold, and he got fresh. She ended up having to punch him. She dreamed of the time she and Micah had climbed into the Cumberland to cut a Christmas tree and become totally disoriented. They wandered around and around for hours. From then on, all the dozing and reminiscing encompassed water and cold, as the temperature in the room continued to drop.

The *Powell Valley News* cut back to one paper a week the first of November. The November 15 edition was late, and turned out to be the last one. Editor Lee Womack, who was on the gas and lights board, felt panic and despair as he placed Sally Wynn's obituary in its nice, neat little box for publication.

~32~
DEERING, IOWA

MATTHEW AND THE BOYS CUT DOWN A LITTLE TREE FROM THE HILLside. They shouldn't have done it, but Karen couldn't deprive the boys of a Christmas tree along with everything else. They covered it with popcorn strings and colored balls. Elsie made truffles and fudge with honey.

Karen wrapped a few books she'd bought just before leaving New York. She had picked some Steinbeck for Ethan and several children's biographies for Troy. She flipped the pages of the books, realizing how much she missed the smell of a new book. She missed a good read, a new book to ponder, to gobble up and then discuss with Jesse. Language, she realized, makes us human. We only truly understand something when we share it.

She thought back to the last family Christmas with Jesse. They spent the afternoon all bundled up watching the skaters at Rockefeller Center. They listened to the concert at St. Patrick's Cathedral before heading home to eat steak and twice-baked cheesy potatoes—the favorite of all the men in her family. The tree in their apartment was surrounded by packages—not to mention the skateboards and electronic games she and Jesse placed there after the boys had given up and gone to bed. It was always so hard to contain their exuberance on Christmas Eve, with the anticipation that Christmas morning would bring such gifts. She had never lost that same warm feeling herself.

Once the stockings were filled with little things—a new watch for Ethan and a really fine new-fangled direction finder for Troy—she and Jesse cuddled on the couch.

Now she was in Iowa, and he was in New York. Or that was where she thought he was. She had tried to call him but the cell towers had gone dead. The generator had gone out in mid-December, and the only heat was from the fire place in the living room. They all had been sleeping together in the one room. The boys complained about Matthew's snoring but eventually adjusted to it.

While she was piling on extra bedding Troy came in to help. "Mom, what do you think Dad is doing now?"

"Oh, I don't know, probably making important plans for the world to change its way to do this or that. He's talking to presidents, and prime ministers, and dictators, and flying around the world."

"I bet he's missing us a lot—it being Christmas and all. We have each other and Grandpa and Grandma, but he doesn't have anyone. Sure must be lonely. I guess he just can't fly here because there aren't any important people in Iowa, huh? He can only make official and important trips. As soon as the plans for Wave II get going, though, they probably won't need him anymore, will they? Then he can come out here and be with us. Huh?"

The three of them were feeling the same emotions but sometimes unable to find the words. She hugged him close. Even Ethan had allowed her a hug or two lately, although at fourteen, he had been avoiding being "mushy." The season caused both of them to know how much she needed to feel them close. She knew that her anger and jealousy over Hannah and not knowing was making her cling to the boys, and that wasn't healthy. But she couldn't help herself.

Troy continued his verbal ponderings, "So we just have to be patient and wait. He's okay, though, isn't he, Mom?"

"Sure, he's okay."

That night as she listened to the boys' soft breathing and Matthew's snoring, she couldn't sleep. She got up, wrapping her blanket tightly around her body, and slipped out onto the porch. It was cold and each breath formed a white cloud. From the porch swing she could see thousands of stars with the big dipper, and Venus bright in the southern sky. The landscape below was pitch-black; it felt to her like there were no lights left on Earth.

~33~
NEW YORK CITY

JESSE AND HANNAH SPENT CHRISTMAS READING REPORTS. OPERA-tion World Salvation was in full swing around the globe. Hannah's office was no longer a neat, orderly place. Papers covered the floor the coffee table, and chairs.

"Let's categorize this stuff, Hannah. Let's see if we can decide where the needs are greatest. We should be able to make some suggestions to the authorities."

Hours later, Jesse looked up from his stack to see that Hannah was just sitting on the floor staring at him.

"What?"

"It's hopeless."

"Why?"

"Listen to this: Fifteen men, women, and children were killed yesterday when their van was chased off an incline into the Arkansas River. The National Guard explained they were just trying to catch the family because they were using fuel and driving a vehicle. That's against the mandate.'"

"And this, 'The bodies of four unidentified children were found floating in the Delaware River. No one has claimed the bodies, and National Guard spokesmen are saying the children, ranging in age from two to six, were very thin and not clothed for winter' And this, 'Fresno, California: Sheriff's deputies have threatened to let neighbors or migrants—anyone who will get crops in the ground—take over the fields of farmers who refuse to plant. The farmers insisted it was too early for planting, but the officials were trying to force them.'

"And there's more," Hannah said, unable to stop. " 'Ten thousand rioters flooded the streets of London yesterday demanding heating oil and food.' "

"I don't know about your stack, but mine is full of misunderstandings between authorities and people. It's full of deaths because people refuse to change their ways. It's full of panic, and misery. It's full of conflict and abuse. Why didn't we anticipate all this?"

"You know why. But there is some good news. Everyone is piling on the clothes as the weather gets colder. People are sharing homes and shelters and food, scrounging bikes for transportation."

"Jesse, New York is a disaster."

"I know."

"The same with D.C."

"I know, but Miami is doing okay."

"Of course, it's seventy degrees. Germany is crumbling"

"You have a report from there?"

"My sister got an email through to me in October. She said they are barely getting by, and she will never be warm again. They have traded furniture, clothes, and bedding for food. She says Ali, her husband, is building bikes with spare parts they are scrounging and stealing. They trade the bikes for food. They have moved into Berlin to be near one of Ali's friends. She wants to know what they should do. German police are very serious about enforcing restrictions, no matter who ends up dead or why."

"They have to be. They have to force people to take the mandate seriously."

"How do we know that? Jesse, I'm afraid. I'm afraid of what the world is turning into—it may not be worth the effort. It's all so . . . so disjointed, so confusing. I can no longer be satisfied in the little victories, because of the big defeats. I'm afraid that we have become what Nietzsche warned us when he wrote, 'Whoever fights monsters should see to it that in the process he does not become a monster.' This may all be a huge mistake. I am so afraid for my family. "' She watched as he buried his head in his hands. "Have you heard from Karen and the boys?"

"No, not since November—the lines have been down, and I guess their batteries ran out. I never stopped to think there was little nuclear power in Iowa. I suppose someone also damaged the cell towers. My whole family could be wiped out, and I wouldn't know it."

"Oh, Jesse, I'm sorry. Here I am so upset about my sister and the children. But it just seems like this whole thing started because of some increased rates in asthma and a few abnormally hot and dry summers.

"We both know it was more than that, Hannah! Thousands have suffered already not only because of a lack of oxygen but also the human suffering brought on worldwide by increased catastrophic fires, collapse of fresh water resources, failing crops, all brought on by erratic and extreme weather patterns we've been experiencing now for more than a decade. People just don't get that climate change is a symptom of the way we've lived our lives the past couple thousands of years. It's a cumulative effect of stuff we put up in the ozone with synthetics and the agriculture practices that have resulted in massive losses of carbon in the soil that has also been released to the air. We have to halt using these things and figure out ways to live our lives as one of a species among many others in a symbiotic relationship. Right now, we are simply in triage—saving lives with the hope we will figure it out going forward. We *are* saving others."

"Yes, I keep telling myself all that and part of me believes it's all necessary. But there's a part that argues, that doesn't want to believe. I can't even reason. The evil is so real, so present so out there."

Jesse walked to the window. It was snowing lightly and too dark to see the street below. "I don't believe evil is a separate entity," he mumbled softy. "We are individually or collectively responsible. It's not out there somewhere but in our own actions and decisions."

He turned around and walked over to where she sat. "Hannah, I want to find a church. Somewhere they are singing Christmas music. I . . . we need to go and find a place where we can get a break from this and a little inspiration. I know you don't believe in God, but it will help us keep our spirits up, don't you think? Will you go with me? A little music won't hurt, will it? Somewhere they are singing. I heard chimes today. What do you say, Hannah?" He reached out with his hand to help her get up.

"That would be hypocrisy."

He withdrew his hand. "Hypocrisy? Why?"

"When I was a child, I saw an old black and white movie of the concentration camps. The commandant was gassing the Jews and then went home to sing Christmas carols around the piano with his own family. Remember Mugabe in Zimbabwe—how he married his mistress right after his wife died, and then created such an economic disaster that he starved many of his people while claiming to be a good Christian? Christmas is an economic farce. Whoever has enough or more can celebrate it while the rest of the world can starve." She got up from her stack on the floor and began picking up the files.

He caught her hand and stopped her work. "Hannah, no! You think I'm like them? I . . . we've made decisions that were according to analysis of scientific information and our own sense of right, not to kill people but to create a world where they can still live."

Pulling away from him she continued to stack files. "Do you really think this is making a difference? Or are we just a couple of self-righteous fools experimenting with the lives around us?"

"Hannah, come on, we've talked this out before! We have to know it is for the best."

After he left, pictures of the gas chamber and thin, naked bodies floating down a river melted together in her vision. She shook her head in disgust. She mulled over her resentment of Christmas. How many Americans—or Germans for that matter—knew or cared what was behind the whole idea? Was there anything beyond the merchandizing? She agreed with many cynics. The West once had a chance to change the world and opted for the Home Shopping Network.

Hannah arranged her stack of reports on the desk. Her individual dismissal was useless in nixing an idea held precious by millions. Maybe if she had just a little faith it would help ease her pain. But if there were a God, why would his so-called "sons and daughters" be running out of oxygen to breathe? Wouldn't a supreme being be able to solve the problem of a little imbalance in the atmosphere? If he couldn't solve something that simple, why sing in praise of him? She felt that old sense of self-justification and superiority as she headed out into the snow.

WAVE II

Future generations will likely condemn our lack of prudent concern for the integrity of the material world that supports all life.

—*Rachel Carson*

"History, if there is any for the human race, will record this as the largest mass migration of humans ever to take place. Billions of people, having ignored the U.N.'s warning to leave the cities and find lodging close to food sources, finally are pouring out of the cities carrying their treasured belongings or nothing at all. Desperate hordes of men, women, and children, old and young are shuffling their way toward an uncertain future." (*The Nation Today*)

"The children, as in all times of tragedy, are enduring the worst. Western children are suffering more than any others, neither they nor their parents have ever learned to provide even the most basic needs for themselves." (*The Nation Today*)

"In most of the so-called "developing world," which is not as dependent on technology or oil, the people have had less trouble complying with the U.N. mandates, and even prospered in the old, familiar ways of producing food and sharing it." (*The Nation Today*)

"In the U.S. the most promising examples of subsistence can be found among the Amish, the Quakers, and some secular intentional communities set up around the country. Having stockpiled food and water and because they still hold on to some of the agricultural traditions, those small communities are surviving and could become examples for the country. However, fear and prejudice on both sides is obviating any help to the masses." (*The Nation Today*)

~34~
ATLANTIC CITY, NEW JERSEY

"Miriamu, she not what she seems. You understand? She is bad. I tell you. I have paper proof if you come and bring money."

Jesse mulled his doubts during the drive to Atlantic City. He should have ignored the call, but on the other hand, the man's concern had sounded genuine. He could tell from the halting but clearly colonial British accent that the informant was from the Caribbean or southern or eastern Africa. He himself continued to be suspicious of Miriamu.

These days, everyone was living a hand-to-mouth existence, and the caller maybe just needed some money for food. But money was becoming less and less important. Barter had become the rule of the day.

The caller had been specific. "Walk along the Atlantic City boardwalk to Pier 84. Light a cigarette. Walk out the pier to the rocks."

So Jesse stood on the rocks at the end of the pier with a cigarette in his mouth and the wind strong enough to almost knock him down. He felt foolish. He chuckled, imagining he was Humphrey Bogart in an old black and white cinema, a film noir, expecting Sidney Greenstreet or Lon Cheney to pop out from behind one of the rocks and say, "Boo."

The sea was continuing to eat up the beach. Here and there, it was still yards wide but dirty and covered with debris. The boardwalk, an accordion worn thin in places, was a treacherous maze. What used to be bustling condos and townhouses and swank apartments were boarded up, like empty shells waiting for the next crab to crawl inside and occupy. Hundreds of ugly gutted tour busses sat empty. Some had families sleeping in them.

He had failed to tell the caller that he didn't smoke. and the lit cigarette kept burning his fingers. After fifteen minutes, he turned to leave—then he saw the man. His dreadlocks hung down to his shoulders, and he was large, very large. He wore a black suit and dark shirt. Moonlight reflected off strands of bright beads around his neck and wrist, making him visible. Jesse resisted the urge to run.

"Thomas Abuto."

Jesse shook his hand, noting there was no watch, which probably made it hard to be on time.

"Jesse Forester. You have information for me?"

"Yes. I work at the U.N. I am on Miriamu's staff."

"How long you been there?"

"For two years—all the time she work with you."

"What is it you want to tell me?"

"Miriamu, she tied to many bad people."

"Bad, what do you mean bad?" Jesse took a half-step closer, wishing he had insisted they meet where there was more light so he could judge the man's facial expressions.

"People who want to see all the world change—all the world suffer like the black world. Rich men who become poor, poor men become rich. But, of course, man who works with Miriamu become rich, very rich.

"Who are these people, Thomas?"

"Some are minister people from her own country; some are big U.S. government men; many are big businessmen—some black, some white."

"I know Miriamu deals with such people. That's her job. What makes you think they are bad? What kind of business men are you talking about?"

"I hear them talking. I think they fix papers."

"Fix papers . . . what papers?" Jesse said as he dropped the cigarette before it scorched his fingers.

"You pay me, I give you papers."

"All right."

"I give you very important paper—paper proof for $500. I show you."

All the way back to New York, Jesse felt sick. Had he sent Karen off and thrown the whole world into turmoil on bogus data? No. He had too many reports about the hottest years on record, increased asthma rates, and the need for oxygen at lower and lower altitudes. But what if he was wrong? What if the data in the papers he was holding were real and he had simply played into their hands? Whose hands?

He looked at the newly acquired report again. It appeared to be a mirror image of the charts and data he and Miriamu had studied twelve months before. But the figures themselves were all different. The balance of oxygen to carbon was normal, and the disastrous numbers that had sent them into emergency mode weren't there. Jesse's head began to spin and the headache that had been threatening all day pounded away.

~35~
SAN DIEGO

ALL HIS FORTY-SEVEN YEARS, THE TV HAD BEEN HIS CONSTANT COMPANION. Now, for some reason, the screen was black. He flicked the remote, nothing happened. He flicked again, dead as a doornail.

Tiny glanced at his wristwatch. It was time to feed the animals. They'd be hungry. Tiny pulled on his tall rubber boots and plopped his broad-brimmed straw hat on his head.

"I gotta feed the animals." The animals were his job; shoveling the food out of the trucks into the feed bins. He got money for it. He got to live in his very own trailer, right at the park. He felt the same pride swelling in his chest as years ago when his momma and the manager first discussed how good he would be at feeding the animals.

"Tiny is very dependable." Momma had said. "He never forgets to do his jobs."

"That's good," the manager had said. "We need someone who will be here rain or shine, day and night, to be sure these animals are fed."

"Oh, I'm sure Tiny is your man." That's just what she said—Tiny is your man—and Tiny's chest swelled with pride. For thirteen years, three hundred sixty-five days a year, Tiny had proven Momma right

Whenever she called and asked, "Did you feed the animals?" Tiny always told her, "Yes Momma, I did."

She'd say, "That's a good boy Tiny. I'm so proud of you son."

But Momma hadn't called for a while. When Tiny picked up the phone the little buzz had gone away. It had changed just like the black TV set, and he didn't understand why. Maybe it was better she didn't call because yesterday and the day before and the day before he hadn't fed the animals. The big trucks didn't come with the food. Today would be different. The food would be there and he would feed the animals and Mr. Nolan would say what a good job he was doing and Momma would call and tell him he was just the man for the job.

He carefully locked the door to his trailer and stuck the key in his pocket. On the way to the animals Tiny puckered up his lips like his teacher had taught him and whistled. Like always, the mynah birds whistled back. He quacked and flapped his arms at the ducks crossing his path and laughed as they scampered out of his way and into the pond. He noticed there were no people. There should be hundreds of people lined up in front of the little train and walking down the paths. Where had they all gone? At least it was cleaner. Tiny had noticed right away the usual paper cups and plates and napkins and straws cluttering the paths were gone, but there were no french fries either. He missed picking up a bag and chewing the crispy little sticks. He always wondered why so much of something that tasted so good got thrown away.

When he got to the first field, he could see that the trucks weren't there yet. The animals were milling around the feed bin, making noises. They stomped their hoofs and pushed each other, going around and around in circles. Tiny had never seen them act that way, it frightened him. Then his favorite little dik-dik_came rushing to him and licked his hand. Tiny got down on his knees, put his arms around her and held her tight.

"It's okay, little girl. Tiny's going to feed you.

He watched as a herd of gazelles shoved away the antelopes and giraffes, only to find no food. He stared in amazement at the beautiful eyes of the giraffe as she stuck her long, black tongue out flicking the back of her baby.

"I'm going to feed you, Mrs. Giraffe. Don't you worry, Tiny's gonna feed you and your baby." He searched to the right and to the left. But he still didn't see any trucks. They would come. They always came. He sat down on an outcropping of rocks to wait.

~36~
LAS VEGAS, NEVADA

SUSAN LLOYD SAW THE STARK OUTLINE OF THE BLACK PYRAMID against the Las Vegas skyline. In the other direction, New York-New York rose up with its roller coaster curving up and over to be swallowed up by the hotel. The sunset drifted down the side of the buildings and disappeared into the desert. The skyline to the west became turquoise while the east darkened to midnight. Minutes later the whole city was a murky black. It had been that way for about two months.

Hustlers still roamed. A bar or two still had a cache of booze. Hawkers sold scraps of food on corners. But the night chased everyone away. The Palms was empty and dark, and the Rio a deserted cube. The sand in the beach had scattered into the stale pool and not a drop fell from the waterfall.

Six months ago, the glow of the city could be seen from St. George in one direction and Barstow in the other. But the lights had left and so had the audiences. Fear to travel in the complete darkness prevailed. No planes came into the city and no planes left.

Susan dumped her backpack out on the bed. Her wallet held two twenties and a five, a useless Citibank card and an equally useless Mississippi driver's license. She shook out her black sequined costume from the Riviera Review, stockings, extra jeans, two T-shirts, and a Levi jacket. In the pocket of the jacket she found a stale granola bar.

Susan lived for the excitement of performing. She had stayed when the rest of the city ran away. When they all came back—the huge trucks with food, the entertainers, and the gamblers—she'd dance again. That was last month; that was last week. But they didn't come back, and the city had become this black hole. Her food had run out; it was time to leave.

She turned on the tap in the tiny bathroom hoping to find a new trickle of water. No luck. When she returned to the window her eyes caught a flicker of light between her and the black speck of the pyramid. Susan stared long and hard. The light was faint and flickering but it gave off a soft glow, a spark of hope, a welcoming sign.

Stuffing the contents back in her backpack, she hesitated at the sequined costume. It was so skimpy that it wouldn't take much room, and who knew? She might be able to dance for her supper. She added Nikes and some shorts and socks but ignored the full shelf of cosmetics, dropping her brushes and some lotion down inside the shoes. Maybe there was an open restaurant and food where the light was.

She took one last look at the place that had been her first real home: the Renoir poster with orange-decked ballet dancers she bought with her first paycheck, the cappuccino machine, and the closet full of clothes so carefully selected. The first and only place she had felt like somebody, the place to which she fled from the stifling heat and darkness of her great-aunt's musty clapboard house. She had promised herself then that whatever happened, she would never go back there.

Blinded by tears, she locked the door and stumbled down the stairs. On the street it became harder to calculate exactly where that light had been. She wandered in the general direction of the pyramid, zigzagging back and forth in the darkness. Down Reno Avenue toward the strip. At the corner of Giles, three scavengers come around a corner, and Susan stepped back into a doorway as they swept by, making herself smaller in the shadows. They were skinheads, with black leather jackets and big boots.

The source of the glow turned out to be a hole-in-the-wall cafe where someone had put candles on the tables, and several young people were seated inside drinking cold coffee. She stood outside, amazed that a small part of civilization still existed.

"What'll you have?" The man was middle-aged, balding, with a dirty apron and a big smile.

"What are my options?"

"Coffee, tea, and lots of stale bagels. That's all's left today. Oh, and some jam—that's not stale."

Susan tried not to gobble down the first bagel, but her hunger made it hard to eat with manners. She finished her third bagel piled high with peach jam and savored the coffee.

"Hey, pretty woman, what are you doing still in Vegas?"

He had entered and come up behind her while she was absorbed in her food. Susan jumped and turned as she raised her fists to ward off an attack by striking first. But the man carefully sidestepped her thrust and threw both hands up in surrender.

"Hey, no offense meant."

They stood staring at each other for a long moment.

"I'm P.J. your ol' D.J.—Paul, Paul Jordan—loud-mouth radio talk show host—formerly of KLVA radio when there was electricity and there were listeners. Now I just coordinate evacuations. His smile disarmed her, and she relaxed a little. Reaching for her hand, he took it in both of his.

"Susan Lloyd, former dancer when there was a Riviera, when there was a Strip, when there was a Las Vegas. Now . . . Now I don't know."

"Can I join you, Susan Lloyd"

Susan looked around. The apron-clad owner was behind the counter making coffee and the other customers were engaged in their own conversations.

"Okay, Paul Jordan, if you promise not to be too loud or tell too many bad jokes."

"Only on the radio. In person, I'm a lamb." Paul signaled the owner, ordering a coffee. He stared at her until she became embarrassed and pretended to be engrossed in her almost-empty cup.

"Give the dancer here some more cold coffee and one of those stale bagels, Frank. I think she's going to faint from hunger."

"No, no thanks, I've had enough actually. I've had three already and lots of jam—a feast. You mentioned evacuation. Do you, I mean are you sure this thing is forever. Are the lights not going to come back on? Is Las Vegas . . . ."

"It's not just Las Vegas, Susan. It's the whole world. The lights went out all over the world. Reverse of that old song. 'When the lights go on all over the world.' " He sang in a deep baritone.

"Then it's true, you think. We have to get out of here, don't we? Go to where there's food and water."

"If we have someplace to go. No place is really safe, and no place holds a guarantee of food. The trucks aren't running, and the food isn't coming in. Even the safe-houses that the government created are running out of supplies."

"So why are you evacuating people?"

"Oh, we find little caches of gasoline and food here and there, and we put the fuel together with the people and send them on their way, hopefully to family or friends. Actually, mostly I help those who can't or don't want to leave."

"How . . . what does it cost? A lot?"

"In Las Vegas, honey, are you kidding?"

He reached in his pocket and pulled out a huge roll of hundred- and thousand-dollar bills. "If money ever comes back in style, I'll be rich. Till then, I'm just Father Paul, the missionary, helping mankind. How about you, Susan Lloyd, the dancer, can I help you?"

"I don't think so. I have no place to go."

"Everyone has someplace to go. Where's home?"

"Mississippi, but there's no one there anymore."

"Do you want a job?"

"A job here? Dancing?"

"Dancing?" He smiled a softness that radiated into his eyes. "I don't need a dancer, Susan Lloyd. I wouldn't know what to do with a dancer."

"That's all I know how to do—I'm a dancer, since I was five. Ballet, jazz, modern . . . I'm good at it. I was the lead dancer at the Rio . . . ."

"Can you add, subtract, organize? Are you strong? Would you mind feeding and caring for elderly people? Could you be a kind of nurse?"

Susan frowned, not knowing how to answer him. Finally she said, "I guess so."

"What I need is a Girl Friday, someone to help me. Come on, I'll show you what I need."

He stood and reached for her hand, and the smile disappeared. "There's important work to be done and I could use some help, please."

She looked at his hand holding hers and into his very blue eyes.

She pulled her hand away and stiffened her back. "But you don't know me. And I certainly don't know you. I never even heard you on the radio. I guess that's because I slept all morning."

He sat down again. "Well, my name is Paul. I hail from Minnesota originally. I'm forty-two years old. I read a lot of science fiction. I love pizza and pasta and Mexican food. Well, I used to. I made $150,000 a year as KLVA's loud-mouth know-it-all until all hell broke loose and I didn't know anything. My hero is Bucky Fuller, and I like people. I admit I especially like pretty girls. Now, do you know me enough to consider the job?" He shrugged his shoulders.

She didn't answer.

"Frank, come and formally introduce me to this girl; she wants to know who I am."

The cafe owner came around the end of the counter. "This is Paul Jordan—masher—seducer—raconteur—general know-it-all. Don't trust him."

Paul grabbed Frank's bar rag and pulled him down so they were eye to eye. "Don't be smart, friend. Where the hell do you think you're going to get food next week to run this miserable excuse for a restaurant?"

"Oh, I get it. You want to impress the pretty lady, so I got to say flowery things about you. Let me see, flowery stuff about Paul Jordan. I'll have to think a while on that one."

"Frank, please."

Once again, Susan detected a playful, gentleness in Paul that his bravado tried to hide.

"Well, that's a new leaf—never had him beg before."

Frank looked at Susan and then at Paul, a huge grin on his face.

"Well, he used to say obnoxious things on the radio. Now he just says obnoxious things in my cafe. And he uses words no one understands, like synergy, holism, and dymaxion."

Paul gave him another pleading look.

"When he's not spouting off, he bargains for food. He's where I got the coffee and the jam. He's the only thing between starvation and us. That makes him a prince, an angel. He's a good guy, little lady. Not that I would necessarily trust him with my daughter. But then, she's only four."

"Thanks a lot, Frank. Tell her I'm not dangerous."

"No, he's not dangerous, just a little crazy." Frank took her empty cup and walked back to the counter.

Susan asked, "What's holism?"

"It's the idea that natural things have no parts; they only function in wholes and patterns of wholes. And the whole is not the same as the sum of its parts."

"What?"

"Susan, it's like water. Hydrogen and oxygen make water. But if you took each of them and studied them individually, their properties would never tell you they'd make water."

She was silent. He waited.

"Please help. But only if you don't take life or death too seriously, because a little levity is what's needed. I promise to make you laugh no matter what the future holds. We have to laugh at what's happening or we'll spend all our time crying, and who wants to spend the rest of a whole lifetime crying?"

~37~
WASHINGTON, D.C.

JESSE SCURRIED UP TO THE HILL AND FOUND A SEAT IN THE SENATE gallery. He stood up so he could see the reaction to Elena's speech on the faces of the members of the joint session of Congress. An aide confronted him with, "Don't stand up." When he leaned over the railing, the same obnoxious aide told him, "Don't lean on the railing." He felt like slugging the guy. He noticed that Senator Cliff Martin was absent. Why wasn't the other senior member of the Climate Change Committee there to support Elena? Of course, the remaining members of Congress were very few anyway. Most had gone home to care for their families. Only a small percentage had been given Essentials status and stayed to run the nation.

What struck Jesse most were the long, sad faces of the members who were still in D.C. Such a contrast to the times he had visited as a Boy Scout or a young college student. The strident, self-assurance of an organization in control of its fate had been replaced with doubt and confusion. Each countenance seemed in shadow. The whole body reflected en masse the dim lights in the chamber.

Elena did a good job. She started with the progress that had been made. Hundreds of thousands of people had found access to food and shelter and fossil fuel use was cut in half during the latter part of Wave I. Rural communities were taking in individuals and whole families that had left the cities, and they were mobilizing to preserve all the food produced that summer and then to expand food production in the coming year.

In some smaller cities, neighborhoods had begun turning every ounce of vacant land into gardens And in northern climates, people were gathering blankets, carpets and rugs and shoring up homes in preparation for the cold. Or they were heading south. Demand for gardening tools went through the roof, and everywhere, bikes were being built, bartered, and cherished.

But as Wave II kicked in and people realized that all use of fossil fuels really was going to end, the weaknesses of a whole society built on this resource blew some regions and industries sky high.

Large landowners and the agri-businesses that cultivated those lands were completely lost. They were told to keep their fields in production—but do it all by hand and draft animals. And to put anyone who showed up to help to work. Many threatened to just walk away. Elena urged the senators from the South, the Midwest, California, and much of the Northwest to force large landholders to get with the program.

The National Guard had to put down riots in New York and Atlanta. And Los Angeles, with its 13 million people and 10 million cars and little public transport, remained a jungle.

Jesse was glad Elena could use some of the basic facts he had given her. He braced himself as she described how they had transferred violent prisoners to areas where nuclear and solar were available and simply released all lower-level offenders. The handful of hospitals that operated on nuclear power were crammed and not accepting new patients. Nursing homes had notified next of kin to come collect any elderly residents who were not on life-support. But many were simply starving to death because no next of kin showed up. And once the equipment was shut off, so did everyone else.

Elena summed up her report by reminding the members of Congress that it was important to shift to entirely renewable sources of energy and actions that would increase food production and create warm shelter for human habitation. She urged them to stay away from looking for someone to blame or creating scapegoats.

Jesse left the chamber with a sinking feeling and walked around looking at the statues in the halls of the Capitol. He ended up staring at a marble figure of Daniel Webster. The inscription read: "When tillage begins, other arts will follow. The farmers therefore are the founders of human civilization." He couldn't help but voice aloud, "Well, I sure hope you're right old boy." The guard across the hall snickered, and Jesse walked away.

Elena had asked him to meet her at The Monocle. The owners had managed to maintain a dark, conservative elegance. The single-page menu boasted canned and dried fruits, vegetables and meats, things left over from last summer's harvests. In another year, none of this would be available.

The place was freezing. Diners sat around in heavy coats, mittens, and hats. There was a small fireplace in the corner of the room but no fire.

Elena was flushed and excited when she came in. She gave Jesse a more detailed view on what various senators were experiencing or how they'd reacted. Senator Morgan from Louisiana had lost a grandchild in the riot there and threatened to urge his constituents to boycott the entire operation. He might find an ally in the senator from South Carolina, where some communities were on the brink of civil war as whites leaving the cities had tried to overrun lands long held by black farmers.

"Jesse, the substitute energy measures seem to be moving quickly into place. Did you know that we could have been transporting a thousand times more products by train without all the pollution and at a small percentage of the cost? General Electric train engines developed way back in the late '90s were easily converted to nuclear fuel and are amazing at conserving energy.

"It's incredible how many alternative energy sources were right at our finger tips. Its moving so fast now that there's a crisis. We were able to locate thousands of wind turbines and solar panels." Her excitement caused her to run on and on, not allowing Jesse to get a word in edgewise.

"I never realized that the wind farm on the Oregon-Washington border generated more power than any other place in the world, even as early as 2002. They are providing thousands of homes with electricity now. And New Mexico they . . . ."

Jesse interrupted her, "Where did the new solar and wind equipment come from?"

"*Jesucristo!* I don't know where they were built. Let me think. Some from the west, Texas maybe; a lot came in from Australia. Senator Martin has all of that information. Why?"

"When was the equipment built?"

"I have no idea. Martin would have that information. All I have is the numbers bought."

"Where is he?"

"I don't know. I expected him to be back here in time for my floor statements. He didn't show, and I'm angry with him. After you came to us last year, well, Cliff has always been surer of all this. It's because he had a more scientific mind, understands the ramifications of your figures better, and was more in tune with the atmospheric problems. Why do you need to know when the machines were built? Why is that important?"

"Do a little nosing around for me, will you? I'd like to have the names of the firms that built the equipment and who is actually receiving payments and when it began."

"Jesse? Is there something I should know about? What?"

Jesse rubbed his eyes and sat with his face in his hands.

"Jesse?"

"Nothing. I'm just curious, that's all.

~38~
SYDNEY, AUSTRALIA

Hendrik,

My Company is not shipping any more. However, if you thought life would be better this way, think again. In fact, things are a mess. Manley Fairy Wharf is a disaster area. The unemployment is creating mass hysteria. You were right, the real farmers are mopping up. But there is nothing to buy with the money they are making. Some are hoarding the funds hoping that life will go back the way it was. At least they are supplying many of the basics beef, sugar, wheat, bananas and oranges from Queensland.

Everything is coming in by horse-drawn cart. We are getting some fish from local fishermen and mutton from outlying stations. But we are choking in the city; the dust and cockroaches are going to win. Yesterday I couldn't see the wharf 50 yards from my window. Lisa and I separated 9 months ago. She is at the station with her Dad. I am heading out there as soon as I can get together some supplies. Thought I should let you know.

Mark

EVEN AS HE POSTED THE BRIEF LETTER, MARK KNEW INTERCONTINENTAL mail was limited to the Essentials, meeting their needs, and ensuring implementation of Wave II. Besides, Hendrik would have to check in Victoria Falls or even Bulawayo for his mail, and it might be months before he received it, if at all. It was futile, but the finality of the whole thing irked him, and he typed it out punching all the right buttons. He had to let Hendrik know. His past life had closed, and Hendrik had always been the unwanted mentor in that life.

Just like the ships, the paperwork had stopped coming in. There was nothing for him to do.

A few wharfies stood around smoking, leaning on the rails, darting furtive glances out to sea. There were no jokes or arguments, just silence and fearful expressions.

"Mr. Mark, more ships comin' in soon?"

Bennie had been BDM's head wharfie ever since Mark was hired. Mark liked the bright-eyed young man. He and Lisa had even spent some time with Bennie's family. Bennie had filled him in on the history of the wharf, especially the battle in '98 when Mac Corrigan had locked out the wharfies because they weren't unloading fast enough. Bennie shared with them his family's panic and struggle during those months. Mark saw the same panic in his eyes now.

"I doubt it Bennie." Mark stood transfixed at Captain Cook's cottage. The brilliant blue flowers that usually adorned the jacaranda trees had faded a little bit more each year—the trees seemed to be gasping for oxygen, water, whatever. Like the men, they looked frightened, desperate.

He found Jerry in their favorite corner of the Waterfront Restaurant, which advertised on its marquee "LAST SHOTS OF WHISKEY TODAY. CLOSED TOMORROW". He downed two straight whiskeys and then announced, "I'm going to White Cliffs."

"When? How?"

"Right away. Walk, I guess. The word on the wire is that all shipping is halted until further notice unless it's nuclear powered, and we ain't got none of them in our fleet."

"Damn. And I guess they aren't going to pay us either. We're out of work in the middle of all this mess."

"Not just out of a job. There was a U.N. declaration attached to it. Fossil fuels can no longer be relied on for ship transport. There will be some nuke ships coming in but . . . ."

"People will starve."

"Lots, but others will figure it out"

"Guess your father was right."

~39~
NEW YORK CITY

MIRIAMU'S RECEPTIONIST WAS WRAPPED UP IN A CHEAP IMITATION fur coat and several lap robes. She looked at Jesse as though he were something foul. He pushed by, chalking her rudeness up to the extreme cold.

"Miriamu, I have been getting bad vibes concerning our data. I want to reconfirm that we have not been duped."

She stared at him with incredulity. "What are you talking about?"

"I'm talking about fake statistics from your office, about data that is falsified for the purpose of alarming us and setting off a worldwide panic!"

"What fake statistics?"

"Someone has indicated all the data may be bogus! I need you to assure me that it isn't. If you're playing with statistics for some personal reason, we'll all be crucified."

"False data? Me, playing with the data? Isn't it your people who've been monitoring the stations for years? Don't *you* get daily reports? Are you accusing me of some kind of intrigue? It was your call to me that started this whole thing. My understanding is that we're using data that's consistent but from a variety of sources. Sit down, Jesse."

She had never called him by his first name before; what might that indicate? Her face was a mixture of fear and confusion. He hoped it was for the right reason. He controlled his anger, sitting on one end of the plush sofa. Her next words were in a low, intimate tone. "You have no idea how difficult it is to be a woman of color and hold a position such as mine among the peoples of Africa. The men are so jealous. They will do anything to make me look foolish or dishonest or to have me fail. I don't know who might be spreading lies about me, but you must trust me."

"I want to see *your* copies of the data—the stuff we first studied a year ago on oxygen levels in the Andes and Himalayas, and compare it again with the other corroborating reports."

Miriamu left the room, returning after several minutes with the documents.

Later, in his own office he laid out both sets of papers on his table and studied them closely. Which figures were real? What was the truth?

While he was examining them, the phone rang. It was Hannah. "Jesse, there is a woman named Mona Freeman here in my office. You remember, her father is the Irish gentleman whose ideas we've gathered to use for the Wave III mandates?"

"Paddy Freeman, yes. I had several talks with him during Wave I. Wise old farmer from Ireland."

"Well, he is no longer a wise old farmer. He's a dead old farmer. And his daughter says we are to blame for his death."

"What?"

"She is in here saying he was murdered and insinuating we know why or had something to do with it."

When he got to Hannah's office, Jesse tried to control his confusion while also presenting a cool demeanor in front of Mona Freeman.

"Miss Freeman, what in the world makes you think that we had anything to do with your father's death, and if you don't mind me asking, how in the devil did you get here?"

"My ex-husband is with the British Air Force. I suppose you could say I stole away on a British Air Force flight to New York. This is why I came."

Mona reached into her purse and handed him a piece of paper. It was stained and smelled of something that tweaked his memory, but he couldn't quite grasp what. He recognized the message as the email he had sent Paddy Freeman a month ago.

Paddy, don't worry about Wave I. It's really just the beginning of a reorganization of the world, as we know it. It is so necessary. As you know, the carbon/oxygen ratios won't rebalance simply because we halt the burning of carbon fuels immediately and over the long term. We have to also restore as much plant life and soil carbon as we can, as quickly as possible. Your ideas will be used. For that we are grateful! Sorry about the violence in Dublin. People have just got to become resourceful without panic. Don't you panic too. Paddy, just want you to know that I really appreciate your ideas about the important project we are working on. Thanks again, Jesse.

Jesse moved closer to the plump young woman and accentuated his question with futile hand gestures. "Ms. Freeman, how does this email incriminate me or the U.N.?"

Without backing down a step, Ms. Freeman spit out furiously. "My father was murdered, Mr. Forester! He was a farmer. He had no enemies that would want to kill him. There had been nothing unusual in the last few days of his life yet he was killed within a few hours of receiving that email."

"But what makes you think we . . . ?"

"You tell me what my father had to do with this office!"

"Your father was just helping us form policy for restructuring food supplies and land usage—just the ideas contained in his writings; nothing more than that."

"I don't believe you! What message from him provoked that email?"

"Why are you determined to connect my email with your father's death?"

"Your email was stuck to a nail in the barn. I found his computer still on. But someone had wiped out any sign of you on the computer. The computer was wiped clean. Whoever did it was very careful, no fingerprints, no tire tracks, no sign that anyone had been there. My father was killed with a rare poison, through a dart, almost impossible to detect for anyone but the forensic specialist I hired. The email seems the one clue I have. I want you and Ms. Koenig to explain to me what part my father was playing in this scheme of yours and why someone felt it necessary to murder a helpless old man

Jesse and Hannah exchanged furtive glances.

"Please, sit down, Ms. Freeman."

Hannah dug through their files, extracting the last two emails from Paddy Freeman. One described what Paddy called a total lack of planning for future food production in Ireland. The second begged for some explanation as to why the civil authorities in Ireland were not using measures to stem the violence. Jesse did remember firing off the quick note Mona had found. But as he re-read Paddy's last email, one sentence he'd completely missed, jumped out—"those Washington guys I met with told me they'd be prepared for this."

"Miss Freeman, do you know who else in the U.S. your father would have been in touch with?

"No, Mr. Forester, you were his only contact as far as I know."

Jesse had no idea what to say to this angry young woman. There were just too many questions he couldn't answer and he hoped she could not see the fear and turmoil rising up from the pit of his stomach.

~40~
WASHINGTON, D.C.

SAMUEL PUT ON HIS HIKING BOOTS AND HIS REDSKINS WIND BREAKER. He took his Big Chief tablet out of his book bag.

> *Dear morris, I heard you say in your sermon it is the end of the world. I have to go to see the president. He will help us. The man in the wheel chair helped the people who were hungry and he was a president. my teacher said that is what presidents are supposed to do. maybe he can keep the world from an end. your son Samuel*

He checked his pocket to be sure he had some money—two quarters and a dime. His father was locked in his tiny study. Samuel went through the kitchen, just in case he'd missed something to eat. There wasn't anything in the icebox or on the shelves. An empty cereal box and empty cans cluttered the sink. He found a small bag of stale peanuts in one of the drawers.

It was dark when he crossed the Roosevelt Bridge. None of the buildings were lit up, not even that big one named after President Kennedy. His class had taken a field trip there once. There were lots of people in fancy costumes. The teacher said they were from other countries and had come to hear the wonderful concert in the hall with the huge glass lights that dripped from the ceiling. He and Alan got in trouble that day for leaning too far over the balcony to watch the planes fly by. He stopped halfway across the bridge to zip up his jacket.

"Hey, kid, where ya goin?"

There were three of them, and one was bigger than the others and had a knife. They were all very thin and mean looking.

"To see the president."

"What a joke —hear that? He's going to see the president. You got an appointment?"

"Well, no."

"Can't see the president without an appointment. If you ain't got no appointment, forget it. Got any food kid?"

"No."

"Stupid dumbass thinks he's gonna see the president. See if he's got any food on him."

Samuel backed away only to find himself up against the guardrail on the bridge. The smallest kid reached into Samuel's pocket and brought out the peanuts.

"I was saving them for an emergency."

"This is an emergency, ain't it?"

He fumbled through the rest of Samuel's pockets and found the coins. They shoved him against the guardrail. Samuel struggled frantically. "Let me be. I didn't do anything to you; let me be. I have to see the president."

Two of them lifted him so high that all he could see was the dark, swirling water below. Samuel grabbed the rail and held on, kicking furiously at them. After what seemed like forever, they set him down and pushed him to the concrete and took turns kicking him.

"Gee, thanks a lot kid. Tell the president hello for us . . . going to see the president—what a dumbass."

As he picked himself up and dusted off his pants, Samuel's stomach growled. He was going to miss those peanuts. He assured himself that when he got to the president's house, there would be more than peanuts.

As he made his way toward the White House, he got more tired and more scared. Everywhere he looked there was nothing – no lights, no people, no cars. His feet shuffled through trash and broken glass. At Constitution and Seventeenth Street, he took a wrong turn. Thirty minutes later, he found himself back at the same corner. He wished he had put on a sweater under his jacket.

He pulled the collar of his jacket up around his neck and walked a little faster. The moon came out and then disappeared again behind the clouds. When it was shining, he saw the trees and leaves making shadows on the sidewalk. When it hid, he just heard the wind blowing the leaves around. He remembered that Morris had said the end of the world was darkness and a void, and the Bible said there was a void before God created stuff. He wasn't exactly sure what a void was, but this sure felt like it. And all the stuff would be created again.

He was concentrating so hard on getting there that he almost walked right past the president's house. He had to stop and think a minute when he saw the big house all dark. It looked blue instead of white because of the moon.

"Halt—who goes there?"

"I'm Samuel." He moved closer to the voice.

"Halt! Stay where you are."

He stood still. "I'm Samuel Perkins, and I came to see the president."

"State your business."

"I . . . I want to see the president."

"The president isn't here. Even if he were here, you could not see him."

"But . . . ."

"Go back from wherever you came from."

"Presidents are supposed to help feed the people. That's what presidents do. I don't think he knows what's happening or he would help us. We don't have any more at our house, and we don't know where to shop now, and the lights have all gone out, and I'm hungry. I had some peanuts, but some kids took them and then beat me up. I need to tell the president that he has to help us; he can do something like President Roosevelt did."

Jupiter Owens lowered his rifle and peered through the dark. He put his hand on the shoulder of the small boy in front of him. Jupiter had no trouble running off the hoodlums that harassed him daily. He was also quite happy to divert the various foreign dignitaries who hadn't gone home during Wave I, were somehow surviving in D.C., and still thought the U.S. president could do something. But this?

"What did you say your name was, kid?"

"Samuel Perkins, sir."

"Well now Samuel, you're cold aren't you, and your nose sure needs to be wiped."

"Yes, sir."

"Why don't you come in my little booth here and we'll both warm up a bit. Then I can explain a little about the president . . . . You see, he isn't here, Sam. If he were here, I would tell you, honest. He's flown off somewhere." Jupiter searched through his knapsack and came up with a small napkin. "Here, son, wipe your nose."

Samuel wiped his nose and blew loudly into the napkin. "But he's supposed to help the people. My teacher took us to see President Roosevelt's statue, and he helped feed the people didn't he? There's no heat in our apartment. I bet he doesn't know that. He'd want to know, wouldn't he?"

"I think he knows, but he isn't here. You see there are a lot of people unhappy with the decisions he's made, and they are very angry with him. He just doesn't feel safe here with us, so he left. Here, Sam, sit on my stool and rest a bit."

"The president went away; he's hiding?"

"Yes, I guess you could say that."

Samuel handed the napkin back to Jupiter and wiped a few tears on his sleeve.

"I think the safest thing for you to do is to go back to your family. Didn't your family get the mandates for Wave I and Wave II? Why are you still in the city?"

"Morris won't leave. He says the Lord wants us to starve. He says we are all hell-deserving sinners, and we deserve to burn in hell. He says it's God's will, and there is nothing we can do about it. .

"Who is Morris?"

"He's my father."

"Damn, damn." Jupiter screwed up his face. He hadn't encountered the narrow realms of religious dogma in a long time, and this was almost more than he could fathom.

"Samuel, believe me, God doesn't want us to give up trying to live. Don't you think God would want you to try to find enough to eat? There is food out there; you just have to find it."

"Morris says we don't deserve to be saved."

Jupiter's stomach growled. His supper for the evening was under the counter in a plastic container.

"Well, your dad's right about one thing. There are a lot of bad people around. But I don't think you're one of them. Jupiter pulled out his cheese sandwich wrapped in old newspaper. "Here, this is for you because you're hungry. I don't want you to starve, and believe me, neither does God, no matter what Morris says. Now, I gotta stand watch here, and I ain't supposed to let nobody into this booth; so you're gonna have to head on back to your house."

Samuel stuffed the sandwich into his pocket where the peanuts had been. Jupiter watched as the little boy lowered his head against the wind and headed back down Pennsylvania Avenue.

~41~
THURLOO DOWNS, AUSTRALIA

MARK HAD WALKED SEVERAL HUNDRED MILES THROUGH THE BRUSH. He had left the Sydney to Perth nuke train because there were just too many Aussies fleeing in both directions. Now he felt he was being followed—not exactly followed but surrounded. He heard footsteps, but they'd stop when he stopped. Sometimes they seemed to be behind him, sometimes ahead. The thick brush made it impossible to see who might be there. For the third time, he checked the pistol fastened to his belt. Soon he would be out of the brush and onto open grasslands. Then whoever it was would have to quit following him or be exposed.

He still had several packages of dried beans, some rice, and two pints of water. He worried mostly about the water. His government map told him there were springs this side of Coonamble, but he wasn't exactly sure where he was. His GPS—thank God for satellites that still worked—told him his location, but the map and the satellite reading were two separate entities. The sun sank into the western sky, and a few wisps of cumulus clouds looked promising. It had been over forty degrees Celsius for two days. He knew if the heat continued and he didn't find water soon, he was in trouble.

He stopped suddenly, listening. The footsteps had ceased. The only sounds came from the dry breeze rustling the gray gum and eucalyptus. Mark was suddenly aware of smoke. A fire coming in his direction could be fatal. He saw no flames. It seemed to be a contained blaze, right ahead of him. He stumbled into a small clearing. There was the fire and a small rabbit roasting over it. There was a small pot of water. Hunched over the fire, with his bony knees jutting skyward, an elderly aborigine slowly turned the rabbit. He looked up and smiled a broad grin.

"Halloo."

"Well, hello. I guess you're the one who's been following me."

"You must have been following me. I got here first."

"So you did."

"But the brush, the rabbit, and the fire do not belong to either of us. Is this not so?"

Mark unloaded his backpack and poured some of the hot water into a pan with some rice.

Both men remained silent as the meal cooked, and they ate. The man cleaned out the pan with a cloth and some sand and settled down near the fire.

"I'm Mark."

"Nappy, short for Napoleon." Nappy sat on his haunches, his leg muscles strong in the fire's glow. His clothing consisted of a worn Olympics 2000 T-shirt and a leather breechcloth. He wore no shoes, but the soles of his feet were padded with calluses. The parts of his body that could be seen were weathered and brown.

"I am going back to my people."

Mark nodded, then after a moment, he confided. "My wife is in Tibooburra—One Tree Hill Station. That's where I'm headed." He lay down and let the Southern Hemisphere's millions of stars wash over him.

"Ah, that is a long way for a white fella."

Mark nodded as he thought about the reason for his long trek. He'd spent the last ten days thinking about Lisa. He'd had no word from her for six months. As things got more and more desperate in Sydney, he'd tried to contact her by short wave, but received no response. Her last note had been short and impersonal. There had been rain, the cattle and sheep were happy. Her vegetable garden and flowers were lush. She was sorry to hear about the fuel problems and the shortages of food. The shortages were perhaps a good thing in the long run.

That last remark angered him. She was such a child, so naive. She would have hated the cockroaches and the dust. They had appeared together as people began fleeing the city and all sewer, trash, and other services came to a halt. He thought of the suffering and confusion as the grocery shelves emptied and people began to realize that fewer and fewer cargo ships were coming. Rural farm people had set up small stands, and some families had remained fishing off the coast. Bartering had become the exchange, no one was sure that money had any value at all. Lisa had no idea how bad it was in the cities. How could the destruction of a whole society be a good thing? Mark realized Nappy was looking at him. But he continued to just stare up at the sky.

"Why is your wife at One Tree and you're here, Mark?"

"We're separated right now."

"You a city man and she's a station woman?"

"Uh huh."

"What will you do when you get to One Tree Hill Station?

"I don't know."

"What did you do in the city?"

"I worked for a big international food shipping company."

"Ah, and that life you depended on is over now."

"Well, Sydney rather fell apart, didn't it?"

"It was foreseen."

"Foreseen? Damn. You sound just like my father." The fire was dying down, and more stars of the Southern Hemisphere offered the only light.

"You white fellas come and go in endless pursuit of what? But the stars and the real man remain the same."

Mark grunted and unrolled his sleeping bag. He couldn't help but remember what Hendrik had always said about the myth of the noble savage. There were no noble savages; man had always polluted and plundered to his own good and caused the demise of the land or some other species. Exhausted, he crawled into his bag and faintly heard Nappy.

"I go beyond the black stump. My wife and children are there. We travel together; it is better to travel together in the face of what seems unknown."

~42~
WASHINGTON, D.C.

THE NEW CENTER FOR INTERNATIONAL SECURITY AND COOPERATION (CISC), had been created to consolidate various U.S. agencies that would be responsible for implementing and monitoring the Wave mandates. Jesse found it housed in a vast convention center a stone's throw from the Hill. A small crew stared at laptops in a central room connected through satellites around the world and using approved backup coal-powered generators as the nuclear power cut in and out.

Everyone wore heavy sweaters and even down jackets. In the summer it would be sweltering because there were no windows. How dependent everyone had become on the flimsy standard of oil. When Jesse finally got the attention of the assistant director, a new appointee named Collins, he felt suddenly at a loss for the words or nerve to tell the man his dilemma. Would he be crying wolf to his own destruction?

Collins gave him a cup of hot coffee and sat on the edge of his desk. He showed Collins the emails and told him about Paddy's murder.

"So you think someone else is in on this, someone who is not associated with the U.N.?"

"I now think that Paddy Freeman had contact with someone who was anticipating the crisis we are facing, and it appears stocks of alternate fuel on the markets in the Orient and in Europe climbed six months before governments began buying them up."

"This is not much to go on. You gotta know we are inundated with gangs, mobsters, and criminals who have quickly organized, not only to survive as we move into Wave II but also to profit off the mistakes and panic of others. We don't have time to research a bizarre death in Ireland. Washington is a mess. If this contact of Mr. Freeman's was someone in the government, he may no longer exist or his organization may be defunct. I am inclined to say you should stop worrying about it." Collins could see from Jesse's face that he was not about to let it drop.

"Okay, I'll snoop around a bit, and if I find anything, I'll get in touch with you. We will probably also have to turn my information over to the National Security Council. Let me know if anything else comes across your desk. I'll also advise the Irish authorities that Mr. Freeman's death may have consequences outside their country, but I doubt it will make any difference. All military and police forces are in the same emergency mode just dealing with day-to-day crises. Anything else?"

Jesse hesitated, but decided he had to be completely honest with Collins. "Well, there was one more thing. I met with an underling from the U.N. who gave me some forged papers, faked to look like the real ones."

"Faked in what way?"

"Different figures on the atmosphere than we had last year—forged to look as if they are official U.N. papers with data that wouldn't send up any red flags about the carbon-oxygen ratios."

"Do you have those papers?"

Jesse rifled through his briefcase and pulled out copies of both sets. He handed them to Collins. "The report in your left hand is from the originals. The other one is the report that fellow gave me. They look the same except for the figures. The problem is, where did he get these? Who would run a set of fake numbers and for what purpose?"

"I don't know if it will help, but I'll put our chemists on it. Maybe they can discern from the watermarks or type of printer, how they were created and when. Who was the informant? Check him out. He may just be trying to cash in on the crisis."

~43~
GEORGETOWN, D.C.

B.J. CUNNINGHAM CAME INTO THE ROOM ANGRY AND AGITATED as usual. The room, cold and quiet, suddenly became hot and stuffy. "Forester dragged the feds into the mix, put Miriamu on notice that there were fake stats floating around, and he's raising hell. Some African on her staff tried to nose into the game. Forester is becoming real suspicious. We gotta ax him."

The other two men in the room shuffled uncomfortably.

Marquez took a swallow of coffee and Senator Cleveland got up to refill his cup.

"You guys getting squeamish? What's the matter, cat got your tongue? We can't let that wacko scientist ruin everything. He's as bad as that preacher yelling hell fire and damnation on the steps of the capitol. Forester should be eliminated too. Cleveland? Marquez?"

"Cunningham, hold on. Let's look at this logically. This is not our problem. We never falsified papers." Cleveland went back to penning notes on his reports.

B.J. jerked the pen from Cleveland and pointed it accusingly at him. "We got the second dumbass black African sticking his nose in our business and Forester snooping around. So I got two more I gotta take out. Bang!"

Cleveland grabbed his pen back and pushed Cunningham away from the table.

Marquez moved around the table coming between them. "Cunningham, you're suggesting an action that might create real problems for us! In the U.S., Forester is a real cog in the whole process! If anything happens to him, lots of people are going to be investigating, and it might come back to us. We should leave Forester alone. Do we not all agree?" The more nervous Marquez got, the more his staccato Spanish accent stood out.

Cleveland nodded his head in agreement. "Manuel's right. So far, we haven't had publicity that would implicate any one of us. We should, however, monitor that U.N. lady. She's important to Wave II continuing. We need her in place. But is she still with us? We need to know that before we make any other decisions. Agreed?"

Marquez jumped in but was calmer this time. "It would seem that the Forester problem is in our friend Senator Martin's lap. Is that not so? After all, his office is the only one directly in contact with appropriations. As long as we don't have an electronic trail, we are in no way linked. If another hit is required, so be it. But let's wait it out and see how Martin handles any scrutiny before we jump on Forester or his informant."

B.J. shook his head, and his auburn hair dropped down the furrow on his brow. "You fuckin' cowards."

"Cunningham, you've got your answer. You're not to touch anyone at this time," Cleveland growled.

B.J. glared at the men and slammed the door as he left.

Cleveland shook his head, "I do believe our charming associate has lost his cool."

~44~
LAS VEGAS, NEVADA

PAUL HAD GIVEN SUSAN WHAT WAS ONCE A LUXURIOUS MANAGER'S suite at the hotel. He had put candles all around her room, which was also near the survival camp, which was once the lobby of the Paradise Club. Large buckets of water and boxes of food were lined up against the walls. On sunny days, the large glass doors allowed enough light for him to sort the supplies he scrounged. Paul had accumulated amazing things in payment for food and water: Tiffany lamps, bronze statues, oriental vases, and rugs.

There was a small chest of assorted jewelry—ruby and diamond ear bobs, necklaces, and emeralds in a gold bracelet—all marked Cartier or Tiffany & Co. A Rolex President watch, an Italian chess set, and oil paintings sat on a counter. There was a diamond-encrusted tiara that ancient Mrs. Radziwill insisted came from some czarina and a clock with a picture of Mount Vernon on it that Paul told Susan was from the 1700s. She loved the old lace clothes and wall hangings that were probably worthless, but he had accepted them as trade anyway. Several beautiful Persian rugs stood stacked against the wall.

"Susan, we have to keep a record of people bringing in food, milk, whatever, and a record of those buying from us. We especially need to keep a record of the money and jewelry. Even make a record of what I scrounge from the government supply house. I've tried to keep up. I need you to clean up my accounting—can you do that?"

"Why?" Susan put the tiara on her head and draped a silk stole around her shoulders as she pirouetted across the room.

"People who have given up precious things—keepsakes—so they can eat may want those things back."

"What if they run out of money or jewelry?" She returned the tiara, exchanging it for a flamboyant black felt hat, and struck a pose.

"I'm extending all of them credit. What's important is feeding people. We'll keep helping them so long as we can find food."

Susan got to know Mrs. Radziwill the next time she came in with a gold and diamond cameo to get some bread and sugar, and Mr. Feldman who wanted to exchange his white Stetson for tea and rice. She spent hours making precise records.

Susan especially liked the way Paul said her name, like it was a blessing. It was probably just a technique radio people learned—how to make everyone feel special. He already included her in his business, saying "we" whenever he talked about the work.

She had only been helping him for six weeks when the Wave II government distribution center outside the Strip shut down. Fortunately, the scavengers who worked for Paul continued to bring in some food—beef and elk jerky, potatoes and some greens and fruit, pulled in by horses or humans.

After seeing an older man deliver the second wagonload of food, she had to ask. "Where are these guys getting it Paul?"

"I don't ask."

"Are they stealing it—harming the farmers that grow it?"

"Well, that would be pretty stupid, like biting the hand that feeds you. No, in some cases these are the farmers. Actually, most of them are feeding their families and just bringing what's extra to us. One fellow told me he and his family had taken some training from that guy Hendrik I told you about when we first met. And he says they're located pretty hidden up there in the valley and able to produce lots of beef and turn it into jerky. They're also growing more vegetables and fruit than they need. So I'm paying them and they take the worthless dollars just in case the good old greenback comes back in use."

They had moved a pool table to the edge of their work area. He taught her how to hold the cue and play the game. There was a lot of time for playing when they weren't distributing water and food.

Paul loved watching her play. Her leg and shoulder muscles rippled as she stretched across into the stroke of the cue. But it was her hands that he couldn't take his eyes off of; like butterflies, they fluttered even when chalking the cue. He knew the muscles were from the dancing. But he had met lots of dancers in Vegas; none of them reflected light and held it in their hands and hair and face like Susan.

One evening, Paul got edgy and a little obnoxious. She wondered if it was because that afternoon, she had beaten him for the first time. She had gotten caught up in the winning, and danced around the table in glee. His face had gone from sharing her happiness to a very different look. Men didn't like to be beaten. She knew even male dancers didn't like it when you showed them up in a routine. And she had never met a male dancer who could match her.

"Paul, it was a fluke, my beating you. It will probably never happen again."

"Yes it will—it wouldn't be any fun if you weren't getting better at the game, not fun for me or for you. Susan, how about you and I go on a date tonight?"

"A date?"

"Yes, out for dinner. Just you and me."

Back in her room, she stared at the few clothes she had dragged over from her old apartment, unable to decide between the red silky dress and the black velvet one. She loved both of them. Since she couldn't imagine where they would be going, she decided not to wear the three-inch heels. Wherever it was, they'd be walking.

Frank had set up a special table for them in a corner of the cafe where they distributed food every day. Someone had scrounged up nice cuts of meat from someplace, and Frank had sautéed vegetables with special spices. He'd even used some of his diminishing supply of jam to make a little torte for dessert. Considering it was all cooked on a single propane burner, it was a feast. Susan was amazed.

Over the torte, she became suspicious that Paul was getting too serious about her. Although he teased her mercilessly about being his beautiful dancing secretary, he had avoided even touching her. While they were still savoring the dessert he sang a familiar song. "Lady in red is dancing with me . . . ." Paul told her he had never seen her look so lovely.

"Susan, how do you feel about me?"

"I . . . what do you mean?"

"Do you like me? Do you find me attractive at all? I'm dying here, Susan; help me."

"I find you most attractive. You are a beautiful man, Paul."

"How about inside me, do you feel that I . . . not just the outside, but the inside is okay?"

Susan laughed, then caught her breath. "I admire what you're doing. Who wouldn't? The people you help adore you. We all know you could have just walked away, but you didn't. Actually I would have just walked away, except for you."

"Will you live with me, Susan?"

"I am living with you."

"You know what I mean, sleep with me in my room. You don't have to answer right away. Just think about it. I can wait."

On the way back to the hotel, he held her hand and then hugged her when he left her at her door. She sat on her bed looking out over the dark city, deep in thought. Her past boyfriends had never asked permission to make love to her. She was floored by a man—any man—with such humility and patience. Paul was definitely an enigma, so outspoken and flamboyant in his talk, yet so gentle.

She realized that he wasn't asking for a fling. He was older and wanted something permanent. She had to be sure that was what she wanted in life. If the world came back one day from the pieces it had broken into, would she want to dance again? How would he feel about having a showgirl as a wife?

Later, she wrapped herself in a blanket and knocked on his door. "Can we talk?" He looked at her as though he had been struck, and she realized he must have thought she was about to turn him down.

"If the world changes and it goes back to . . . to like it was, I have to dance."

"And?"

"And how will you feel about me dancing?"

He threw his head back and laughed—that laugh she had come to love, the laugh she didn't hear nearly often enough.

"Susan, I don't want to change you, I just want to love you. He slipped his hands inside the blanket and held her close. Then he kissed her eyes, her nose, and her mouth softly. "Susan, my beautiful lady in red, how will you like living with someone who works weird hours, and often makes a jackass of himself on the public airwaves so that people hate him? The other thing you must consider, I am older—I'm forty-two, almost forty-three. When you're forty and still young and vibrant, I'll be sixty. Have you considered that?" He kissed her again, and this time it wasn't as gentle.

~45~
DEERING, IOWA

MATTHEW WAS WORKING IN THE BARN WHEN KAREN SAW THEM ride up in a Land Rover. She knew instinctively they were trouble. No one had any gasoline. And if you did, you weren't allowed to use it. And no one in Deering owned a Rover. That big guy, still wearing the plaid shirt, who Matthew had befriended a few weeks back got out of the car. Matthew came out of the barn, held out his hand, and instantly pulled it back. She heard splintered parts of the conversation: Matthew pleading with him and loud, ugly curses from the visitor.

She reached for the loaded shotgun behind the kitchen door and aimed it through the screen. Two other men got out of the Land Rover—one tall and thin, the other short and squatty—and went in the barn. They brought out the little heifer and tied her behind the Rover. When they came out again, they each had a squealing baby pig tucked under their arms. Matthew was waving his arms and shouting. Finally he lunged at the man he knew, tackling him around the waist. They both fell to the ground.

"No!" Karen yelled as she burst through the door, gun held high. She pulled off one shot. "No!" again, as she pulled off another shot as she moved quickly toward the three men standing over her father-in-law who was still on the ground.

The tall, thin man grabbed a shovel that was leaning against the barn and hit Matthew on the head till he lay in a silent heap. Karen trained the gun on the thugs as she moved closer. The gun suddenly discharged, peppering the ground at their feet, startling Karen and giving the largest of them a chance to lunge at her and tear the shotgun from her hands.

He ordered the other two men to find more food as he dragged her into the barn tearing at her shirt and jeans. In the semi-darkness, she felt his hot breath and smelled the sweat on his clothes. Karen tried to calm herself for a minute and think clearly. She lay still as he stood jerking the fasteners on his pants. She slowly reached over her head in the darkness of the barn and grasped a small scythe Matthew must have dropped when he heard the car approach. She tightened her grip and waited. As he lowered his body reaching for her, she swung the scythe with all her might, catching his shoulder and neck with the blade. He made a sound like a small animal, and she felt and smelled his warm blood spilling out onto her face and chest. She choked as he grabbed her neck, and then swung again and again with the blade, hitting his head and back until he stopped moving. Twisting out from under him, she pushed his body aside. Karen crawled out of the barn. The other two men were nowhere in sight. Matthew was still on the ground behind the Land Rover. She picked up the gun and ran to the house, perching herself just inside the screen door where she could see them when they came back.

Karen watched as the two men rounded the barn, laughing as they each carried a handful of chickens by their feet. She watched them stuff the chickens in the car and listen at the door of the barn, smirking. She waited. They stopped laughing.

They cautiously stepped inside the barn. They came out one at a time, the little guy looking from side to side, the taller one dragging her attacker. He was covered with blood and very still.

Karen was now calmer; she had planned her next move. She couldn't let them take any of the animals. She stepped out on the porch and aimed the gun.

"Stop right where you are. Stop right there or I'll shoot both of you, and you'll be as dead as your friend."

They looked at each other and hesitated for a moment. Karen tightened her hold on the gun and started down the steps.

"Untie those animals right now. Move!" She fired a shot, kicking up the dust at their feet.

The thin man stuffed his lifeless buddy into the back of the Land Rover while the squatty one untied the heifer, dropped the chickens, and let the pigs out. The engine roared, and the Land Rover peeled out, leaving chicken feathers and dust in Karen's face.

Hours later, when the boys came across the field with Elsie, Karen was still sitting, sobbing and holding her father-in-law's head in her lap. Matthew was dead.

~46~
HARARE, ZIMBABWE

JESSE WOKE AND TRIED TO REMEMBER WHERE HE MIGHT BE. WHITE stucco walls and mesh curtains with a breeze wafting across his torso. He closed his eyes again. In his search for solutions to implement during WAVE III he'd been on too many planes and in too many strange hotels in the last few months.

He lay still a minute, trying to gather his thoughts. Then he remembered, the Meikles Hotel, Harare—famous as the hangout for foreign journalists during Zimbabwe's civil war in the '70s. After an eighteen-hour flight from New York City on the most godawful uncomfortable military transport plane, he'd fallen into bed the night before, fully clothed, and slept like a baby.

He sponged off in a small basin with water from a bucket and pulled on khaki slacks, a soft blue polo shirt, and sandals. He'd always wanted to see the big game of Africa, but he could never have imagined the circumstances that would finally bring him to this corner of the world. His meeting with Hendrik Johnson wasn't until noon. Meanwhile, he'd take in the city and try to get his bearings.

As he wandered through the hotel lobby, Jesse tried to recall the recent history of the nation once known as the breadbasket of southern Africa. Just before Wave I, it had finally thrown off its "president for life," Robert Mugabe. A smart man, Mugabe had risen from civil war rebel to president in the early 1980s. He went on to rule well, welcoming the whites to stay and help build a new Zimbabwe. But after ten years, he chose ego, wealth, and ruthlessness over the welfare of his entire nation. The men and women sitting around the lobby wore fine clothing; their cologne and jewelry couldn't be missed.

The perimeter of the lobby featured little boutiques, selling the latest from London and Paris in ties, shoes, and safari clothing. They must have had a huge backlog when Wave II hit, because no foreign goods were being shipped in now. Then it hit him. There weren't any tourists anymore either, no one but local residents left to buy all this expensive, gaudy stuff.

Out on the street, the blast of heat and the smell of sweat reminded him of New York City. In fact, if he closed his eyes he wouldn't know the difference. But the farther he got from Meikles and surveyed the dilapidated roads and buildings, the more it seemed as if all of Harare's builders and public works employees went on holiday long before Wave II hit. Harare, once a beautiful and well-groomed city, had long ago deteriorated beyond the point of reclamation.

Still, the sidewalks buzzed with people, mostly black, a few white. It was like other large cities he'd seen after about four months of Wave II being in effect in the so-called "developing world." Those who hadn't fled in the first Wave had found some means to go on with their lives. And after the initial looting and pillaging, things had gone back to a tentative normalcy. Open-air markets, still common in the twenty-first century in most African nations, simply shifted everything to a barter system, while groceries shut down. In fact, Africa's cities had survived better than most around the world. City dwellers often had extended families in the villages. And almost everyone had a garden and some chickens right there in Harare. They grew what they could and then went to their village home regularly to get other food, especially beef and pork, and come back—selling or sharing what they could not use themselves.

At 11:45, Jesse began looking for the Cafe Mutare. He felt sweaty and agitated. He had never liked crowds. During the two weeks he and Karen had spent in Istanbul, she had never tired of the crowded streets, the markets, the haggling with cab drivers, and the bargaining with shop owners over a cost difference of just a few American dollars. Here, she would have been in her element. But Karen wasn't with him. When he closed his eyes to bring her face into focus, he could conjure up only a vague image of her peering up at him on that last night when they had held each other in what felt like desperation. He felt again the deep sadness and weariness that he couldn't shake. Then, Hannah's face came sharply into view, and guilt rose up in his chest.

The cafe was clearly a local hangout where few whites ventured. Jesse got there first, thinking he was prepared for the old man's arrival. He had heard about Hendrik from Karen when she began her editing job in New York. She had come home one night and spread out the contents of her briefcase on the dining room table.

"Jesse, will you look at this? You have got to read what this fellow from Africa has been saying for decades. Here, listen, this is from an article in *Time* from March 1960."

> *For centuries humans have been drastically altering the micro-biotic and micro-climactic conditions of billions of acres of the Earth. It would be naive and stupid of us to think that this would not, eventually, have a macro-biotic and macro-climatic effect. There is no mystery to the loss of plants and animals, the changes in weather patterns, the increase in frequency and severity of catastrophic drought, fire and flooding. The end result will be changes in our climate that will, then, in a viscous cycle increase the intensity of drought, fire and flooding.*

"And this is from the *Christian Science Monitor Magazine* from June 1985."

> *The grasslands of the world, where 1.5 billion people live and from which they derive their food and income in livestock, are collapsing because there are too few animals, not too many, on the land. The soils, plants and the grazing animals co-evolved. Without the animals, the grasslands will continue to turn into deserts. The ground is increasingly bare. It is dry and as I walk on it the crackling is like the rattling of my own bones. The grasslands*

> *will become deserts, fresh water systems will collapse, and more people will starve.*

"And Jesse, as early as 2010, his team of scientists calculated that the world could become carbon neutral just by increasing soil carbon content by 0.4 percent. Think of it, without even addressing the output of fossil fuels, we could be carbon neutral if we just focused on soil carbon! He wrote and spoke four decades ago about the very things we've been experiencing for years now and he offered solutions that not only addressed climate change but also improved food production, groundwater reserves, and wildlife habitat."

"Sounds like a prophet."

"No just a guy with a lowly bachelors in botany and zoology talking about the loss of biodiversity as a crucial—and fixable—precursor to and cause of climate change—carbon released from damaged soil into the air. He was warning us. But I guess no one was listening. I think he's still alive. I did a little internet research and it appears he still lives in a village called Dimbangombe in Zimbabwe. It's near Victoria Falls, almost on the border of Zambia. He'd be in his eighties now. This last quote really hit home to me, love, when I think about all of your efforts to halt environmental collapse:"

> *There is no evidence, in all of human history, to indicate that humans have ever been pro-active in averting an oncoming tragedy. All the evidence suggests that humans do not act until there is a crisis. And by then it is usually too late. Or at the minimum, there is a great deal of human suffering that could have been avoided.*

When he and Hannah began identifying solutions that might be implemented by people—as part of Wave III—to restore civilization to some semblance of normalcy, he had dug up the articles on Hendrik Johnson and contacted the Harare-based Essentials. He was relieved to hear that the old fellow was still alive, and that his colleagues would get him a message to see if they could get him to come to

Harare or Jesse could be invited to Dimbangombe. Johnson's reply came quickly, indicating a day and time he'd meet Jesse in Harare. In the note, he'd described himself as eighty-five, medium height, slight, gray hair, and long of tooth. Jesse expected a grizzled, bearded old coot. So when a dapper gentleman who looked to be no more than sixty-five—dressed in hunting attire including a Tilley hat—approached the table, he was thrown a bit off guard.

"I'm Johnson. Since you are the only who doesn't look one bit Zimbabwean, you must be Jesse Forester?"

Jesse jumped to his feet. "Yes. Yes, I was expecting someone . . . uh."

"I am no more nor less than myself. Would you like a passport, a picture ID, perhaps a witness who could assure you who I am?" Hendrik's Rhodesian accent was soft, faint. When they shook hands, Jesse felt the strength and calluses of a hand that knew how to till soil and pull calves.

"No, only you do not look like I expected—you don't look your age at all. Please, Mr. Johnson, sit down. I'm so honored that you took the time to meet with me."

"No, I am the one to be honored. The messenger who brought your request to me in our little village caused quite a lot of excitement, ya know. Your reason for contacting me must be pretty important; I only come to Harare twice a year. And with the new U.N. mandates, it's a long way by ox cart."

"Mr. Johnson—may I call you Hendrik?—Karen, my wife, researched your work for me, and I believe I have read almost everything you ever published, starting in 1950 right through to 2015."

"Depressing, isn't it? Even I can't stand to read that stuff now. You must have had a lot of time on your hands, young man. Why did you find it so interesting?"

"Well, I'm one of those responsible for creating and then implementing the U.N. mandates. As my note said, I'm an Essential. And I believe—many of us do—that climate change and the reason we had to implement Operation World Salvation is entirely anthropogenic. And if it is caused by humans, humans can probably fix it. Well, and I think, from reading your reports, that you can help us."

"Help you to do what, Mr. Forester?"

"Help us . . . well . . . help us save the world."

Hendrik threw back his head and roared. His laughter resonated less of humor and more of pain. "You are insane, young man, and not a little naive. I once thought the world would beat a path to my door; but the scientific community dismissed my ideas, vilified me, banned me from university campuses. Your own U.S. agriculture scientists tried to have me thrown out of the country when I was first there on a lecture tour. I spent my whole adult life looking for ways to help humans change what we were doing and its impact on the Earth. And I helped thousands of individuals and families along the way. But it wasn't enough to shift the titanic impact that the combination of fossil fuel use and soil carbon loss has had on this spaceship Earth. Mr. Forester, I have had too many disappointments. Why should I now reopen that door? I am too old for any extended battle."

"Mr. Johnson, I have put my own life and career on the line. My hope was that you would help me work out a plan to leave this world a better place in spite of the mistakes made in the past. I was sure you were a fighter. I guess I was not just naive but wrong." Jesse stood up as if to go.

"Now, young man, you came even farther than I did to make this meeting. Surely, you are willing to give an old man a little time to consider such an offer. Sit back down; don't be so quick to push off. You're brave *and* naive. Let me apologize for finding your request just a little painful and ironic. Let's have some food and drink. I've had a long, dusty ride. A little sustenance won't hurt before we discuss . . . what was it you called it? . . . 'saving the world.' "

~47~
DIMBANGOMBE, ZIMBABWE

NIGHT HAD FALLEN BY THE TIME THEY ARRIVED AT THE VILLAGE. A few fires burned here and there, surprising Jesse since in the rest of the world people were being shot for burning any sort of fuel. Hendrik, sensing his confusion, offered, "We have permission from the government to burn a small amount of wood every third evening to cook meat for the next few days and boil water for the local clinic's use. Partially, that's because we are growing and replenishing all of our own forests—both softwoods and hardwoods—and our grasslands have been tested as the highest in the world for locking up carbon and producing oxygen."

As they passed a cluster of huts, people stared at the vehicle made available to Jesse as one of the Essentials. They parked in front of a hut that sat a small distance from the village. It was a bit larger than the others and decorated with colorful designs. Its windows were covered with screens where other huts windows were just open. Bright fuchsia bougainvillea arched the doorway exuding warmth and a sense of home.

A woman stood in the doorway, watching and waiting. When Hendrik got out, she heaved a visible sigh of relief. This was part of their routine. He left and she waited for him to come back. It was never really clear to her why she waited with such apprehension. Perhaps it was because his life had seen so many senseless and tragic turns that she wanted only for the rest of his days to be peaceful.

"Hello there, love," Hendrik called out. "Look what picked me up in Harare." He laughed. "This is Jesse Forester. Remember those guys we heard about on the BBC one night when they first announced

Wave I? Those guys called the Essentials? Well, Jesse here, he's one of the Essentials. Essentials get cars and petrol. I didn't have to ride that bloody horse and cart all the way back. Of course, I will at some point soon have to figure out how to get it back here, won't I?"

"Jesse, this is Katherine, my current wife; my *indlovukazi*."

Jesse could see a grin light up Hendrik's face as the oil lamp glowed behind Katherine, who had waived him off at the *indlovukazi* remark. The word meant queen elephant—an endearment to Hendrik but not necessarily one Katherine fully appreciated, nor that Jesse understood, given that the woman was tall and lithe.

"Hello, Jesse, glad to meet you. Hopefully, you won't find our sparse accommodations too rough during your stay."

"I've waited all my life to see Africa, and I can't imagine a dirt floor, thatched roof, or outdoor latrine that would deter me. Your accommodations beat the hell out of New York City without any electricity, gasoline, natural gas, or fireplaces—especially in the winter."

Over tea, Jesse relaxed enough to explain his visit to Katherine. "The U.N. didn't put in place sanctions and then call it quits. We now have to quickly adapt our lives in a way that continues to not produce any additional carbon and lock whatever there still is into the soil, oceans, etc. The time to do all this was yesterday, of course. We know that now.

"Now, we have to take the next step and begin creating ways to restructure how we live. How will the human race build some semblance of a livable world without petrochemicals. I've been visiting various communities that have survived the meltdown. My research has shown that there are common links, and I am following up on them."

"And you heard about our little village here?" Katherine seemed incredulous.

"Well, more than that, Mrs. Johnson."

"Katherine."

"My wife, Karen, found articles about your husband's work. And eventually, his writings. I must admit that early on, I couldn't get beyond his advocacy of livestock as crucial to grassland ecosystems. He was so controversial. But I've met a few people who are now living in communities influenced by his work. These communities have figured out how to produce what they need in food and shelter, without depleting—in fact, while replenishing—their resources. They don't depend on imported resources, so the lack of fossil fuels with the implementation of Wave II has hardly impacted them.

"Who all have you been in contact with?" Hendrik asked.

"There's Kim Lee, a Japanese fellow, actually a friend of mine from college and a somewhat modern-day follower of Mr. Fukuoka. Kim went back to Japan to try to influence his government to find ways to be less dependent on the West. He never made a dent in influencing his government, but he's influenced small farmers all over Japan.

"I met with a contingent of Aussies last month. They have been using your ideas too. There's a group of ranchers in the northern Great Plains. Then there was a fellow in Ireland, a Paddy Freeman . . ."

There was a long pause as Mona Freeman's accusations came back to him. He shook it off and continued.

"And there is one whole country, Argentina, which in the midst of Wave I and Wave II is doing quite well. Its minister of agriculture met you many years ago and began pushing your ideas into all levels of government policy. Let's see, her name is Camilla something. She's powerful, impressive from what I have read. What she's been able to do is amazing. There's been almost no civil unrest. Years ago, under her guidance, they began reorganizing their large cities and making sure all people had access to food without huge transport systems. And making sure that all food and other production was achieved while replenishing any natural resource on which that product depended."

When Jesse said "Camilla," a quick flicker came to Hendrik's eyes and a small curve touched the corners of his mouth. Katherine stiffened just slightly. "Olivas," said Hendrik. "Her last name is Olivas." Then there was silence, and Jesse sensed that their pleasant evening had come to an abrupt end.

~48~
BUENOS AIRES

CAMILLA OLIVAS, MINISTER OF AGRICULTURE FOR THE GOVERNMENT of Argentina, strode down the dark halls of the departmental building. She nodded to important men as she passed. It was her policies and her determination that were keeping Argentina at the top of food production, not those of the mustached, bearded men in dark suits and shiny shoes. Her actions had also led them to hate her.

She had long endured jokes and envy from the males who far outnumbered her gender in the field of agriculture. They began when she was the only woman on the research station in the Pampas during her third year of university and followed her to this day. When she'd arrived in the U.S. for an internship at the Sevilleta Reserve in New Mexico, she was only twenty-one, and even more captivating than she had been at sixteen. She had retained all of her pride without the hastiness of her youth. Even in modern-day America, when it came to agriculture, especially rangeland, she was still one in a hundred. But her passion for and knowledge of the land was deeper than anything the others could muster.

Her days were long, full of riding horses, gathering and analyzing grasses, making field notes on the behavior of wild species that roamed the mesas and the bosque along the Rio Grande. She had applied four years in a row for this internship, and was determined to squeeze every ounce of learning she could from it. After years in the smog and clutter of Buenos Aires, peppered with too few and too brief field trips to the Pampas, she relished the desolate landscape that was southern New Mexico. The smells of the sage and the chamisa were intoxicating; the ridges of purple mountains etched in rows one on top of the other took her breath away. She felt at home among the mountains that turned pink and red and purple with the setting sun, and a sky that was so vast you could see rain that was still fifty miles away.

Camilla also needed at times to see the city lights, to sit in a small cafe drinking coffee and watch people go by. Many weekends, she would hop a ride with one of the Sevilleta staff to either Albuquerque or Las Cruces, both university towns where she could usually find a party and a young man willing to sip coffee or beer and later share his bed with a lovely Argentinean. She would sleep late, peruse the university library or a bookstore. She attended an occasional party or concert on Saturday night and caught a ride back to the Sevilleta by noon on Sunday.

One weekend in Albuquerque, she saw an advertisement for a lecture by an African renowned as a "range revolutionary." Hendrik Johnson was known as the "guru of grass" to a small handful of people around the world who had trained with him and adopted his management ideas. To others, especially those with Ph.D.s in grass, biology, or wildlife, he was a charlatan, a snake charmer, even a cult leader. Camilla had read his book in her first year at university. She remembered only that he had some pretty radical ideas.

When she arrived, the hall was only a quarter full, mostly ranchers sitting in the back as if they were all in church. In her usual way, she glided to a front row seat. Voices lowered, eyes followed. She was early and began reading a small pamphlet that had been handed to her when she came in. Slowly she recalled that this was the fellow who thought the grasslands of the world had co-evolved with large herding ungulates and pack-hunting predators. He also thought that if one simulated the wild herding behavior of the buffalo or the elk, even with cattle, one could increase the overall diversity of species and completely restore the grasslands.

When he stepped out on the platform, she saw a wiry middle-aged man with sandy hair, hazel eyes, and a somber, smooth face. However, when he spoke, his eyes lit up and his voice reverberated with passion and thunder. After two hours, she was convinced of two things: He was probably right in his theories, and she wanted to be with him. She wanted more than anything in her twenty-one years to hold, love, and share with a man who spoke with such knowing of grasslands, animals, water, soil, and wind-swept skies pierced only by the screech of a hawk. She had never heard a man speak with such tenderness and compassion.

Later, they would laugh that embarrassing lilt of new lovers when he would tell her that when his eyes had first rested on her, his knees had gone weak and he'd been unsure whether he would be able to continue. As he spoke, he felt every tilt of her head, her eyes on him intent, serious, searching. And at moments, it was as if he were speaking only to her of these things he knew from the core of his being.

When the floor was open for discussion, he fielded the usual barrage of praise from some farmers and ranchers who had followed his work and changed the way they managed their livestock. From the others, he got only vindictive stares. They were a mix of environmentalists and traditional cattlemen, the latter unwilling to change their management even slightly, smug in their rightness while their grasslands and families collapsed around them.

She had lingered by the exit sign while he shook hands with a dozen or so cowboys. When the last of them finally wandered toward the exit, Camilla approached Hendrik. He had been watching out of the corner of his eye, tracking her every move, silently hoping she would stay. He was not yet sure what he would do if she did remain, fully realizing she was young enough to be his daughter.

"My name is Camilla, I'm from Argentina, and I'm here on an internship at the Sevilleta near Socorro, and I want you to help me bring these ideas to my country. Can I buy you a drink?"

~49~
TAUSHIMA, JAPAN

NIKO RAN THROUGH THE ORCHARD, STUMBLING ON THE MELON VINES that grew between the peach trees. In her running shoes, she would go fast to Mr. Omira's store and be back before anyone knew she was gone. Brother Matsoi had been coughing for a week, and no one was doing anything about it. Niko didn't understand why her father had not gone for cough medicine. *When I bring the medicine back for him, he will get better, and I will be a hero.* Perhaps she would also buy a bag of candy—or maybe Mr. Omira would give her some like he always had in the past.

She stopped to catch her breath, then leaped across the irrigation canal and turned right toward the small road down by the bay. She ran all the way to Omira's, stopping only once to tie the laces on her Nikes.

As she approached the store, she couldn't believe her eyes. The main road past the store was full of people. She had never seen so many people except in Tokyo. Thousands of them walked in the same direction, with bundles of clothing and sacks of food on their backs. A few pushed or pulled handcarts and wagons. Some rode bikes. Their faces looked like statues, their eyes staring straight ahead. No one spoke; everything was quiet except for the sounds of the carts and feet crunching on the roadway. Niko stopped and stared.

She turned into Mr. Omira's store. It was empty. There was nothing on the shelves. Where cans of food once had been piled high, there was just dust: no rice, no buns, no meat; even the ice cream cooler was empty. The little corner where the cough medicine and aspirin and bandages should have been was bare too. Niko turned around and around, trying to imagine where everything had gone. The windows had been broken, and the floor was covered with glass.

"Mr. Omira, Mr. Omira?"

The back room, where Mr. Omira had a TV and an easy chair, was empty too. There was no teapot on the stove or dirty cup in the sink.

"Mr. Omira, hey, where are you? Mr. Omira, it's me, Niko. All her life, she had been coming to Mr. Omira's store for her mother, and now it was empty.

"Mr. Omira?"

No one answered. Matsoi would die. A shiver ran up her spine. For the last couple of months, her father had been telling Niko not to leave the farm. She had promised. She must get back.

In her confusion, she ran into the road where all the people were. Now, there were even more than before, and they surrounded Niko before she realized what was happening. There were so many people moving that her arms were pinned to her sides and her feet set in motion in the direction the crowd was going. It was the wrong way. She tried to turn and climb back up the hill, but she couldn't. A man with a cart almost ran over her. A woman with a baby fell in front of her, and she couldn't keep from stepping on the baby.

"My farm, my father. Please let me go. Stop. You are pushing me. Let me go the other way. Please."

But they didn't hear her, or they wouldn't listen. There were too many of them, and they were all walking somewhere. Niko didn't know where. She began to use her elbows and to slap with her hands. It gave her a little space but not for long. The people looked at her with their blank faces, and a few slapped back. As soon as she stopped punching, she was enclosed again by the mass of people all moving down the road.

"Please, let me go. Please let me go. My father will miss me. I must get home! Please, please."

Hot tears streamed down her face, and her nose began to run. Her Nikes had come untied again, and she concentrated to keep from tripping on her laces.

"You don't understand. I must go the other way. Please, I must go home." Finally, she gave up trying to be heard or to reverse her steps. She allowed herself to be swept along. Eventually, they would have to stop and *then* she would walk home. For now, she must not trip on her shoelaces. If Niko fell, they would surely trample her to death.

~50~
SAN DIEGO

"MR. NOLAN, WHERE ARE THE TRUCKS?"

Bob Nolan looked at Tiny with compassionate frustration. "There aren't any more trucks, Tiny."

"No trucks? I have to feed the animals."

"Don't worry about the animals, Tiny. I'll take care of the animals. You have to go home to your mother."

"I have to feed the animals. Momma expects me to feed them!"

"I know you think you have to feed the animals, Tiny, but things have changed and there's no more food so we . . . you can't feed the animals."

"The animals are hungry."

"I know they're hungry."

"The animals eat more than ten tons a day Mr. Nolan. You said I feed the animals. I'm just the man for the job. You told me so."

"Yes, Tiny, but it's different now. There aren't any trucks to bring the food. The board hasn't made provisions, alternate plans; I can't give you food I don't have."

"The animals are hungry. They need food."

"Tiny!" Mr. Nolan came around the desk and put his hand on Tiny's arm. "You need to go home, Tiny. There is nothing you can do. There is nothing anyone can do . . . go home to your mother."

"No, Mr. Nolan, I'm just the man for the job. That's what you and Momma said."

Bob Nolan shook his head and rubbed his eyes. For two weeks, he had sat at his desk with his 130 I.Q., his master's degree in wildlife biology, and twenty-five years in endangered species captive breeding and management. Still, how to feed the animals eluded him. His compassion turned to anger.

"Go back to your trailer and wait, Tiny! Wait until I figure out what to do. Tomorrow . . . tomorrow, I'll figure out what to do."

In his trailer, Tiny stared at the black TV screen and waited. All the time, he heard the animals crying out. He heard the deep hoot of the rhinoceros, the bleating of the antelopes and goats, the sharp cry of the giraffe. The lion's roar woke him in the middle of the night, and he sat on the side of his bed thinking. The trucks didn't come. They didn't bring the food anymore. He had to find a way to feed the animals. An idea came to him. Tiny's chest swelled with pride.

He slipped on his tall rubber boots, plopped his broad-brimmed straw hat on his head. He carefully locked the trailer door and put the key in his pocket. He whistled softly as he passed the mynah birds, but they were asleep, and no ducks crossed his path.

The door to the work shed was locked. Tiny used a sharp stone from the path and with several blows broke the padlock. After his eyes adjusted to the darkness inside, he found the tools he needed.

When Tiny approached the animals, they looked up, but they continued to circle around and around, keeping their eye on him and pushing each other aside. The little dik-dik came up to him. He patted her head as she licked his other hand. It took him a long time to cut the fences. He cut carefully and rolled back the fence so the little keiker and the little giraffes wouldn't get their hoofs caught in the wires. There were twelve pastures in all for the gazelles, giraffes, rhinos, and kudus. He cut them all.

"Come on out now, little animals. You can get out and eat trees and grass outside now. Come on—but be sure to come back tomorrow. Mr. Nolan's gonna figure it out by tomorrow, so come back and there will be food."

Tiny approached the lion's hillside hesitantly. He was afraid of them. The pride was calm, ignoring him. The wires were heavier, and he began to sweat in the cool night. Forty-five minutes later, only half of the fence was down. As he cut the last strands, he stretched on his toes beyond his full six-feet-four for the wire cutters to reach the top of the ten-foot fence. The sweat dripped off his face and arms, mixing with the blood that oozed from cuts.

There was a ditch between him and the lions, so he found some planking that a construction crew had left. He hauled it back to the lions and placed it across the ditch.

"Hey, there, Mr. and Mrs. Lion, there you are. Tiny's letting you out too. Go get some food. But be sure to come back tomorrow. Mr. Nolan's sure to figure it out; he's so smart. The trucks will come back tomorrow."

Tiny stuck the wire cutters under his arm and headed back across the pastures, whistling. His happiness knew no bounds. "Skip, skip, skip to my lou, skip to my lou, my darling. I'll find another one better than you; I'll find another one better than you, skip to my lou my darling."

* * *

At 6 a.m., everything was too quiet. Twenty minutes later, Bob Nolan found the cut fences. The wire cutters and the trailer key were intact. Tiny's body, boots, and straw hat were shredded and covered with blood. Hundreds of African animals were roaming the hills of San Diego. Tiny Grant had fed the animals.

~51~
FAIRBANKS, ALASKA

THEODORE SANDS SPENT HIS LAST DAY ON DUTY EMPTYING HIS DESK and wiping out all his files in the computer. He wasn't due to fly out until 0600, and he had time to waste. He cleaned out his personal cubby and packed his duffle bag. He felt glad to be leaving, mixed with some concern about dealing with the chaos in the lower forty-eight. There were no planes flying for civilians and once he stepped off the flight he would in fact be a civilian. Maybe he could jump a nuclear-powered freight train. He had never seen himself as a stowaway on a railroad car, but he would do anything to get home, even walk.

His crew hadn't been surprised when the order came to cut the contingency down to a skeleton crew. There had been few cargo planes landing, and the supplies were scarce. The Pentagon obviously had much more pressing things to deal with than bases in remote hinterlands. He emailed his wife, thinking that the electricity from the nuclear plant was probably not supplying north Texas, and even the wind turbines in west Texas that everybody had complained about so much might not be enough. He decided to send one last letter off to the guys. He had fun compiling it.

To the soothsayers and prophets:

The gang from the good old Alma Mata: Were we right? We sure cashed in. Hocus Pocus, zammo-whammo—and the world followed our lead down to the last unpredictable incredible detail. I'm winding down in old Alaska, wondering how I will get home, and wishing I could see you guys one more time.

Let's hear it for the four of us one day soon strolling across the golf greens and beating it out on the tennis courts in the sunshine.

Regards, Teddy

He sent it off knowing that, like the one to his wife, it might not go anywhere. Then he wiped all personal emails from the deep recesses of the computer, shut it down, and trudged to the snack area in the hope that maybe, just once, there would be more than stale bread and cold coffee.

~52~
NEW YORK CITY

WHEN B.J. CALLED AND INSISTED ON A MEETING, HER BLOOD RAN cold. Miriamu had insisted that they meet in a public place. Ever since Haile's murder, she had been afraid. Miriamu assured him in their brief messages that she still was sexually attracted to him—just afraid of their getting caught.

The cafeteria at the Metropolitan Museum looked empty—no tourists or art lovers. The skeleton crew of guards and curators protecting the treasures munched on sandwiches. They made her feel a little safer. B.J. was late as usual. She sipped her tea and noticed how early the trees in Central Park had leafed out this year. There were also a lot of dead ones. What had killed them, she wondered. Poor care? Lack of oxygen? Surely, the experts hadn't convinced nature as well as the human population.

"Ciao, beautiful."

"You're late."

"Couldn't find a parking place."

She frowned.

"Just kidding, I had to walk, and I got lost down near that mausoleum and had to find someone to give me directions. It's hard to find a New Yorker who still lives in New York. Let's go into the park and talk."

"No. I . . . I'm hungry. I want to order a sandwich first."

"Whatever."

She munched the vegetable sandwich slowly as he watched her every move. "We can talk here, no one to hear us. What is it you need to talk to me about?"

"The leak in your office, my dear, and your black friend."

"I told you before he is an idiot. There is no permanent damage."

"Mr. Abuto decided to take information to Mr. Forester, who in turn contacted the Center for International Security and Cooperation. Don't play games with me, Miriamu; it isn't smart! Remember, my job is to take care of you, woman." B.J. smiled broadly.

She studied his face, finding his expression neither threatening nor supportive; she couldn't resist noting how muscular and handsome he was. "I thought his accusations unworthy of my attention. Jesse Forester is always coming up with problems concerning me and how I do my job. As for Thomas Abuto, I told you he's not too bright. I told him he will be sent back to Africa. He admitted he had gone behind my back for money. I think Jesse has taken into consideration how desperate the African nations are and how Thomas might stretch the truth."

"And the papers?"

"I have the real ones—Jesse knows Thomas's were forgeries. He had them tested in D.C."

"Good girl! Let's take a walk in the park."

She had hoped to avoid being alone with him but was out of excuses. They didn't talk as he steered them toward the lake and the most remote part of the park.

"How romantic. Let's take a little ride in one of these cute little row boats."

Fear griped her once again. "I have to be getting back. There is a committee coming. It's too cold to . . . ."

"Bullshit. I haven't seen you in months." He launched the little boat and took her hand to help her in. He didn't talk, just smiled that engaging, toothy smile of his until they were near the middle of the lake. He stopped rowing, carefully putting the oars in place along the inner side of the boat.

He took her hand and ran his other hand down her thigh, still smiling. She breathed a sigh of relief, so familiar was his ardor, convincing herself that sex was his ultimate goal. He kissed her mouth, running his hand across her breasts and down her belly. Then that hand reached between her legs, while the other one twined around her waist. She relaxed and moaned. Very slowly he began to apply more and more pressure. She looked up at him for reassurance, and her eyes widened in fear. His arm through her crotch lifted her completely and twisted her around, throwing her in the water. She sank down and tried to paddle away, but he grabbed her by her long, black hair. He held her under the water and then pulled her up.

"Be sure you are more careful in the future, my dear." He held her under again, jerking her by her hair. She saw his beautiful face become a twisted gray mask through the distortion of waves. She came up gasping for air.

"If we can't trust your actions, I will have to solve this little problem another way. Don't make me have to eliminate you."

She gasped for air before he pushed her farther down. He held her under longer this time, then let go and rowed to shore.

He carefully tied the little boat up to the pier and left, not turning back to see her choking and struggling to reach shallow water or gain some foothold in the muddy bottom.

~53~
WASHINGTON, D.C.

MORRIS HADN'T COME BACK TO THE APARTMENT FOR THREE DAYS. Samuel's stomach growled, and once he had barfed into the toilet. He'd started sleeping with his old teddy bear—a habit Morris denied him when he was home. The sun filtered through the cheap lace curtains of his bedroom as he lay there thinking. Morris was never coming back. Or there was an accident and he had got run over or lost and couldn't find his way back to the apartment. Samuel was sure that Morris hadn't done anything bad or evil to make the police get him.

There wasn't any food, no cereal in the boxes, no cans on the shelves. He remembered Old Penny always had stuff in her kitchen. Old Penny lived in the next apartment. She went to Kentucky. She said Kentucky was heaven because there was green grass everywhere and white fences and lots of horses. When he had asked Morris if that was heaven, he just snorted and disappeared into his study.

Samuel grabbed his book bag, climbed out onto the fire escape and went through Old Penny's window. Her things were just as she left them. Her checkerboard was on the coffee table from when they last played. In the kitchen, he threw open the cabinet doors and found a can of Spam and several cans of cat food. Penny had taken the cat with her. Samuel had never been able to get the little key off the top of the Spam before. This time he twirled it around the can until he could jerk the top off. He cut his finger digging out the meat and had to suck the blood off because there wasn't water to help stop the bleeding. The sink was full of those big brown bugs Morris said were dirty.

He stared at the bugs with the little feelers on their heads and lots of legs. They weren't so bad, and there sure were a lot of them. He decided right then and there he would eat them if he had to. He opened one of the cans of cat food and ate that. It didn't taste so bad and he decided he didn't need to barf. There was a little milk in a carton in the icebox. It tasted awful but he drank it. Morris always said milk was good for kids.

There was some dry cat food and he put that and the other can into his school bag. He found the hard mint candy in the glass jar where she always kept it for their checker matches. In Penny's bedroom he found a box with two candy bars. He got his Big Chief tablet out and wrote:

Deer Penny, I took some cat food spam and candy. when I come back or morris comes I will pay you. your friend Samuel

Back in his own apartment, he cautiously opened the door to Morris's little study. It was filled with books and papers. On the desk was an open Bible, and Samuel read what Morris had underlined in red. "The nations were angry and your wrath has come and the time of the dead." There was no food.

In his room, he stuffed his book bag with an old C.D. of Elvis he kept hidden under his mattress, his baseball glove, and his Bible with "To Samuel with all my love, Mother." Then, he added the old worn bear.

Samuel knew better than to go toward the city. Twice, he had been on field trips with his class. Once they went to a farm where cows and chickens and horses lived. Another time they went to a place where there were beautiful flowers and trees everywhere.

After five blocks, he heard gunshots. Someone was shooting from an apartment window. He hid in a doorway until it was quiet. Then he moved on to where a lot of people had turned over a man's cart. It had green stuff in it and some potatoes. The people walked over the man, carrying off the green stuff and the potatoes. Their faces were all alike, with drawn on painted angry expressions. Samuel waited patiently until all the people had left. The man must be dead, he thought, because he didn't move at all, even though his eyes were open. The cart was empty, but he could see green stuff peeking out from under the man. Samuel pushed with all his might and turned the man over. There sat two potatoes and a squashed head of lettuce. Samuel put the vegetables in his book bag. Morris always said he should eat vegetables.

~54~
ONE TREE HILL STATION, AUSTRALIA

NAPPY LEFT MARK AT THE BRONZE SQUAT STONE THAT MARKED BLACK Stump. They had become companionable, if not exactly friends. Mark had always carefully avoided any contact with the aborigines. He was surprised at the man's stamina and his innate knowledge. He knew where the game was before they came across it. He knew where the water was before it appeared. Often, it seemed to Mark, it wasn't just the old man's familiarity with the bush.

It was a genetic knowledge that Mark couldn't even begin to fathom. In his growing admiration for Nappy, he began to question Hendrik's conclusion that native civilizations made the same mistakes as modern ones. Hendrik claimed that Australia, before the introduction of man, was once covered with grasslands filled with beasts, including hoofed kangaroos. Now there were not enough animals to cycle the vegetation, fertilize the ground, and prepare the soil surface for rain and seed.

"I show you the next three places to find water." Stooping down, Nappy drew on the ground the terrain Mark should look for. He gave Mark what was left of the kangaroo they had hunted and all of a rabbit. Then he gathered up his sack, slung it over his back, and walked away.

Mark missed him immediately. He checked his map often to be sure he hadn't missed a turn here or a way marker there. Finally, he crossed the Darling River and skated past Wilcannia. He followed an empty dirt track for a while and then headed northwest toward White Cliffs.

One Tree Hill Station was a million hectares. He walked for three days before he came to the buildings. Heading around the shearing shed, he heard a cacophony of voices, and electric clippers, telling him it was shearing time. The aroma of lamb on the grill came from the cook's house. But he kept moving toward the main house. He was filthy and smelly, probably worse than the animals, and neither the jackaroos nor their cook would know him.

Two hundred yards farther stood the house with its wide veranda. As he approached, he heard a baby crying. On the north side of the veranda hung a white cradle with painted pink roses covered with a light netting. The crying continued, then stopped, then started up again. Mark climbed the steps and walked over to the cradle. The baby had lots of dark red hair but brown eyes. It looked up at him and was silent for a moment, then let out a true wail.

Mark heard the heavy breathing an instant before he felt the blow to the back of his head and fell to the wooden deck. He woke up tied to a post in an out-building. The smell of roasted lamb mingled with hay and sheep dip entered his nostrils. His head hurt, and he was disoriented. He strained at the ropes that entangled his hands and feet. He began yelling at the top of his lungs. "Hey, is anyone out there? Lisa, damn it; untie me. Did your dad do this? Sean O'-Malley, you bastard, I didn't leave her; she left me. Hey, is anyone listening?'

On the veranda, Kitty was tending the baby, pushing the cradle with her foot and humming tunelessly. She ventured halfway to the sheep shed, cocking her head to listen.

"Has everyone here gone crazy? I'm not a robber. I'm not a murderer. I'm not a drifter. I'm Lisa's husband. God, Lisa, where are you? Do you really hate me this much?"

"Miss Lisa, Miss Lisa, come out here. Listen to this man. He says he's your husband!"

"Who are you talking about, Kitty?"

"That man Nick tied up in the shed, he's yelling like a banshee out there!"

It took Lisa some minutes to get the cords off Mark's wrists.

"Damn it, Lisa, why was I hit on the head and tied up?"

"Nick didn't know who you were. He probably thought you were a marauder; they've been stealing sheep and food. You sure look like one of them, and you sure do stink."

"He could have asked first. Did he have to whack me over the head?"

"He thought you were after the baby!"

"What did he think I would do, eat it?"

"Maybe. People who make it this far are desperate!"

Mark massaged his wrists and then took her by the shoulders. "I've walked over a thousand miles. I didn't expect a warm welcome, but I didn't expect to be whacked and hog-tied either. Lisa, look at me." He shook her, making her raise her eyes to his. "Lisa, where did the baby come from?"

"It's my baby."

"You mean it's our baby."

"No, it's my baby. You didn't want any children, remember? You just wanted Sydney and the nightlife and the money."

"I remember. But you're not being fair. Those things don't exist anymore, but the baby does."

"Oh, yes, but one day those things will exist again, and you'll be off chasing them."

"I doubt it."

"Even if they don't return, what you wanted isn't here. You made that very clear last year. You said you could never live with the smell of sheep dip and dry winds. You could never handle the isolation and limitations. You didn't want to live here, remember?"

"I said a lot of things. But maybe now I know what isolation is."

"What?"

"Sydney left to the cockroaches and the dust."

"What makes you think you can come busting in here and . . . ."

"I don't think anything, I don't know what I want now. I wanted to know you were safe. I wanted to see you and touch you again. I've missed you so much. Lisa, can't we just . . . ."

He drew her closer and kissed her. "Lisa, I love you. I've never stopped loving you."

A shadow crossed the doorway followed by a rifle, in the hands of a very tall man.

"Lisa, honey, just back off from him. Mister, take your hands off her so I can kill you."

Lisa backed away. Mark let his hands fall to his sides.

"Nick, this is Mark, my husband."

"Mark this is Nick. Nick is . . . ."

"Yes, just who is Nick?"

~55~
DIMBANGOMBE, ZIMBABWE

BIRDS SCREAMING, CACKLING, AND WARBLING SHATTERED JESSE'S SLEEP as the sun rose on Dimbangombe Village. A pot had been placed on the little round table by his bed, along with tea, milk, and sugar. He lay still, drinking in the cacophony of sounds, letting the day overwhelm his drowsiness. He dressed quickly, no shaving, a quick comb through his hair and a brush of his teeth, the same clothes he'd worn the day before and his bush sandals.

Katherine and Hendrik were sipping their tea quietly as he entered. The look on Katherine's face spoke of acquiescence that comes with having lost an argument. Breakfast consisted of more tea, fresh fruit, mangos, papayas, scones, eggs, cheese, and a little impala sausage.

"A little protein for the day," said Hendrik with a wink. "So, Mr. Forester, are you ready to see the real Africa?"

"Sure, but please call me Jesse."

As they stepped out into the cool morning air Jesse felt the weariness from the last two years give way to excitement. Not a sound could be heard as Hendrik walked barefoot down a path toward a distant cluster of huts. Jesse winced at every snap and thud of his own sandaled feet.

"Jesse, when I was a much younger man and my first marriage had crumbled, I was exiled from my homeland and lived for a time in the U.S., lecturing about my work. I met Camilla when she was just a college kid, doing an internship in New Mexico. I was old enough to be her father, but over a period of about five years, she became a dear friend, sometimes a lover. After I had met and married Katherine, I spent some time with Camilla in Argentina, helping her plan the strategy to revitalize her country. That was the only time Katherine and I ever truly fought. I have not seen Camilla for many years. Katherine, is not generally a jealous woman, but she has zero tolerance for my affection toward Camilla. She is a smart woman, this Katherine of mine.

The two men approached a small grouping of huts. Hendrik continued: "Most of our people live in clusters of four to five huts, generally, these represent extended families. Katherine and I, and a few others, choose to live a little farther from the center on our own. We have no true biological extended family here."

Jesse wondered if Hendrik had family and if so where his children might be, but decided that that subject, like Camilla, might be too sensitive. He couldn't help but note how the brisk walk came so easy for this older man.

"This area we are walking through used to be barren of any vegetation or wildlife. The boreholes all went dry, and what soil there was ran off into the Dimbangombe River.

The river, which you'll see around the bend, was a seasonal wash last century, though records show it was a deep perennial river in the late 1800s with wide, sloping banks, hippo, crocks, fish, and humans everywhere. We've restored the land and the river in the last fifteen years." His voice became choked and his eyes were misty.

They rounded the bend, and there indeed was a deep, wide river. "If you like, I can show you photos back at the house of what it looked like twenty years ago. You won't believe it is even the same river."

Jesse stood, drinking in the quiet, the beauty of the river's reedy banks and its soft meander through the valley. They ascended a hill and entered a larger settlement. Chattering, singing, and laughing came from every direction. As they wandered through the village center, even children stopped to greet Hendrik. He was greeted as "*Ixegu.*" Hedrick explained that it meant old man. Even though Jesse could not tell what they were saying, he sensed a deep respect, maybe even devotion, from everyone.

"I began spending a lot of time in my homeland about two decades ago. I have been here continuously the last fifteen years. Our village and the surrounding area has been virtually untouched by these world events, except for the hordes of people leaving the cities who want to stay with us."

As they approached the very center of the village, Jesse saw a large rondoval filled with children—obviously a school. On the edges of the school, women drew water from a borehole or pounded grain in small groups. Further out, men and women tended garden plots. Children too small for school ran from one group of adults to another in what appeared to be a game of chase. Jesse wished fleetingly, then angrily, that his boys could be here with him in this safe haven. How strange it was to wonder what twist of fate had made them Americans rather than Zimbabweans.

"So, Hendrik, what is the secret of your success?"

"It's really only one thing . . . and it affects everything we do here. Long ago, I discovered—or felt I discovered—that all the ills of the world, except for true natural disasters such as earthquakes, are really a result of human activity on Earth. We have human problems that arise out of the way we choose to live our lives. Since the dawn of time, humans have made decisions in a way that is mechanical or linear if you will. This is very successful in the short run to create and build mechanical things, and disastrous in the long run especially in managing living things or natural resources. It does not take into account the holistic nature of the Earth and universe. The results have wreaked havoc in the natural world. History shows that even native peoples all over the world hunted many species to their decimation."

"So we have built great buildings, bridges, and bombs at the expense of the natural resources that actually feed, water, clothe, and shelter us. The very oxygen we breathe is the product of all those plants and animals and minerals and microorganisms that we just didn't care about. They are our life support system."

"But how do you implement your ideas here?"

"We have a common vision of the kind of life we want to live. Here in Dimbangombe we look at every action, every tool we use, every major effort we undertake in terms of how it will replete or regenerate the resources we depend on and impact the social fabric of our community. If an action we are considering will clearly deplete our natural resources or harm our social values or both, we find some other way to do what needs to be done."

A group of strapping young men approached. He acknowledged them with what seemed to Jesse great respect. They strutted by, their heads held high. "Good morning, Ixegu," they all greeted Hendrik as they passed. "Good morning, Abelusi," he responded.

"Those young men have reached a position of great importance in our society. Let me see . . . how to explain to a self-described 'environmentalist'? One of the things I also discovered, along with the role of human decision-making in environmental destruction, is my theory how grasslands—two-thirds of the Earth's surface—evolved.

"Contrary to what has been thought and practiced for the past nine thousand years, the Earth's grasslands are dying from a lack of the grazing and trampling that once took place across about two thirds of the Earth's surface—the seasonal rainfall grassland areas, such as your Great Plains. The only way to restore this vast portion of the Earth's surface and re-sink billions of tones of carbon in the process is to get vast herds of grazing, trampling animals on the land.

"It does not matter whether they are domestic or wild stock as long as they behave like ungulates—bunching, trampling, grazing, dunging, and urinating and all on a constant move. Best case is that there are also pack-hunting predators in the mix because that's what keeps them bunched and on the move. But human management can also simulate the behavior. That is why we now have a river here, and plenty of lean protein in our diet.

"I remember that was the part of your work that I refused to buy into," Jesse whispered.

"That's no surprise. Neither does the rest of the civilized world. Jesse, what you see here is the result of our making the livestock work for us. It's the animals and how we manage them that have brought back the Dimbangombe River, the water that gives this village its name. They restored the soil on which the river and the underground springs depend and now they keep it healthy and provide us with the bulk of our protein. The young men, those you just saw, herd them during the day and kraal them at night. And they are held in high esteem by all."

"How many animals does the village have?"

"Oh, about ten thousand, and they run in a single herd, just as if they were zebra or waterbuck or any of the many animals that once roamed the African savanna. In your country, it was antelope, bison, mule deer, and elk that created the vast grasslands. Losing all those herds is one of the greatest causes of desertification and climate change. I warned the scientific community that we had to rethink the seasonal rainfall and the grassland environments of the world. I set up a whole organization to help others create grasslands and learn to make holistic decisions. I failed, despite forty years of effort. So I decided to just come home and make a difference in the place where I will one day die.

~56~
LAS VEGAS, NEVADA

SUSAN CRINGED AS JAKE SPAT ON THE FLOOR AND STUCK A FRESH PLUG of tobacco in his mouth. She wondered where in the world he got it. Jake shifted from one foot to the other, his greasy tan hat tilted way back on his head. The elaborately stitched and fitted leather jacket he wore looked brand new and out of place with the torn jeans and dirty boots.

Paul was writing rapidly and folded the letter and stuck it in an envelope, carefully sealing it. He handed it to Jake along with a wad of bills.

"You'll be sure this gets to Dallas, right?"

"Sure thing."

Susan knew Paul was trying to reassure himself as he looked into Jake's eyes.

"Got it, man." Jake put the letter in his jacket pocket and started out. Paul caught him by the sleeve and grabbed his hand shaking it vigorously.

"Remember, I need that to get to my kids. They don't know if I'm alive or not. Tell them . . . well, the letter will tell them."

"Yeah, I'll get it to 'em."

She came up behind Paul and watched as Jake skirted the slot machines and blackjack tables. The place was a messy conglomeration of boxes, barrels, and miscellaneous debris. The slot machines looked like ornate iron robots waiting for somebody to command them.

"I don't trust that guy."

"He has a horse, and he's going in the right direction."

"But he's, there's something not quite right about him. Like that jacket and the tobacco."

"Like I said, he's headed the right way."

Susan went back to her desk and began sorting lists of people still living in Las Vegas who depended on Paul to get them food and water. It read like who's who in the geriatric department of the Mayo Clinic. Mr. Longmire, past president of CBS, who got caught in Vegas in a wheelchair. Mrs. Krieger, the widow of a Conoco Oil executive who was almost bed-ridden. Then there was the Cramer family, a brother and two sisters in their late seventies. Able to leave but too stubborn to go. At least half were like that, just too stubborn.

As long as Paul found new suppliers who were willing to comb the valleys for farmers growing food, they were in business. But how long could this last? It seemed to Susan that she and Paul were on a seesaw teetering between life and death, and she had her doubts about the stash of money he was accumulating. What use would it ever be? And even if it wasn't valuable now, the bands of thieves and marauders might think it was worth killing for.

The gold and jewelry were even more dangerous. As Paul felt they should, they kept a record of who had paid what, just in case they wanted to buy it all back when this was over. When this was over? The elderly and even Paul kept that hope in the back of every deal, every load of food or water. But Susan felt deep down inside that it would never be over. Or it would at least never be the same.

She watched as Paul dealt with two men pulling handcarts loaded with beans and kale. Meat was what she craved. The fellow who had been supplying it hadn't been seen in weeks. She hadn't had any meat since their romantic dinner. If there were still ranchers in Nevada, they were keeping most of it for themselves.

"Hey, kid, let's take a break. Let's go for a walk."

Susan grabbed his hand.

The streets were deserted. The last real residents who weren't Mafia or showgirls were gone. Every once in a while, one of the casino owners would wander in, look around at his holdings, and then wander out of town again.

"Paul, do you really think this will all come back again?"

"No, at least not like it was."

"Then why are you doing all of this—collecting the money and caring for all these old folks like it will be over tomorrow and the world will be right side up again?"

"What else should I be doing? I don't care about the money or the valuables. It's just something to keep my hands busy. As my mom always said, you could be out stealing hubcaps—remember in the musical *Grease*?"

Susan always learned something new talking to him, and she loved the fact that he knew so much about life. Since music had been so much a part of her, he could identify with that too.

They climbed the steps of what used to be a crosswalk over Paradise Boulevard and leaned over the empty musical fountain pits.

"Eventually, the food that others are supplying us will run out, won't it?"

"Not so, oh ye of little faith. The whole economy will change, but it will not disappear; take heart. Doesn't it make sense that the farmers will get better at what they're doing? Even without the fossil fuels, there were farmers supplying people with food in the Fertile Crescent and in ancient Mesopotamia and Egypt and Rome. Civilization through the ages has adjusted to plagues, wars, floods, and all kinds of disasters. We just need to be patient with the change and wait."

"I'm trying. I know what I'm doing now is more important than dancing, helping all these old folks. Not as much fun maybe but a good thing. When I see the look on old Mrs. Jennings' face when I bring her a little fresh water and some cheese and how Mr. Means sings me a tune every time I come in with vegetables, I can't help but feel good."

He stopped, caught her hands in his, and turned her to face him. "I love you Susan. I'm sorry if I held you back. I know you would have rather left when the leaving was good."

"Where would I have gone?"

"I've seen you staring out the window in the middle of the night, and I know you sing to yourself and dance when you think I'm not looking. I'm so sorry the music stopped for you. I wish I could make it come back. I wish I could play that stupid piano. When we do get some electricity, or the minute I can trade for batteries or a generator, I promise there will be music for you."

He kissed her tenderly; she responded to his touch with urgency. She tasted like sweet mint. "I wish all those cowardly men of the cloth hadn't run away so we could get married."

"Married?"

"That used to be what people did when they were in love, or have you forgotten?"

"In my crowd that's not exactly what people did. We were all sure every man was a one-night stand and chancy, at that, especially with AIDS and STDs. My kind never hoped for a long-term relationship. I take that back, I guess *I* never did."

"Well, you got one now, kid, whether you want it or not."

He tucked her hand under his arm and continued down Paradise Boulevard.

"What was Beth like?"

"I met her in college. She was studying sociology. I was a philosophy major and running the student radio station. She was a real beauty, a nice lady, but she was into rich. She couldn't settle for a mediocre radio announcer."

"Then why did she marry you in the first place?"

"Cuz I was so good looking."

"I know that, but I mean why you if she was so rich and could have had . . ."

"We were in college and young and stupid. We made love everywhere we could be alone. I guess we were just infatuated with sex and our emotions. Anyway, she decided the only moral thing to do was get married. So we did."

"And had two children before you decided it was a bad deal."

"Before *she* decided it was a bad deal."

"You would have stuck it out?"

"Yes."

"Aha! My competition."

"No, that was another world and another life. It's over and done."

They had meandered over to the impressive models of Egyptian gods surrounding the pyramid. Paul stopped and chuckled.

"What's so funny?"

"I'm thinking how the ones in Egypt got covered up with sand over the centuries and now these poor stupid imitations are about to be covered up too. Civilization has a weird way of laughing at humanity's creations. This is not the way Bucky said it would be."

"No? So, what did the famous Mr. Fuller say would happen?"

"He believed our very lack of specialization and innate creativity would save us, that man is unique because he is not specialized. He is penetrating, exploring, adapting, inventive, and dexterous."

Suddenly, Paul yanked her in the opposite direction. It was too late. They came from around the black obelisk and surrounded the couple. Paul fumbled for his revolver but hesitated just long enough for the leader to grab his arm and the gun. There were three women and two men dressed all in black with tattoos on any skin that was showing. They had knives and guns hanging from their belts, and began rattling the chains around their necks and waists.

"You two got food somewhere; where is it? Been eatin' good ain't ya? Where's the food?"

"That's enough. We don't have anything you want. Leave us alone."

One of the women spat in Susan's face, and as she tried to wipe the spittle out of her eyes, the woman ran her hands up and down Susan's body. A man with a patch over one eye and boots with cleats held Paul while another woman searched his pockets.

"Maybe you don't have anything on you but you're alive and look like you been eatin' good, so where's the food?" The gun was jammed into Susan's breast. She clenched her fists determined not to cry out.

"I'll get you food, but you have to leave her alone."

~57~
NEW YORK CITY

MIRIAMU WAS DESPERATE TO SEND THOMAS ABUTO BACK TO AFRICA. But he was determined not to go. New York, even without fuel and food, was better than trying to compete with millions of his black brothers for a patch of land and a few cows. His family had disappeared when the Kenyan government began wiping the Kibera slum off the face of the Earth. He really had no place and nothing to go back to.

He had packed only a few possessions, keeping the bag light, since he had every intention of getting away. Then the note from the Senate office came, demanding he meet with someone about the papers. He debated whether to ignore it and just disappear but had second thoughts. Maybe someone was about to take that haughty Kenyan woman down a peg or two. That would be very satisfying. If the officials wanted more information on her, he would try to oblige.

He still had access and could nose around the U.N. building without anyone suspecting anything. He sat down at a computer and logged in with his old password to see if he could get email. Then he used his secret backdoor to check the general UNEP email traffic. He intercepted several messages from D.C. and some of the other African commission notices, but nothing came up that he considered suspicious.

Thomas had decided to wear his suit and tie and gold necklace to the meeting to be sure anyone meeting him would take him seriously. He took the same reports he had copied for Forester, hoping he could get transport out of New York in exchange for the papers. He left his room a little ahead of time, so as to impress the official. Just to show him that Africans were not always late or thoughtless about time.

The meeting was at 7 sharp and was to be secret, so the U.N. people wouldn't suspect anything. Squirrels, the only other occupants of San Gabriel Park, were busily gathering acorns. At a quarter past 7, he looked at his fake Rolex and decided there must be some mistake. Just as he was about to leave, a man dressed in a suit and tie approached him. He was very big, larger than Thomas, and he smelled of expensive after-shave.

"Thomas?"

"Yes sir."

The man had a beautiful smile, "Let's sit down and talk, shall we? We were most grateful for your information and wanted you to know that."

"I have the papers right here." He fumbled in his jacket pocket to remove the papers.

"Yes, we could use those too."

"I tried to get more information for you, but Miriamu's office has been more secure lately. I was wondering if you guys could get me a transport out of New York to . . . maybe LA, or Chicago . . . quick. She's sending me back to Africa. I can't go back to . . ."

Two men approached from behind the bench. Quietly, they took Thomas by his collar and lifted him off the park bench.

"Hey, what is this? I'm a U.N. employee. I have immunity! What are you doing?" He twisted around to see the fellow from the U.S. government sitting calmly, smiling.

B.J. listened and watched as the two men beat Abuto mercilessly with fists and clubs, stripped his body of the gold chains, rings, and fake Rolex. They dragged the unconscious man into a mass of shrubs and dumped him there. B.J. took some bills and coupons from his pocket and gave several to each of them. Then he walked away.

~58~
BUENOS AIRES

IN HER MORE DISILLUSIONED AND LONELY MOMENTS, CAMILLA REminded herself that her challenges had been of her own making. The web, the fine silk that had woven the pattern of her life was as clear as the green eyes with which she penetrated the souls of friends and enemies alike. She had been able to turn her penchant for older men into advantages she otherwise would have missed.

Father Emanuel was thirty-two when she was fifteen. He was the only adult she listened to. Her parents, who were poor and uneducated, only piqued her anger and resentment. Even though she was the youngest of eight, her knowledge of life surpassed them. As she combed local garbage dumps for clothes, shoes, and on the worst days, food, her resentment toward her parents became uncontrollable.

"Camilla do you remember the sixth commandment?"

"Yes, father, I know all the commandments, Immaculate Conception, a hundred rosaries, the prayer of saints, and catechism. I know them like I know my own body. You have taught me well." She said this gazing longingly into his eyes like no fifteen-year-old should ever look into the eyes of a priest.

"Why, if you have learned well my dear child, do you not then honor your father and mother?"

"I am no longer a child and I find nothing to honor. I see only ignorance and a blind faith for a nonexistent god and a promise of salvation that will never come." Her green eyes remained steady, her chin slightly lifted, and Father Emanuel caught his breath as he felt his own soul being stripped for all to see.

"Camilla, I cannot argue the issue of a salvation I have not experienced. But I know God exists and he is an equally loving and wrathful father. I despair at the bitterness you carry in your heart for two simple, kind mortals. Child, I am afraid you will become a hard woman."

"Father, is it not better to be a hard woman if I am to survive in this world of simple people and powerful men?"

She reached for his hand, a common gesture for all her fifteen years. As a little girl she had grasped his hand as he walked down the center aisle of their small cathedral. But now, returning her intent stare, trying to penetrate the soul of this woman-child, and so heal her bitterness, he knew he had utterly failed. He abruptly withdrew his hand from hers.

"Yes, you are no longer a child and I am still a priest."

As she grew older, Camilla became more rebellious toward her parents, the nuns, and Father Emanuel—burying layers of anger and frustration. In the parish, she was seen as haughty, disrespectful, and unruly.

But the church was her tie to education, the bridge she knew would eventually carry her away from poverty and people she couldn't really love because she didn't respect them.

When Camilla was sixteen, she learned a woman might stoop to groveling and become subservient to a man. It was then she felt a surge through her loins and her breasts ached that strange and longing ache satisfied only by caresses. Alejandro was eighteen, lithe, with massive jet-black curls wrapping large brown eyes. He was studying at the university. When Camilla sashayed down the aisle at mass he was naturally attracted. They began meeting secretly, exploring each other's hidden places with abandon. Custom forbade Camilla more than one man but allowed Alejandro any young woman he could lure to his bed—as long as he didn't get caught.

Her parents and Father Emanuel suspected but were frightened to confront her. They worried needlessly. She soon satiated her own interest in sex, and his parents found a young woman for him, someone of respectable lineage, demure, obedient, and quiet.

Through all this, Camilla maintained the highest marks in the parish school's history. But she would have disappeared into obscurity were it not for Father Emanuel.

"Camilla, do you want to go to university?"

"That is a stupid question."

"If you are admitted, are you willing to work hard and be a credit to our little parish and your parents?"

"When I am admitted, I will work hard and be a credit to myself. Whatever credit goes to anyone else let them lap it up as dogs do crumbs under the table. My achievement will be for me and no one else."

"Camilla, must you be so hard on us mere humans? Ah, never mind. I have wonderful news, and I had hoped it would make you a little more humble."

"Why would it be wonderful for me to grovel? Why should my own self-worth and pride be destroyed in order to get an education?"

"Someday, young woman, you may learn pride and humility are not exclusive. Be that as it may, we've received funds from a Catholic foundation in the United States that will allow you to attend university. You begin next month."

The university became the laboratory where Camilla eventually discovered her passion. But it did not come easily. Her first year at the university in Buenos Aires was in pre-law—a course few women pursued in any Latin American country. After her second year, her love for good-looking men and a debate over civil rights was abruptly sidetracked by a love for the land.

The boy who spent the most time in her bed that first year had invited her to his father's estancia on the Pampas. She had never ridden a horse, never smelled dew on long grasses, never seen the shimmering sun sink to meet the Earth and disappear.

"I will begin taking courses to earn a degree in biology and environmental science, with an emphasis in range-land agriculture," she announced at the beginning of her second year.

Her adviser, Professor Lopez, stared at her in disbelief from behind his thick bifocals. "What in heaven's name will you do with such a degree? It will be absolutely worthless to you. If you think law is a male-dominated bastion, what the hell do you think agriculture is? There are no women. You will not find work, you will make no money."

"I will succeed, and I will make money. And I will help my country. This is what I will do with my life."

And succeed she had, beyond anyone's wildest dreams. The last ten years, she had put into practice everything Hendrik taught her. When Antonio Ortega, Argentina's U.N. ambassador, informed them there would be no more use of fossil fuels, her plans were already at work across the nation. Who would have predicted the world would be forced into such drastic measures? No matter, the Pampas was alive with grass and cattle; the farms were small, organic poly-cultures—and there were thousands of them. The people in Buenos Aires and Rio de Janeiro might grumble about going without heat and air conditioning, walking, riding bicycles, and being cut off from the Internet, but they would not starve.

She had dismantled the most predatory of agri-businesses. Chemical companies hated her, but every speck of vacant land in the cities was growing fruits and vegetables. Re-processed and filtered sludge was being spread on gardens and croplands. Soils were as rich as they had ever been in recorded history. Large estancias, lost to absentee owners and moribund from an agricultural perspective, had been transformed.

Of course, it wasn't just Hendrik's ideas. Her husband, Enrique, was another part of the web of her life that allowed her so much freedom. After they had been dating a few weeks, she learned he owned thirty thousand hectares of the Pampas. Shortly after that, she told him she was marrying him because she loved his land.

"You will learn to love me too, Camilla. And I promise you will be allowed to make all the decisions concerning the land. I will only interfere if you fail."

She had not failed. And she had learned to love him in her own way, accepting that he didn't understand her any better than the other men in her life—with one exception.

~59~
ONE TREE HILL STATION, AUSTRALIA

SUPPER HAD BEEN A CHILLY AFFAIR. MARK AT LEAST FELT PHYSICALLY better. He had bathed in the big tub, shaved, and put on some of O'Malley's work clothes. His father-in-law was the first to break the awkward silence.

"What's happening in the city, Mark?"

"People are leaving in droves. The ones who are staying are developing small garden plots. Pineapple and citrus is being brought in by carts from the north and carcasses of animals are hanging in open markets. Fishermen are selling along the wharf. There is a lot of dust and cockroaches. Many people have gotten desperate."

"I want to know how you got here, a yank like you on foot, over the Blue Hills and all the way to White Cliffs just doesn't make sense, the heat and all, how'd you get water?"

"I had a companion part of the way. Nappy, an abo, he knew where the water was and how to find food. He was something else."

"You traveled with a black fella?" Lisa was astonished.

"Yes, I traveled with a native. He and I shared food, water, and conversation. I learned a lot from him."

She shook her head, and for the first time a slight smile crept across her mouth. "Why, Mark Johnson, I didn't know anyone could teach you anything."

The baby let out a cry. Mark crossed to the veranda to pick her up. He rocked back and forth on his heels and she whimpered and was quiet again.

"You've messed everything up," Lisa whispered as she came up behind him.

"Why, Lisa?"

"I sent the divorce papers months ago."

"Well, I didn't get them. Honest, I never saw them. It doesn't matter—I wouldn't have signed them. What was the plan, divorce me and marry Nick? Is that why he keeps looking at you with those dreamy eyes, and why he's threatening me with a gun and dirty looks?"

"He thought you meant harm!"

"Now he knows I don't. He can call off the dogs, and the guns, and the looks. What did you tell him about me, that I'm a heel, that I beat you? Did you tell him I made you come out here and have our baby alone? You were going to divorce me and marry him, right?"

"I don't know."

"Well, he sure thinks you're his."

"I can't help what he thinks."

"Come on, Lisa. No man looks at a woman the way he looks at you if he hasn't been encouraged."

"To hell with you, Mark Johnson, I know about all those women in Sydney! I'm not supposed to get lonely too? To hell with you! I tried to not even think about you, about men at all. I know I can get along just fine without you or any bloody male."

He put the baby back in the cradle and tried to take her hand. "Lisa, I never stopped thinking about you—never. I don't want to live without you."

She pulled away; her eyes clouded with tears. "I had it all figured out. Now, you've confused my life again, just like you did three years ago coming out here—just like you always do. I don't want to be confused any more. I want . . . ."

"Lady, the whole world is confused right now! Nothing is the same! Sydney's not the same. Australia's not the same. I'm not the same."

"Well, this land is the same!" She climbed down the veranda steps and gazed out into her rose garden and the land beyond.

"No, it's not, and you know it. The markets will all be local. The transportation of cattle and sheep is different. Everything that was, is not. It's a whole new . . . ."

"Markets! Markets! I'm not talking about markets! I'm talking about me. I'm the same. And I'm talking about the land. It's the same. I still want to live here and as soon as this is over, you will want to be somewhere else. I know you will. Don't come into my life again and mess it up."

"That's your problem Lisa. You look at the world from such a narrow perspective; such blinders." He sat on the porch steps, looking out over the land and gesturing. "As long as everything is running smoothly at One Tree Hill Station and Lisa has her way, we won't worry about the fact that people are starving and desperate and dying! Don't you understand? Can't you get it through your thick skull that what we said and did last year or even last month has no bearing on today?"

"God, Mark, is this really you? Talking to me about caring about the world? When did that come before your cocktail and your vacation in Singapore?"

The silence was broken only by the sound of insects whirring and sheep bleating in the distance. She sat down next to him on the steps, and after a long time he took her hand in his and rubbed the place where her wedding ring should have been.

She gently pulled her hand away. "Maybe you have changed, Mark. But it's too late."

~60~
DIMBANGOMBE, ZIMBABWE

"HENDRIK, I RAN INTO A YOUNG NURSE EARLIER TODAY, AND SHE says that, based on her observations over the last few years, the people here are healthier than most. Why do you think that is?"

"Well, my theory is that, for ten years we have eaten only clean meats, fruits, grains, and vegetables. The soil, water, and air are clear and bursting with microorganisms, minerals, and life. And after a few years and many discussions, the villagers have rejected the practice of the men taking multiple sexual partners, which is common among most of these tribes."

As Jesse walked the hills over the next few days, surveying the wildlife, listening to the birds and the laughter of children, he decided humans were not really meant to live in cities like rats in tall, grey boxes with little windows. The only sign of the tumult beyond this village were the daily streams of desperate people looking for food and shelter. About half the time, the community would hand out some food, water, and clothes, and then send the bereft group on their way; the other half, an individual or small group was allowed to stay.

One evening, about a hundred women, men, and teen-agers gathered at the rondoval. When Hendrik and Katherine entered, an ancient man crossed the floor. Hendrik explained Jesse's presence at the gathering, seeking approval for a stranger to listen in.

The old man held up his hand and began talking. Katherine translated for Jesse. The remarks constituted a welcome to all the villagers and a reminder about their common agreement concerning behavior during meetings. People were to stick to the point, not repeat themselves, not repeat what another has already said unless to expound on it further, keep it short, and listen when not speaking. The evening's topic was the relentless onslaught of people streaming in from the cities.

Katherine whispered, "Each adult or older teenager represents one extended family living here. And it's his or her job to bring the concerns and wishes of that family to the discussion."

A tall, handsome young man stood. All eyes focused on him. He spoke with passion, his eyes flashing. "His family's main concern is our food reserves and the growing influence of 'outsiders' on our way of life, teaching the young people ways that are not ours and enticing them to want things we do not cherish here," Kathryn whispered in Jesse's ear.

An elderly woman spoke next with a soft voice but powerful fluency. She expressed concerns about the turning away of families that came seeking shelter and food, reversing a long-held tribal tradition of taking in those in need.

An older gentleman followed. Katherine whispered, "He's reminding us that if we take in more than we can feed, we will not need to worry about our culture—we will all starve to death."

There followed ten more speakers, each adding a new twist to the main themes. Hendrik and the elder took turns asking a series of questions and eliciting a nod of approval or a shake of disapproval. Katherine whispered, "Based on what has been said, they're coming to an agreement that we will now have to begin refusing entrance to almost everyone. The only exception will be elderly parents or grandparents of existing members and small children who have been abandoned and whose only remaining extended family lives here."

Jesse sensed that not everyone would have chosen that path, but that all would commit to it. As they left, the people began to sing in a low, rhythmic, melodious tone. Katherine elaborated in a soft voice "Because there is deep concern about the effect this will have on the culture we have built here over the past fifteen years, they will meet again in one month. That meeting will focus on identifying any early warning signs that the decision we made tonight was not sound. To be truly sound, they have to be environmentally good, socially good, and financially good, and lead us toward the kind of community we are seeking."

At the hut, they sat down for one last cup of tea, since Jesse would be leaving very early the next day. After a long silence Jesse asked, "Hendrik, I have to ask you again to consider returning with me to the U.N. headquarters in New York to help us plan a worldwide strategy for developing communities like Dimbangombe."

The silence that filled the hut for some minutes was broken by the screech of a leopard. Hendrik grinned from ear to ear. "Oh, I doubt it Jesse!" His eyes met Katherine's. "I'm quite old now. And I want to live every day in the bush among these animals and sleep every night with this beautiful woman. I told you. I long ago gave up the illusion that a worldwide strategy for sustainability or restoration could ever work. It takes lots of grassroots effort, one family, one community, or one village at a time."

"But we cannot simply let the entire human race perish! We've got to do something!"

"Friend, I knew it would come to this, even with all the warnings. But the scientists, including me, just confused people. Survival is linked to the elephant, the lion, the spotted owl, the timber wolf, and ultimately something so humble as the soil."

"It can't be too late. I have a wife and children—what about them? What about all of those people now misplaced and roving? How can you not care? How can you not help me do something?"

"Whoa, young man, I cared for years, cared deeply. But no one left me, or you, in charge. I'm no savior. I spent forty years of my life trying to get the U.N., international NGOs and numerous governments—including yours—to listen. I have five, maybe ten years of life left here on this Earth. I'm not going anywhere. There are textbooks and materials based on my work in your libraries. You can do it. You have the ideas. There are hundreds of people around the world trained in those ideas. It is the ideas that are important, not me."

Silence closed in on them. Katherine removed the cups and teapot from the table and retired to the bedroom. Then Hendrik whispered,

"Ask Camilla to help you. She's a contemporary stateswoman. She's been more successful on a bigger scale than anyone else, including me. You said yourself that her country is faring well. Remind her of the starving children in other nations; she has a soft place in her heart for the children. If you have to, if she seems reluctant to help, ask her to do it . . . for me."

~61~
WASHINGTON, D.C.

HE HAD TO LAUGH OUT LOUD, THINKING HOW THE UNITED STATES government and the whole United Nations was helping him, B.J. Cunningham, to achieve his goals. Now it wasn't just the mountains where people were poor and hungry; it was everywhere and everybody. He turned the corner and climbed the slope to the Red River Grill. Across the street, the Heritage Foundation had finally boarded up its building, and the surrounding apartments were vacant.

The Red River's poolroom was still noisy. The red walls seemed to accentuate the noise. He picked a table as far away from the clamor as possible and looked at the hand-written menu. The choice was pitiful: fish or cold cheese enchiladas. He hated fish almost as much as he hated Mexican food. He ordered a draft.

Cliff finally came in and sank into the booth across from him. He'd aged and was perpetually exhausted. He ordered a martini and the fish. His voice was hushed when he spoke. "Lenny says there's a leak in Miriamu's office. Where do you think the woman's head is now? Is she stable? The others seem real concerned about her."

"Don't worry. I have her under control."

"Yeah, but one slip could blow everything. Did you hear about that Abuto guy?"

"Nope, never heard nothin'."

"He worked in Miriamu's office up there in New York City, and he was murdered.

"Didn't I tell you, I have it all under control."

"Well, Miguel says some guy named Collins from the CISC was asking questions yesterday. Did this Collins talk to you?"

"Nope." B.J. shook his head.

Cliff lowered his voice further. "I have a hunch someone alerted Villanueva, and she asked CISC to investigate."

"What kind of stuff was this Collins guy asking?"

"He wanted information from GAO and appropriations."

"So?"

"Miguel told him the information was already available in public records, which is what he has to say."

"So stop worrying."

"Yeah, you're right. I wiped out all my personal records a month ago. We should be okay. How about you?"

"Ditto."

"You haven't been doing any talking, have you?"

"That's a stupid question," B.J. growled.

There was a long pause as Martin finished his martini, then looked into B.J.'s eyes.

"Tell them all transactions are over. We are no longer in business. This is the last time we'll meet."

B.J. laughed again on the way back to his room. He found the papers Abuto had given him and set fire to them, then waited a bit and put the ashes down his toilet. Man, was he glad he was an Essential and still had a flush toilet! Then he got out his automatic rifle and handgun and whistled as he cleaned them.

~62~
NEW YORK CITY

WATCHING HANNAH HOLD NICHOLAS'S DEAD BODY AND SOB LEFT Jesse disoriented; it made her seem so vulnerable. As they left the hospital and walked to her small room in the secure building where Essentials lived, he figured silence was probably best.

As if on autopilot, she put water on the Bunsen burner, got out two packets of instant Nescafé and two cups. She stood at the kitchen counter waiting for the water to boil, staring at the wall.

When the coffee was ready, she made her way to the sofa, handed Jesse his cup, sat down with her legs tucked under her, and wrapped a wool shawl around herself.

"I never told you I have a daughter. Her dad was killed working in Africa. Anna Marie lives with my sister in Berlin. I gave her up when she was three months old. So you see, we are both child deserters."

"No, you never told me that."

"No one here knows. I was so determined to make a difference. It seemed the right thing to leave her there. They have a real family, a little girl a year older than Anna. Do you know why I became a lawyer? Why I went to work for the U.N.? What I hoped I could accomplish?"

She dropped the shawl and began searching through the books on a shelf by the window. She found what she was looking for and held it to her breast. "Did you ever read *Letters to Freya*? No, probably not. I don't imagine a book by a German lawyer would be part of U.S. science curriculum. This book has everything to do with my goals and my life."

She dropped the book in Jesse's lap and went back to the couch, recovered the shawl and wrapped it tightly around her body again. "Helmuth James von Moltke was a count and a lawyer under the

Weimar Republic during Hitler's rise to power and the war. He wrote volumes of letters to his wife, which she hid in beehives and eventually spirited out of the country."

"Von Moltke knew it was all wrong. He was a moral, ethical man, a humanitarian. He tried desperately through his knowledge of international law to put a rein on Hitler's bloody government. He pleaded for them to comply with international law, but to no avail. He failed, was arrested, tried, convicted, and executed just before the war ended.

"The U.N. is not Hitler's war machine but it has needed reform for a long time. There have been financial scandals and worse things such as thousands of women being raped by U.N. troops who were deployed to nations to protect those very women. There have been U.N. troops completely unable to do their jobs, resulting in hundreds of thousands being slaughtered. I have always hoped I could not only be at the leading edge of international law but also, in a small way, help it reform from within."

She heated more water on the Bunsen burner and then poured herself and Jesse a warm cup of coffee while he examined the book. "I was in gymnasium and only sixteen when I read that. His story taught me that every person has to try, even if he fails. Now, I just wish I could feel as hopeful—feel that our actions really will turn out to have been the right thing to do, as he felt those last nights in prison, waiting to be executed."

"You mean he wasn't angry or sad? He didn't give up?"

"No. That's what's so profound about his story. The very last day he wrote Freya that he knew good would eventually triumph and he felt his work had not been in vain."

Jesse moved to the couch and took her hand. "How do you think someone like me ended up here? I understand perfectly. We're quite alike in some ways. I became a scientist for the same reasons. I suppose von Moltke heard daily of those being shipped off to camps and gas chambers, of children as well as soldiers dying. I've spent my life viewing data on the demise of various species, the changes in atmosphere, and the collapse of river systems. These spell the end of any prosperous life for our children just as surely as the gas chambers did. It's just more subtle and happens over a longer period of time."

Jesse dropped her hand and got up, moving around the room. "Hannah, if only you could have been with me in Africa. There is a village there proving it's possible to sustain life on a higher basis. They have lived through all of this change while sustaining decency and well being without the stuff our modern culture thought it couldn't live without. I saw with my own eyes a harmonious community where the land and water, and the children, are thriving."

"So Jesse, how did a species that is supposed to be so intelligent bring itself to the brink of destruction? We had Carlson and Johnson and Freeman and many others warning us to change. Why didn't we?"

"Maybe we aren't particularly smart after all. We problem solve but don't look at the big picture. Hendrik says our brain software is faulty," continued Jesse. "Humans process decisions in a linear pattern, while the natural world, the Earth, our biological support system, functions in wholes."

"So we did this, made all these mistakes on purpose?"

"No, humans don't sit up in the morning and say, 'I think I'll destroy a bunch of habitat today,' or 'I'll go out and put carbon in the atmosphere.' We just make millions of decisions within a linear framework, and the consequences for a world that is holistic are complete biologic meltdown. Hendrik says we're not stupid or evil; it's just faulty programming."

"So, friend Jesse, how are we to reprogram the world population?"

WAVE III

Mankind faces almost no real problems—except the odd earthquake, hurricane, or tornado. He faces only the consequences of the deterioration of Earth's resources, and that is a direct result of his own decisions and the actions that flow from those decisions. It's entirely within his control to reverse the course of human history.

—*Allan Savory*

~63~
TAUSHIMA, JAPAN

LEE'S RAKE HIT SOMETHING HARD. SHE REACHED DOWN TO PICK IT UP then let out a little scream and dropped it. Her hands rushed to her face and her breath came in long gasps. It was a human bone. It looked like a femur, a leg bone—white and gleaming, picked clean of any tissue. Only around the top, where it should have been connected to the hip, was there a little black, wrinkled flesh left. The leg had been severed with a sharp object. It smelled horrible, sweet and musty. Lee tried to wipe the smell from her hands then covered her face with the scarf from her neck.

Her rake hit another hard object. The skull of a small human with matted black hair stared up at her. She raked until she unearthed the bones from two children and one adult. Their flesh had been mostly eaten away and in a few patches it seemed to have been sliced from the bones by a knife or hatchet. Lee dug a shallow grave for the bones. She buried them on the side of the hill a little away from the orchard and left no marker.

Despite feeling an urgent need to do so, Kim hadn't gone to search for Niko when she disappeared. He needed to stay close and protect Lee and the little ones.

"After the planting is done, I will go and get Niko. She is well. I know she is."

"Yes."

"What do you mean, yes?"

"Just yes—I know you must go and find her."

"I know she is well, Lee. I know we will find that she has been with a family somewhere near."

"No, no, surely she is not near.

"Niko is a clever girl; she will have found a safe place. She is probably just waiting for us to come for her or for an opportunity to come home. I know she is safe."

Kim put his arms around his wife and patted her back. He felt her shoulder blades sharp against the palm of his hand. He ran his hand down her back, each vertebra feeling as if it were about to break through the skin. He held her at arm's length, realizing she was so slight that even her soft facial features had sharpened and darkened.

"Lee, you must stop giving your food to the little ones. I cannot live without you; you must be strong. This year will be a wonderful one for our gardens. Even if the stores do not open again, we will eat. It is not necessary for you to starve yourself."

"Yes, I must try to eat more." She turned away from him and went back to her sewing. Each day she told herself that she could eat again. But each day she ate and lost the precious food outside on the ground. She had been careful to hide her suspicion about Niko's fate as she sat at the table with Kim and the children. Kim shouldn't have to worry about whether she ate or not. But then each day in the food on the table, she saw the little skull with matted black hair.

~64~
PARKVILLE, PENNSYLVANIA

OLD CALEB FOUND THE BOY IN THE BARN WHEN HE WENT TO SLOP the hogs. He thought the child was dead, but while carrying him into the house, he realized there was warmth and faint breathing coming from the little fellow.

"He be one of those city folk, Rebecca. Keep him warm and when he wakes, we shall feed him."

"We dare not keep him."

"He be a child—we shall keep him so long as needed." Caleb found Samuel's book bag under the straw a few days later. He didn't look inside, but took it to Samuel and watched the tears well up in the boy's eyes as he pulled out the worn bear and the small black Bible. Later, Caleb read the inscription on the inside cover of the Bible. It helped to be able to call him by his given name, but it didn't reveal anything about the lady who wrote the inscription, who she was or where she might be.

The boy was a hard worker. By the second week, he followed Caleb around to milk the cows and feed the pigs, and he gathered the eggs for Rebecca. Caleb taught him how to harness the mules and drive them around so he could help with the plowing. He ate, he slept, he worked, he responded to them, but he didn't talk. Samuel was mute.

"Caleb, how can we care for a mute? He must be someone's son. How can we find out where he belongs?"

"We cannot right now. God put him into our hands to bless us. God works in mysterious ways. We must care for him like our own. There be others who have come from the city; they say many are starving. The Elders have said it would be wrong to turn him away."

Samuel heard them talking about him. He had only vague memories of the moment Caleb found him in the barn. It was all a blur, and at the time, he wasn't sure if he had died and gone to another world or was still in the old one. If his father was right, he should be burning in hell. But he had been cold, not hot, and so hungry. He had walked and walked. He hadn't had anything to eat for days, and he had been sure the straw bed he found in the barn was a last place to lie down in this world.

Samuel tried to tell them about Morris so they'd know they were doing the best thing and how grateful he was, but he couldn't. He couldn't even tell them about his visit to see the president and the nice man who gave him the cheese sandwich. He couldn't tell them about all the dead bodies on the road. No words came out. Most of all he wondered at what they said about God. He knew their God must not be the one Morris said hated so much. But then he knew the other God was out there somewhere because he had seen all of the hungry people. After all, Morris knew God better than anyone. A kid couldn't argue with God's person on Earth.

Every time he thought he would just open his mouth and let the words pour out like they always had before, they didn't. His throat closed up and his head got all messed up. The faces of dead people surrounded him, pressing in. And he couldn't talk. He knew they were hell-deserving sinners and God had smitten them.

~65~
DEERING, IOWA

THEY DUG ALL DAY TO BURY MATTHEW. KAREN SAID A LITTLE PRAYER and Elsie put that year's *Farmers' Almanac* carefully beside the body of her husband. Then she ran and got her copy of *A Gift From the Sea*, a book she had found comfort in during their often-contentious marriage. Pressed inside the pages was the white gardenia she had worn on her lapel when they stood before the justice of the peace in Mayfield that warm June night. It was yellowed with age, but still had the faint smell of gardenia mixed with the aging paper.

"Why did you do that?"

"Don't need that book now, there's no more marriage."

Karen held her a long time before she and the boys slowly walked back to the house.

"But he's not there, is he, Mom? He's not really there in the ground is he? Doesn't grandma know that?"

"No, Ethan, he's not there. But that grave is just . . . is just a symbol. It is the last hold your grandma has on the life she has known.

Several times since Matthew's murder, Karen heard the Land Rover in the middle of the night, but it always sped away before she could get outside. In the morning, they would find fewer chickens or there'd be a small pig missing.

One morning, the county sheriff appeared on their doorstep. "Elsie, 'tain't much I can do in these times. I got me no deputies and no gasoline. Me and Lilly think we'll mosey on down toward Texas way.

"Granville, you're a coward! People here need you. You can't just go and let these hooligans take the place! Where's your backbone? What's to become of them that can't move?"

Four days later, two neighboring farms were set on fire in the middle of the night. One farmhouse had been vacant since April. In the other, the Smiths, a family of four, died in the flames. By the time Elsie and Karen hitched the horses and got there, all the animals had been hauled off. Karen thought the tire tracks were the Rover's, but couldn't be sure.

That night, Karen found Matthew's old Colliers Atlas and began contemplating leaving. She spread it out under a candle on the round oak table and combed through the pages. She remembered the discussions with Jesse about sustainability. Water and a long growing season were important. It was easy to decide where they might grow food, but now no place seemed safe.

Curled up on the couch, she remembered conversations she had with Kim and Jesse. She had encouraged them to read classics. They considered Hemmingway and Fitzgerald fluff but tolerated *The Grapes of Wrath*. Then Pearl Buck hit a nerve. Both identified with Wang Lung in *The Good Earth*. When greed stepped in and Wang Lung stopped making the land a priority, his life fell apart. Now, Karen saw her own world as a kaleidoscope of the sorrow of ancient China.

For the hundredth time, Karen ruminated about her marriage. Her friends in the English department at college had laughed when she began dating Jesse. He was that quirky guy with a bushy beard who didn't own any pants that weren't ripstop khakis, and laid down in the road to keep people from cutting down trees. It took her only a few dates to realize that behind that beard was an incredibly discerning mind, and under the pants and work shirt were muscles. But mostly, she had fallen for his honest desire to make a difference in a world he felt was headed in all the wrong directions.

That night, Elsie admitted, "Fear's got aholt a me at night; I fear someone will set us on fire."

"Elsie, we have to go south. I don't think Texas is as good a place to aim for as a river valley in Colorado or New Mexico. Fewer people, maybe secure water."

"All right, let's pack up and get movin'."

Deciding what to pack in the limited space of the old wagon took much thought. Warm clothing, blankets, food, and seeds were the most important. The old plow and the salted meats had to be included along with the canned and dried fruits and vegetables. Books were a luxury.

* * *

The day they left, Elsie and the boys carried the old trunk to the cold cellar. Elsie carefully folded the good quilts and on top she laid the fragile photo albums she had inherited from her grandmother. She took time to show Ethan and Troy her accumulation of Jesse's school pictures and his old report cards.

"What's deportment, Grandma?

"That's how you act around other people. I'm afraid your father got frustrated and angry at teachers."

"He got a D in deportment?" The boys hooted and giggled.

"Look here: When he learned to focus on science, he got all A's. If someone else comes to live here whilst we are gone, they will respect these treasures. If those men who are traipsing around burning down houses come, well, the cold cellar will be the safest place. So, when we come back, these things will be here."

Ever since Matthew's death, her usual organized nature had begun to fissure. Nothing made sense. She had never realized how much she really depended on him. Through the years, she had learned not to question his decisions even though her innate female instincts told her he was often wrong. Why had he befriended that horrible man? Why hadn't he taken Karen's advice and sent him packing?

She hid her copy of Emily Dickinson's poetry in her personal knapsack along with her reading glasses and a bundle of letters tied up with a ribbon. She was the last to climb into the wagon. Taking a deep breath, she determined not to look back.

The black mare and the roan filly jogged along unbalanced in the harness. After half an hour of jolting, it seemed normal. That didn't keep Troy from complaining.

"Ah, Mom, it's too rough back here. We're getting all tossed around. We keep hitting the side of the wagon."

"Take a blanket and pad the side."

"Be quiet Troy—don't you know it's hard enough for Mom without your constant whining?" Ethan had been such a help, and Karen was so grateful. He sensed whenever she was really stressed and needed him to support her decisions. He had been included in the plans to leave, and that confidence caused him to leap into a new maturity. That leap was unfortunate for someone still so young, but she couldn't help being proud of him.

~66~
WASHINGTON, D.C.

MICHAEL COLLINS TOLD SECURITY AT THE MOTEL NOT TO EXPECT HIM. "I'm going to be working late."

"Exactly when should we expect you, sir?"

"I'm not sure. I may pull an all-nighter. Just don't worry about me."

With the brutal killing of Thomas Abuto fresh on his mind, he was determined to get to the bottom of these murders. He'd had his doubts about Jesse Forester from the beginning. The scientist had seemed so nervous when they talked. Jesse's information that Paddy Freeman had been murdered unsettled him the most. After all, he'd been named for one of the great Irish heroes of independence. Still, he was careful not to let the U.N. scientist think he had any personal interest in the investigation.

He decided to follow up on a hunch. The electronic system was still up, operating on generators, and capable of sorting through random emails. Collins felt the old excitement of his earlier career when he was tasked with uncovering data no one else saw and handing it over to the investigators so they could find and bring to justice a wide variety of criminals. What had been sent in the past should still be available in the CISC's archives. He found it particularly easy to access U.S. military and classified personnel records. There had to be an electronic trail.

His career had begun as an electronics specialist. After five years in the think tank at Microsoft, he had signed on with the National Security Agency, intercepting emails, faxes, and mobile phone calls from individuals living around the world and in the U.S. who had been identified as possibly belonging to terrorist cells.

Taking the job at the new Center for International Security and Cooperation was a bad move, but at least he hadn't been sent overseas.

Although he spoke Arabic and Farsi, he had no desire to set up a lemonade stand in Riyadh and spy on the Saudis. He knew that the many terrorist cells had to be infiltrated, but he didn't want to be the one to do it. The nuts and bolts of technology he loved. Without a computer screen in front of him, he felt a little lost.

He grabbed the last cup of hot coffee from the makeshift counter in the lobby and wrapped his extra coat around his body. The screen showed no emails sent to or from Paddy Freeman except those to Forester at the U.N. If Paddy had been in touch with someone in Washington, it must have been a private individual on a personal computer. He looked for anything suspicious coming to or from Abuto at the U.N. Nothing there.

Next he began an exhaustive search of the data sources that fed the U.N. and the U.S. concerning the atmosphere. There were 2,562 exchanges, during the period in question, between Forester's office at the U.N. and environmental stations around the world. None had been deleted and they all substantiated a decrease in oxygen. Nothing unusual there. Forester didn't seem to be in contact with anyone suspicious.

Collins pulled the coat tighter around his body. The temperature must have been below fifty in the building. Realizing he would have to dig deeper, he began to explore *all* messages sent to and from those environmental stations. There were 4,793 if he included the personal stuff as well as those that had been sent to government or military instillations. At midnight Collins made himself a tepid cup of instant coffee with the Bunsen burner in the lobby and sat down for more long hours at the computer.

It was 4:10 a.m. when the screen caught something that looked out of the ordinary. It was a personal message sent from the environmental station in Adak, Alaska, to locations in D.C. and Saudi Arabia. One of the recipients in D.C. set off an alarm in his head that became more insistent when Collins realized he was related to the recipient in Saudi Arabia. "Bingo," he said under his breath. The sender's name was Teddy. Reading the message he smiled, knowing his long night's work had just paid off.

~67~
NEW YORK CITY

"JESSE, YOU'RE MAKING IT ALL TOO COMPLICATED. IF I DON'T UNderstand it, how can we expect the average person to know what to do?"

"Hannah, if we don't teach people how to consider the consequences of their decisions on the whole environment around them, they are doomed to repeat the same mistakes. It's not enough to just say 'go out and grow food or put in solar panels or dig a well.' We have to teach them how to consider the impact on the rest of the living world."

"Jesse, we know that they will starve if they don't just grow food, and they know that."

"They should know that by now, but there will continue to be many more decisions than that. What part of each community's culture will be kept? What part will wild animals play in the future of the world? Does the decision to grow a particular plant increase or deplete the soil nutrients for next year? Do we stay here or move to a better climate? That's a biggie! Once they have some food, do they share it, and with whom?"

"People must always help each other! Always! Even in the worst of situations, humans rise up and help," insisted Hannah.

"Not necessarily. Some people have continued to rob and maim and kill. You have to make a decision about your family or the one next door. Who would you save? How about me? Would you let me starve while saving a child you didn't even know?"

That silenced her. She removed the comb from her hair and caught the loose strands on her neck and her eyes became wet. "Oh, Jesse, you are so unfair!" She turned away from him.

He grabbed her hand, turning her around. "Hannah, to figure out how to rebuild some basic society we have to look at things logically, not emotionally. We have to get information out to the communities that are functioning that will help them fundamentally change the way we've always done things."

"Jesse, most of us had no idea we were making mistakes."

It suddenly occurred to Hannah that Jesse never asked about her own mistakes about her likes or dislikes. He asked nothing at all about her personal life. But then, she never offered information either. He probably thought of her as cold and incapable of real affection. It bothered her that Jesse seemed to be a combination of Karl and her late husband.

Remembering Karl, she felt anger rise up. He was clearly a big mistake. During law school, she had let down her guard and fallen head over heels in love with him. In her young eyes, he was handsome beyond belief and so intelligent. They met working on a difficult case concerning the economic and political ramifications of Turkish workers gaining German citizenship. They spent hours putting together the brief defending the workers, and their presentation brought acclaim from the whole law school faculty. They became engaged a few months before graduation, and he moved into Hannah's flat.

One rainy afternoon, Hannah returned early from a canceled appointment to find her fiance in bed with another law student. She completely lost her cool. Later, she couldn't believe her fury. She threw his suitcase at him and gave him thirty minutes to get out of her apartment and her life. She never regretted her action, just the overwhelming anger and betrayal she had allowed herself to feel for too many years after the event.

Jesse dropped her hand and walked to the window to gaze over the empty river. No boats, no barges, nothing to ripple the water. Still-life reflections of the buildings etched in the calm water. The river, like the city, had become a quiet mausoleum, a burial place. Then, he saw a small boat. A man and his son were fishing. Jesse's eyes begin to water and he was afraid to turn around.

Finally, she cleared her throat, "I am just afraid you are making it much too complicated. If we expect anyone to follow the mandates, they must be simple."

"Okay, let's decide on just a few basic things. I know, if a small village in Africa can learn how to make wise decisions, surely other communities can."

~68~
MIAMI

THE LITTLE GIRL SIFTED SAND THROUGH A SIEVE AND INTO HER BUCKET, then poured it out. She built hills and valleys for her dolls to walk through and ran cars around them on make-believe roads. Every now and then she repeated a limerick Pricilla had taught her. "Hickory dickory dock, the mouse ran up the clock," or she chanted "and when she was good, she was very, very good, and when she was bad, she was horrid."

She finished a sand castle with a balcony on both sides and a moat. Then she saw the pack of dogs. There was Felicia, a full-sized white poodle who could have been mistaken for a sheep. The lady she'd belonged to lived in a high rise in Fort Lauderdale, and had left her in a park when she could no longer feed Felicia. Then there were two Labrador retrievers. Both had identification tags: One said Princess McClure; the other said Buster McClure. Their family had fled north and left the labs in the back yard. Eventually, starvation drove them to jump the fence.

There were four mutts. Missy with the pink collar had been adopted by a large Cuban neighborhood that no longer existed. The two large curs and the husky had no collars. They came from the suburbs and had been roaming, eating out of garbage cans even before Wave II went into effect.

The Great Dane wore a black collar with silver letters that read 'Saturn.' Because of his size, he should have been the leader, but when he challenged the husky mix, he lost one ear and gained a bloody scratch down his right side. From then on, he was happy just to follow the others. They were all perpetually on the brink of starvation.

When they saw the child, they stopped and momentarily retreated. They hadn't seen a human in weeks. She held out her hand, and after some hesitation they surrounded her.

Lucy's mom, Priscilla, sat about fifty feet back from the edge of the tide typing on an old Smith Corona scrounged from a second hand store. Camping out with her daughter in the deserted cottage had been ideal for her work as a journalist. Someday the printed word would be valuable again, and her documentation of Operation World Salvation would sell. The struggle for food, the reappearance of farmers' and open markets, the exodus from the high rise apartments and condos, the closing down of all the things that made southern Florida a mecca for the rich and famous. She'd hammered out pages of material that was stacked around her.

Priscilla got up to turn the salted white fish on the drying rack and glanced out toward the sea. She did a double take and froze at the scene in the sand. Grabbing a broom from next to the kitchen door she slowly walked across the scorching sand. She had forgotten to put on her sandals but her feet didn't even register the heat. The dogs eyed her suspiciously, and the larger ones began to growl and bare their teeth.

"Lucy, honey, don't move. Momma is coming to get you."

"Look at all the dogs that came to play with me. Do I have to go in, Momma? Can't I stay and play?"

"I see them. You must come in for a little while; nice doggies, nice doggies." Pricilla continued to move slowly. Entering the circle of dogs, she carefully reached down for Lucy and scooped her up under one arm and backed slowly away. The pack followed her toward the cottage. Just when she thought she might make it inside, the husky lunged at them. Lucy screamed. Pricilla struck him on the head with the broom handle and then lowered it, allowing him to grab it in his teeth. He began shaking it violently. The sand made it hard for him to gain traction and he slid backwards, but wouldn't let go of the broom. Pricilla fell forward, barely able to keep her balance. For just a moment, time stood still for the ravenous dog and the terrified woman.

Then the other dogs crept forward snarling through clenched teeth. Lucy screamed again and buried her head in her mother's shoulder. Pricilla kept moving backward slowly, shaking and twisting the broom handle. She crept past the patio table with its typewriter and her precious writings. Five feet from the kitchen door she jerked the broom handle from the husky and jammed it hard into his mouth, then turned and ran, slamming the door behind her. Leaning back against it, gulping in air, she clutched Lucy to her breast.

"Momma, Momma you're hurting me. Momma, let go of me!"

The dog pack stayed for some time. They grabbed the broom and fought over it. The husky chewed on it, while the others turned over the table, crashing the typewriter to the ground. They fought over the manila folders, leaving them and Priscilla's papers a chewed, soggy mess.

~69~
WASHINGTON, D.C.

Miguel was the only legislative aide left in Senator Martin's office. Computers had been set up in the lobby so the senators had access to information coming over the emergency wires from around the world. As his world collapsed around him, Miguel tried to hold on to some semblance of normal. His stomach was churning from the thoughts in his head. Sitting at his desk, he tried to come to terms with his fears.

The senator's attitude bothered him most, specifically his indifference to what was happening. Miguel had admired the man he worked for but the senator had become gruff and uncommunicative. That left B.J. Cunningham in charge. It was a mystery to Miguel why the senator had chosen B.J. as his chief of staff. But then it did seem everyone but him loved B.J. Miguel could see beyond the handsome face and flashing white teeth, and didn't like what he saw. He often caught a look of pure evil on the man's face, and wished B.J. had fled with the others.

People in New Mexico were hanging on desperately or relocating to a place that looked more promising. Miguel's family in Gila had decided to stay put on their land. When he left for the nation's capital, he had felt little pride in their two hundred acres of green chilies, corn, and beans. He had been almost ashamed of his father, who had never been out of New Mexico. He was even more dismayed that his sisters and brother didn't even care to get college degrees but instead seemed satisfied to just stay there. Now he was all too aware that the stupid poor farm might be the salvation of his whole family.

Months earlier his mother wrote, "Today I bought two ewes and a great big ram named Bubba. Last week we got two pigs from the

Garcias, and my flock of chickens is multiplying. Don't worry about us; we will be eating good." He felt a certain amount of pride that they were so independent. He knew his dad and brother still had their hunting rifles, and certainly knew how to use them. He hoped they'd never be needed for anything other than fresh elk or deer.

No one came into the reception area, so he spent his time scanning the information that had come over the wire. While sipping a warm Coke, he ran across email traffic from the individuals at the U.N. in charge of the creation of Wave I and Wave II. Slamming the empty bottle down on the desk, he had an idea. He copied down the names and email addresses and raced back to his own cubby and his computer screen. Miguel once more typed in the senator's code for the private account he had accessed earlier. It was gone. It had been wiped out. The account information he'd seen earlier on a company called SOLYN something and the huge payments it was taking in had disappeared. He began to search frantically through his own files to see if he had kept those emails and the attached lists anywhere.

~70~
NEW YORK CITY

"MR. FORESTER, PLEASE SIT DOWN. I'M HOPING YOU MIGHT SOLVE a mystery for me."

The Ethiopian ambassador hesitated. "When my assistant Haile was murdered last year, the police called it a robbery. I have been, shall we say, doubtful—indeed suspicious—concerning his death. Just before he died, Haile was convinced there was some sort of special operation unfolding and that it was essential the poorer countries make a bid to be involved." The U.N. ambassador walked back to his desk, and shuffled through several drawers.

Jesse drummed his fingers on the arm of the chair, impatient to catch his Air Force plane to Argentina.

Finally, the ambassador found what he was looking for.

"Haile evidently had a meeting with Ms. Miriamu concerning this issue. He was increasingly passionate about our country and its plight. I told him that no such operation existed. Later, I assumed that it was Operation World Salvation but really Haile's rantings began prior to that. I want you to assure me that Miriamu, you and others are involved in nothing more than saving the planet. Perhaps, Haile just stumbled on the plan earlier than its inception. However . . . ."

"Ambassador, please get to the point. What has this got to do with me?"

The ambassador sat down behind his massive mahogany desk. "There's the autopsy. It indicated that he had been beaten about the shoulders and stomach and stabbed."

"That's not unusual."

"It might not be, except that some of the wounds were old, inflicted prior to the robbery. I have been remembering that after he confronted Miriamu and returned from a trip to your capital his movements seemed painful. He refused to tell me what had happened."

Jesse leaned forward in his seat, suddenly stirred from his apathy. "When did this happen?"

"The murder was in early April of last year. However, I noted his distress weeks earlier. I also remember his anger, his vehemence that we should demand to know the truth about this plan of Ms. Miriamu and its ultimate effect on Africa. I am sure that was late February."

"Ambassador what in the world gave Haile the idea there was some plan afoot? He couldn't possibly have had that information before April."

"The first thing that made him suspicious came in this memo. Haile received it by mistake."

"What memo?"

"I have it here along with some notes he made about his meeting with Miriamu. Please, Mr. Forester, I'll be very grateful if you can assure me that Haile's death was purely due to a robbery. Although Haile was of no real note in this country, he was the first-born of a highly ranked general in Ethiopia, someone who is also a long-time friend and colleague. My country, as yours, struggles with the compliance. That is enough to handle right now."

He handed Jesse the memo from someone in the Hart Office Building, Washington, D.C. It was a cryptic note:

> **M, bait taken; a billion minnows in the pot; $$ fishing good for dark, push harder, all fish and sharks will tumble, more later, B.**

Attached to it was a list of dates and names, with amounts of money alongside each.

Jesse recognized only one name. The dates were from January through December the year previous to Operation World Salvation. Jesse read the note three times. He shook his head and frowned.

"Ambassador, why are you bringing this to my attention now?"

"Yesterday, I reviewed the autopsy and police report again in much detail. Haile evidently came home and went into the kitchen and was stabbed with a knife. The first stab wounds were in his back followed by many in the front—many more stabs than necessary to kill him and complete a robbery. A robber would have no reason to kill Haile. I'm going home to my country; I am needed there. I leave uncovering the truth about this in your hands."

Later, Jesse confronted Miriamu with the cryptic email and Haile's notes. She examined them, denying that she was the M to whom the email was sent and that she had any idea what it alluded to.

"Jesse, there are, and have been, many 'M's at the U.N. Why bring this to me?" Miriamu countered as she sat down in the receptionist's chair.

"Miriamu, the ambassador believes Haile's death was not a robbery but a brutal murder. Thomas Abuto was killed in much the same way. Both of these killings lead back to you," he said as he dropped onto her entryway couch in sheer exasperation.

"Me?" she said as she exploded out of the chair. "Are you accusing me of murder? I'm not the one the ambassador contacted. He contacted you. Those murders lead to you as much as or more than to me." She paced back and forth between Jesse and her desk. "Damn Haile. That young man was a problem here from the very beginning—a troublemaker. Anyone in his delegation can tell you. Always questioning everything I did."

"What else did he question, Miriamu?"

"That's none of your business. But I can tell you I don't have time to be responsible for his anger and fears, or for Mr. Abuto's deception."

"But why were they murdered?" Jesse growled, making a gesture like a blow in the air.

"How should I know? I refuse to be responsible for their stupidity. Maybe they were just in the wrong place at the wrong time. Or they offended the wrong people. I don't know. You and I both have trusted that the copies Abuto was selling were forgeries. What more proof do you need?" She wadded the paper he had handed her and tossed it into the wastebasket. Then she rearranged her bright blue wrap and dismissed him with a wave of her hand.

Jesse left quietly. But he had a feeling she was reaching a panic point, and he'd never discerned any fear in Miriamu before.

~71~
BUENOS AIRES

JESSE THREW WATER ON HIS FACE AND SHAVED. HE WAS MEETING Camilla in the lobby. His recent arguments with Hannah, the meeting with the Ethiopian ambassador, and his confrontation with Miriamu had created a low-level migraine that flew from D.C. to the capital of Argentina with him.

But even the little glimpse of the country he'd gotten in the ride from the airport to his hotel had brought him new energy to push on.

The streets of the city were bustling. To be sure, the cars, buses, and trucks had been replaced by wagons, horses, and bikes. But unlike D.C. and New York, where only the indigent remained, eking out an existence, the largest city in Argentina was thriving.

Shops were open selling clothing, handcrafts, leather goods, and all manner of hand-powered equipment. There were open-air markets with fresh fruits and vegetables. Carcasses of lamb, beef, and poultry hung in front of butcher shops. Even more astonishing, the pedicab driver accepted money for the ride. In Argentina, the feel of normality was all too evident.

The scene in the hotel bar reminded Jesse of the last scenes of *Butch Cassidy and the Sundance Kid.* A wizened old man plucked classical pieces on a guitar. The overhead fans were still, so it was hot. Most of the occupants—some in work clothes others in suits and ties—seemed to have purpose and were grabbing a bite before siesta.

He was not in the least surprised when the beautiful brunette coming toward him turned out to be Camilla, the only one who looked cool and very comfortable. Her bronze complexion was clearly darkened by hours spent in the sun. When she sat across from him, he realized he had never seen such deep green eyes.

Jesse ordered a beer, she a glass of wine. "Mr. Forester, why are you here? Is there not enough to do in the United States? What we hear from there is not encouraging. People rioting, people starving, people roaming from place to place, it is a mess, no?"

Jesse tried not to show his anger. "It's been difficult. From what I've seen so far here, your country is certainly doing better. But then, you do not have nearly as many large cities as we do, 15 million in Los Angeles alone, not to mention New York City, Boston, and Chicago. When we told them to get out of the cities and find food, many panicked, yes. But others are finding their way. The reports probably don't give out that information."

"We also have large cities. We, however, were prepared. You were not. I admit we were still more of an agrarian country, we depended less on imports, but we were much smarter in deciding years ago to become independent of other countries. The fewer trucks and ships necessary to supply your people, the easier it becomes to do without fossil fuel, no?"

"If I may be so bold, how did a woman get the position of agricultural minister in a South American country?"

"My husband had the land. I had the ideas and the desire. Actually, I had picked Hendrik Johnson's brains enough to know the pitfalls of old land policies and how to succeed where others had failed."

"And your husband—it's all right with him?"

She shrugged, lowering the silky white shawl from her shoulders. "Enrique . . . he is very busy being a government solicitor. He cares little for the land. That is sad but true, and that very sad fact became my golden opportunity. I find America's current condition so ironic."

"How so?"

"Hendrik spent time in the U.S., you know. Beyond the dependence on oil, he couldn't understand the bureaucracy. He traveled across your country and was just amazed. His very words were 'this is the most diverse, fertile country in the world—able to grow anything. Yet the government is subsidizing food.' He was incredulous. He considered it the ultimate of lunacy."

"Yes, the government interference in agriculture was stifling. But it wasn't the only problem: being so dependent on imports, farm practices that depleted our aquifers, paving and destroying farm land."

"Will the people of the United States have enough food to get through this winter?"

"Not all of them."

"And what will they do?"

"They will starve, Camilla."

"Yes, they will starve. And you will feel more and more responsible. Is that not so?"

Jesse cringed at her directness. She cut right to the painful chase.

"I was in Zimbabwe with Hendrik only a month or so ago. I spent a week with him and his wife Katherine. He sends his regards." He stopped to see how this turn in the conversation hit her.

Her face softened and broke into a smile. "And how is the old gentleman, as obnoxious as ever? Did he enchant you with his theories and the stories of his incredible life? Ah! How I have missed him."

Jesse sipped his beer and waited as she stared off into space, focusing on a scene, a place he could not share. Then she was back staring at him with those piercing green eyes.

"So, now you are here. He sent you, did he not?"

"Well, I guess you could say that. He refused to leave Zimbabwe and help me himself."

"Why?"

"He said, and these are his words, 'I am old and I want to spend the few years I have left here in Africa with the land and the animals.' " Jesse purposely left out the part about sleeping with Katherine, not wanting to offend the beautiful woman across the table.

"And he does not want to leave his Katherine? No? Is that not a part of the reason he refuses to come to the U.S. or Argentina or anywhere else? She is his love now.

"So, he wishes me to help you. To show you what is working here in my country and help you to make it happen in the rest of the world?"

"Camilla, he asked that you do it—*for him*."

"The old fox—for him, hmph. Do it for him?"

~72~
NEW YORK CITY

REPORTS COMING IN FROM AROUND THE U.S. AS OPERATION WORLD Salvation continued left Hannah on an emotional roller coaster. She tried to concentrate on the good things.

Operation World Salvation—U.S. Conditions

• Coming soon, to land near you, a farm! There's a farm in your future! Georgians are working hard to make that come true. New peach and pecan trees have been interspersed with rows of corn, beans, squash, and peanuts. Cotton has been interspersed with melons. The only thing that could interfere with our success is a drought.

• Across the Midwest, some communities have finally realized that food will no longer be shipped from Mexico and California. Small cold cellars have been dug into the ground to save whatever fruits and vegetables they can for as long as possible.

• Around the country, large consolidated districts have dissolved and each community has set up small schools that are not dependent on buses or cars. Parents and teachers are alternating between instruction in the homes and classrooms and working the fields. Groups have formed to carry out the basic functions, such as trash pickup. Debris and garbage on the streets and fields has almost disappeared. The roaches have not.

• Wind turbines in New Mexico and Texas are increasingly producing energy.

• Train tracks across the nation are being refurbished in anticipation of new solar-powered engines arriving sometime soon.

• Riots broke out in Detroit and Chicago this week. The program to retrain truckers to drive horse-drawn wagons went on uninterrupted.

Hannah marked a few items to share with Jesse when he returned from Argentina so that together they could consider the deployment of additional U.N. troops to areas where the violence was most desperate. Munching on a squash sandwich, she opened an envelope that had been dropped off earlier.

The address on top read: HANNAH KOENIG, LEGAL DEPARTMENT UNITED NATIONS, but there was no return name on the document or the envelope. She skimmed five pages of purchases made in the solar, wind, and nuclear market. Hannah shoved the pages aside. Why would anyone feel the necessity to send her this information about purchases of energy equipment?

After lunch she read through reports she had received on the conditions in Western Europe:

• The London winter had been cold and wet and, without heating oil to burn, many had died. Now there were floods like the ones in 2000 and 2003. Dublin finally got its act together and citizens received excess food from warehouses. People there were taking Paddy Freeman's writings seriously and growing a large variety of crops and raising a lot of sheep and some cattle.

• Austria was depending on French nuclear trains for transporting food.

• Eastern European countries faced insurmountable problems. Romania never recovered completely from the communist years. Older citizens who lived with such deprivation through Ceausescu were more able to cope than the youth. Everywhere life depended upon this year's growing season, the abundance of rain, and its distribution. Transport of food was highly unlikely anywhere. The few agencies still working at all in Eastern Europe fear thousands, perhaps millions, will starve next winter.

• Can the U.N. offer some support to Eastern Europe and the Middle East? The Kurds will be decimated again and probably beaten if a U.N. force does not step in or food is not forthcoming from outside; even that may not prevent wholesale famine.

The reports highlighted a pattern she was beginning to see often. Nations like Romania, where the systems for food and shelter had remained more primitive, were faring okay. Nations like Hungary, which had quickly mechanized and become dependent on fossil fuels after the collapse of the Soviet Union, were struggling to convert and keep people fed.

Hannah shook her head and gathered all of the reports into a pile and stared at them. She had no idea how she and Jesse would figure out where to deploy troops. The United Nations forces were already spread too thin. All peacekeeping and problem-solving units were already deployed, and sending more people—even if they were control units—into an area where others were already starving didn't make any sense. Images of the massacre of Rwandans while U.N. troops sat by flashed across her mind and her hands grew cold with sweat.

She sat back in her chair, allowing some time to just think. She missed Jesse terribly. In spite of their fights and arguments, they had come to depend upon each other for companionship. When he was down she was up. They had a good relationship, a good friendship, and she didn't regret the few times she had let him hold her perhaps a bit too close.

Like Tam—the husband she had loved so briefly and still cherished in her heart—he was a good man. They had been working for the International Criminal Tribunal in The Hague, part of a team of four young lawyers investigating genocide around the world. The work took them to danger spots in Central America, Africa, Asia, and the Balkans.

Tam was a young Vietnamese whose family had fled to the United States in the '70s. The youngest of five children, he had graduated with honors from Harvard Law School and done pro bono work before he joined the tribunal team. There was a whirlwind romance of hard work in places most people never heard about. There was little time to be alone and less time to consider the consequences of their relationship. Tam was the first person whose passion for humanitarian justice matched hers. He never backed off when the confrontation meant revealing the truth about military despots, political tyrants, or mere low-life army thugs.

Six months after their simple civil marriage in Brussels, he was sent to the Sudan. A few weeks later, his body was found in his tent mutilated by an ax. When she was able to think clearly about his death without melting down, Hannah was sure he was getting close to those truly responsible for the bloodletting. He had probably let his anger replace logical reasoning concerning his own safety. What was he thinking when he took his last breath? Wasn't that what this was all about, taking the last breath?

Since then, she had substituted her passion and dedication to work for any personal or emotional relationship. But then there was the little girl. She had avoided thinking about Anna Mai. What kind of a mother was she to give up the child so easily? Had that been justified? If it became necessary, what kind of a mother would she make for the little girl? She knew so little about being a mother. Once more, she closed that door.

"Enough of this. Back to work," she mumbled, turning to the papers still on her desk. Her eyes fell again on the anonymous memo and list from Washington. For the first time, the dates of the purchases jumped out at her.

~73~
PALM SPRINGS, CALIFORNIA

IT HAD ALL STARTED THREE YEARS EARLIER, SITTING AROUND A POOL in Palm Springs sharing a six-pack of Coors. The four of them—Manuel Marquez, Senator Cleveland, his brother Pete, and Teddy—had been friends since playing soccer and tennis at college. After college, once a year, they left families and jobs to rendezvous someplace interesting where they could sweat it out on the tennis court or a golf course, joke about their growing waistlines, and just enjoy each other's company. But their conversation that March had gotten very intense.

Marquez started it with, "Pete, my man, when are you going to come back to the States and get a real job? Haven't you cheated the U.S. taxpayer long enough?"

"If you think living in that hell hole called "The Kingdom" is easy, you can have the job."

Teddy asked, "Should we believe the adverts that say BP is really going to help the world get anywhere near having a sustainable fuel source?"

"Hell, no, don't make me laugh. Those bastards only care about the next great oil reserve."

"You should read *The Prize,* by Yergin. It's a veritable tome, but long hours in the frozen north made it pretty good reading. He's convinced we could be driving cars powered without gasoline, but the oil companies keep all those new ideas shelved."

Senator Cleveland interjected, "Yeah, when you're in the Senate you see it happening right in front of your eyes. You don't need a book to explain how ideas are squelched by Exxon, Mobile, Chevron, British Petroleum. Big daddy oil is determined to remain king."

"But all the scary predictions about warming and the environment hasn't come about. Has it?" Teddy asked. "We're not showing a lot of change up north where I am. I have a theory that the so-called extreme climate events were actually natural fluctuations in weather, exacerbated by the Earth's collapsing ecosystems. In many areas of the world, the soil simply cannot hold the rain any more, *voilà*, increased frequency and severity of droughts, fire and floods."

"But Teddy, don't you think stuff is happening but just not showing up on the charts?" Peter took a sip of his beer and added, "And what would happen if those figures did show carbon rising and oxygen dipping? Would that jolt the world into a change for the better?"

"And who would profit if we could not use fossil fuel?" Manuel asked.

"Those who invested in renewable energy," replied Peter, as he crushed his beer can and tossed it into the cooler. "Let's make it happen."

"What?" Manuel was incredulous. "It won't work."

"Why not, Manuel? I bet Teddy here could hack into the systems that track atmospheric data for the U.N. and various governments and change the numbers. You can be like one of those rogue hackers who use their skills to do things that are illegal but that they think should be done anyway. "

"That's crazy," said Manuel. I know eventually we will have to stop using stuff that mucks up the atmosphere, but we can't make it happen. It'll come, but I wouldn't want to be part of trying to make it happen. That could be dangerous."

They spent the next three days hatching details. Teddy would use his computer skills to get into carbon/oxygen data gathering systems around the globe. He'd let the others know if he succeeded. Meanwhile, the senator would look for others on the hill to get the government to invest in renewable energy technologies. He had one very powerful and useful friend and colleague, Senator Cliff Martin, who was the chairman of the Joint Congressional Committee on Climate Change.

The four friends pooled $15 million to begin the venture. At Palm Springs International Airport, they toasted their future with more Coors, assuring each other it was no less a sure thing than the stock market.

~74~
WASHINGTON, D.C.

THE NATIONAL GUARD JEEP WAS THE ONLY VEHICLE ON THE ROAD. The driver remained silent then stopped in front of the Washington Monument and lit a cigarette. Hannah waited impatiently and finally said, "I'm in a hurry. I have an appointment . . . and you should know that smoking in a closed vehicle is not permitted."

He looked at her in the rear-view mirror. "How come you were able to fly in here?"

"I work for the United Nations. I have important business with a senator."

"So, you're one of those who created this mess *and* you're a foreigner. What do you know that we don't? My wife and kids are hungry. The government feeds me, but there isn't enough for them. When is this going to be over?"

"I don't know. I wish I did."

"You better make it soon."

"I don't have any control over that—it's out of my hands."

"Well somebody made all these damn decisions, and my guess is it was you and your U.N. gang."

"The U.N. made those decisions to make sure you and your family can breathe. I certainly didn't create this scenario. I'm just a lawyer."

"A lawyer lady. Ho, that's rich. I always knew the fucking lawyers would do us in! The lowest cockroach on the block—lawyers. A German lawyer! Old Hitler didn't do the trick, so you just thought you'd try to finish us all off? Is that it, lady? You don't even have to put us in gas chambers or work us to death. Just let us starve out here on the streets."

He looked into the rear-view mirror and was surprised to see tears streaming down her cheeks.

Hannah broke the silence. "I wish I could tell you I know this will be over soon. I have family in Germany, they are much worse off than we are here. I despise everything about Hitler and the Nazis. I am sorry that you distrust me so because I am a lawyer, and sorrier still that you hate me because I am German. I have an important meeting with one of your senators, and I must get there." She started to open the door but he twisted around and caught her arm.

"I must get to this meeting." In her face he saw not just determination but fear. He released her arm and watched as she dug in her purse for a handkerchief and blew her nose loudly.

"Sorry, lady, you can't walk. It's too dangerous. If I let you walk, I lose my job and my family and I starve for sure."

In the Hart building, senator Villanueva read the five pages of orders twice before she looked up. Hannah sat on the edge of her seat twisting a strand of hair that had come loose from her bun.

"Where did you get this?"

"It came by special express yesterday with a D.C. courier."

"Who is it from?" asked the senator.

"I have no idea. I dismissed it as unimportant, so the courier was gone before I could ascertain who had authorized it. As you can see, there was no return label. I thought you would know who ordered all of those items."

"A Senate committee was put in charge of the purchases. There are purchasing agents assigned by them, but that didn't go into effect until April before last. These orders are from a year earlier."

"I know," replied Hannah. "That's why I am here."

"I'll call Cliff and . . ."

"Wait a minute!" Hannah rose and walked to the senator's desk. "If someone wanted to instigate an international crisis and thereby make a lot of money on the deal by swaying statistics and policy, would that be possible? Who would do something like that? Would there be someone here in D.C. that powerful?"

"This didn't start here in D.C. It began with you at the U.N. Remember: Jesse came to me, not the other way around. It started with him and the atmospheric tests around the world."

"But the money is not coming to the U.N. The money—at least purchase of these items—appears to have come through Washington," responded Hannah.

"Just because it's on U.S. Senate letterhead doesn't necessarily mean it is the act of a U.S. senator. It could be someone who works for the senate, or a hacker who just happened to stumble on this information," said Senator Villanueva. "Remember the great climate debacle with hackers back in 2009?"

"But no matter who sent the information, it appears that someone knew how to cash in on this crisis before we knew it was coming! How could they have? What did they know that we did not?"

"Did Jesse have the scientific data earlier?"

"No. At least no conclusions were drawn before then. And as best I know, no conclusive data showed up earlier."

"Can you be sure?" asked Senator Villanueva.

"Senator, this whole thing has been as hard on Jesse as on any of us. I cannot fathom he had any data before he made it known to his superiors and me—and then you and the rest of the Climate Change Committee."

"What is it you want me to do, Ms. Koenig?"

"I want to know who here in Washington has been responsible for buying alternate forms of power prior to the announcement of Operation World Salvation."

Elena shook her head. "Money is no longer even valuable for exchange today—only food and water."

"That doesn't keep people from stockpiling for a later date."

"I'll contact the members of the senate committee who are still here. We'll set up a meeting for 8 a.m. tomorrow."

~75~
WASHINGTON, D.C.

MIGUEL RECEIVED THE THIRD CALL IN AS MANY HOURS FROM SENATOR Villanueva's office at 5 p.m. "Senator Martin is in conference."

"This is Senator Villanueva, and I need to speak to him right now, I don't care if he is talking to the pope!"

"Yes, sir, uh ma'am, uh senator. I'll interrupt him, hold on just a moment."

He resisted the temptation to listen in on their conversation, wondering how Elena Villanueva fit into all of this. He rummaged through his desk for the profile on senators. She was born in East Los Angeles. Her grandparents emigrated from Tijuana in the late '50s. On the other side, her grandfather escaped from Cuba just before the Bay of Pigs disaster. No one in her family went beyond grade school. She obviously made up for the rest. A B.A. in Romance Languages from UCLA, a J.D. from Stanford Law, and a doctorate in the legal system of Mexico from San Diego State. Immersed in politics, she became student body president and fought for illegal immigrants to be eligible for schooling in California.

She had all the advantages of an American with a "wetback" in the closet. Miguel understood that kind of a genealogy. The Latino population in Southern California considered her their champion. He remembered several years back when she had fought for a young woman from Columbia to be allowed to remain in the U.S. She lost. The woman had been shipped back and immediately imprisoned. It had made all the cable channels and the front page of the *Post*.

From world history class, he remembered the Spanish commander Pierre Villeneuve, at the battle of Trafalgar when Nelson was killed.

It was a different spelling but an interesting bit of trivia. Cleaning off his desk just before six, he heard loud voices coming from behind the senator's closed door. Villanueva's name came through loud and clear amid an explosion of profanity.

Miguel was at the reception desk pretending to be busy when Cliff stumbled out of his office muttering to himself. Looking more depressed than ever, he walked right by Miguel and slammed the lobby door behind him.

B.J. came out a few minutes later with a smirk on his face. Miguel had learned to hate that expression.

"Go home, Miguel."

Miguel hesitated, "I've got some more work to do before I can leave."

"In the morning Miguel. I said go home now, little man."

~76~
WASHINGTON, D.C.

"I NEED TO GET TO MY DESK."

"Sorry, senator, not until the experts get here and check for fingerprints."

"But my fingerprints will be on everything anyway. I won't interfere with their work."

The room was roped off with yellow tape, and Security was conducting an investigation. The building had been locked down the night before at 6:45 p.m. No one had been allowed in or gone out after that.

Elena Villanueva's office was a disaster. The only item still intact was the picture of her late husband sitting atop a file cabinet. Files and papers covered the floor. Her computer was upended and smashed. Her desktop was empty of the stacks of papers she had been going through the day before.

Elena worked her way through the papers on the floor. Most of the things she had been working on were still there. Then she remembered the lists Hannah had given her. She'd slipped them into the top of her second drawer on the right. That drawer was on the floor; the contents all missing.

At 9:30 a.m., Elena and Cliff Martin sat alone in her conference room. Hannah Koenig was an hour and a half late. The other senators and the requisition representatives left at 9 a.m. Elena had called the army barracks where visiting Essentials were housed. The person on duty said that Ms. Koenig had left the barracks at about 7 a.m.

"Or Ms. Koenig decided this wasn't as important as you thought. I'll leave these papers you asked for Elena. I have other issues needing my attention. If you want to reschedule I'll be in my office."

"Cliff, can't you see the importance of someone ransacking my office and removing only the papers Hannah left with me yesterday and her now being late to a meeting she insisted I set with you?" Cliff shook his head and left the room.

Elena skimmed through the file that the requisitions department had pulled for her. The records listed fifteen hundred wind machines on April 30, just as Wave I began, then solar reflectors on May 15, and so on. It was entirely different from the list Hannah had left with her. No order appeared before that fateful April. Elena wondered if Hannah kept a copy of the papers. She called the government barracks one more time. No word from Ms. Koenig. She called the Air Force base, inquiring if any Essentials requested a flight out that morning. She called the National Guard Transport. Hannah Koenig had simply disappeared.

~77~
GILA, NEW MEXICO

THEY HAD STOPPED BETWEEN TWO RIDGES, ATTRACTED BY THE WATER, the lush valley, and the fact that there seemed to be no one else to compete with. There was an abandoned, modern house, totally useless without the electricity, two outbuildings, a barn, and a tiny adobe cabin. The chicken house resembled a hotel; she smiled, thinking someone had really loved chickens. It had carved wooden boxes and a way to access the eggs from the back without disturbing the fowl inside. She would have to figure out how to get some chickens.

The silvery chamisa was blooming, covering the hillside with its golden fuzz. Above the chamisa and blue grama grasses, the cottonwoods were in full leaf. As the wind caught the leaves, they fluttered, reflecting back at the sun in myriad shades of green and gold.

"We can't travel any farther, boys. It's already August, and we've got to get ready for winter. This has got to be it."

"Looks great to me, Mom; it's a pretty big house for us, though."

"Ethan, I don't think we can live in the house. We have no way to heat it, but we can stay in this little adobe. It faces south and has a fireplace. Are you ready to chop lots of wood, young man?"

They spent their first night in the little adobe, and found that the fireplace worked like a charm. Some of the windows were broken, but they could cover them to keep the cold out. Karen discovered they were not the only residents in the adobe. A pair of raccoons had a nest in the rafters just above the back door and scattered noisily every time someone barged through.

Ethan and Troy waded and splashed in the small creek. They relished the cool feeling of water running over their toes and finally being somewhere besides the back of that wagon. Karen watched, squelching the latent fear she felt about water. She searched the mountainside above them, then up and down the canyon, and decided the stream was safe for now. She began transferring items from the wagon.

Karen figured the creek would provide irrigation water. Unpacking the seeds, she contemplated starting a vegetable garden. But then she wasn't sure how long Indian summer would last in New Mexico. Ethan detected game—deer droppings, elk maybe, and rabbit. They still had ammunition for the shotgun and the pistol. *We'll be safe,* she assured herself as she cleaned the dust and leaves from the two rooms. This is so isolated, men in Land Rovers won't likely be visiting. From the looks of the place, no one would be visiting.

She was wrong.

"Mom, Mom, there's a guy coming over the ridge. He's got a gun!"

Karen grabbed the shotgun and ran out into the blinding sun. The horseman made his way down the west side of the ridge and then through the large boulders ringing the other side of the creek bank. His horse carefully picked its way through the water and across the small pasture. Karen raised the gun, aiming it at his chest.

"Whoa, hey, don't shoot," he said. "Put that away, little lady. Name's Wilson; my place is over the ridge a way. I saw the smoke last night and thought the Garcias might have come back."

Karen moved around so the rider wasn't in the glare of the sun and saw a short, elderly fellow sitting atop a sorrel mare. He had a broad smile under an old black slouch hat and didn't look dangerous. Troy stood behind Karen, but Ethan placed himself a little in front of her, folding his arms across his chest in defiance.

"My boys and I need a place to settle for a while. We've been traveling since May. If this place belongs to someone else, we'll move on."

Wilson got off the horse, letting the reins drop and offered a hand. Although the hand was calloused and worn, Karen immediately recognized it as a female's.

"Karen Forester, Ms. Wilson." She offered her own hand.

"Glad to make your acquaintance, Karen. This place belongs to a family named Garcia—bigwig contractor fellow over in Phoenix, used to come in with horses in the summer and stay a month or so. They haven't been back since Wave I set in. Guess they don't need it right now, and you and your boys do. Actually no one's used the old adobe since the hippie generation. Where you hail from? Looks like you come a far piece."

"The boys and I . . . we came from Iowa, in this wagon. We just need a place to settle that is safe, a place where we can grow food, hunt a little and . . . Ms. Wilson, will we be safe here?"

"Name's Annie. Safety's not something anyone can promise any of us these days. But folks coming through scavenging for food has slowed to a trickle. The cities are damn sure not where you want to be. And this here's a nice community; the locals won't harm you or your sons. So, I guess safe as can be. Now, let me help you unload this here wagon."

"Annie, have you had any word? Is this thing over yet? I haven't had any information for months."

"Can't help you there, all my means of communication gave out about two months ago."

~78~
NEW YORK CITY

JESSE HIT THE TARMAC RUNNING. IN HIS HAND WAS THE MESSAGE from Hannah's secretary. After the National Guard transport dropped him at the U.N. building, he skirted around the group blocking his way and took the stairs two at a time to Hannah's office.

Petra had been crying, mascara running down her face. He wondered where on Earth women still found make-up or the time and energy to use it.

"Petra, why did Hannah go to Washington?"

"I don't know. She was in her office going over all those reports. Suddenly she came out, kinda agitated, and ordered me to get her on the next military transport to D.C."

"Did she take a suitcase?"

"I guess so. That was at 2:30 and the flight was at 4. She must have gone back to her apartment first."

"Did she get to D.C.?"

"Yeah, that Villanueva lady said she had met with her Thursday. She's also the one who told me Ms. Koenig was missing. She's called at least five times. Ms. Koenig was supposed to meet them Friday morning at 8. She just didn't show and now the senator is really worried."

Petra dabbed her handkerchief at her eyes and looked sadly at the black marks made by the mascara.

"Did Elena tell you why Hannah was meeting with her?"

"No, sir."

"Put in a call to her for me and get me a seat on the next transport to D.C."

Jesse went through the papers on Hannah's desk. Like her apartment, her desk was clean and neat. The Eastern European reports she had been dealing with were on top, with red marks beside the emergency areas they needed to address. Next to them was a stack of memos from areas where good things were happening around the U.S.

Another stack concerned South and Central America. On top was the booklet written by Camilla. Jesse searched the drawers and when the phone rang he still had no idea why Hannah had flown off to D.C.

"Jesse, I'm so glad you're back!" exclaimed Senator Villanueva.

"Did you find Hannah yet?"

"No. She was supposed to meet Cliff, a few others from the committee, and me at 8 a.m. Friday morning. She simply didn't show!"

"Why were you guys meeting?"

"Well, she'd given me a printout of lots of items that had been purchased solar, wind, the stuff we've been buying helter-skelter."

"So?"

"The printout showed that lots of it was ordered and paid for long before you came to us with the data on oxygen—paid for by a private concern and the U.S. government at least a year earlier. To Hannah, that just didn't make any sense. I agreed and asked to meet to see what we could learn.

Jesse was silent on the other end of the line.

"Jesse?"

"Where did she get that information?"

"She said it came in a packet from someone at the Hart Building, but it didn't have a name on it and she didn't pay attention until it was too late to find out from the carrier. That's what led her here, and it's one of the things we hoped to learn from discussing it with those on the Climate Committee left in town, but then . . ."

"Is there any indication that she returned to New York?"

"No. The Air Force says she did not. And Jesse, another thing: my office was ransacked night before last, things thrown everywhere. The lists Hannah left with me are the only thing missing."

~79~
ONE TREE HILL STATION, AUSTRALIA

MARK'S EMACIATED HORSE CAME BACK TO THE STATION FIFTEEN DAYS after he rode off. The saddle was gone and there was no sign of the packs it had carried. Nick found the horse, hungry and thirsty, wandering outside the corral. He gave it water and food and a rub-down. Then he hid it in a dark, back stall so Lisa wouldn't stumble on it before he had time to tell her.

Mark had left the station with enough supplies to last several weeks. The day before that, he and Lisa had been out riding, returning exhilarated but covered with dust. Mark had begun to warm to the feel of the landscape and the possibilities of making a go of it on the station. He climbed the steps to the veranda and checked that the baby was sleeping in the shade. After a sponge bath and some fresh clothes he got himself a beer and sat beside the cradle.

He drank his beer and watched as Lisa mulched saplings she had planted a month earlier and pruned some roses. Then he walked up to her, catching her hand and pulling her up so he could put his arms around her. She didn't resist. The last month had been like a second honeymoon; he'd been happier than he imagined and could sense that Lisa, too, was content. But they'd run out of batteries for the short wave, leaving him frustrated by the lack of communication with the outside world.

"I'm going back to Sydney."

"I know."

"How do you know?"

"Because I know you need to know what's going on out there."

"Yes, even if I'm happy with you and our little girl and I can see the possibility of being here for good, I can't simply forget the rest of the world exists."

He dropped his arms, and took her hand, leading her to the veranda steps. "It's complicated. It has to do with Hendrik, and me, and BDM. He was right about food production, shipping things around the world and me thinking it was a good thing. I was wrong. I'm so sorry, for him, and me; for all of us."

"I've realized these past months I'm more like the old man than I've ever been willing to admit. He used to say 'think Mark, think.' Well now I'm thinking, and I can't just sit here and eat egg curry and Dundee cake and down beer. I just have an idea that maybe I'm supposed to do something to help the rest of the world since it's my dad who has come up with some solutions. You and the baby are safe here. Lisa, will you wait awhile, for the divorce I mean? We probably can't do anything legally now anyway; give me time to see how things are panning out in the rest of the world. Then, if you don't want me, I won't contest it."

Lisa reached her lips up to his for a long, sweet kiss—interrupted only by a cry from the baby.

~80~
GILA, NEW MEXICO

THE BOYS HAD RIDDEN OVER TO ANNIE'S ON THE HORSES AND BROUGHT back five chickens in exchange for several cans of peaches and green beans. Karen knew the chickens were much more valuable than the canned goods, but she didn't question the elderly woman's generosity.

Ethan and Troy both seemed happier than they'd ever been in New York or Iowa. The vastness of the mountain range to the east kept inviting them. When they weren't on the horses looking for animal scat they were playing in the stream or helping her secure the house for winter. It was like camping out, which they had always loved.

"Time for bed, boys."

"Mom, can we go hunting tomorrow? We better get us some meat. I saw deer scat on the way back from Annie's."

"We'll talk about that tomorrow, maybe I'll go too.'

"Ah, Mom, we'll be safe."

"Ethan, go to bed."

Even with the boys gone, though, Karen could find no peace. The tragedy of the flood that had struck them seemingly from nowhere invaded her thoughts every day. Like images of the men in the Land Rover and Matthew, she found it hard to believe she had been so blind-sided. No one had told her that rain in the mountains miles and miles away could make arroyos on the plains flood like that.

They were crossing just west of Springer, New Mexico. Over the mountains to the west, ferocious lightning and thunderheads shrouded the peaks. But the sky above them was clear blue, and Elsie was asleep in the back of the wagon. The dirt road went right through what looked like a little ditch. She could see that other vehicles, wagons, and horses had gone that way. She was hesitating atop the crest when she saw a large man on a horse coming behind them with such speed that she panicked.

She urged the horses off the crest and down through the arroyo.

Too late, she saw the torrent of water coming around the bend bearing down on the wagon. She only had time to yell at the boys to hang on as the horses and wagon spun completely around, and then the horses caught ground and hauled them out. The horseman was behind her, but suddenly he lost his mount and went under. She couldn't help him.

Once on dry ground, they turned to look in their wagon—Elsie was gone, swept, they realized, from the rear platform into the roiling stream.

Though the incident initially thrilled the boys, their loss became overwhelming. Karen tried to comfort them, Troy sobbed but Ethan's eyes were dry. He just seemed dazed. They ran up and down the bank calling for Elsie. But had to wait till the water subsided to do anything more.

Karen found Elsie's body two hundred yards downstream. It was cradled in the arms of a tamarisk tree whose branches reached out across the arroyo. Karen couldn't tell if she had died of drowning or the shock of being swept away. Her face looked as though she was at peace, almost smiling. On the other hand when she uncovered the body of the stranger from the mud his face was screwed up in what seemed to be such anger and fear, and she had to turn away from it.

Karen and the boys dug a grave in soft soil some distance from the arroyo and buried Elsie under a tree with lovely magenta plumes. Then, they buried the horseman nearby. The boys collected all they could of the blankets, canned goods, and tools that littered the arroyo. She caught the horseman's mount and secured it to the back of the wagon. Tied to the horse was a beautiful tooled leather jacket. She quickly ruffled through the saddlebags and jacket pockets. She discovered a very large bundle of money and a hand-written letter. She spread it out in the sand to dry. Some of it was still readable.

To: R ck & Dan. l
Dallas, TX
From: Dad
Las Vegas, Nev. March 2014
To my boys:
Dear sons, I miss you so much. I know y r mom is taking good care of you. I am still here in Las Vegas, and doing well, so don't wor about me. W i crisis is over I will get up to see you and maybe y u can come down for vacation like you did before. Don't ge your Mom grief. Remember what we decided out you two being the men in the family now. And since t re are two you and only one of me, you will do better I could ever have done in taking ca of your

The rest was so blurred from the water that she couldn't read it. The whole thing made her ache. Some father was trying to communicate with his sons. But the guy they'd just buried couldn't be the dad who wrote the note because if he was going from Las Vegas to Dallas, he sure didn't know his geography. Where did all the money come from? Maybe it was just as well he was dead. Thinking thoughts like that made her sick. What if this had been a letter from Jesse that never got delivered because he was dead in a ditch somewhere?

* * *

Karen walked outside and sat on a big, flat rock near the water to watch the dying sun change a layer of clouds from pink to purple. The east side of the canyon changed colors at the same time, and a rabbit scampered down to the stream. The rock was warm from the sun's heat.

The days had been beautiful—each and every one of them. She didn't know the sun could shine for so many days in a row. They had planted lettuce and peas and squash and greens. There were already some tiny green sprouts above ground. She and the boys had carried water to the rows from the creek. In the spring they planned to create some irrigation channels.

All day long the music of her past had been running wild through her head. It wasn't surprising that the music she hummed today was all about the sun. She'd loved John Denver's lyrics about how wonderful sunshine was on his shoulders, but only now was she beginning to realize that sunshine everywhere was such a blessing. Jesse would howl at her revelation. With a jolt Karen realized it was the words to Sheryl Crow's "Soak Up the Sun"—her favorite in college—that perfectly fit how she was feeling.

Each day, it became clearer to her that no matter what else life threw her way she was going to survive. She was a different person now—stronger—and not dependent on anyone for keeping herself and the boys alive.

Was Jesse a different person too? Would he blame her for his parents' deaths when she was supposed to be taking care of them? What about Elsie's death?

How would their love ever survive all of this? Would they end up like people who endured years apart in the military and discovered they had nothing in common after it was all over?

The stars began to appear. She and the boys had marveled at how many they could see in such an isolated place where there were no lights to interfere. As she climbed down from the boulders, her hands felt the deep impressions in the rocks—indentations she and the boys had decided the ancient people used for grinding corn and catching water. Did other women appreciate the stars long ago as they sat there waiting for their men to come back from a hunt or battle?

Karen was too tired to contemplate the vast implications and intricacies of human love. Besides, the warmth of the rocks no longer seemed to be keeping away the cool evening breeze that came each night as the blessed sun disappeared behind the mountains.

~81~
WASHINGTON, D.C.

THAT MORNING, HANNAH HAD SEARCHED FOR A RESTROOM ON THE ground floor of the Hart Building. Then she noticed an elevator in operation and later she remembered thinking it strange, because none were in service the day before. When she entered, she realized she was not alone. A large, meticulously dressed man was there. He had a beautiful smile, with lovely white teeth, and curly auburn hair. She felt a little better. At least he wasn't going to accuse her of destroying his life like the National Guard officer had yesterday morning. The elevator closed and she smiled weakly back. A few seconds later, her senses told her the elevator was going down, not up. The man stepped smoothly behind her, then clamped a damp cloth over her nose and mouth. He was so large and powerful that her struggle against him and the pungent smell was useless. He pinned her arms to her sides and kicked her legs out from under her.

Later—she didn't know how much later—Hannah opened her eyes. She couldn't see anything. It was dark, frigid, damp, and silent. Her hands and legs were shackled with something rough. Tape covering her mouth restricted her breathing. The surface beneath her was rock hard, and her body ached as she lay there helpless. As she regained her senses, the last thing she remembered was B.J.'s blue eyes and beautiful smile as he snarled: "No one is going to find you except the rats."

Squirming around to figure out where she was, her head hit a wall and she groaned. Slowly, equilibrium returned and she pushed herself against the wall to achieve a semi-upright position. Then, something warm and alive brushed against her. Two red eyes were peering up at her. Her muffled scream sent the rat plunging back into the dark unknown.

Hannah remained still, peering into the darkness and praying there was only one rat. She turned toward a clicking sound and saw a small red light. She must be in a basement and the ticking came from a transformer running what power was still being used in the Hart Building. But she had no idea how long she'd been unconscious and wasn't sure she was still even in the Hart.

She made a conscious effort to work on the problem at hand. She had always been good at concentrating, even in terrible conditions. She had proven that working in Asia and Africa. Several times, she'd had to stay calm amid violent, desperate situations. This was no different. She would figure out what had gone wrong. Who was the man on the elevator? Certainly, his attack on her confirmed at least some of her suspicions concerning a plot behind the lists and the data—and the murders.

The hum of the transformer box became almost comforting. Then the two red eyes appeared again and she squirmed and made the loudest noise she could. The damp air in the room put off a foul smell. She fought off the desire to vomit, knowing that with the tape over her mouth that would be fatal.

~82~
GEORGETOWN, D.C.

A SENSE OF ANXIETY PERVADED THE ROOM, BUT NO ONE SPOKE FOR a long time. Manny broke the silence. "What's happening in the Hart building now? Word is that the CISC guys are on to something. Is Martin handling it? What will be the fall out, Cleveland?"

The senator responded: "Martin's dealing with Villanueva; she's the one making all the waves. Her office was ransacked yesterday morning and that female attorney from the U.N. disappeared. As far as the records are concerned, I told Martin to wipe out everything weeks ago. Our contact out west closed down all communications and disappeared." Senator Cleveland paused as that information sunk in. Then, he continued. "I don't know where the leak in our operation came from."

"How did Villanueva and the U.N. get company lists? Manny, did it come from your operation? Lenny, where is B.J.? Has anyone been in contact with our violent friend?" There was another long silence into which no one wanted to step.

"Cleveland, you know I never had any of that on my computer or in files at the Energy Department." Manny paused then went on: "The mole had to come from Martin's office. If he has wiped out the files, we could recreate memos indicating purchases from SOLYNDRIX came to his office from Phoenix. After all, he's the only one of us on the Joint Climate Change Committee and should be the prime suspect. Lenny, you give B.J. the word to create a fake trail back to Martin." He rose to leave. "There is nothing more I can do in D.C."

"Hold it!" Cleveland stood up and put his hand out to stop him. "That would be a dangerous move. Who knows what our friend

Martin would do if he were confronted. If he were to implicate us, what is our defense? We could all be fingered. It would be stupid to make it easier for anyone snooping around. But we should have a plan; we all need to be on the same page if we are dragged into an investigation. What's our story?"

Manny sat back down and took a deep breath before responding. "Let's keep a cool head and reason this out. After all, we really aren't responsible for all the turmoil. The U.N. and various heads of state and ministers around the world made all these decisions. Like good citizens we just kept our heads down and were led. It's not our fault if they didn't check the facts more carefully."

Cleveland returned to his seat. "Well, we haven't really committed any crime. There's no law against locating alternative forms of energy and selling them. There's no link to us in the original data, so no one can tie acquiring that equipment to us. I guess you could say we did a good deed, didn't we? Helping to prevent a national crisis? Like, we were warning people about a hurricane, or tornado. We're really heroes, aren't we fellas?"

~83~
TAUSHIMA, JAPAN

KIM SEARCHED FOR THREE WEEKS. HE TRIED TO IMAGINE WHAT A twelve-year-old girl would do. Where would she go? As a small girl, Niko had always been fascinated with the idea of the big city just beyond her reach. Had she roamed purposefully into Kyoto? It was easier for Kim to accept that she had run away of her own volition than to think that she had been kidnapped or harmed in any way. But deep down inside he knew his daughter wouldn't have run away and the other alternatives were the only ones that made sense.

Taushima was almost deserted. The homes of Niko's friends were vacant. He showed her latest photo to several people on the street, and asked if they had seen this small girl in the last couple of weeks. They answered him with vacant stares, then hurried on.

He trudged through mud up to his knees. But it didn't bother him as much as the mess that the city had become. Most Japanese were still not exactly sure how to deal with the mandates. He did see some open-air markets where people sold fish, vegetables, and fruits. Rice was abundant because the last growing season had been good. But there were makeshift tents and hovels and people everywhere, especially along the shore. Some were cooking on open fires, others just eating fruit and raw fish. The lack of sanitation meant a stench came from each and every place humans gathered.

The authorities were no help at all. Everyone in Japan seemed to be lost. He filled out a missing person's report with the International Red Cross in Kyoto, and the agents promised to share it with other surrounding cities. But Kim felt little assurance. The only sympathy came from one minor official whose two small children had been crushed by a crowd pushing its way to a government food distribution center. Cultural norms wouldn't allow them to speak of it, but sharing the pain eye to eye as they spoke brought Kim some relief. He would have given up sooner but he kept thinking about Lee at home and the look on her face if he returned without the girl.

She was bent over weeding the garden when he trudged back up their hill through the peach trees. He stood looking at her tiny form for a moment, not wanting to speak, needing her love to come and meet his grief. Finally, he approached her softly, calling her name and putting his arms around her from behind. He let her body sink into his and he held tightly. After a few moments he felt the wetness of her tears dropping onto his hands and his own tears fell into her hair. Silence said everything that was needed.

~84~
WASHINGTON, D.C.

THE SENATOR GOT OUT OF THE VAN AND CAME TOWARD HIM, CAUSING him to flinch, a reaction he always had when confronting a person much taller and bigger. He hadn't known the Mexican bitch was so tall. Mexican women were supposed to be petite and dark. She had red hair and was a good six inches taller than he was. As she neared, he saluted her, the uniform giving him more bravado than he felt.

"Good evening, corporal. You're new? Where is Corporal Miller?"

He hadn't expected her to know actual names of guardsmen or recognize a change in who was on duty. He poured on the old Southern charm he always used as a kid with women he felt inferior to. He knew that always led to disarming them.

"Yes ma'am, senator. Just brought up from Quantico. Guess these guys up here could use some relief by way of some new recruits. Looks like we might have a little rain and it will be a tiny bit cooler this evening."

"Yes."

"Now you just let us know if there's any little thing you need, senator."

"I'll do that, corporal. It's been a long day."

"Just pleased to be of service, ma'am." He shut the door behind her, wishing she were not so tall. She reminded him of his mother. She'd been tall and he had always felt she'd seen him as somehow inferior because he was so short. He'd never played any of the sports she wanted him to play because of his size. Eventually, through earning a black belt and working out at a gym, he had learned to feel somewhat important.

* * *

Elena's rooms were, like those of the other Essentials in D.C., on the third floor of what had been an old Holiday Inn, and they were messy. Since her husband's death, she hadn't felt any need to keep a place neat. Clothes lay draped on chairs and strewn on the floor. She often wondered if this was a general reaction to widowhood or just her own neurosis. She felt bone tired, and for some reason she was shivering, despite the August heat and lack of air conditioning.

She undressed as she pondered the events of the past twenty-four hours. Deep down, she knew Hannah was not the kind of person to drop the issue and just leave. She had carefully examined the lists that Cliff left. She couldn't find a single item purchased by the requisitioned orders of the Climate Change Committee before that April. What were the lists that Hannah had left with her? Who had ransacked her office? Tomorrow she would throw the whole thing in Jesse's lap and maybe he could get Security and the others to investigate Hannah's disappearance.

She heated a pan of water on her Bunsen burner and poured it into the tub. Then she heated another and another. It was wasteful, and there wouldn't be enough heating fuel to cook her food next week. Still, she sank down into the six inches of warm water and reminisced on the luxurious baths she'd enjoyed in the past. She dozed off for a few minutes, until the water got too cold.

As Elena dried herself, she heard a noise from the front room. Had she slipped the chain lock on the front door? She probably just wasn't used to all the creaks and moans the old hotel made. But then there was another sound, soft like cloth being moved across the floor. Elena quickly wrapped a towel around her body and walked silently into the bedroom.

The small .45-caliber revolver her husband had bought her was in the bedside table. Elena put three bullets in the chamber. Her husband had insisted that if she was to be out on the street and in parking garages alone, she had to know how to shoot the gun.

Her stomach knotted up, and her heart beat loudly as she thought to herself, *Thank you, my dear.* She stood behind the door to the living room and waited, listening. Her hands were sweating, but the warmth of the bath had left her body.

She hugged the wall as tightly as possible so she wouldn't be hit if the door swung open. Instead, the door inched open slowly. Her ruse about being in the tub had worked. The light pouring from the bathroom and across the floor showed a wet streak, and she prayed that the intruder wouldn't notice. As he started across the room, she raised the gun and aimed it at his back.

"Turn around slowly so I can see your face, mister." The man in a guard uniform turned quickly, using her hesitation to lunge. Her first shot went wild, but the second caught him in the shoulder. She fired again, then felt a searing cut as he lashed out with the knife in his right hand. The third shot hit him in the chest. He fell on her as the knife clattered to the floor. The last thing Lenny thought was that his mother had been right: he was too short. He'd sliced a gash in her left hip but missed anything vital. Elena struggled to get out from under him, realizing it was the soft-spoken Southern corporal who'd been on guard when she came home. She feared for her friend Corporal Miller.

~85~
GILA, NEW MEXICO

"SADDLE UP, BOYS, WE NEED SOME TIME AWAY FROM THIS PLACE."

"We goin' hunting?"

"No, we're going into town."

"Aw, Mom"

"Don't argue with me; let's explore this little berg before winter comes on."

She saddled the big horse for herself, and the two boys rode the mare and filly bareback. They had been in the adobe by the creek for six weeks, and needed a break.

Annie had been right. It was safe to ride into town. A few old men were sunning themselves in front of what had been the town cafe. She waved at them, and they waved back. Karen had told the boys about the old men who'd sat around the stove in the country store outside Olympia when she was a girl. For the elderly, habits were hard to break. The only other business in town was the now-deserted gas station.

An ancient woman was in the post office. The official tag on her blouse said she was Josie Martinez.

"Do you have any means of communication with the outside?"

"*No más.*"

"No mail coming in or going out?"

"*Nada.*"

"Do you have any idea when the mail service will start up again?"

"*No, señora.*"

"Does anyone in town have a short wave? A cell phone? Any way to communicate?"

"*Creo que no.*"

"Thank you señora."

"*De nada.*"

The little adobe library next to the elementary school was open but deserted. The note on the door said, "Gone home, be back tomorrow. Pick your books. Fill out the card and return them in two weeks." It was signed "Flora."

Karen smiled to herself. How wonderful to find a library in the first place, and even more special to find a place where people trusted each other to fill out a library card and return the books. It was like a whole new world. No, it was like a whole old world where one's word meant something and everyone expected others to simply do the right thing.

The shelves contained an interesting mix of mostly old books, probably ones that had been donated by larger institutions or people passing through. Karen looked through the biographies, mostly presidents and movie stars. She was determined that the boys have things to read, and felt hungry for some diversion for herself. If they were to spend the late fall and winter holed up in the adobe by the creek, she would have to be the teacher. Competing with the call of the outdoors and riding the horses in the mountains was not going to be easy. She felt a lot of respect for home schooling and those parents who had struggled to raise standards in past years.

She selected two biographies, on Einstein and Jefferson, and then came across one of Bruce Catton's Civil War histories.

"Hey, Mom, here are some cowboy and Indian books."

"I'd rather you read biographies."

"Mom."

"Okay. We'll get a couple by Zane Grey too, and let's take this one, *A Distant Trumpet*. It's probably about the Army in the West."

She searched for a book that might hold Troy's attention, and decided to start him on C.S. Lewis. He'd already devoured all the *Redwall* series.

She was totaling up her borrowing when she stumbled upon a shelf marked "Southwest Literature"—books by Lafarge, Eastlake, and

Waters. She had never read any of them, and the whole Native American scene, especially in the western U.S., was a mystery to her. Casinos and corruption in the BIA were all she'd ever read about Native Americans. Then she found a book on flora and fauna of the Southwest, and decided it would make a great teaching tool for the winter. Paper was at a premium, and she hoped her neighbor Annie might be able to help her find some notebooks.

The ride back was exhilarating. The boys galloped ahead through the brush and around rocks. They held onto the horses' manes and crouched low over their heads like jockeys at Churchill Downs. Both of them had lost their fear of the unknown and were perfectly comfortable with their surroundings. Karen had made the right choice. She had told Jesse in her note that this was where she was headed, generally speaking anyway. She meant to be where he could find her.

Karen slowed her mount and threw her head back, drinking in the early October sun. Late autumn sages and flowers blanketed the hillsides. Annie had told her their names. There was purple sage that made the air smell like dressing at Thanksgiving. The last of the golden chamisa was hanging on, and in gullies, the brilliant coral known as Indian paintbrush peeked out. She stopped to take in a whole meadow of purple desert asters, their faces also soaking up the sunshine. The beauty made her happier than she had felt in months, and a sense of relief and well being swelled up from inside. She and her boys were going to be fine. They would make it through whatever the winter ahead held.

Later, under a blanket in the adobe she felt her euphoria melt away. As she finished reading *Laughing Boy,* her eyes were wet with tears for the first time in weeks. If only Jesse were there to share it!

~86~
WASHINGTON, D.C.

THE ONLY PICTURE HE HAD BEEN ABLE TO FIND OF HANNAH WAS THE official one in the U.N.'s Law Journal from a few years back. It made her look so uptight. But then, ever since Wave I went into effect, she had looked uptight. Elena had been right: there was no record of her returning on any military flight.

Neither of the Saturday drivers at Reagan National had been on duty Thursday or Friday. He would have to talk to their counterparts who had the weekday shifts. It would have been either Private Coe or Private Merriman.

Jesse found both men at home with their families. Coe lived in part of what had been the guardhouse to the British Embassy. He and his wife shared the building with three other families. Blankets covered the windows, and there was a small vegetable garden where a manicured front lawn had been. Private Coe didn't recognize Hannah from the photograph. On the day in question, he had transported only a general to and from the Pentagon.

When Jesse pulled up to the New Hampshire Street address of Private Merriman, two little black boys stood like statues behind the iron-gate entrance to the small yard. Their eyes were big and their faces immobile as they followed him to the upstairs apartment. They hid behind the man who opened the door.

"Private Merriman."

"Yeah?"

"I'm Jesse Forester. I'm with the U.N. Do you recognize this woman?"

Danny Merriman frowned at the photo and stepped back as

though he might shut the door, but Jesse jammed his foot in the opening. He pushed into the room and grabbed Danny's collar.

"Private Merriman, you drove this woman around on Thursday, didn't you?"

"Why do you want to know?"

Jesse tightened his hold on the collar. "Damn it, private. She's missing. And if you saw her Thursday and don't come clean with me, I'll see to it your life isn't worth the powder to blow it to hell!"

"I didn't mean any harm! I didn't like her at first, but she's really a nice lady. I shouldn't have given her such a hard time, I know. I didn't mean anything calling her a foreigner. It's just that . . ."

Jesse pushed him farther into the room. "What did you do with her? Where is she?"

Danny threw up his hands in a gesture of surrender. "Hold on, man! I didn't do nothing but give her a rough time while we were driving to the Hart building."

"And you were the last one to see her. Where is she?"

"I don't know anything about her being missing. I just drove her to the Hart."

"When?"

"First thing Friday morning, around 7:30."

"And that's the last you saw of her?"

"Yes, sir."

"Did anyone meet her there?"

"I didn't see anyone. She got out of the car and went into the building. That's the last I saw of her. What do you mean she's missing?"

"She didn't show for her meeting at 8 a.m., and no one has heard from her since."

~87~
WASHINGTON, D.C.

JESSE AND PRIVATE MERRIMAN HAD JUST PARKED IN FRONT OF THE Hart Building when a squad car careened around their vehicle. Collins and two other plainclothesmen and another officer jumped out and surrounded them.

"Please step out of the car, Mr. Forester."

"What is this, Collins?"

"I'm afraid I have to arrest you."

"Arrest me, for what?"

"Forester, all that you come in contact with seems to turn into mayhem. You informed me of Paddy's murder. We have confirmation of two U.N. staff—a fella named Haile and one named Abuto—who are now dead, and now there's been an attempt on a senator's life. You are the only person connected to all these people. And I've now got a pretty good idea who your fellow conspirators are. So we're taking you to headquarters while we get it all sorted out. The violence has got to stop and you are the linchpin."

"Wait a minute—what conspirators? What are you accusing me of? I don't know anything about an attempt on some senator. What senator?"

"Elena Villanueva confronted an assailant in her room at the old Holiday Inn last night. Fortunately, she had a gun and put him away before he could do any damage. She's at the Essentials medical clinic right now. Unfortunately, the corporal whose uniform the assailant used wasn't so lucky. Lieutenant Winter here says they found him stuffed in a trash can in the alley behind the hotel."

"God no! Collins, my colleague Hannah Koenig has been missing since Friday. Private Merriman left her here on Friday morning, but she didn't make her meeting with Elena and the others. I flew down this morning to try to find her."

"Let's go, Forester." Lieutenant Winter grabbed Jesse's arm and the two pushed him toward the car. Jesse jerked away and stood squarely in front of the two officials.

"No, no, Collins, this doesn't make sense; I need your help. Taking me in is not going to find Hannah or help Elena. I already told you everything I know. Hannah disappeared from here, and maybe she's still in this building. I can't tell you any more than I already have. We're wasting valuable time standing here."

The two other men held Jesse while Collins and Winter walked away a few paces to talk. After what seemed to Jesse an eternity, they shuffled back.

"Okay, Forester, but don't get out of my sight. I don't know that finding another dead body will help your case, given three murders, an attempted murder, and a robbery already pointing back to you."

"Can we just get on with a search?"

"Where do you suggest we start?"

Using the one copy machine operating in the lobby, Jesse made copies of Hannah's photo. The officers went out in different directions. Jesse and Collins began in Elena's office, questioning her two remaining staff members. No one had seen Hannah on Friday morning. Jesse and Collins went from Elena's office to Senator Martin's. Although Martin wasn't in, Miguel was at the front desk.

"Miguel, have you seen this lady?" There was a brief flicker of recognition in Miguel's eyes, and Jesse immediately jumped on that bit of hope. "She's a friend of mine, and Sergeant Collins and I are searching for her. Son, we're afraid she may be in danger. Did you know Senator Villanueva was attacked last night?"

Collins jumped in. "Sandoval, let's have the truth. Where is Ms. Koenig?"

"I don't know, sir."

"Have you seen her here in the building?

"I'm not sure."

Jesse was hoping that Collins' sharp attitude wouldn't scare the kid. "Miguel, please tell us anything you know." Showing him the picture of Elena's attacker, he asked, "Son, have you ever seen this man in the building?"

"No, sir."

Jesse smiled in an attempt to reassure the anxious young man. "Miguel, someone from this building sent Ms. Koenig information up at the U.N. She came down here because of that information and then disappeared. I promise no harm will come to you if you do know anything. Please tell us what you know."

Miguel felt the shock of guilt. Finding those figures and sending them had brought harm to that lady and possibly also to Senator Villanueva. He took a deep breath and was just about to speak when B.J. walked through the door.

"Mr. Forester, Officer Collins, this is B.J. Cunningham, Senator Martin's chief of staff."

Jesse immediately recognized the man from their brief encounter in Miriamu's office. She had lied about not knowing anyone in D.C. What else had she lied about?

~88~
DIMBANGOMBE, ZIMBABWE

THE TEA FELT WARM IN HIS HAND AS THE CHILL OF NIGHT BEGAN TO dissipate. Kathryn moved quietly toward him with two plates of fruit, meat, and boiled eggs. The night had been full of a lion's roar, the snorting of passing warthogs, kudu, and impala. It never bothered Hendrik to be awakened by these sounds even though he felt increasingly tired by the simplest of days. Several mornings now, he had found huge paw prints of a roving lion just behind the hut.

He'd been unable to get his thinking straight about Mark. The little runner had brought a message from Lisa through a short wave in Bulawayo that Mark had spent about a month at the station and then headed back for Sydney. She had written that Mark wanted to make a difference and was "changed." Hendrik wondered what exactly that meant. She said his horse had come back without him, and that she had been unable to find any indication Mark had reached Sydney. Kathryn tried to keep her husband from dwelling on the possibility of his son's death.

"I wonder if Jesse was able to accomplish anything when he went back to the U.N.," Kathryn mused. It had been three months since his visit.

"BBC announced just recently that there's an investigation to determine if the data the 'hole watchers' used was falsified," Hendrik said. "They reported that perhaps folks had cashed in on the buying and selling of renewable energy systems. But the reporter said nothing is conclusive yet, only allegations."

"Well, it doesn't matter does it? I mean, if the data was contrived, this was just a foretaste of what is to come, wasn't it?"

"I certainly believed something like this would happen." Hendrik was silent and then added, "We just didn't know then what it would look like. It was predicted that we would experience cataclysmic weather events. We didn't know it would come as something so silent and deadly as the level of oxygen falling. After all, it had only changed slightly over eight hundred thousand years, according to studies of the ice cores in 2016. Of course, the increase of carbon dioxide percentage in the atmosphere had accelerated over the last hundred. And no one believed we would all begin *proactively* making the changes needed. It always takes a crisis for us to make any change. No one will believe something is happening next time, even if it is. Our species has such an infinite capacity for just 'going on with the party'," Hendrik sighed.

"Let's walk down the elephant trail and check on the herders. Then let's pop over to the school and see how the children's gardens are doing. Maybe we'll hear from Jesse one of these days. He's such a nice young man, so full of passion for the natural world. Reminds me a bit of me at that age," mused Hendrik.

"And maybe he will also bring us word of Camilla. You did tell him to get her help."

Hendrik looked askance. "You heard?"

She shrugged, and with that small gesture released years of jealousy and doubt. "You told him when you wouldn't come to the U.S. to help that maybe she would. And husband of mine, I hope he did find her, and her work is used by the U.N. as an example the rest of the world could be replicating. That, as well as Dimbangombe, would make such a fitting end to the many years you toiled to share your ideas with so many people."

"Ah yes, Kathryn, that it would." He took her soft hand in his leathery one and led her down the trail.

~89~
WASHINGTON, D.C.

"CUNNINGHAM, WE'RE JUST ASKING MR. SANDOVAL SOME QUESTIONS. Could we ask you to step back outside until we're finished? And please don't disappear, since we'd like to ask you a few questions too."

As Collins pushed B.J. through the door, Jesse saw the vicious look he gave Miguel, and Miguel's veiled but panicked response. "Miguel, you saw Hannah didn't you?"

Miguel nodded, but he couldn't make words come out of his mouth.

"Where did you see her?"

"In the elevator." It was a barely audible whisper. "With . . ." he motioned toward the door with his head.

"That man?"

Miguel nodded.

"Then what happened?"

"It was Friday morning when I came in, and I saw Cunningham with a blonde lady. I didn't get a really good look at her, but I know everyone who comes in these days and had never seen this lady. It sure could have been her."

"Did you see them later?"

"No, and that was kinda strange because they didn't come up here."

"Do you know where they went?"

"No, sir, Mr. Forester, but for some reason the elevator was running Friday morning. I think they went down, not up, on the elevator."

"What's below the lobby?"

"The basement and the little train to the Capitol and the Dirksen Building."

Jesse's heart sank—Hannah could be anywhere. They would have to search not just one building but several, and an underground tunnel to boot.

Collins went out to start interrogating Cunningham. Miguel led Jesse and Merriman to the basement stairs. They found a security officer with a flashlight and stepped out with him into the darkness to examine the cavernous passage to the Capitol. Flashing the light up along the tracks, Jesse could at least see that the dust hadn't been disturbed by footprints. He called out Hannah's name repeatedly, but the only sound was water dripping from somewhere in the tunnel.

Realizing they would need a whole National Guard contingent to search the buildings the tunnel connected, Merriman left them to call his superior and see if more men might be called in. Jesse stepped into the tunnel and called out again. There was a faint sound, like a thumping, but Jesse couldn't tell where it was coming from. He called out again. Miguel, standing back against the wall of the opening, realized that the thump wasn't coming from the tunnel but from the other direction.

They had missed a metal door opposite the track because it blended into the wall. Jesse pounded on it and kicked it. "Hannah, Hannah—are you in there?" This time, they could tell the sound was coming from behind the locked steel door. "Hannah, we'll be back and get you out of there, hang on! Don't give up, you hear?" Leaving Miguel in the basement, Jesse ran back upstairs.

★ ★ ★

In Cliff Martin's office, Collins and B.J. were having a heated conversation.

"Mr. Cunningham, did you or did you not see this lady on Friday morning?"

"No, sir, I never saw that lady Friday or any other morning."

"Mr. Cunningham, do you know this man?" The picture of Lenny stopped B.J. for a moment.

"Nope."

"And I suppose you know nothing about the files missing from Senator Villanueva's office."

"Now, why would I want to steal anything from a senator?" As far as the big, handsome man was concerned, he didn't know anything about anything.

Jesse burst through the door, caught B.J. by the collar, and pushed him up against the wall. Cunningham's hands flew up in the air as he tried to look innocent and indignant. "Hey, mister, I didn't do anything."

"Where's the key to that room, you asshole?"

"What key to what room—I don't know what you're talking about, friend."

"Don't call me friend. You locked Hannah in the basement, and I want that key."

B.J. emptied his pockets on the conference table and, although there were several keys—to his room, the Senate office, and a file cabinet—none looked as if it would fit a heavy metal door in the basement. Jesse grabbed the keys anyway and headed to the basement with Merriman, who'd just wrapped up his call to his boss.

When none of the keys fit, Jesse prayed silently that Hannah would be nowhere near the door when Merriman began shooting at the lock. The first bullet did absolutely nothing; the second and third left a small hole. It took five shots before the knob fell off and Jesse was able to swing the big steel door open.

The beam of light caught the other side of the room and he jerked it into the corner—nothing. As he moved it around the room, something moved. It was Hannah, curled up in a ball. The light startled two large rats as they scampered across the room and up the pipes. They had been chewing on Hannah's feet.

Jesse gave the flashlight to Miguel, picked her up in his arms and carried her up the two flights of stairs. He laid her on a couch in Martin's reception area, tore the tape from her mouth, and began untying the cords on her hands and feet. The rats had already gnawed some of the cords, and there were small and large bites on her toes and ankles. Miguel brought water and paper towels, and Jesse carefully wiped much of the blood away. Hannah was only semi-conscious. As soon as he had the cords undone, he massaged her arms and legs, trying to put some warmth back in her body.

"Hannah, remember you have nine lives—like a cat, you told me—you haven't used all of them yet. Come on, wake up—we need you. I need you.

Cliff Martin came through security and stopped abruptly when he saw Jesse.

"What the . . . !"

"Senator Martin, that big handsome, vicious thug over there in the corner handcuffed to the radiator is responsible for kidnapping and almost murdering this U.N. official. Miguel will testify to what he saw your chief of staff do with Koenig just before she disappeared. We just found Ms. Koenig in the basement, left to die while rats ate her. What kind of a Senate office are you running here?" Jesse glared at him, and the senator watched as Jesse wrapped his ezpensive Navajo rug around the unconscious woman.

~90~
WASHINGTON, D.C.

TWO WEEKS LATER, COLLINS' INTERROGATION OF SENATOR CLIFF Martin turned ugly and then tragic. He admitted knowing about SOLYNDRIX, the company set up to buy solar and wind machines a full year before the mandates. He had been in on the initial investment with Senator Patrick Cleveland, his brother Peter, Manny Marquez, and Theodore Sands.

"So you know that Paddy Freeman was murdered in Ireland when he began to threaten some of your crew with exposing the meeting he had with you around SOLYNDRIX?

Martin looked puzzled and slowly shook his head. "I never met anyone named Paddy Freeman, and know nothing about his murder." He reached inside a pocket and fumbled with a stick of gum. Wadding the paper, he rolled it around with the fingers of his right hand.

"How about Haile Gebremichael? I suppose you never heard of him or his brutal murder either?"

"No, I did not and have not." Martin clenched the wad of paper tightly, then relaxed again.

"We've gathered enough evidence in the last couple of weeks to charge B.J. Cunningham for the murders of both Gebremichael and a UNEP staffer named Thomas Abuto. Do you deny that you knew about Thomas Abuto? Or who attacked Elena Villanueva, or how Hannah Koenig ended up tied up in the basement of the Hart building? Senator Martin, how can you deny knowing about the orders coming from your own office and carried out by your flunkies?"

"I never gave any orders to tie up, kidnap, or murder anyone."

Collins had linked Cleveland and Marquez through fingerprints from a Georgetown residence. They all had received the email Theodore Sands sent from Alaska. He had yet to find out who fudged the figures, but he knew it was just a matter of time and interrogation.

"Martin, you were chairman of Appropriations. You sank millions into SOLYNDRIX. You used taxpayer money and knew you were violating Senate ethics rules. B.J. Cunningham was in your employ."

Collins handed him Leonard Picket's picture. "Do you recognize this man?"

"That's Lenny."

"That's the man who attacked Senator Villanueva, the man she shot in her apartment two nights ago."

"Oh, my God. No, no," Cliff buried his face in his hands and began to shake. He sat down and blew his nose into a handkerchief. He sounded so genuinely shocked that Jesse began to wonder if he too wasn't just a pawn in someone else's game.

"Give me a few minutes. I need to pull some of this together," the senator said.

"You mean you need time to make up more lies?"

Jesse got up and moved to the window. It hurt to look at the senator, his eyes bloodshot, with heavy bags. If Jesse didn't know better, he would have thought Martin had been on a two-week drunk. He probably hadn't been sleeping.

Collins knew he had him on the run and decided to close in. "So you do know this man, you did have dealings with Leonard Picket?"

"I exchanged messages with him, and initially I attended several business meetings where he and others discussed SOLYNDRIX purchases."

"How about your chief of staff—was he at these *business* meetings?"

"Can I go back to the beginning and try to explain, Forester? Collins? You need to understand where I'm coming from, why I got involved in the first place. Not that I'm completely innocent, but I . . . I honestly didn't know anyone was going to end up dead. Believe me—oh God, I was so naive, so stupid."

"You were giving orders to B.J. Cunningham, to kill and kidnap—that doesn't sound so naive to me!"

"No, no, no. B.J. was my chief of staff, yes, I gave him . . . we were . . . he was part of the group, but I never, never instructed him to kidnap or kill anyone! I . . . did he tell you I did? Did he?"

"Yes, in your offices, just before we officially arrested him."

"He was kind of a go-between. Cleveland encouraged me to hire him. He brought me information on when I was to meet with Cleveland and the others. He didn't come to me about any killing. I also met with Lenny, but we never talked, just traded info on the numbers of units we were selling and what we were earning."

"And it never dawned on you with so much money involved, someone might get hurt if they interfered?"

"No—God, I didn't know. I thought we were all doing it for the good of the world. I thought we were all in it to help the environment, to reduce climate change, get the oxygen levels back up. That was what we all talked about at the start. It wasn't about money. When I was elected to the Senate from New Mexico, I really thought I could make a difference. What a mess!" He put his head in his hands as Collins turned off his tape recorder.

Jesse needed to know what made this man tick. "What in the world forced you into this bogus scheme? Didn't you have enough to do as a senator?

"The party machine was too entrenched with the big industry lobbyists. Only if it meant we would win the next election could I get support for cutting emissions. The party dictates were almost always at odds with the best decisions for the people. You had to compromise with the other side of the aisle. Oh, we passed legislation that looked good and soothed the demands of the people, and then it never would get the funding, or never really be put into law. So many times I was hopeful and had my ideals dashed to pieces . . ," Cliff's voice trailed off.

"Martin, I don't feel sorry for you—there are a half-dozen people in our own networks who lost their lives in this scheme of yours, and millions more who are dead or have had their lives crushed by the U.N. mandates."

Jesse left the room ruminating over a quote he had heard a long time ago, something like "heaven keep us from well-meaning people who become misled and create a mess of other people's lives."

He was as guilty as Martin.

~91~
KISUMU, KENYA

"JAMBO," MIRIAMU CALLED OUT AS SHE DROPPED THE HEAVY BAGS and sat on a log to rub the feeling back into her sore feet. The walk from where the matatu had dropped her hadn't been that long, but her Saks Fifth Avenue shoes had not been made to walk on Africa's dusty, rutted roads—really little more than cow trails.

She had hated the ride from Nairobi in the stinking, crowded Mitsubishi bus. Would her people ever learn to wash and use deodorant? By the time she'd covered the short distance to the village, her beautiful shoes were filled with dirt.

"Jambo" she called again.

Her father emerged from the dark, cool room that served as her parents' kitchen and sleeping area. "So, you have returned."

"Yes, where is Mother? Why is it so quiet? Is someone dying?"

"No, we are being shunned by the others in the village, and we are in mourning. Nairobi papers said one of our children had brought great shame by being untruthful."

So, she thought, even here, I can't hide from the rumors, innuendo, and half-truths. She felt the old anger welling up in her. "Well, I guess it doesn't matter what actually happened. You're not interested in the truth; all that matters is what the papers say."

"You are correct. There is only what the people have been told and what they choose to believe. Nothing you do or say will change that."

The gulf widened as the silence embraced both father and daughter.

"What are you planning to do? There is no place here for a haughty girl who looks down her nose at others. They say millions of innocent people are dead and homeless. The U.N. scheme you were involved in even led to the death of two of your own brothers. Your presence here will only make our shame and grief worse."

"I have done no wrong. I did only what was required of me, what I believed in my heart was right for our people. I have nothing to be ashamed of, and certainly you and mother have nothing for which you should be shunned."

For a brief moment, Miriamu felt a twinge of guilt. But it was quickly overcome by her distaste for the squalor of the place, her hatred for the cow dung and chicken shit. She hated the men who sat hour after hour under the shade trees, smoking, laughing, and drinking while the women worked from sunup to sundown in the heat.

"Miriamu, why are you here? You left so big and full of yourself. You told us this village was going nowhere, and you would never come back.

"I need a quiet place to stay temporarily."

"This is no longer a place for you."

"Surely, there is a hut for someone who was once a daughter."

He shifted, sighed, and softened. "Take the hut farthest from the kitchen that was grandfather's. One week, no longer."

She flung her Prada handbag over her shoulder, lifted the two bags she'd come with, and walked to the hut she had loved as a child for the sweet smell of her grandfather's pipe. Her father shuffled back into the kitchen, where she knew her mother had been lurking trying to catch details of their conversation.

Miriamu went through her bags, the clothes and treasures from her New York apartment. He was right: The villagers might talk with her, even invite her for a meal, but in the end, they would believe the Nairobi papers.

Where could she go? All her colleagues had either been rounded up for questioning or left quickly for home—no forwarding address—as Operation World Salvation melted down. She couldn't stay here, even if they would let her. There were no cars, no electricity, no plumbing, and no means of communication. The simple life in this village would be worse than prison. But she had to lie low. The U.S. or the E.U. might seek extradition once they learned of her role.

How had it all unraveled? Was it Haile? Abuto? Forester? She had failed. None of the money had even gotten into her bank account. If she were caught, that might at least be a point in her favor. In the end, it was her fear of B.J. that had made her run.

She sat on the dirt floor under the hut's cool, thatched roof and looked out on her childhood home. These people she had looked down on and considered ignorant had survived much better than her fellow New Yorkers. No—they had thrived. But she couldn't bear the thought of living the rest of her life without running water or a flush toilet.

~92~
DIMBANGOMBE, ZIMBABWE

KATHERINE RECOGNIZED THE HANDWRITING THE MINUTE THE DUSTY letter arrived from Harare—the firm, looping script so much like Hendrik's. It had been months since they had received the note from Lisa. Of course, there wasn't really any good way for Mark to reach them while Wave II and III were being carried out.

Hendrik, true to form in his endless forbearance with this difficult son, had made her promise, just before his death, that she would make an effort to find Mark when it was all over. At the time, she didn't know how she would manage that. Mark had never taken to her, but it was so important to Hendrik.

During his last few weeks, he had turned inward, not distant or morose but enveloped by a quiet, self-satisfaction. He wasn't as observant of the prints of lions or the calls of the birds. Their walks became a bit shorter, and he slept later each morning, napped in the middle of the day, and went to bed earlier. She had joined him in this new routine so it would not feel like an abrupt change to Hendrik, and spent every minute possible with him.

She sighed, biting her bottom lip and hoping against hope that the letter held something positive for her to hang on to.

Dear Dad,

You were right there isn't much left when all the support systems bottom out. Lisa and the baby are well. (Oh yeah, you didn't know it but you're a grandfather!) I stayed out at the station. I was with them for a few months during Wave II. Getting out of Sydney was a nightmare! But I came back to

Sydney, thinking maybe I could do some good, and you know how I hate being in the outback with truly nothing to do.

But it's all crap here. Nothing is left intact. It'll take decades to rebuild some semblance of a society even with all the government and U.N. effort. Everything I loved about BDM and my life here has proven—as you said it would—to be as "worthless as the paper on which the transactions were written" once the oil-based systems were shut down.

I hope to see you one more time; I want to tell you in person that you were right all along. That's not an easy thing for a son to say but I can sure see it now.

Give Katherine a hug for me. Tell her that I never did dislike her. I just let my selfish anger at you overwhelm everything when I was around you two. IF you get to Australia, we'll go see Lisa and the kid. She was already beginning to look like her old man when I saw her last. If she's lucky that will change and she will be beautiful like her Mom.

Dad, I am so sorry,

Mark

Katherine read it twice more and then laid it on the small table near the cook stove. She felt a sob well up in her throat. *NO! No more crying. I'm done with the crying and sadness.* But the tremendous loneliness still would visit on so many nights. She slipped on her flip-flops, grabbed the letter, and stepped out into the bright, warm afternoon. The letter needed to be with Hendrik. There was nothing she could do now to help either of them. But maybe if she laid the letter to rest where she had last seen him alive, he would know how Mark came to feel.

She walked the soft path along the river, crossing just above the game pools. She climbed, looking out over the plains below. Together they had climbed the escarpment on the last day she had seen Hendrik. By then, she had ceased arguing with him over what to do with his remains. She wanted to give him a proper, if simple, burial, not too far from the hut where they had lived the last twenty years, and where she planned to remain.

He balked. After all, he pointed out, "I am nothing but a bunch of bones and water. There is no reason why I cannot go off, die somewhere in the veldt I love, and be recycled like any other species."

It felt callous of him, but she knew that was not in his nature. He was just being pragmatic and taking control of his own destiny even in death.

So early one evening, she had accompanied him, kissed him lightly on his cheeks, and left him. The path home was drenched with her tears. It took her a week before she could bear returning to the baobab. There was nothing there, and she did not search—just sat for a long time looking out over the land he loved, remembering the sweet and hard times of their twenty-five years together.

Later she called the villagers of Dimbangombe together to tell them of Hendrik's death. There was silence for a long time after she spoke. Then the chief herder began a song known by all the villagers from school age up. It was the song of honor for a loved one who has passed to the spirit world beyond. The song went on for many, many rounds, and when it was over, the villagers returned to their homes in silence.

The next morning, two young men came to the hut to see Katherine. "The chief of our village wishes that you would move closer so we can all watch over you. If you will not move closer, he has asked that you let us build a hut near yours so there is always someone strong and young who can help you with the firewood and other chores that may be too hard for you in the coming years. This is the wish of our chief and our council and all our people for all that you and Elder Johnson have done for our people." Katherine knew then that she would stay among these people for the rest of her days.

~93~
NEW YORK CITY

"SO WHAT'S NEXT FOR US?" HANNAH DIDN'T LOOK AT JESSE AS SHE shuffled papers on her desk into a briefcase. For the past month, after the plot was uncovered, they had been closer. He had protected her from the press, often slept on her couch, and comforted her whenever she'd felt the recurring nightmare of that dark cellar. When she cried out, he would shake her gently and let her know she was safe.

"Yeah, the bad guys have all been caught, the lies exposed, and everyone is gearing up to bring us back to all that good stuff humans think they can't live without. The work you and I were asked to do was not only impossible, it was useless."

"How can you, of all people, say that? Jesse, it isn't just about the bad guys. What about all the corroborating evidence? What about Hendrik and Paddy and Camilla—all their work? There's still a real problem. How can we let people go back to supporting what is most surely self-destructive?"

"I just don't know."

"What has happened to the young man who came to me two years ago and asked me to keep the human race from self-destruction? Did I spend two days tied up in that cellar with rats for nothing? Jesse, do you doubt that a change is needed?

Jesse was silent, somber, weighing the choice—to walk away or to continue. The first U.N. decree to the world would be so important in how it influenced what would follow.

"He's as sure today as he was three years ago that we are headed for much more extreme disruption," Jesse said. "He's certain. But he's tired, Hannah. He never wanted to be a front guy, someone leading a platoon into battle or behind some U.N. mandate. Together, we're an awesome team working like we've done the last two years. But . . ." he halted. Suddenly the deeper meaning of her words hit him. He looked at her, shoulders pushed back and lips pressed together. "Hannah?"

"What?"

"Do you want to talk about *us?* Isn't that really what this is about? We can't bury that discussion under all this bullshit about helping guide U.N. policy down a better path! We both know that I have to make a decision to stay because I want to be with you or to go try to find Karen and the boys—and that has nothing to do with the rest of the damn world.

"And Hannah, I desperately want to do what is right for us all," he said softly, moving toward her and reaching to put his arms around her. She stiffened a bit but didn't pull away. Then she wrapped her arms around him and buried her head in his shoulder.

"What's there to talk about, Jesse? What can I possibly say?" she whispered through her sobs. Jesse stroked her hair. Since the kidnapping, she had been so much more vulnerable. He fought to keep his composure without seeming cold. Inside, he felt torn apart.

"I won't—can't—ask you to stay, Jesse," Hannah whispered. "I don't want you unless this is where you want to be. I would never deny you your family. Then again, maybe I would if I thought you'd forget them and that I'd be enough."

Hannah stopped, pulling away from him just a bit. When she looked into his eyes, she knew he was leaving; perhaps she had known it all along. He needed to find some resolution to the life he once knew. And he could never do that if he stayed in New York. And Hannah knew she had to pull away as well. She needed time to think and to relieve the overwhelming sadness and anger she felt.

Jesse sat down, leaning back and pulling her down beside him. "Hannah, do you remember the book you loaned me, *Letters to Freya*? I finished reading it last night. Did you know that George Kennan said von Moltke was the most moral man on either side of the war? I've tried to equate my position with his—but I keep coming up short."

"What do you mean?"

"In his last letter to his wife, he said he didn't mind being executed for something he had tried to do if it was a worthy cause. He had a great desire not to have died in vain."

"Your head is not on the chopping block, Jesse."

"No, but hear me out. Von Moltke was convicted in the end because he and the others had *thought together* about the future of Germany. They never plotted the overthrow of the government, never even produced a pamphlet or a leaflet—just shared ideas."

"So?"

"Don't you see? We produced pamphlets and leaflets; we *did* overthrow, not just the government but the whole world order—at least as we knew it."

"Our intention was to make the world a better place."

"So was his, and in the end, he had a feeling of absolute protection, because of his belief that his cause was just."

"I see where you're going."

"He says he'd finished the task God gave him to do and God had taken infinite trouble with him. I only wish I had that feeling of such absolute protection in knowing what we did was the right thing to do. In some ways, he and I are so alike—and yet so different: a wife . . . two boys . . . two years separation."

"Jesse, this is a different era and a whole different set of circumstances."

"Is it really? Or is that just a copout to excuse our mistakes? Poor Cliff Martin when he spilled his guts. He was so sure he was doing it all for the best—just like us. Do the means always justify the end? Who will I be and what will I do if I can't find Karen? What will I do if all that's happened in the last two years is too big of a gap for us? She didn't want to leave me; I made her go. I don't own Karen, nor can I expect you to just wait around on the off-chance I might come back. Hannah, what are you thinking? What are your plans?"

"I don't know where I'll be when and if you might come back. I can't continue to fight . . ." she paused, ". . . without you. I'll have to figure out what I'm going to do now. My sister Marta is dead."

"What? How?"

"It was a misunderstanding with the authorities. German police have always taken their authority much too seriously." A badge, a gun, and they are the controllers. So she was shot."

"Accidentally?"

"Maybe. Her husband, Ali, hasn't been heard from, and my uncle, Franz Dietrich, said he may be dead also. My hope is to bring Anna Marie and my niece back here, if that's possible. I don't know. I do know Franz Dietrich doesn't need two more children to care for. I don't know if Anna Marie will even accept me. I will go home and get reacquainted with her." Hannah smiled at that thought. "I have to figure out how to be a real mother. Then I'll come back here and continue to fight. I'll be all right, Jesse—honest, I will."

"And I have to find Karen and the boys."

She looked at Jesse again, and her eyes softened a bit. She couldn't help remembering the times they'd disagreed, fought, and then found some way to make up and get back to work.

A peaceful silence enveloped them. Finally, he turned to her and grinned. She felt ready, then, to let him walk out, not knowing if she would ever see him again. She hugged him and then, holding him at arm's length, smiled.

~94~
DEERING, IOWA

HE SCROUNGED UP A MOTORCYCLE WITH A SIDECAR, AND ENOUGH GAS to get him to Iowa. He'd been saving food rations for months. He stayed off the main roads, traveling fast because all reports indicated that most of the country was still full of bands of desperate, hungry people. There were no authorities or police to depend on.

People could use gas again, but it would take months for most of them to have access to fuel, consistent supplies of food, and other necessities. He avoided the cities, going around them on small farm roads and even dirt paths when necessary.

Here and there, Jesse could see small clusters of human habitation—villages of sorts. For some, the situation had stabilized. Many of them had armed guards staked out around the entire community.

He was determined not to stop. But at three-hour intervals, he had to stretch his legs. He carried a pistol tucked in the front of his jeans. He slowed down to eat jerky and dried fruit, guiding the handlebars with one hand. He rationed his water, filling the canteen whenever water was available and looked relatively clean.

The ride went without incident. He tried to imagine what the boys would look like—his only images old and faded. He struggled to prepare himself mentally, trying not to build up expectations.

Childhood memories flooded in as he hit Deering. There was the corner, one county east, where he and his drinking buddies almost ran the car into a Mack truck while racing one summer. He passed his old high school, a red brick building where kids from all over the county had been bussed. It was deserted. Windows had been broken out, and part of it set on fire. He passed the big Walmart that came to town when he was about fifteen and put Green's General Store out of business. Deering was not as deserted as he had expected. Big houses in the wealthy part of town were vacant, but farther west toward the farm, he passed a cluster of occupied homes. A few people on bikes or foot passed him on the roads, men were working in the fields, and he saw a woman hanging clothes on a line. The sight flooded him with false hope.

Jesse took one look and knew the farm had been abandoned. He pulled up and looked all around, making sure no stranger was there before he turned off the motor. It felt eerily quiet. Dismounting, he took out his gun and stuck it in his belt. He headed toward the long, low porch.

The door was open, and the screen banged behind him, just as it had every time he'd run in hollering for his mom when he came home from school. This time, the banging door was met with silence. Jesse looked for any clues that would tell him when they'd left or where they had gone. He tried to recall if he and his mother had ever had a secret place to leave notes to each other. They had mostly used the little chalkboard above the phone. Someone had wiped it clean.

He checked each room. Upstairs, in the room that once was his, he found bunk beds and a twin—Karen and the boys had shared that room. They'd left behind clothes, baseballs, footballs, and hats. Jesse rummaged through drawers, including his parents'. Matthew's dresser had an odd, unused feel about it. His shaving mug sat right where he probably put it after the last time he shaved.

He stepped outside into the warm autumn afternoon, determined to find something that would lead him to answers. The barn was empty but for the old tractor and leftover hay, hand-tied into tall bunches. Behind the barn lay the orchard with its small graveyard in the far corner. Even before he could see the details, his eye told him there was a new headstone. Not a real one carved by an engraver, just a beautiful, large river stone from the nearby stream. Someone, perhaps the boys, had etched a scraggly "M" on its face and a date.

So Matthew died last April. How? Why? Despair gripped him when he realized that unless he found the rest of his family, he might never know the answer. It would become just one more missing link in his life's story.

When he got back to the house, he remembered an old Irish trunk where his mother had kept a handful of important things. He searched the attic for it, knowing that after they'd bought the trunk at auction, they found its secret compartment where immigrants had placed their important papers. It wasn't there.

As he looked out the dormer window, his eye caught the door to the cellar behind the kitchen. He'd forgotten about the cellar, but it was probably a safer place for them to leave things in the hope he'd find them when they packed up and left.

Sure enough, the trunk was sitting in the middle of the small room. His heart beat rapidly as he lifted the lid and moved the board to the hidden compartment. A single piece of paper, neatly folded, was tucked inside.

Jesse, his mother's neat scrawl, so comforting, began.

If you are reading this, then you can see that we have gone. Where? When we left, May 25, we were not sure except somewhere with a warmer climate. Somewhere where we might find a village we can join or a piece of land where life is safer. Someone has been stealing animals and burning down houses.

Your Dad was killed by one of those hooligans last spring, trying to keep Karen from . . . well, let's just say being hurt, perhaps killed, herself. I miss him so much. Your boys are growing. They're so handsome, and Karen's been a good mom and a better daughter-in-law than I ever believed was possible. I feel sometimes like Naomi and Ruth. Do you remember that story from when you were a boy and we would read the Children's Bible together? Oh, sure, we had our differences. But they all paled in the face of the troubles we've overcome together. We haven't heard from you in so long that no one knows if you're alive. The boys quit asking a

long time ago. We're determined to survive, and that means doing whatever we must. Perhaps someday this madness will end, and we'll find one another again. I have cried many nights wanting you to return. I'm done crying now. Stay safe, my son. I love you.
Mom

They were alive, he said to himself. Four months ago, they were alive.

Jesse had read about the conditions all over the globe when Wave II went into effect. But being an Essential had kept him separate, mostly protected from the desperation and ugliness. Now it wasn't someone else's story; it was his.

Somewhere with a warmer climate—boy, that was helpful. Anger welled up inside him. He had no clue what to do now, where to go, or how to find them. Winter was coming on, and he was alone and especially vulnerable to gangs. He'd brought just enough food and fuel for his trip to Iowa.

In his head, they were going to be here or be dead. He would be reunited with his family or would somehow get back to the U.N. The idea of searching farther for his family had never occurred to him. Maybe he'd known all along the only option was to go back.

He sat for a long time on the floor, his mind racing from Karen to Hannah to the boys to the last two years of exhausting work which in the end had come to nothing, really hadn't even been needed. The world would go back pretty much to the way it had been before Wave I.

Once communication systems returned to normal, it would be easy for Karen and the boys to track him down. They knew exactly where he was last and who to contact to find out if he was still alive. Would they? If he didn't search for them now, would they come looking for him? Would they understand why he went back? How would they feel if they knew he didn't come looking for them after he'd come this far? Would he be a "slug" in their eyes for returning to the U.N. and just waiting for them to call? No, he had put his personal life on hold for almost three years. In leaving New York, he had been so sure it was time for him to tell the rest of the world to take a flying leap.

As he stood up, he noticed a note tacked to the back wall.

In the cold cellar, Karen had nailed a note to the wall behind the trunk. It was in Karen's handwriting:

Dearest Jesse,

It got too dangerous for us to stay. I doubt that we can make it through another winter. I know, I promised we'd stay here, but I just couldn't keep that promise. We're heading for southern Colorado or somewhere in N.M.—someplace by water with a milder climate, hopefully fewer people. The boys and I are fine. Your Mom is with us. I will try to get in touch when we settle down. Oh Jesse, I hope you get to read this. I love you so much I ache, and I'm not giving you up. You belong to me—Maybe saving the rest of the world was important—I can't judge that right now—but one thing I do know. I am your partner and you are my dearest friend and husband, and I don't want to live without you.

If you don't find me, I will find you—that is a promise!

Karen

He read it three times with tears streaming down his face. He felt ashamed of his doubts about her—unable to justify his actions. All he really wanted was his family—the rest of the world be hanged. It seemed until now he had all his priorities mixed up. He wanted to hold his wife in his arms and love her. He wanted to see his boys grow into men, to encourage and protect them. He felt deep down inside that they were alive and well. Perhaps God had taken infinite trouble with him after all.

He went through the old house one more time. When he got to his room, he gathered one item each that had belonged to Ethan and Troy. In the living room, he pocketed the small picture of him with his parents, which was still on the mantle.

~95~
LAS VEGAS, NEVADA

GOOD MORNING, ALL YOU OUT THERE IN RADIO LAND THIS IS P.J. YOUR ol' D.J. It's been a long time since we've talked. A generator came to us from Denver yesterday. I put together some short-wave stuff. A technician I am not, but here goes nothing. I hope we are once more on the air, and some of this is getting out to listeners far and wide, at least to those of you who have short-wave radios. News flash, for any of you that are old listeners. I'm a married man now. My lovely lady, Susan, was a dancer here in Tinsel Town.

Now, back to our business at hand. I plan to be on the air for an hour each morning and an hour each evening. Then, as we can replace equipment, regular programming will continue.

The country has been through a storm, almost three years of turbulence. I'm not going to say I know for sure how or why all this happened. But since I'm running this show and don't have any program manager to tell me to cease and desist, I'll be giving you my opinions and facts as they come my way. If you listened to me before Wave I, you probably know I had some doubts about the way things were going long before the U.N. and our own government took it on themselves to mandate those changes in our lives.

Now it's time to reevaluate—and I will be mouthing off about the future and how we might use what we've learned. Also, I plan to broadcast the following:

1. Information on where food, water, and other essentials can be found whenever they become available.

2. Safety information for the residents of Las Vegas and the surrounding areas.

3. Government information whenever available.

4. Your personal information, for example if you are looking for a loved one, come into the station or send me a message if you can and give me the information on name, age, descriptions, and where they were last seen. Hopefully, this will help those of you out there wandering around to find each other.

But for God's sake, don't wander into Las Vegas. This place is a ghost town—no casinos and the only live entertainment is from counting the rats and mice and roaches. There are no bright lights or loud music, and only one dancing girl: my lovely wife, Susan. Let's just say that right now, she don't dance for anyone but me. There is no fresh water supply and won't be any food until either next season or when trains start delivering from California or someplace east. The same is true of Phoenix, Tucson, Albuquerque, Denver, and Salt Lake City. I don't know about farther west. But I would bet California is no better off. Any big city is still a mess.

So if you and yours have an abode where there's water and a little food, stay there for now.

Along the same line, you still need to stay where you can grow food, where there's safety from gangs. Remember, when the government could no longer sustain the prisons, most of the prisoners were released. They are out there, so beware.

Now, for today's personal stuff:

Judy Mitchell is trying to contact her parents—Olga and Mitch—age 55. Judy last saw them leaving from Vegas for Texas at the beginning of Wave II.

Marie Van Staten is looking for her son, Barry. Barry is twenty-five, six-foot-two with blue eyes and blond hair. She last saw him two months ago in Bountiful, Utah.

Yesterday, a New Yorker, Jesse Forester, rode through looking for his family—his mom, Elsie, his wife, Karen, and two boys, Troy and Ethan. He says Karen is a beautiful brunette with soft brown eyes, and the boys are now twelve and fifteen. They were headed from Iowa to the Four Corners area. If you know or see any of these people, tell them he is looking for them. As soon as they get the cell towers back up, call me and I will try to help make connections.

Meanwhile I'll just play a little music … and be back on the air at 6 p.m. tonight. How about something appropriate for a world trying to reclaim its soul. . . .

Hello darkness, my old friend
I've come to talk with you again
Because a vision softly creeping
Left its seeds while I was sleeping
And the vision that was planted in my brain
Still remains
Within the sound of silence

In restless dreams I walked alone
Narrow streets of cobblestone
'Neath the halo of a street lamp
I turned my collar to the cold and damp
When my eyes were stabbed by the flash of a neon light
That split the night
And touched the sound of silence

And in the naked light I saw
Ten thousand people, maybe more
People talking without speaking
People hearing without listening
People writing songs that voices never share
And no one dared
Disturb the sound of silence

"Fools", said I, "You do not know
Silence like a cancer grows
Hear my words that I might teach you
Take my arms that I might reach you"

But my words, like silent raindrops fell
And echoed
In the wells of silence

And the people bowed and prayed
To the neon god they made
And the sign flashed out its warning
In the words that it was forming
And the sign said, "The words of the prophets are written on the subway walls
And tenement halls"
And whispered in the sounds of silence

AFTERWORD

THIS BOOK—ITS CHARACTERS, SCENES, AND CONVERSATIONS—IS A work of fiction. A few of its characters are loosely framed around individuals whose work we felt important to include. Here and there, a real individual and his or her work are included to tie the events to things with which the reader might be familiar.

Most of the environmental, health, and weather data is taken from actual media articles or institutional publications over the last fifty years. We purposefully kept all that very simple because the factoids are, after all, not the point.

Recent media have portrayed global climate change and species extinction as one big cataclysmic event. This book portrays them rather like drops of rain that eventually become a flood. The raindrops are coming down all around us, but we refuse to pay attention. They are the consequences of billions of human decisions (followed by actions) made over thousands of years to build our communities and live our lives with little or no thought for replenishing the resources needed to sustain our existence.

In the history of humans, there is no evidence that any society—much less all the societies of the world—has ever foreseen catastrophe and mobilized to make the changes needed to avert tragedy. If history repeats itself, we will not attempt what the characters in this book did. We will, rather, destine our children and grandchildren to the consequences of our poor decisions and materialistic lifestyles.

One character in the book—Hendrik Johnson—is based on a real person: Allan Savory. Although the details of his life and the relationships in this story are part of the fiction, Savory's ideas and life's work are not. His efforts to save the grasslands and their attendant herbivores and fresh water habitats around the world are unparalleled. His contribution to agriculture, environmental science, and reversing climate change will one day be universally recognized. He's long been a thinker ahead of his time. One knows that instinctively by the opposition: mainstream agriculture and the environmentalists who have railed against him personally for fifty-plus years without being willing to even look intelligently at his ideas.

Long before Al Gore knew anything about global climate change, Savory was writing and speaking about desertification and climate change as "two sides of the same coin." Human-induced massive loss of topsoil worldwide, with its release of billions of tons of carbon into the atmosphere, represents the biggest raindrop—and has for centuries. If one understands micro and macro systems, it is clearly the other side of the coin called climate change. It's a cause, not a symptom. And we already know how to reverse it. We simply lack the political will to do so.

As shared in this book, Savory's practical and simple idea—that humans can reverse the collapse of spaceship Earth by changing the way they make decisions—is profoundly elegant. It's not rocket science; if our decisions lead to actions that destroy biological diversity, we logically can change the way we make decisions and thus reverse our destructive actions. Answers to the most complex challenges have always come through the simplest of lenses.

Around the world, small pockets of people are already creating change. In these regenerative communities, one sees two abiding characteristics: a focus on family and community rather than *things* and a sincere love for the plant and animal kingdoms that sustain all of us. Things never made anyone happy. That also is true and simple.

And yet, simple does not mean easy. There is work we all must do.

If you have enjoyed this story and wish to learn more about the ideas we've shared, the best source of information is at www.SavoryInstitute.com.

In Zimbabwe, just south of Victoria Falls, a committed group of individuals has been creating the Dimbangombe College for Agriculture and Wildlife, managed by the Africa Centre for Holistic Management. It's not yet all that is described in this book. But it's a start. Where there was once bare ground and dried up rivers, grasslands are flourishing, streams are flowing again, and animal-based agriculture is producing both food and healthy land. People, soil, plants, livestock, and wildlife are all living and working together in harmony. That's what it's all about.

—Vicki Turpen and Shannon Horst (2019)

ABOUT THE AUTHORS

Vicki Turpen's clan includes five grown children, ten grandchildren, and six great-grandchildren. She has a M.A. degree with an emphasis on writing, and is an award-winning teacher who has taught drama, the Bible as literature, and English at the secondary level for many years in New Mexico and Colorado.

Vicki co-founded the Durango Lively Arts company and has taught environmental education. She is a member of Albuquerque's Rotary del Sol club and Southwest Writers. She has written articles and editorials for the Christian Science Publishing Society and is a member of the Christian Science Church. She's an intrepid gardener living in an intentional family community on a farm in Albuquerque's South Valley.

Shannon Horst also lives at the farm in Albuquerque's South Valley where she and her husband raised their two boys. Her educational background is in languages, linguistics, and communication. She is a former editor of Africa affairs for the Christian Science Monitor. Shannon spent three decades working with Allan Savory to help people change the way they make decisions. Currently, she's the executive director of Tree New Mexico and community relations manager for the Principle Foundation. She is an avid gardener and flyfisher. Second only to her spiritual path, Savory's ideas have fundamentally changed the way she cares for the people in her life and her part in replenishing spaceship Earth.